The Organic Underwear Conspiracy

The Organic Underwear Conspiracy

Paul W. Jackson

LifeRich Publishing is a registered trademark of The Reader's Digest Association, Inc.

LifeRich Publishing books may be ordered through booksellers or by contacting:

LifeRich Publishing
1663 Liberty Drive
Bloomington, IN 47403
www.liferichpublishing.com
1 (888) 238-8637

ISBN: 978-1-4897-2209-6 (sc)
ISBN: 978-1-4897-2208-9 (hc)
ISBN: 978-1-4897-2207-2 (e)

Library of Congress Control Number: 2019903574

Print information available on the last page.

LifeRich Publishing rev. date: 4/11/2019

For my father, who taught me that a dog is the only friend you'll ever have who will always be glad to see you and never ask where you've been.

Prologue
1935

The vote was 4-3, but the city council had slandered Alan Jovial's good name. It would be damaged beyond repair unless somebody did something. It was brutal. Unfair. Malicious and untrue. The public would read about it and believe it unless something were done, and fast. The reporter busily scribbling notes in front of the room couldn't be trusted.

Two ignorant city council members obviously knew nothing except how to parrot what they'd heard on the streets. The Jovial family's reputation was at stake, not to mention the honor and legacy and economic potential of Jovial, Michigan.

Let others sit back and let history be revised in error. Alan Jovial II would not, could not.

He was successful, as always, at hiding his anxiety about the public plea he was about to make. But Alan-the-Second—he hated the tag "junior"—knew how to turn things to his advantage. His father had taught him well. There was always an advantage to be found, no matter the circumstances. The trick was finding it. The greater accomplishment was selling it.

"Thank you, Jovial city fathers, for the sweeping mandate you've just issued," he said, his voice exuding even more pomposity than normal. "I know this magnanimous action on your part was difficult, mainly due to cost, and I applaud your fiscal concerns. This is the taxpayers' money you're spending, and the decision is never easy. I understand that fully, having been on this very council for years, as was my father, the founder of this town." He stood a little straighter and taller than at first.

"You young first-timers on the board, in particular, I'd like to congratulate," he said, trying and failing to make eye contact with Calvin Leonard, a wet-behind-the-ears pastor serving his first stint on the city council.

Leonard, who ran for office on a spending control platform, had been vociferously opposed to spending taxpayer money on what he termed a "frivolous, if not sinful" statue of the town's not-so-righteous patriarch.

"Let only God be honored, not man," he'd said at least a dozen times throughout the lengthy council meeting.

He was strong just a minute ago, but now he won't make eye contact, Alan deduced. He wanted the cowardly young pastor put in his place. He wanted to pierce the young hypocrite's armor and strip him of it like a butcher strips hide from a deer. But Alan was never one to burn bridges, so he continued.

"My father founded this town in 1875, with his own funds and the sheer power of his will," he said. "And despite what the young Pastor Leonard might think he believes, history—if investigated at all—reveals a great man of vision whose legacy will reach beyond a stone or brass tribute. Does it really matter, fifty years later, that there are false rumors about how he received the money to purchase this township? If it would, I'm here to set the record straight. I know how he sacrificed for this town, and I know his financing was completely legal. He told me that himself. Would any of you deny that this town—his town—is among the finest places to live and raise families in this entire United States?"

He straightened his back and felt his chest muscles expand. Nationalism always did that to him.

"Our respected young pastor may think he's standing up for some social cause," he said, "but I know the truth. My father's reputation has been tarnished by wagging tongues, here less than a year after his passing. But let the record show that he was a good man, with high ideals, real vision, and a philanthropic nature."

He wiped his right eye. He'd found his advantage. It was time to sell it.

"This board has done well, today, to choose to honor my father's name with such an outstanding mandate," Alan said, recovering emotionally.

"I stand before you today to thank you for the outstanding respect you've chosen for him, and in keeping with my father's legacy, I'd like, single-handedly, to protect this council from the threat of fiscal criticism. I'd like to donate the money it takes to commission and build his statue, with only two conditions."

"Here we go," muttered Pastor Leonard. "There's always a catch."

Alan sent him a quick, piercing glance, and moved on.

"I, being made in my father's image, should pose for the statue. And I, because of the considerable expense of the project, request the council's permission to find the right man to create it."

"Have someone in mind, Alan?" Asked Mayor Macintosh Benz.

"I don't presently, Mac," Jovial said. "I know enough not to jump ahead of this council. No, I think we should send to New York, or maybe even London or Paris, and find one of those sissy boys, you know, a real sensitive type who may or may not enjoy the company of women, and get this tribute done right the first time." Each member of the board except the pastor snickered.

The council huddled for a moment. It made sense that Alan pose for the statue. It was common knowledge that the son was the 'spitting image' of his father. Both were more than six feet tall, with sturdy waists and broad shoulders. The characteristic Jovial family's thick, black hair was showing no signs of thinning, and baby-blue eyes could turn fiery and almost metallic when incensed. And this really was the prudent thing to do fiscally, Reverend Leonard pointed out.

"No other strings attached?" Mayor Benz asked when the huddle broke.

"Just those two," Alan said, standing even more proudly than before. "The statue, when complete and installed in the central city park, will be the sole and exclusive property of the City of Jovial. Free of charge. I'll sign any papers you want to draw up."

This time, the vote was unanimous. The statue project would move forward.

The next morning, the *Jovial World* featured a front-page story with the headline: "Statue for Founder Goes Ahead Thanks to Mandate, Philanthropy."

Alan Jovial II had primed the pump.

Fulton Gray walked onto the Jovial City Park grounds as smoothly as a boat drifting into a slip. He looked systematically to his left and right, but his followers were unsteady as sparrows on the crumbling, neglected, and uneven concrete sidewalks.

"It's almost 1 a.m.," said Fulton's right-hand man, Vince Halport, whispering as they approached the statue. "When are the lights going off?"

"Your watch must be fast," Fulton chided. "Be patient. We'll have plenty of time for this. You got the bag?"

Vince patted the backpack slung across his right shoulder and nodded. "You sure this is such a good idea?" He asked. "We could get in a lot of trouble if..."

"If we get caught," Fulton interrupted. "That ain't gonna happen. You want to make a stand or not? C'mon, man, grow a pair."

"I just don't know if anybody in town will get it," Vince said. "You call it protest art, but the cops will just call it vandalism."

The statue of Alan Jovial stood prominently, proud as the old man himself, in the exact center of the Jovial City Park. It looked as if the entire recreational site had been built around it, but the truth is, when the marble and bronze tribute was completed, ten mature trees were cut down to make room for a sizable circular concrete pad, and the firewood was buried in a new dump just outside the city limits. It was, as most patrons of the park agreed, an uncommonly well-done and detailed statue.

Alan Jovial's effigy stood, marble legs spread wide and even, in his Civil War uniform, a musket resting with its stock at Alan's feet and his right hand gripping it by the barrel, leaning slightly away from his body to the right. The bayonet, appropriate in scale to the bigger-than-life Alan Jovial, rose a foot or two above his head.

The uniform coat was made of expensive dyed bronze, turned as blue as the New York artist could get it. The soldier's cap was almost lifelike, too, but it was the damaged coat that made most respectable citizens turn eyes away from Alan's backside.

What had impressed the artist immediately upon meeting Alan Jovial II was his hair. He instantly determined that it should be a focal point, so he made it appear as if it was waving in the breeze below his Civil War cap, even though Alan had always preferred a short-cropped hair style, unlike his son.

The artist also made the coat appear to flap horizontally in an imaginary breeze as old Alan pointed west with his marble left hand, looking determinedly with his dyed-blue bronze eyes that were only a slightly different shade than the hat and coat.

The group of young men approached the statue from behind, and Fulton started sniggering.

"It cracks me up every time I see old Alan's buns out there like he's mooning the whole town," he said.

About twenty years ago, a tornado had touched down twice in Jovial, sparing most parts of town except its only mobile home community and the city park. It had toppled one tree, which fell directly on the back of the hero's coat, snapping it jaggedly between the knees and waist, exposing the buttocks.

Since times were hard and there was little money in the city treasury, the council decided it would be best to grind the uneven coat down so children wouldn't be hurt by its sharp edges. Though it was too high for children to reach, many city council members won several reelections, campaigning on their record of thinking always about the town's children.

Unfortunately, the city maintenance department had put its least-talented and least-experienced grinder to the task, and he'd slipped enough times to shave the coat down far too much. He'd even sanded down the pants, taking much of the color with it, and today, it looked like old Alan was wearing an ill-fitting skirt that billowed in the breeze like Marilyn Monroe's famous photo. His buns appeared bare and polished, tight and marble-solid.

The city worker had been fired, of course, and even went to court on a lewdness charge, but there had never been an urgent desire on the council's part—or enough money in council coffers—to cover Alan's shame. Those buns were almost irresistible.

Fulton called his other two companions to huddle up just outside the statue's three spotlights, installed in the ground and pointing up.

"You all clear about your jobs?" he asked. "Let's go over it one more time." Just then, the lights timed off.

Satisfied after a quick, whispered recitation that these three, Vince, Sam Perkins and Jalen Yearwood, were up to the task, Fulton, his eyes now accustomed to the dark, marched ahead toward the statue with straight, determined strides, graceful as an eagle riding a thermal as his companions flittered behind him. His tall, athletic frame tapered from broad shoulders, and he breezed through the darkness as if to dare anyone to challenge his right to be there, even at 1:05 a.m.

A worn cowboy hat darkened Fulton's square jaw and high cheekbones, and his long, straight, thick black hair fell nearly to his shoulders. He stopped, removed his hat and gathered his hair. He tucked it under his hat. Why hadn't he cut it? It was too hot for this.

Earlier that day, as he'd walked out of the hardware store with a couple cans of white spray paint in a brown paper bag, Melissa Hawthorn rushed up behind him like an impatient spider hungering for an elusive, delicious fly.

"Hi, Fulton." She sang as she touched his shoulder. "You sure look hot today."

"Yeah, it's way too early to be this humid," he said, teasing her.

"No, I mean you're really hot with your long hair," she said, flipping her own long, blonde hair across her left shoulder. "I haven't seen you for awhile." She gently rubbed his bare arm, then squeezed it tightly. "You're getting a tan already. If I didn't know better, I'd swear you were an Indian, and what could be hotter than that in a place like Jovial?"

"I don't know." Fulton replied, smiling against his own wishes. "Maybe you, Melissa. But I know from experience that you cool down in a hurry."

"I was just too drunk that night, you know that," she said, puffing out her bottom lip in a mock pout. Clearly, she remembered one evening, but Fulton was referring to her frustrating mood swings. "Give me another chance and we'll blow our hair back together," she said.

"I won't have mine for long," Fulton said. "I'm on my way to get a buzz cut right now."

"Fulton Gray, don't you dare! Why, you'd probably end up looking like some chocolate ice cream cone with plain old vanilla sticking out of the top." She giggled. "Hey, that doesn't sound too bad right now. Want to get an ice cream with me? The shop's open already. Seems like a month earlier than normal."

She gripped his upper arm with both hands as he shook his head. Her long nails were painted bright red. She leaned toward him. "Well, then, meet me tonight at the Pump House?" She whispered.

"How will you know it's me without my hair?"

"You won't cut your hair."

"Maybe I will."

"I'll be mad if you do," she said, flipping her hair again. As she walked away, she turned back to look twice. Both times, she caught Fulton watching her. He shook his head and smiled. Then he walked past the Jovial Barber Shop, and headed to Jalen's house.

Fulton picked up the pace and jogged into the darkness, swift and light-footed, like Tonto on an old black-and-white TV screen. His three buddies followed, giggling, pawing and jostling each other like children floating on an inflated inner tube. Sam looked lost. Fulton had told him not to eat that brownie.

"Shut up, you guys," Fulton stage-whispered. Jalen started getting the duct tape and butcher paper ready. "This has to be perfect." Fulton growled. Sam started wrapping the statue's legs with the smaller pieces of butcher paper. Jalen and Vince giggled and Sam poked them both on the shoulder, almost toppling them when they collided. "And don't make any stupid butt jokes!" Fulton ordered, his voice louder and more fierce than he'd intended. His three companions disrespectfully shushed him with exaggerated fingers to lips and giggled like grade school students. How did he ever end up with such immature friends?

Once the butcher paper was tight enough for Fulton's satisfaction, he prepared the stencil. The holes in it left open the perfect shape of boxer shorts, an accurate likeness of the very first one—made out of locally-grown wool manufactured at the Jovial Undies and Woollies Factory, founded in 1939. The original name was outdated, of course, because the factory, a shell of its former glory, now went by the acronym JOU–Jovial Organic Underwear.

Fulton reached into the bag for the paint cans and felt something strange. He commanded Jalen to shine his flashlight, and he grinned. "Jennifer, you're amazing," he stage-whispered. "Always thinking."

Another stencil with a block of letters inside the bag had adhesive on the back, protected by a strip of clear film. Fulton pulled off the strip and pressed the block just below the bottom of the butcher paper that covered Alan's belt buckle. Fulton did a quick check of where the brand-name of JOU was on his own underwear. The stencil's words read: "Eat Jovial Shorts." It was perfect. Jenn continued to amaze him with her cleverness. Who knew she agreed with Fulton on this stuff? Two ballot proposals ridiculed with one stencil. Dullards in this town needed things spelled out for them if they were ever going to understand.

Fulton laughed, but was quickly hushed by his companions. Time was getting tight.

Fulton pulled one paint can from the bag and shook it, but suddenly stopped and stared at everything except the can, as if someone had just tripped over a sleeping, vicious dog. The can's pea made a lot more noise here than it had this afternoon in the store. He waited a moment and listened. No dogs were barking.

He removed his T-shirt, wrapped it around the can as a sound suppressant and riled it up again. Keeping the shirt on the can—it was a surprisingly effective muffler—he began spraying smoothly, left-to-right, then back right-to-left.

Careful to be sure the stencil letters would stand out, he suavely rocked the can back and forth at the front of Alan Jovial, then underneath the coat, between the statue's legs and back up the rear and sides. By the time the second can was half gone, a tight, white pair of boxer shorts appeared. Perfection.

"How long does it take for paint to dry in this weather?" Fulton asked. "I didn't read that far on the label."

"We can't wait long." Fulton answered his own question. "A patrol car comes through this area of town at 1:30, if it's on schedule." Fulton pulled out his cell phone and checked the time. 1:29. Hopefully, the cops were late.

"One more thing to do," he said, grabbing the bag that Vince easily surrendered. He athletically leaped onto the statue's upper platform. The bayonet was still too high, so he wedged his right foot into the stiff folds of the bronze uniform and boosted himself up, balancing on one foot and one hand grip. He calmly reached into the bag with his free hand and started piercing old produce onto the bayonet. First a soft head of lettuce, then a smelly cabbage. Then a couple of overripe apples, a cucumber and—the cherry on the ice cream—a browning tomato. In this heat, they'd be quite raunchy by tomorrow morning.

He jumped down onto the lower platform and ripped at the butcher paper. It tore easily, loudly, and he cursed at the mess. Headlights rounded a corner on the other side of the park, and Fulton hastily reached under the statue's crotch to pull the rest of the papers off Alan's legs. Tacky paint smeared on his arm, and he stuffed the ripped stencil into a trash container next to a nearby picnic table. The group's next task suddenly became urgent.

"Stop right where you are, you kids," shouted a voice from the darkness.

"Run!" Fulton cried, and as practiced, three of the four ran in different directions. But Sam, reactions slowed as he admired the work he and his buddies had just completed, appeared frozen. He'd been warned about that brownie.

Fulton paused once he was in darker shadows and looked. Sam, too slow, tried to run when he finally realized it was the cops, but was grabbed by the back of his T-shirt by a deputy. Fulton couldn't see who it was. But he was certain he saw the officer pulling Sam's head while Sam gyrated desperately to slip out of the shirt and the policeman's grasp. Fulton started back to help, but after two steps forward, he ran back into the shadows again. Discretion. Survive to fight another day. Him in jail wouldn't do Sam any good.

It took him nearly twenty minutes to circle the park widely, his eyes on the too-bright police lights searching the park's perimeter as he made his way to the Pump House for last call. Melissa would almost certainly still be there. He needed a drink. He'd catch up with news about Sam tomorrow.

He arose as dawn was waking spring birds, and slipped out of Melissa's back door. He was clear-headed, though emotionally cloudy. See? He could control his drinking. He jumped into his Dodge Power Wagon and felt an unfamiliar lump beneath his buns. He reached down and looked at the wadded panties Melissa had left there.

"Oh, boy, Fulton," he said to the steering wheel. "Dude. Was that really worth it?"

He decided to go to work through town. He drove by the city park, under the twenty-five miles-per-hour speed limit. The boxer shorts on Alan Jovial were obvious from the road, and sharp eyes could even see writing on the waistband. "Now that was worth it," he said as he sped up and out of town, past the city limits.

Static. Relentless, hazy, infuriating white noise. It had to be stopped.

Garit West cursed and mashed the radio search button again. His parents were freaking idiots.

"Do you mean to tell me they paid sticker for that Jeep Cherokee?" he'd asked the family lawyer, Tom Saxe.

"Yep," Saxe replied. "Didn't even haggle over price. Just walked on the lot and put it on a credit card."

Spending too much money for a car wasn't really like his dad, but letting the free satellite radio offer run out sure seemed to fit his parents' pattern. Airheads, both of them. Neither ever followed through on anything. That was their lives in a nutshell. Idiots. Self-absorbed sellouts who thought themselves open-minded. But yet, here Garit was, holding the bag. Their bag, not his. Their stupid, aimless, overpriced bag to which only other hippies could relate, he supposed.

The search cycle landed, but not on static. "Rush Limbaugh!" Garit shouted to the dark starting to give way to light. He popped the search button again as if it would burn his finger to press it gently. "What have I gotten myself into?" What choice did he have?

"You could work at the produce terminal," his best friend in Decatur, Illinois, Doug Pratty, suggested the night before Garit left.

"And make nine dollars and fifty cents an hour on the graveyard shift the rest of my life?" Garit replied. "No, I think Saxe is right. I have to get away. A clean start. You're the only person I even know here anymore, Doug, and we haven't been in touch at all since I left to follow those idiots Acrid Reins."

"No, you went to follow Sandra," Doug corrected. "And then you end up leaving her behind?"

"She changed," Garit snapped. "And remember? My parents?" Doug looked down and became silent. The topic was too raw. The guy was still hurting too much to be confronted right now, and Doug was inadequate in finding the right words, ones that wouldn't make things worse or cause some uncomfortable scene in this crowded bar.

"OK, but Jovial, Michigan?" Doug said finally. "Way up there? Why go to the frozen tundra, man? There's got to be something you can find around here."

"No, " Garit said firmly. "I'm done with this town. Things are what they are. Messy. And they always will be here. I need something brand new and foreign, you know? My comfort zone is nonexistent, so why not push the limits? I'm not going to waste my time picking up a bunch of pieces when I didn't break anything. Seems like my only choice, and Saxey-boy will take care of things here."

"For a fee," Doug said. Garit smiled for the first time that night. "That's right, for a fee. A big fee. You could help, though, and buy my parents' house. That would help move things along."

"Yeah, right," muttered Doug.

Static again. Garit tapped the search button, then picked up his phone. Still charging, and only one bar. What a great metaphor for his life. All he wanted to do was recharge, if that were possible. If his idiot parents could make a comfortable upper-middle-class life for themselves in spite of apparently hating themselves, he sure could. All by himself. Who needed his parents? They were irrelevant now.

Garit bashed the radio search button again, if only to shake his mind from the reminder of just how alone he was. Something resembling a rock song blipped into the Jeep, then right back out. "Come on, come on," he snarled as he slammed the button. A sign zipped past him, but it was still too dark to read at this speed. Vote for something. Would his first job be covering an election? Great. Small-town politics. Useless stuff. Nothing of world-changing importance, that's for sure. Just another bunch of old white guys trying to be big fish in a small pond. Useless. A country station faded in and out between button punches.

Less than a week ago, he'd sat in his parents' living room and sorted through old photographs. He'd formed two piles. One small pile to save, one large one to throw into the trash. Their land-line phone had echoed through the empty space and silence.

"Garit West? Wally East calling. Say, Garit, I wonder if you're still interested in a job here at the *Jovial World*."

"I might be. Where are you?" Garit had delivered resumes to every newspaper in every town the band had passed through, but only because he had promised his mother before he left on the tour.

"We're up here in Jovial, Michigan. Have you gotten anything else lined up yet?"

"Not quite yet."

"Tell you what. You're in Decatur, Ohio?"

"Right."

"Where is that?"

"Down in the center, an hour from Bloomington."

"Got no idea where that is. Tell you what. You get the cheapest flight you can get and come up tomorrow. I'll pay for the trip if I hire you. Sound like a deal?"

"Yeah, I guess I can do that."

Garit hung up and took a deep breath to slow his breathing. A job? With all this crap hovering around him?

He called the family attorney. Tom Saxe was more than an attorney, though. He was a trusted family friend, a former college roommate of his dad's who went right after graduation while his dad went left.

"Should I do it, Tom? I really got nothing else," Garit asked.

"To be honest, I think it would be better if you left town and started over," he'd advised. "Take the Jeep. Possession is nine-tenths of the law. I can handle things here. No use in you being dragged down any further. It's going to get a lot messier before it's cleaned up. Go. Start a new life. What's left for you here?"

The next day, Wally held the interview over lunch and offered Garit a job by the time dessert arrived, but only if he could start the next Monday.

"Take your time, son," Wally said, scooping fudgy, steaming cake into his mouth. "What do you say? Got any better offers?" Moist crumbs flew from his mouth into his still-full water glass, sitting next to the third empty whiskey sour.

"I just didn't think things happened this fast," Garit babbled.

"You ain't in college anymore, son. Or on some artsy-fartsy adventure with some Satan-worshiping band. And this ain't *Rolling Stone*, thank God! We gotta get things done and on deadline! You want the job?"

"What's it pay?" His college counselor's only real advice was to avoid the salary topic, but Garit had already resisted his desire to correct Wally's impression about the Acrid Reins. But this was all so sudden, rules were out the window like a cigarette butt.

"I like that, Garit. You cut right through the bull," Wally had said. "Three hundred and fifty bucks a week after taxes, plus you can live in my apartment above the office for free. Whattaya say?"

It was at that very moment, when he reached out to shake Wally East's hand, that Garit's mind began to divide and the lump began to grow in his stomach. What were his options?

He couldn't go back to the concert tour. He'd burned that bridge right down to the water. But he couldn't stay in Decatur. It was where dreams went to die.

Rush Limbaugh popped into the Jeep again. It wasn't better than static.

Garit thought about what his mother might say.

"There's no reason to be apprehensive," he said to himself, mocking her. "Look at the bright side. Fear never got anyone anywhere. People leave far more farther behind every day. A weekly small-town newspaper? It's the best place to start. Not as much pressure as a daily deadline, and a chance to get into some real in-depth reporting instead of being shoved into the social media department somewhere in a big city." She was an idiot. But he told himself she would have been right, had she said it.

It all made sense as he drove. He continued aloud: "The downside? Having to write about everything from beauty pageants to prize heifers, which might be surprisingly similar stories, truth be told." He pushed back the humor. It couldn't be appropriate.

A classic rock song popped up and stuck suddenly as the Jovial County line swished behind him. It was a song his parents had liked, although he had always been apathetic about their hippy tastes.

Garit quickly pressed the set button and made it number one on the channel list. He pulled the button that rolled the window back up. He turned on the air conditioning.

Dawn was finally breaking. If he was going to do this, it was time to give it his all. He would have a positive attitude, despite himself. His drive to succeed had always been strong and internal. Hard work was not in his genetics. But he would succeed, on his own. He didn't need his parents, anyway.

A large political sign sped by, then another. Garit slowed to read them.

"Save our lives! Vote Yes on Prop. 1." Seemed logical enough.

"Stop the monopoly! Vote No on Prop. 1."

Garit could feel the sun's heat now. Seemed a bit early to be this hot.

"Stop the poison," read the next sign. "A vote for Prop. 1 is a vote for your children's health."

"Want good food? You got it! Trust your farmers! Vote no on Prop. 1."

"Don't bring Detroit crime here. Vote yes on Prop. 2!"

"Prop. 2: A waste of time! Vote no!"

The signs were getting more frequent as Garit saw the first outline of what looked like civilization. The issues would take some time to understand. But he was a good reporter, a good writer. Why only Wally

East saw that, he couldn't know. More signs zipped by. "Vote No! Vote Yes! Save our Children! Save our rights! Visit our website. Don't be fooled! Vote Yes! Vote no!"

He slowed as he came into town. The Jeep moseyed past a sign on a squarish building under construction that proclaimed there were ninety-nine days until the grand opening of some store.

The ache in his stomach subsided a little. He was almost home, like it or not. Here was his new start.

Fulton pulled his pickup truck into the
main farm's driveway. Two big, fluffy white dogs pranced up, silent with
tails wagging.

"Hi, guys," he said, cupping each one's chin under his hand as they
greeted their friend. He shut the truck door quickly, because Scully
would have jumped in. Mulder, the bigger of the two Great Pyrenees
dogs, always held back a little. He was the enforcer. Scully was the
charmer. They bounced ahead of him as he walked toward the house,
just as Jennifer Dogues stepped onto the large deck attached to the
farmhouse.

"Gettin' in a little late, dude." She smiled. Fulton knew better than
to take the comment as judgment. It was just a tease.

"Hey, Jenn, thanks for the stencil. It was perfect!"

"Just don't ever tell anyone I even knew about your dirty deeds," she
said, giggling. "Not even Coney."

"My lips are sealed," he said, noticing she'd gotten a haircut since
he saw her last, two days ago. Not much. Just enough to let it fall gently
on her broad, yet feminine shoulders. Her blondish-red locks hadn't
faded into gray at all, even at her age, and she was still as attractive as
ever. Maybe even more so. Her experience and wisdom had formed fine
spider-web lines from each eye outward, and they gave her a weathered
look that accented her mesmerizing blue eyes, and made Fulton proud

that men in his family could keep such beauty so close for so long. Maybe someday he'd know their secret.

"Where's that husband of yours?" He asked, knowing she was off to give a store progress report to a city council committee.

"Not sure, but I know a cow went down this morning. Don't know details, just that he's been up since about three this morning and hasn't taken a break for breakfast. Find her and you'll find him."

Fulton called to the dogs: "Mulder! Scully! Where's your daddy?"

He heard a bark coming from the side of a free-stall barn closest to the house, and headed that way.

"Coney!" He shouted. The dogs appeared, stopped and ran behind the barn to a smaller barn where dry cows roamed in and out to their feeding troughs and, in summer, out to pasture. Down the short cement walkway, Fulton found his uncle, Cornelius Dogues III, kneeling beside a cow lying on her side, bleeding and groaning.

He approached in silence and put a hand on Coney's dripping wet shoulder, and noticed he was milking her by hand. He knew how hard his uncle took things like this.

The cow was bleeding from several holes in her head, neck and side, and she lifted her head, moaning when the dogs rushed to her. One eye was punctured, and it spurted blood. Fulton shooed the dogs away, and they left for other tasks. Fulton stepped back a little and noticed the cow's ear tag.

"Fifty-five?" he asked. "What the heck? I thought it was thirty-one who was having all the calving trouble."

"Nope. She did just fine, Nice little bull calf." Coney shifted his weight to relieve his knees from the hard, rough-textured concrete, then resumed milking her into a pail that was lying on its side.

"So what happened here?"

"Don't know exactly what put her into labor, but she had a small heifer," Coney said, pouring a small amount of the colostrum into another pail, which was now about half full. "Sure not big enough to tear her insides out like this." He pointed behind the cow, and Fulton noticed a massive rupture. Rancid afterbirth was sitting like road kill, steaming even in the too-early spring heat.

"Where's her calf?" Fulton asked. "And why is she here instead of in the birthing pen?"

"She was still three weeks away," Coney said, pausing for a moment to flex his hands. "Look over in the corner, there." Fulton walked over and picked up one of several thin wires, each one about twenty feet long.

"What the heck does this mean?" He asked.

"Look against the wall."

Fulton saw, propped up, a sheet of plywood with dozens of nails sticking pointy-side up. Not just any nails. These were ten-inch long construction nails, used mostly for holding retaining walls together.

"All I can figure," Coney said, "is that someone put the trip wires across the cement to tangle her feet, and put the plywood in just the right spot so she'd fall onto it. It's like someone wanted her to suffer."

Fulton looked at the massive animal's front legs. They were cut, just below the knee, where she apparently tangled in the wires and fell. She had rolled partially onto the board, and when Coney found her, he'd pulled the plywood out with no little sweat and difficulty.

"Animal rights people?" Fulton asked.

"Could be. I hear they've come back now that it's warming up."

"How'd they get past the dogs?"

"Don't know," Coney said, looking up. "Get me that clean pail behind you, will you? I have to get her colostrum to her calf ASAP. She's a tiny little thing, but healthy for being premature."

"So the trauma sent her into labor?"

"That's how I got it figured." Coney handed Fulton the milk he'd gotten and took the new pail. " Only God's grace that none of the nails hurt the calf. She's in the newbie barn. Feed her right away, will you? I have maybe enough for her first meal. I hope I can get enough for three meals, but I don't know."

Coney continued squeezing and pulling milk from the dying cow until his hands cramped like frozen vice grips and his wrists ached all the way up to his elbows. He flexed his fingers, then milked her more, from his haunches.

"I'm sorry about all this, girl," he said, and patted the animals side, gently. He couldn't get enough colostrum for a full three-day ration, but he'd gotten some. Hopefully it was enough. He flexed his hands again.

His knees felt all that crouching, too. The dull ache of middle age was unmistakable.

"This is not cool at all, Lord," Coney prayed. "But thank you again for the calf. May she milk better than her Mama and be just as gentle." He stood just as Number fifty-five took a deep heavy breath. Coney heard a gush of more entrails and blood, saw it flowing from her back end and from lacerations on her sides and neck. Then she sighed and died, and Coney wept for her pain as he collapsed onto her body.

Coney recovered, milked her a little more, then gave up. She'd done all she could, and so had he. He shook a kink out of his left leg, and stretched his entire body.

"It's enough, Lord," he said. "Thank you. And about the people who did this?" He looked up at the sky. "I know you want us to bless those who do us harm, and I pray for your grace that I'll have the right attitude to do it. But I also pray that there's a specially dark and cold place in Hell for people who attack innocent animals."

He took the colostrum and poured it into three two-quart bottles, the kind most farmers used to hand-feed calves. All three came out about half full. Not perfect, but enough to give fifty-five's calf what she needed to build her immune system. He labeled the bottles with masking tape on which he'd written '55', and was putting them into the refrigerator just as Fulton came back into the milk house with an empty bottle.

"She drank it all down," he said. "Pretty little thing." Coney grunted and fought back tears.

"Want some good news? We put a nice set of boxer shorts on old Al last night," Fulton said. His smirk burst into a giggle, and it reminded Coney of his late sister, Fulton's mom. Coney wasn't in the mood.

"They're gonna catch you if you don't watch out," Coney said sternly. "Botsdorf won't be able to help you then. You'll have to pay your own fine, because I won't bail you out." He lied.

"Oh, relax," Fulton said. "Jimmy Dulogski couldn't catch a cold in a pneumonia ward. You're just down about losing a good cow, dude. Can't blame you. All I can tell you is what you tell me. It's a part of farming. You knew that from way before I was born."

"Still doesn't help. And boards full of nails aren't a part of farming."

"I know. It's a stupid saying," Fulton said and walked toward the door. "Going to the store meeting? We're already planning which bull will get loose at our grand opening."

"At least you know your history," Coney replied. "But I don't have time for a meeting, and neither do you. Get over and get that first celery in the ground. Labor won't get here until next week, earliest, so you can just forget about your pranks. I've got to wait for the cops and the insurance man, then bury fifty-five."

Fulton started to defend himself. This was not a prank. It was a political protest. But he turned and got into his truck, headed toward the river and the rich, black muck that grew such amazing vegetables.

By the time Coney came into the house for lunch, Jenn was back and putting a sandwich and some fresh vegetables on the table.

"We got to keep an eye on Fulton," she said. "Sometimes he's just too smart for his own good, and the problem is, he knows it."

"What did he do now?"

"Oh, nothing all that big. Just painted underwear on the statue."

"Kids have been doing that for years."

"Yeah, but this year I have a bad feeling," she said. "They keep talking about this gang proposal at the city council. They all seem to think it's a great idea. I have a feeling it's just an excuse to get some grant money, and I'm afraid there will be some unintended consequences if they push things through too fast."

Coney grunted his agreement and stretched his fingers.

"His bigger problem is getting that muck ready," he said. "We'll keep him planting for the next week or two before he gets another day off. He needs to get his mind off politics and girls and onto his job."

As was his custom, Coney flipped open the Bible on the kitchen table.

It fell open to Ecclesiastes. Chapter three. 'A time to kill, and a time to heal. A time to weep and a time to laugh. A time to plant and a time to reap'.

The dogs burst in through the farmhouse's dogie door and walked by, their noses skimming along the table edges. "Some guard dogs you are," Coney said. Scully looked at him and yawned, and both dogs laid down on the kitchen floor.

It was after nine a.m. when Garit pulled the Jeep behind the *Jovial World* offices.

The parking lot surface was cracked and decaying. Its edges were crumbly, falling outside their lines like wandering scribbles in a kindergartner's coloring book, but the yellow parking lines appeared brand new and so bright they reflected the sun.

The air was humid and heavy as he stepped out of the Jeep. The asphalt, hot already under a thickening sun, peeled one of the yellow line decals back as it tried to escape the ground heat.

The parking lot held two identical boxy yellow Kias with rusty wheel wells—10 years old if they were a day—each of which had a legal-sized, laminated paper on the dash that read "PRESS" in large, bold, printed letters.

He walked around the *World's* reinforced and aging cement loading dock and through a larger, newer paved parking lot in front of the building, on Jovial's Main Street.

He imagined that the immigrants who traveled to this country so many decades ago felt just like he did today. Everything was foreign. The sun hadn't come up where he'd expected. Tree buds were in earlier stages of development than back home in Illinois, which didn't make any sense, considering how far north he was now. Birds sang differently and the air smelled peculiar, as if it lacked something. The architecture in the town was roughly similar to central Illinois, but just different enough to make him wonder if he would know which language he'd hear as he reached for the handle to the glass door of his new life.

Immediately to his right, once the heavy door shut behind him, he noticed an ancient, huge copy machine, and its sudden sound spun him around. It purred and spit out sheets of paper like Play-Dough seeping through a toy meat grinder.

On the wall at his left, beyond the inner-office door, hung three framed photographs. He stepped closer to read the laminated newspaper clipping inserted into each frame. Various people were caught on film accepting giant novelty keys from someone. Wally East, editor and owner, was in the last photo, the only one shot in color. Wally looked much different than Garit remembered from his job interview. Maybe it was the bushy sideburns, like the ones he'd seen on his dad in the old pictures Garit had pitched into the trash just four days ago.

He turned around. Behind the counter in front of him, Garit could see three messy desks in a row along a bland light-brown three-quarter-height panel wall that held tacked-up calendars and snapshots of children, horses, cats and dogs, and the occasional husband-wife shot.

Wally East appeared from behind a partition and silently leaned on the counter behind Garit. A pair of bifocals on a chain dangled from Wally's neck, and when they clacked against the reception desk, Garit jumped.

"How do you like our awards?' Wally asked. Garit shrugged. "This paper is 144 years old, and there have only been four owners," Wally said. "Three of us are on the wall there. Someday I want to get one of the Debbies to colorize the old boys and Photo Shop all of us together, like a family reunion photo or something."

"So what are the awards for?"

"For being newspaper owners. Isn't that enough?" Garit smiled, hoping that was a joke.

"Let's get you into the newsroom," Wally said, cheerily.

He was short and stocky, with a flat-top haircut that made him look like a drill sergeant. Streaks of gray the color of an ancient glassed Civil War uniform crept into the light browns of stubble on his head. His face was round but hardened, with a wide nose flattened as if it had been punched too many times. Garit could tell Wally was smiling at him, but his mouth curled downward, making the smile appear reluctant, like approving disapproval.

"Shouldn't I change first?" He asked. "I just drove in, and didn't know I'd be on the job so fast."

"Don't bother with that right now," Wally said. "I don't want you to wear that T-shirt when you're working, but the jeans are OK if they're clean. We're informal here. If we all wore suits, people might think we were up to something. Or making too much money."

Garit stepped around the counter and Wally swept his arm broadly as if it required great pomp to usher Garit in. Wally wore newer jeans and a light blue dress shirt.

The carpet ended at the door behind the reception counter, and the back room's floor was clean, smooth, bare cement, though not cold under Garit's Nike tennis shoes. From a distant room, a clacking sound repeated itself continually, in rhythm like a back beat of some foreign machine or a rusty train leaving a station.

Garit and Wally shook hands, and Garit stifled the shot of pain that accompanied it. Wally wore a ring on every finger of both hands, even the thumb, and one of them had bitten Garit's pinkie the first time they'd met, just like now.

Wally urged Garit to follow him toward two girls' backs. They sat at adjacent desks, two computer screens on each desk.

Debbie One, a sharp-chinned redhead with striking green eyes, and Debbie Two, a brunette with a broad welcoming smile and flat chest, giggled obligatorily when Wally introduced them.

"I never could tell them apart. That was why I named them Debbie One and Debbie Two," Wally said, grinning. They each tossed Garit an uninterested glance after he lightly shook their hands, and they immediately went back to work. "They're building ads," Wally said. "Don't disturb them too much. They keep quite busy."

"And we're already quite disturbed," said Debbie Two. Both Debbies giggled without stopping work as if one was Betty Rubble and the other Wilma Flintstone.

Wally led him to a far corner of the room.

"This is the sports desk," he said. "Jeff, our sports guy, keeps odd hours, but he gets the job done. You might never see him, but he gets me clean copy. I'll never get used to his filing method. This desk just looks like a pile of junk to me."

"Lots and lots of piles." Garit agreed.

"Over here," Wally pointed, "is by comparison a neat and tidy proofreader's desk. Over there by the walls are the sales reps' desks. It's always good if they're not here. They shouldn't be this time of day. The darkroom is right there next to them."

The darkroom, Garit noticed, trying to decipher this new northern language, was nothing more than a curved metal black door with a sign above it that said "darkroom," but it bulged out of the wall and had no knob on it.

On the wall to its left, so high it was completely out of place, was a regulation wooden door, with a small wooden platform under it and wooden stairs built of two-by-fours held together with particle board. Wally spun around, and his glasses on the chain followed.

"You just missed the staff meeting," he said. "Monday mornings at eight sharp. Then go do your job. That's my policy. That's all I ask of my employees and myself. I'll never work anyone harder than I'll work myself."

"Sounds fair enough."

"I work until the job gets done," Wally said. "So will you. And now, the editorial department," he said, and pointed Garit to a spotlessly clean desk pushed against the back of a free-standing three-quarter wall partition. Next to it was a very messy desk. The nameplate on it read Aspen Kemp.

He'd seen the name in the three back issues Wally had given him at the job interview. He'd read them all cover to cover, every word. She was a good writer, better than Wally, in his opinion. But who was he to judge?

The only things on Garit's clean desk were an older desk-model flat screen monitor, mouse and keyboard, and a shiny black nameplate, bearing his misspelled name.

He and Wally walked over, and Garit picked up the nameplate.

"What's wrong?" Wally asked, noticing his discomfort.

"Not a big deal," Garit said, "but my name is spelled G-A-R-I-T, not G-A-R-R-E-T-T."

"You're the first person I've ever seen who didn't like his first nameplate," Wally grinned. "Are you gonna dis your first byline too?"

"I've had a few, remember?"

"Ah, the *Rolling Stone* gig. Gotcha. You'll be writing real news here, not entertainment news." The way he emphasized the words made Garit believe the man had great disdain for entertainment and all that went along with it. Garit liked that about the man.

"Tell you what," Wally said. "Organize whatever stuff is in your desk, check out the computer and get passwords set, get settled and look through the files in the drawers. When Aspen comes in, she'll get you the paperwork you need to fill out for taxes and stuff like that. Then check the story list on the wall behind Debbie two." He pointed over his shoulder without turning his head. "See if anything interests you for your first feature." Garit nodded. Wally marched to the only enclosed office in the room, opposite all the other desks.

The drawers in Garit's desk were empty except one at the bottom right that was packed with old newspaper clippings in file folders. He read through the headlines, but they meant nothing to him. They told stories about city council meetings and voting records and grants from the government, and one thick file was only labeled 'history'. Pretty tame compared to the antics of an acid-rock band touring the country. This job would probably be easy. He needed that.

Garit went to the clipboard hanging on the wall near Debbie Two, who didn't look up as he took it. He stood by her desk as he read the list of story ideas.

"Uh, excuse me, but am I supposed to know anything about any of these things?" He asked Debbie Two. "Everything here just confuses me."

Wally suddenly yelled "Undies" from his office, and began laughing. Garit looked up, but the Debbies didn't.

"I don't see how you could know anything about them," Debbie Two said to Garit. Her face was suddenly tight and unfriendly. "You just got here from where? Ohio?"

"Illinois," he corrected.

"Sorry. Look. I'm just a designer. I don't know anything about editorial. You'll have to ask Wally or Aspen."

The darkroom door, a turnstile of black, squeaked open just then with a swoosh and a clang as it hit a stopper. The room became brighter as Aspen Kemp stepped from the blackness into the room.

She was tall and thin, with Carpathian walnut-brown hair that was lighter, almost blonde, at her part, just slightly to the left of center. She took a double-take and smiled when she saw Garit, and her bright blue eyes sparkled in the room's flat light, defying all laws of illumination and reflection. She stepped toward Garit.

"You must be the new reporter," she said, extending her hand. Her arm, bare to the shoulder, was tanned, toned, firm, and long with no sharp curves or tightness from over-conditioning.

"Wow." Garit blurted and began to turn red as he accepted her hand. "I mean, wow, did I misread you." *Good catch*, he thought, wondering if she saw through it.

"What do you mean?" Aspen asked, tilting her head in a way that made Garit believe she saw right through him.

"I read all your stuff from three issues, and I tell you, I had you pictured a lot differently."

"Oh? How so?"

"As an older woman, maybe plainer. For sure fatter," he babbled.

"Well, I don't know if I should be flattered or insulted," she said, and withdrew her hand from Garit's.

"Oh, take it as a compliment, for sure," he stammered. "Your writing is full and straightforward. Yeah. That's what I meant. And mature. Like you have insight beyond your years."

She turned her head with a natural, unconscious, and uncontrived sensuousness. When her eyes darted back at him, they were mischievous.

"Right. You tried to carry it a little too far, but, nice catch, uh ..."

"Garit West," he mumbled, putting his hand out again, then dropping it.

But she reached out again, and they shook hands again, lingering over the touch.

"Aspen Kemp." She smiled as their eyes met again. "At your service."

"I'm flattered," he said. "And glad to hear it, since I put my foot so far into my mouth just now."

"No troubles," she said. "Have you gotten all your paperwork filled out?"

"What? Oh, yeah. Wally said you'd take care of it."

"He did?" She turned toward Wally's office.

"Wally, darn it, you can't even get the tax stuff together?" She complained.

"That's your job now, remember?" Wally's voice replied.

"Oh, yeah," she muttered, shrugging her shoulders and raising her eyebrows as if the joke was on her. "I'll get it."

She disappeared behind a partition and returned with a pile of papers. She put them on Garit's desk.

"Just read all this over and sign where you're supposed to," she said. "If you need anything, I'm right here." She pointed to her messy desk.

"One thing," Garit said, and leaned forward as if he were about to tell a secret. Aspen leaned over and their heads nearly touched.

"What is a darkroom, anyway?" He whispered. Aspen laughed and stood upright. "You're just all brand-new, aren't you?" She giggled. "Fresh out of school?"

"I been out a few months."

She smiled beams of sunshine on him. "Got no bad habits yet?"

"I don't know about that." He grinned.

"I mean bad writing habits!"

"Oh. I guess not."

She tilted her head as if contemplating him.

"A dark room used to be where they developed film and printed photos before they invented digital cameras," she said. "But now, the darkroom is just a place to hide. If you're ever stressed out or need a break, go in there. No one can get in if the door's shut, and there's really only room for one, maybe two if you're willing to be uncomfortable. It's got a comfy chair and a stereo, a fridge with some non-alcoholic beverages. The joke around here is, what happens in the darkroom stays in the darkroom!" The Debbies laughed but didn't turn from their work.

Wally grumbled loudly in his office, and Garit thought he heard

him say "boxer shorts! And "rotten produce?" in the middle of a group
of profanities.

"Maybe this afternoon I can give you a tour of the town," Aspen
said, her smile a perfect complement to her deep three-dimensional
eyes. They speared him as if he'd taken a peek at a solar eclipse. "Did
you unpack yet? I hear Wally's renting you his fixer-upper."

"That's not how he described it, but I only have a carload of stuff."

"No furniture?"

"Nope."

"Fridge? Stove? Couch? Bed?"

"I have an air mattress that I bought on the way here. For the last six
months I slept mostly on the floor of a van on a cot mattress in a sleeping
bag. So the new mattress is probably my most valuable possession,
except for my computer and the Jeep."

"Wally!" She yelled toward the office. Her eyes flirted a dance back
and forth between him and Garit. "Will you at least get Garit here a
fridge and couch? Maybe a kitchen table and chairs?"

"What? What for?"

"For Garit and your apartment. Man! You'd forget your head."

"I'll take care of that later," he said, appearing at the door of his office
with a phone pressed to his chest. "Right now I need Garit to go see
what's going on in the park. Someone painted another pair of underwear
on old Alan, and from what I hear, they did a really good job."

5

In the center of the one-square-acre city park, shaded partially by barely budding, tall, mature hickory, maple and beech trees, Garit saw the stately statue, about six feet high from its base three feet from the ground, a slightly larger-than-life likeness of town founder Alan Jovial.

Garit parked the ancient company Kia, waited for the engine to sputter to an end, and observed the scene, imagining it as an establishing shot from a movie.

Three policemen sat at a single picnic table, and another policeman was standing, addressing them. Garit walked to a picnic table behind them, sat with his feet on the seat and took out the point-and-shoot camera Wally had tossed him.

The camera squeaked power on. He pointed it toward the police and pressed the shutter. He was too far away to take a decent photo, but he could hear clearly. He turned on the voice recorder in his phone.

"Now I've never kept a count, but I guess I've seen at least fifteen statue paintings. Maybe twenty," the police chief told his deputies. He reminded Garit of his high school football coach. He wore his uniform sloppily with no tie, and a few long hairs protruding from his shirt made him seem unusually wiry for someone slightly overweight. His hat hadn't been washed any time recently, and he wore long, broad sideburns, the kind that were worn by Garit's dad in the 1970s.

"I even knew a kid in high school who did it," the chief said. "Some stoner whose name I forget now. But this time is different. This time it's serious. Deputy Smith, you've inspected the scene. What can you tell us?"

Deputy Smith rose to his feet, his shirt buttons straining against the pressure of his belly.

"I walked slowly around the statue checking for footprints or discarded paint cans or brushes, but I saw nothing out of the ordinary except a stencil and butcher paper in the trash can," the deputy said. "Either this year's vandals were careful or someone already corrupted the scene."

The chief scribbled something on a small note pad that slid easily from his shirt pocket. "Not a bad observation, but there's more," he said, and walked toward the statue. He cautiously touched the paint.

"This paint is dry, he said. "How long does it take paint to dry in this weather?" No answers.

"I don't know either, but we need to find out," he said. "If we find out what kind of paint it is, maybe we can track it to where it was bought. What else do you see?"

"They did a good job," Smith said "It's neat, with no over-spray. Not sloppy at all." The chief sighed.

"That's good," he said, turning to address his other two officers again.

"You know, kids will always be kids, but this one is different. You have to admire a job well done. But we can't afford to do that. Neither can the city or the county, for that matter. This is not about youthful rebellion anymore!"

His voice began rising, like a thunderstorm billowing in. "No more laughing and turning away. No discounting it as kid stuff as if it could be forgiven like all the others. We're in a new era, men, or we will be when the gang ordinance passes. This was no freehand job. Using a stencil is a sign of premeditation. Great. Just when we get somebody with some pride in their work, we gotta go after him. And the rotten produce was a nice touch." He smiled, paused and turned.

"You know, boys, this should make you angry," he said after a dramatic pause. "You're all servants of the city of Jovial, after all, and when the city council directs the police to crack down on painting the statue, by golly, we'll do it, even at the expense of preventing real crime. Our personal feelings can't get in the way of our duties to the city. If this is what the people want, this is what we'll give them. If obeying directives brings respect—or better yet funds—to the city, it's worth it. I just hope I'll see the day when fighting crime is funded for the right reasons, not for politics. But more than all that, it should make you angry that you have to come out and scrape paint off a statue's crotch!" His voice was billowing again. "You all have better things to do. You know it and I know it. But we're public servants, and we'll do it, by God."

He bent under the statue awkwardly. "Now look at old Alan's buns," he said. See this tiny smear?"

"What's that mean, chief? said a deputy who Garit thought looked about his age.

"Maybe something, but nothing too important," the chief said. "It's just noteworthy enough to get in the notebook. Just in case." He slipped out the notebook again and scribbled. "Alright, let's get to it," the chief said.

Garit stepped to the ground and checked the camera, which was still on. Probably too old to have a timed shutoff feature. He approached the working deputies, who glared at him.

"Get back to work," said the chief. "Never mind the press. I've got a citizen's visit to make."

The smallest deputy, a blonde, square-shouldered and square-faced officer built like a half a brick, held a can of paint thinner in one hand and a rag in the other, and he began rubbing Alan Jovial's posterior intently, with his tongue sticking out of the side of his mouth, his head cocked sideways. He reminded Garit of a childhood acquaintance who spent one whole summer peeking under his neighbor girl's doll dresses.

Garit pulled a lever that activated the camera's zoom function and pressed the shutter. All deputy face in the frame, but blurry.

Facing the statue's front was Deputy Smith—a dark-haired, broad man—holding a wire brush and another can of paint thinner. He scrubbed with surprising vigor right where the underwear had the most value as concealer of the town patriarch's private parts.

Garit checked his photos on the camera, deleted the blurry one and looked up. The deputies were working, but watching him too.

"It hurts just watching those wire bristles work," he said. Deputy Smith smiled, but the blonde brick deputy sneered.

Garit took a closeup shot of the corroded stone and scratched paint. He took another far-away shot. The blonde officer's vigorous, accelerating speed blurred his hands in the camera's viewer as he brushed the statue's crotch up and down with an obvious degree of enthusiasm. Garit zoomed the lens to get as close as the camera would allow. The deputy's left hand gripped Alan's posterior. Elbow grease, mixed with sweat, flew up and dripped from his face.

Unsure about this camera, Garit pulled out his cell phone, zooming in with the camera application and shot several times, getting closer to the deputies' faces with each shot. He turned the camera feature off and checked the audio recording, just to be safe and to accurately quote whoever would agree to an interview.

"How many times have you had to do this?" Garit asked of any of the deputies who would answer. "I mean, there's clearly wear on this, er, um, area of the statue."

"What else do you see?" Asked the chief, who was suddenly standing over Garit's shoulder. "Look deeper, son." Garit paused, trying to appear thoughtful.

"This statue's rear shows wear," Garit said, finally. "As the paint comes off, I can see pock-marks and tiny potholes of erosion, particularly on these, um, shall we say prominent buttocks?"

The chief put out his hand, and shook Garit's heartily, gripping firmly.

"Police Chief James Dulogski," he said, grinning. "You must be the new reporter Wally's told me about. From Ohio, right? Most people just call me Chief."

"Garit West, from Illinois," Garit replied. "So what's this all about, Sheriff Dulogski?

"I'm not a sheriff, I'm a chief. What do you think it's all about?"

"Well, Chief Dulogski, to be honest, right now, I'm thinking how cool it is that this is my first story ever for the *Jovial World*," he said. "I expected some boring city council meeting or obituary or a traffic accident or something. I'm thinking how lucky I am. How often do people get to see cops scrubbing a statue's crotch and butt? Or get to journal it with words and photographs? I couldn't have asked for a more unusual start to a career."

"Well, now, that's an interesting perspective, West," Dulogski said. Garit held the phone up to record the chief's words. "But let me take you a little deeper than that. If you stay in Jovial any length of time, there just might be some other unusual things to write about. But can I give you a little friendly advice?"

"Please do."

"What you said just now was all about you, wasn't it? No one wants to read about you, son, no offense. They want to read about the statue, and about who did it and why they did it. That's your real story. Now if we catch who did it, that would be a real story."

"I agree," Garit said. "But for now, Wally just wants a picture. I don't even know if I'll get to write the story for sure. I hope I can."

"I'm sure you will," the chief said. His pager squawked, but he paid no attention.

"So what *is* the story?" Garit asked. "Who do you think did it, and why? Is it just a prank, like painting the water tower on graduation night?"

"Ain't no big story here, if that's what you mean," Dulogski said. "It's just a bunch of copycat hoodlums who've probably heard about this urban legend." He looked at Garit's cell phone and pointed at it. "This is off the record, but you might need it for your own understanding, if you're going to be here awhile. I hope you are. Wally's been going through reporters like beer through a horse over there. Most people in town know all this stuff, so there's no need to write about it."

Dulogski tipped back his hat, put his hands on his belly and sat on the picnic table the deputies used for their supplies.

"Back in the early 1900s, the story goes, when old Alan Jovial here was still around and kickin', there was this group of his enemies, for lack of a better word, who formed an anti-gov'ment group against his mayorship, and they called it the Jocular Society. They were just a bunch of drunks who liked to tell dirty jokes, but they captured the ear of the local press at the time, which made them into a kind of folk legend. But the truth is, they never really did anything to improve the community. That's where the truth ends, for the most part. But part of the legend, with no proof, is that one night, after old Alan fell asleep at his concubine's house—see there never really was any concubine, because Alan Jovial was a Christian man—this group of boys come in and painted his bare-naked bottom with this bright red paint, and Alan, so the story goes, never fully got it out of his skin until the day he died. They think maybe the lead in it killed him. That's all they had back then was lead-based paint. Not like today."

Garit was happy he was recording this, but regretted that it would all be off the record.

The chief resumed. "It was a nice little fictional tale in this town's past, interesting enough to be a kind of reward for people interested in history, like me, even if it isn't altogether true. Time tends to let fact blend with legend in these cases. But one day back in the 1960s, I think it was, some hippy liberal teacher happened to dig up the story and tell it to her high school history class as a hoot. Well, some of them boys in her class decided to paint old Alan's statue the same way, for the sake of history, I guess. Maybe they got extra credit, I don't know. And to this day, somebody seems to pick up the habit every few years when it warms up, just like—you said it—painting your name on the water tower. Just a bunch of drunk kids, is my theory. And besides, boxer shorts are an inaccurate rendition of the story. I don't know if they even had boxers back when Alan was alive. Probably didn't have elastic bands."

"Then why was it called the Jock-ular society?" Garit asked.

The chief looked at him and turned his mouth sideways.

"You're a writer, right? You know words and stuff?" Garit twitched.

"You know what jocularity is?"

"Oh!" exclaimed Garit. "Duh."

"No kiddin'," Dulogski smiled, showing no annoyance.

"Guess they thought they were pretty clever," he said finally. "Some folks say there still are some of the descendants of that original Jocular Society around here, but I don't know. Probably wouldn't matter much if they were. That name comes up, just because it's part of the legend. And them boys in the '60s called themselves the Jock-ular society." They spelled it j-o-c-k. "I always thought it was more subtle to just spell it the way it's supposed to be spelled, but they probably were punks and still so young they snickered about the jockstrap factory."

"Jockstrap factory?"

"You didn't know? Jovial at one time was the jockstrap capital of the Upper Midwest, courtesy of Alan Jovial the Second. It all would have went under in the seventies, but a big bailout by the town helped them switch to men's organic underwear, and a few other less-profitable products." Suddenly, the chief's radio squawked again. He checked it quickly.

"I gotta go, Garit, will you be OK?" Garit nodded. "Just call me for whatever you need, quotes and such," Dulogski said, and sped off.

Garit turned off his phone and slipped it into his back pocket. He took a few more photographs with the *World* camera, including several of the officers drizzling paint thinner on the ground, and got back in the company Kia. It sputtered and backfired, but finally started.

He waited for a moment, listening for the engine to smooth out. When it did, he looked up and saw the short, blonde, brick-built deputy outside the window, one hand on his gun.

"Give me that camera, kid," he snarled, holding out his hand.

"What for?"

"Because I said so, kid. Hand it over!"

"This is newspaper property," Garit said. "You can't just steal it."

"I didn't steal anything," the officer said. "There is no camera." He drew his gun, widened his stance and pointed it directly at Garit's eyes, no more than a foot away.

"What, you're threatening me?"

"I'm not doing anything, kid. Hand it over."

Garit frowned to hide his terror, reached to the passenger seat and handed the camera to the officer. He holstered his gun, dropped the camera on the ground and stomped it with the heel of his black boot. It didn't break. Unfazed, he stomped it again with the other boot, but it remained intact.

"Guess you're no match for Chinese technology, huh?" Garit said. The policeman threw a punch into the car, but Garit ducked. Returning his attention to the camera, the deputy shoved it with his toe under the Kia's front tire.

"Too bad some stupid kid reporter is so clueless that he doesn't know when he accidentally ran over the company camera. Go, kid! Now!" He shouted. Garit backed up the Kia, and heard the camera crunch under the tire.

The deputy grinned, turned his back, then turned around again.

"You'd best be going back to work, kid," he grinned as he put his gun into its holster.

Police Chief James Dulogski pulled into the Dogues' farm driveway and was greeted by furious protective barking. Mulder and Scully were usually friendly, but as Jenn looked out the kitchen window, she took note of their behavior. After the initial "Woo-Woof!" and growls, which was standard for the pair, they didn't approach the car. That was unusual.

As he emerged from the patrol car, the dogs sat, maybe twenty feet away, and watched him. They growled a low but patient rumble, as if waiting to assess this funny-dressed person fully before passing judgment.

Jenn stepped onto the porch, wishing she had changed out of her council meeting clothes into something less flattering.

"Hi, James," she shouted. "Kids! It's OK!" The dogs looked at her and turned to walk between her and the chief, with Mulder, the enforcer, getting in the last word with a grumbling refrain of staccato, guttural woofs.

"Jennifer," said the chief, tipping his hat. "I came to see Coney." Jenn pointed toward the barns just as Coney appeared, walking slowly as if it was the end of the day, not merely late morning.

The three sat at the family's solid oak, century-old kitchen table, and Coney showed the chief pictures on his phone of Number Fifty-Five, the trip wires and the board of nails. Jenn offered no coffee or water or refreshments.

Dulogski shook his head.

"Tragic," he said at last. "But this is really a job for your insurance adjuster, not me."

"The insurance man has been and gone," Coney said. "I wanted you to come out because this is beyond insurance. This is criminal activity. I've reported a lot of suspicious stuff since last summer, James. But now they've gone beyond protesting and opening the milk tank spigot over at Brenner's. Now it's come to destruction and killing and trespass. If something like this happened to Pinckney's ugly little rat dog, he'd have pushed for murder charges."

"So what do you want me to do? Do you have any suspects?"

"How about a patrol out here now and then? How about keeping an eye on the animal rights folks? This is no different than a serial murderer, James. They start with animals. You know that better than I do."

"Believe me, I do. And we are watching Pinckney and all the others who follow him." Dulogski lied. "The problem is, we don't have the resources to watch your farm. And you have these vicious dogs. Aren't they enough?"

"Somehow they got past the dogs," Coney said. "If they can do that, who knows where else they've been? Who knows what else they're capable of?" Dulogski paused.

"Have you ever thought of a camera surveillance system?"

"I have, and it's way too expensive. You know how tight things are in the farm economy. I can't justify it right now."

"As long as you have insurance, anyway," Dulogski muttered.

"What's that supposed to mean?"

"Nothing, nothing," the chief replied. Jenn's face was turning three shades of red deeper than her hair, but she held her tongue. Her eyes, however, could not hide her rage at the implication.

"Look," Dulogski said. "If it were up to me, I'd have my boys set up cameras for free. That last grant got us six more and a network, but the city council has made it clear. All resources have to go into catching the vandals who keep painting underwear on the statue. As we speak, my entire staff is setting up cameras all over the park. It's priority one, and there's nothing I can do about it."

"Really!" Jenn blurted, her self-control finally at its end. "So you're telling me that you believe it's more important to catch some teenage pranksters than to catch people who are obviously capable of some very vicious, malicious crimes. People who have no regard for private property or the life of innocent animals! Your priorities are really messed up, Jimmy." She practically spat the man's nickname, one he despised.

He looked Jenn in the eye momentarily, his pride trying to burst out, but he dared not hold her gaze long. Jenn was a very strong woman and carried great influence. If only he could match it.

"Tell you what I can do," he said. "I'll put in for another grant for a camera or two. I can't guarantee anything, and we may have to borrow from next year's budget, but if we get them, your farm will be top priority. It's all I can do."

"And in the meantime?" Coney asked.

"Just keep your eyes open," he said. "Report any suspicious activity."

"It's what we've been doing for a very long time," Coney said. "A lot of good a bunch of files in your computer does us. Maybe it's time to take this beyond the police."

"What's that supposed to mean?" Dulogski asked, defensively. "Be careful what you say, Coney. I don't want to know. I'll do everything I can, believe me. But you'd better not be thinking about taking things into your own hands. Be patient. Get your farmers out to vote for Prop. Two, and we'll have more teeth to enforce stuff like this as gang activity. That could end this vandalism once and for all."

"This is way beyond vandalism, and way beyond small-town political games to get more government money!" Jenn said, again calm. "Your duty is to protect the citizens of Jovial. Are you going to do your duty or not?"

"I've said I'll do all I can," the chief said, picking up his hat from the table. He pushed open the screen door to see Mulder and Scully, sitting alertly on the deck, enduring an all-too-early hot sun.

"Stay, kids," Jenn ordered.

Dulogski walked warily past the dogs and back to his car.

Garit steered the sputtering Kia back
into the *World* parking lot, and only then noticed that his teeth were
clenched together, grinding. That explained the headache, but not the
reasons he picked up such a bad habit in response to stress.

He forced himself to relax his jaw. How would he explain to Wally
that he'd not only failed to get a valid interview on his first assignment,
but had also ruined the company camera?

If things in his life had been normal, he'd have called his dad for
advice. But that time had passed. He was on his own. Fat lot of good
his dad's advice ever did him, anyway.

Garit shook his head to remove the ridiculous thought. He'd
resolved to do the opposite of what his old man would do. Seemed like
the best policy, since dad and mom apparently hadn't thought clearly for
months. Maybe even longer. There was no way to hide from this. He'd
have to just blurt it out.

Wally wasn't in his office when Garit walked in, but Aspen was
eager.

"So, how did it go?" She asked, beaming as if she was questioning a
kindergartner after the first day at school. "Did you get a good photo?
We've held a hole on page one for it."

"Well," Garit said with a sigh, "I was threatened at gunpoint, ran
over the camera with the Kia and don't have enough facts to write much

of anything. But I think the police chief liked me." He told Aspen the entire story.

"If this isn't obvious to you, I think your real story is the threat at gunpoint," she said when Garit finished the tale. "The statue painting is secondary compared to this. We can just run a cut-only photo with that." She hesitated. "But Wally might think differently. What about this? If Chief Dulogski likes you, why don't you report it to him?"

"Should I?"

They were interrupted by Wally's voice coming from the loading dock.

"Give me a hand with your stuff, West." Wally shouted in a tone that could have been playfulness, but Garit couldn't be sure.

They spent the next couple hours moving things from Wally's pickup truck, off the loading dock, through the *World* offices and up the wooden stairs. Garit didn't count how many trips it took, but he noticed that the Debbies didn't pay much attention.

The room that would be his home was open and large, without inner walls except for the bathroom, After the refrigerator was in and a worn couch and coffee table put in place, Wally brought in an old kitchen table that he announced would be Garit's home work station, and he turned on the gas to the four-burner stove that was already in place.

Hardwood floors that covered the entire room were dusty, but as Wally handed him a dust mop, Garit needed to confront the situation before he wasted time moving the contents of his Jeep all the way up the stairs.

When Wally announced a short break, Garit followed him onto a small outdoor porch that overlooked the *World* parking lot, a row of older houses and a view of Phil's Philling Station and Garage. The deck held four plastic camping chairs, and Garit thought it was his best chance.

He explained what happened up until the deputy threatened him as Wally listened, intently at times and at other times distracted.

"Let me see your photos," he demanded.

"I need to talk to you about that," Garit began. "Some deputy—square-headed bully type—pointed a gun in my face and made me run over the camera with the car. I have a few shots I took with my phone, but I haven't really looked at them to know if they're good enough for the front page. More immediately, I need to know what to do about getting threatened at gunpoint. That seems like a pretty big story to me."

Wally ignored Garit's editorial advice, took Garit's phone and looked at the photos. He smiled. "Did Deputy Schoen know you took these?"

"Probably not, since he seemed so intent on making me wreck the camera," Garit said. "He never asked for my phone, and I didn't offer it."

Wally appeared contemplative for a moment as he looked at the photos more intently, not revealing approval or disapproval.

"Let me take care of it. You weren't hurt, were you?"

"No."

"You seem a little shaken. Were you traumatized? Will you lose sleep over this?"

"I don't know about that."

"As long as you don't need psychological help. That's too expensive for our insurance plan. Well, let's go see if the card is still there," Wally said. "You'd better hope it is!"

They climbed in Wally's now-empty pickup.

"This is new to you, West, so I'm not going to take the camera out of your pay," Wally said as they drove toward the park. "Next time, just remember that Deputy Schoen is a real piece of work. Stay out of his way. And next time, resist more. Don't be such a wimp. If he'd have shot you in the head, we'd really have had a good front-page story."

Garit laughed uncertainly. "Yep. That would have shown him! So you're going to talk to the Chief about him?"

"Don't be naive. That wouldn't do any good. It would only be his word against yours, and I'll give you one guess about who the chief would believe. Best to let it lay for now. I can't afford to have enemies in the police department."

"Seems to me like I'm already an enemy to at least one deputy."

"Don't be so melodramatic, Garit. Stuff like this happens every day. Nothing ever really comes from it. It's best you just forget it. Schoen probably has by now."

"Forget that a cop threatened me at gunpoint? Isn't that illegal? Aren't cops supposed to uphold the law? Isn't the press supposed to expose this kind of thing?"

"In your little Ohio college world, I suppose. In a perfect world, sure. But sometimes in the real world, you need to be a jerk to catch criminals. And Schoen has caught a lot of criminals."

"I didn't know it was against the law to be a reporter." Garit blurted. "But I did think it was against the law for anybody, even a cop, to pull guns on people. How is it any different than if he'd been a gang banger or some other sort of real criminal? It doesn't feel all that great to see a gun pointing into your eyes, you know. Have you had the pleasure?"

"Just relax," Wally said. "Don't be so dramatic. Worse stuff than that will happen to you before you're through. And let me write the story. You're too emotionally attached to it to be unbiased. Did you record anything?"

"On my phone, with the Chief. But most of it's off the record."

"Leave it with me, and I'll see what I can get from it before I call Dulogski for an official statement. You'll learn. Some things need to be handled delicately in a small town. This isn't big-city Ohio."

"Thanks for the reassurance. And it's Illinois."

Wally sneered at Garit and grunted as they pulled into the park's small parking area. "There, over there," Garit pointed. "Looks like they never cleared up the evidence."

"Then it's your lucky day," Wally said.

They found the camera's flattened remains in a neat pile on the tar parking lot, as if they had been broomed into a pile and left there. Wally ran his hands over the rubble. Under a piece of silver metal, he picked through and found the tiny blue card that held photos, but it was bent and chipped.

"Lucky for you Schoen has the memory of a fish," he said. "Let's just hope we can still use this card, or we'll have to use one of those low-resolution phone shots.

"I want you to get to know this town," Wally said as they drove back to the office. "I'm assigning you the Yesteryears beat, because you'll be able to learn while you work. See how efficient I am?" He looked up and smiled, and when he did, his eyes opened wider and his eyebrows raised, bringing wrinkles all the way up to his hairline, like a tire tread pattern on wet blacktop.

"What's Yesteryears?"

"Look in the back issues and see how Aspen did it," Wally said. "Just go to the library and get into the microfilm. The librarian—Betty—can help you get started." Wally paused, as if having second thoughts. "She can, but I don't know if she will. You're going to have to sweet-talk that chilled head of lettuce to get what you want. Just lay on the charm. I assume you have charm?" Garit shrugged.

"I want stuff from old *Worlds* from a hundred years ago, fifty and twenty-five. About 500 words, verbatim, for each week. Since we go to press today, you'll have a week to do it. I'll get you a laptop and you'll have to transcribe what you find by hand. And do a good job! Try not to ruin the microfilm machine like you ruined my camera. Betty will probably watch you like a hawk. Don't mess with her. She doesn't put up with any crap. But, it's getting late now, and we're due to send galleys to the printer in..."—he looked at the clock on the car dashboard—an hour!" Finally he looked at Garit.

"It's been an interesting first day for you," he said, picking up his phone and putting it to his ear. "Why don't you get your stuff moved in and let me finish this edition? You can start in fresh in the morning for the next issue. And by the way, I appreciate you thinking far enough ahead to use your phone. It's always good to have a backup plan."

It was a tedious task, since he had to carry things two-at-a-time, but before long, Garit had moved all his earthly belongings from the Jeep except for one big box that contained odds and ends, a bag of weed and some rolling papers he'd found while going through his parent's stuff, and an old 27-inch flat-screen TV.

As he entered the apartment with his last load, Aspen climbed silently up the stairs behind him and followed him into the room.

"So? Can I help with your decorating plans?" she asked.

"Must be the paper has been sent out," Garit said.

"Put to bed," she said. Garit looked at her.

"That's the proper term for it," she said. "The paper has been put to bed." He nodded.

She spun around like a confused top and bounced about the bare room as her spirit led her. "You should put a dividing wall over there. Give you a little privacy, and maybe even a bedroom. Maybe put a free-standing divider in front of the bathroom door," she said, cocking her head at various angles. "The light really changes quickly up here. You need some plants. Don't mind me, Garit. I'm just drifting, thinking freely, using stream-of-consciousness to snap sparks into the wind."

"That's good," Garit said. "Snap sparks into the wind." Aspen didn't appear to be listening, but he watched her roam the room.

"I don't know what to do," he said, finally. "Isn't that up to Wally? He owns the place."

"He'll follow my advice," she said, and snapped her fingers. "He's wrapped around my little finger. I think I've got it. About the colors?"

"What colors?"

"For the walls. Du-uh. I'm thinking a nice birds-egg blue along the entry wall and around the front door, and maybe even out into the front stairwell, even though nobody ever uses that entrance. Then a brighter, maybe light yellow wrapping into the kitchen area, and back to a darker blue across into the living room. What do you think?"

"I think I'll leave it like it is."

"You're not serious." Garit had been, but he smiled to hide it. "What's birds-egg blue? Sounds kind of gay."

"It's not gay!" She rolled her eyes, and Garit noticed that they were like bright, precious marbles that sparkled in a child's hand when she was enthralled. "I'll tell Wally to build you a wall for a bedroom area. I'll take you out next week after you get your first check and we'll buy a comfy chair and some kitchen chairs, maybe a new table. This one doesn't look all that sturdy."

"I don't need a table. I can eat at my desk or over the sink."

Aspen rolled her eyes again. "Stereotypical bachelor statement. What about dishes?" Aspen said it with real excitement. Garit smiled at her and shrugged.

"You don't have any. Don't worry, we'll get you some of those too."

"Someday," Garit said, motioning Aspen to move ahead of him down the stairs. "I have enough paper plates for awhile. Right now I have to get stuff out of boxes."

The next morning, Garit walked two
blocks to the Jovial Public Library, a handsome brick building with long, narrow windows that started at the roof line and dropped dramatically to the ground. It looked like a medieval castle, all the way up to its peaked copulas.

The library checkout desk was built so high that Garit, at six-feet, one- inch tall, barely could see over it. Above him, peering down over her bifocals, was Betty Raeusidout, or so the nameplate said.

"Good morning, Betty," Garit enthused. "May I introduce myself?"

"You need my permission, hot stuff?" Betty replied. She learned forward over the desk and peered over her glasses, set precisely in the center of her Roman nose. She was not unattractive, Garit thought, for an older woman in her thirties. Her blonde hair was curled tight to her head, making her long jaw look like an empty stem under ripening white grapes.

"I'm Garit West, the new *World* reporter," he said, reaching his hand up over the counter. Betty ignored it.

"Isn't that nice," she snarled. "I thought you hot-shot reporters were supposed to write books, not read them."

"Can't I do both?"

Betty took off her glasses and paused, as if the question deserved an answer. "I suppose you can. But will you?"

"Betty," said Garit, stretching on his toes to get closer. "Let me ask you something. You've been in Jovial a little while, right?"

"Born and raised," she said flatly, as if bored by her existence.

"Well, let me ask you. If a police officer threatened someone with physical violence, wouldn't you think that would be a criminal act?"

"In a lot of places, I suppose that would be true," she said. "What's your point?"

"Then why doesn't anybody seem to care in Jovial?"

Betty leaned forward over the desk again, her smallish breasts bumping a short stack of books, pushing the top one off. Garit caught it.

"Who was it?" she asked, her face seeming to calm like lake ripples dispersing.

"Is this all confidential? I don't want any rumors getting out that shouldn't. But I think a reporter's job is to expose corruption, right? To tell the people the truth?"

"You been here from Ohio what? A few hours?"

"Illinois. And almost two days."

"Ooh, two whole days!" She snided. "And you think you already dug up some dirty little secret in Jovial?" She leaned back in her chair. "Which one are you, hot shot? Woodward or Bernstein? You can cut the B.S.," she said, her face returning to its pale, tight white ripples. "What must I do you for?"

"I'm sorry," Garit said, raising his hands defensively, palms toward her. "I didn't mean to offend you. It was me, OK? A cop put a gun in my face yesterday, and Wally East thinks I should just let it go. But if you're not interested either, well, I'm only here because Wally told me you could teach me how to use the microfilm. I'm taking over the Yesteryears column."

Betty sighed heavily and pushed her glasses back up her nose. "I meant who was the cop?" She said as she came around the long, narrow desk and stepped down three steps to get to the main floor. Her top half appeared normal, proportionally, but when she came down the steps, Garit had to pull his eyes away from her backside. It blossomed from her rather normal-sized waist like a hot air balloon half-inflated and just starting to lift off the ground.

"I don't remember his name," Garit said. "Something like Scone?"

"It's Schoen," Betty said, spelling it. "Sounds like scone, but not nearly as tasty. Come with me," she said, waddling ahead of Garit down a straight staircase into the basement that smelled like a funeral home. "And don't you dare look at my butt."

"Wouldn't even think of it."

"What's that supposed to mean?"

"Whatever you want, Betty," Garit sighed and his shoulders slumped. "I'm not here to con you or pick a fight or to comment on your body. I'm just trying to start a life here and do my job. You can either help me or fight me. I don't care. Just let me know which one you want."

They locked eyes, and Betty was first to pull away.

"Fair enough," she said. She pulled out a chair for Garit beside a very old, bulky computer terminal. "Make yourself homely." She moved to a closet that opened on to a dozen or more shelves stacked with white boxes.

"Let's see," she said, looking back to see if Garit was watching. "You need one hundred, fifty and twenty-five years ago, right?"

"Perfect. You know this better than I do."

"I've been here longer," Betty said, sighing. "A lot longer."

"C'mon," drawled Garit. "You're not that much older than me."

"I meant in Jovial," she barked. "And it's not a matter of me being too old, but of you being too young."

"Too young for what?"

Betty paused and looked at him, and Garit thought he saw signs of a smile, perhaps even empathy. "Too young to have a cop shove a gun in your face," she said.

She came back from the closet with three boxes, and opened one.

"See, you thread the old film onto the left spool like this." She said, deftly putting the film into a slot in the middle of an empty spool as if she were threading a needle. "Once you get the film started, you click it." She clicked it into place behind a metal guide. "And set the full spool onto the other side. That's all there is to it," she said. "Now just press the arrow that points left for backward, and right to go forward. Knock yourself out."

"Thanks, Betty. You've been a big help."

"Yeah, yeah," she said. Her butt created the illusion that she was floating up the stairs as she left. "Don't put the spools back yourself. You'll ruin my whole filing system. Just drop them off by the book return slot."

Garit untucked the latest *World* from under his arm and flipped to the Yesteryears section. Despite what happened yesterday, this job would be a piece of cake. Just type in interesting tidbits from the same weeks as the present publication they were working on, and that was it.

He found himself most engaged by the 1919 archives. Athletes hawking cigarettes, fledgling automobiles on sale brand new at the local dealer for $400, and one, a smaller ad near the back of the newspaper, asking people to join a new society dedicated to jocularity. The word instantly caught his attention. That Jocular Society stuff was real?

> "Tired of Old Man Jovial hogging all the fun?" The ad asked. "Join the Jocular Society and see what the good life in a fine Northern town can offer you. Call Riverside 345."

He typed it, word-for-word, into a file on the laptop.

He moved on to the proper edition's front page. The bold, large headline captured his eye immediately.

"Bull rampages through town on Founder's Day!" the headline proclaimed. Garit began to read:

> An unusual and frightening event took place in Jovial this past Founder's Day that left many citizens frightened and maimed. A bull, owned by citizen Tommy Johnson, adult son of Harrison Thomas Johnson and Mary Johnson, tore through Main Street and was finally shot to death, but not before inflicting serious property damage and no little trepidation among the good citizens of our fair town.

Startled by the shotgun blast that officially starts the Founder's Day parade through town, the bull overpowered his handler Mr. Johnson and bolted, butted and kicked his way up Main, where he collided with four parade walkers, who became gored and bruised, but were quickly comforted by town attorney Merrill Flaxstone, Esq., whose offices are at 523 Oak Street.

The bull's attitude then changed, and he began a pernicious rampage, attempting to mount the secondary school equine club's horses, pouring the girls astride them into panic. They screeched and spurred their fillies and geldings, and tried to bolt away, but were understandably and refreshingly clumsy with the fear of impending male-driven assault arching from their terrified eyes.

Finally, tired from the unproductive lustful chase, the bull turned angry and wrecked nearly half the storefronts in town, kicking and head- butting and snorting out long streams of foaming slime, spinning and running over anything in his path.

Suddenly, he turned and seemed to be looking for someone. He ran with apparent purpose and didn't stop until he spotted Mayor Bill Spencer. Just when it appeared the nasty, beastly bovine had gone out of his way to try to crush the Mayor between a park bench and the wall of Benjamin's General Store, home of the two-for-one baling wire promotion, he suddenly saw himself staring into the eyes of Alan Jovial. As if the legendary town founder somehow had summoned supernatural intervention, his glare bored into the bull's brain like a drill breaking through tin. The bull then turned his attention away from the Mayor and spun away as if in a stupor.

Finally, after ramming through the summertime swinging doors into the Pump House Saloon, the bull was shot to death by Jovial police officer Heathcliff Brady as he leaped over the bar. He killed it with one clean shot from a 12-gauge double-barreled shotgun donated to the police department by gunsmith Justin Holmstead of The Holmstead Gun Shop, 776 Maple Ave.

Saloon owner Frederick Tunney, being a clever fellow, butchered the bull out right there on the bar as his patrons went about their business and citizens swelled about inside to see the sight. Never one to miss an opportunity, Tunney offered half-price draft beer as long as the bull was in the saloon. Then he fried up the tough but free steaks for the rest of the day and served them outside on our town's modern and clean wooden sidewalks. The aroma was said to have reached all the way up to Sventon, carried on an unusual hot wind out of the Southeast.

Not only that, but Tunney's action sparked a new promotional idea. Every Friday, he said, drinks will be half-price for three hours, the same amount of time it took to butcher the bull. See his advertisement on page 8. So come on into the Pump House Saloon this Friday between 4 o'clock and 7 o'clock p.m., and enjoy what Tunney calls "Happy hour."

Garit smiled. He transcribed it onto the laptop.

The 25-year-old *World* couldn't even come close to holding his interest like that story, until Garit realized that this would have been his parent's youthful era.

The quality of the print had deteriorated, making the computerized scans difficult to read in places, but there were more pictures than in the older archives, some of them even in color. He landed on one of the items for the column. A photo of a young man and a teacher, standing side-by-side, hoisting a giant check and holding hands. "Young honor student wins major grant," the caption read. Apparently, it was big news 25 years ago for a high school student to win $1,000 to start a landscape business. It promised to employ other students during summers, and let them earn money for college.

Garit copied the words, making doubly sure to get the names right. The long-haired young teacher, complete with big, bushy sideburns and a mustache that was barely visible, was named Dan Pinckney. The student's name, however, struck Garit as either evil, misspelled or unfortunate.

He saved the information on the laptop and put the film spools back into their boxes. He went upstairs and put them in front of Betty, who looked up, her face much softer than before.

"You know a Jim Deadfrick, Betty?

"Deadfrick? Yah, I know him. Why?"

"Oh, he was in the 25-year-old edition. Wonder how a guy with a name like that turns out?"

"Depends on who you ask."

Garit lingered at the library when the
weekly edition of the *Jovial World* was delivered to the Jovial Police
Station and the rest of town. He was still there trying to understand
Betty's undulating moods when Deputy Sean Schoen pulled open the
door of the *World* offices and marched straight through the unmanned
reception desk door to the editorial area.

Without closing the door to the office, he threw the paper on
Wally's desk and pounded his fist on top of it. The two Debbies turned
and looked at the sound, looked back and made eye contact with each
other, and silently decided it was time for a break on the loading dock.

"I demand my rights!" Schoen screamed. "You have violated the law,
my privacy and my dignity, and I will not leave here until you retract
this story and photo!"

Wally listened, calmly, and stood, walked past Schoen and closed
his office door, although it made no difference. Aspen could hear every
word from her desk, and she made no effort to join the Debbies.

"What's wrong with it?" Wally asked when he sat behind his desk
again. He didn't offer Schoen a seat.

"What's wrong?" Schoen's face was turning red, starting with his
thick neck and moving upward. "This makes me look like some kind of
pervert, rubbing a crotch like I was enjoying it!"

"Why do you say that?"

"Look at the angle," Schoen shouted. "I look like I'm gay or something, caught in some faggy act. All I was doing was trying to undo the damage some punk kids did, and this is the kind of respect I get for it? I'm the best police officer on this whole God-forsaken force, and this is how you treat me?"

Wally picked up the paper and looked at the photo again.

"I think it's a great shot," he said. "It's close, it shows the hard work and sweat you're putting in, and it shows the damage done to the statue. I think you come off looking pretty good. You grip a wire brush very skillfully."

Wally's attempt at humor went way over Schoen's head.

"Don't give me that," he retorted. "It shows a lack of appreciation for what me and the whole police force does for this town, and I'm sick and tired of it. I demand respect. Is that too much to expect from a veteran officer with commendations all over my wall?"

"You earn respect. You can't demand it," Wally said. "Have you read the story?"

"I got the gist of it."

"Anything wrong with it? Are the facts right?"

"We don't have any facts yet," Schoen said. "What's there is accurate enough, I suppose. But one thing that's completely wrong is that we have a suspect. You need to print a correction about that. But the bigger issue is this photo. I want you to tell me right now how you even got it?"

"Oh, you mean how did my new reporter get the shot after you destroyed my camera?" Wally accused.

"That's a lie," Schoen blurted. "I didn't do a thing to that camera."

"Only intimidated a kid fresh out of Ohio State at gunpoint," Wally said. "Did you even notice that I didn't report that? You could be in some deep manure if I had. I could have called the state police and demanded an investigation. That would have looked pretty good on the front page, and you'd be back doing third-shift security at the Sventon Wholesale Mall. And besides that, you'd better remember next time to pick up the memory card and destroy evidence a lot better than you did."

"Never happened," Schoen said, calming slightly. "You can never prove it. Those allegations are lies, probably made up by your new punk reporter, come in here from Ohio to try to be a big man. I think you should fire him right now for running this photo," he said. "It violates my rights, and I'll see you in court!" He slammed Wally's desk again with his fist.

"In court over a privacy claim?" Wally said. "Now that's going to be a pretty long ladder. You, a public servant on public property, doing your job. Doesn't the public have a right to know what you were doing?"

"It's none of the public's business," Schoen said. "Even if it was, they have no interest in the day-to-day things we do. This photo was purposefully manipulated to make me look like some kind of pervert who gets his jollies by feeling up a statue. I want this kid to hang, Wally! Are you too stupid to know that this is why people hate the press? Cut your losses and dump this stupid Buckeye, Wally. I can make his life plenty miserable."

"You just leave him alone," Wally said. "He's my employee, and I'll take care of it. You're just lucky I wrote the piece. He had a recording of your Chief saying things that don't exactly line up with city council policy, you know."

"Well, you just better keep a firm grip on this punk," Schoen said. "I'll be watching him!"

"And you just better keep your gun in your holster," Wally replied.

Schoen reached for the door knob.

"Don't expect any favors from my department if this kind of thing keeps up," he said.

"Your department?" Wally asked. "As far as I know, it's Dulogski's department. If you get elected chief, then we'll talk. Until then, get out of my office."

Schoen stormed out and was reaching for the front door handle as Garit reached for it from the other side. Garit won the race and held the door open for the deputy.

"I'm watchin' you, pissant!" Schoen said, pushing his nose as close to Garit's as Garit's stubbornness allowed. "Don't you ever cross me again. Lucky for you you're too green to know any better, but from here on out, you'll never get close enough to take a picture of dog poop if I have anything to say about it, and I do. You better watch every step you take in this town, because I will be. I give everybody three strikes, and you got one, maybe one-and-a-half!" He raged.

Garit surprised himself that he didn't retreat, and let Schoen's nose come within a fraction of an inch of his. As Schoen jumped angrily into his patrol car, Garit was both proud of that courage and confused about why his heart was racing, shooting a warm bolt of heated adrenaline up his back.

"Hey," Aspen enthused from her desk as Garit arrived. "Great photo for your first one!"

Garit picked up the paper, and noticed his name under the photo. The image caught Schoen scrubbing the statue's crotch, dead center on a bulge in front with a wire brush, rubbing vertically so quickly that his hand was blurred. In focus was the officer's face, and his hat tilted back. Beads of sweat were on his upper lip, dripping from his nose and over his eyebrows. His gaze was a textbook study in concentration and humidity, and his tongue peeked out of a corner of his mouth.

"Yeah, it is pretty good," Garit replied, smiling.

Wally came into the newsroom, betraying no emotion. He stood there, arms folded, saying nothing, even when the Debbies came back and delayed getting back to work.

"New editorial policy," he said to the entire room. "Always take a few photos with your phone for backup. Keep using the digital cameras, but always, always, use your phone too." He looked around the room.

"Good job, Garit" he said, waving his hand. "Question authority. It's what we do."

"Within certain political limits," Aspen muttered.

"What do you mean?" Garit asked.

"Let's just say it's a small town," she said. "You'll learn."

10

During the next couple weeks, Garit was assigned various feature stories and one hard news story when marijuana was found on a high school student, which led to a complete shutdown and evacuation of the campus. He'd even done a story and photo shoot of a mentally challenged third-grader who gardened a potato that looked like Abraham Lincoln. Turned out that it looked more like Oprah Winfrey than Lincoln, but Wally edited out that little bit of Garit's editorializing.

Wally had assigned him to the Jovial City Council beat, and as his first meeting neared, Garit increased his visits to the Jovial Library. For a reason he couldn't explain, he felt comfortable there. Betty was warming to him. He could feel it. Once she had even opened up about her love for detective novels, and boasted that she could see a plot line thickening before the author could.

It also was obvious that she knew just about everything that went on in Jovial and the surrounding Jovial County, which took its direction from Jovial, the county seat.

One day, Garit finished his Yesteryears work at precisely noon.

"Betty, how about I go get us a couple subs and we have lunch on one of the reading porches?" He asked. She agreed.

"You know, Wally told me you'd kick my butt if I crossed you," he said as they ate, and she laughed. "Must be you've kicked his butt before. Can't think of anyone who'd deserve it more."

"I've been known to have my moods," she said. "But you're different than most kids Wally hires. He likes weak sycophants. You stood up for yourself your first day here. Not many guys do that, especially ones your age."

"Does that mean you like me now?"

"Take it easy, killer. I don't *like you* like you," she grinned. "I'm a cohabitating woman. Committed. One thing I would like to know, though. What's a good-looking young man like you doing without a girlfriend?"

The question stabbed at Garit, who had hoped when he left Illinois that he could put Sandra out of his mind. But Betty pressed him. "I won't tell," she said. "I hold more secrets than anyone else in this town, you know."

"Prove it," Garit said.

"Oh, you'll have to give a little to get a little," she said.

Maybe this was a good time to reveal a little something about himself. Being closed off from the world hadn't yet earned him a single friend in Jovial, although he found Aspen's company to be exciting.

"Alright," Garit told Betty.

Garit and his roommate Marty had gotten separated in the crowd as they pushed toward the doors to the University of Illinois's Foelinger Auditorium and the Acrid Reins concert. An obese ticket taker looked Garit over twice dispassionately, ripped the stub off the ticket, and dropped it. Garit knelt through the turnstile, and as he grabbed his stub, he saw her.

She was off to one side of the door, bending over, reaching for her boot. Her tanned, smooth legs were the color of light maple. She wore a thigh-high denim skirt and a cowboy hat over her thick, wavy long blonde hair, which fell over an Acrid Reins sleeveless t-shirt and her shoulder like pure creek water spilling over a smooth rock. She reached into her cowboy boot and pulled out a bottle of some kind of liquor when their eyes met.

She held the gaze a moment, smiled, and then, distracted by a friend, turned away and disappeared into the flowing crowd.

"I just saw the hottest chick I ever saw in my life," Garit told Marty when they'd met again in their bleacher seats.

"That's what you always say," Marty replied.

"She was just steamin,' man. Keep your eye out for her. Hot blonde, cowboy hat and boots, long kinky hair. Great legs. Perfect." He sighed, resigned to a life without her. "Now who are these Acrid Reins, anyway?"

Just then, the house lights went down and the band came onto the stage.

"That's Tony Finn at lead guitar, the brains behind it all," Marty shouted as the band started a morbidly driving deep base beat. Headbangers, obviously. Garit had always been quickly bored with headbangers.

During the third song, Garit and Marty found themselves surrounded by sweet-smelling, thick smoke. He inhaled the ambient air deeply. It flowed over him again, stronger this time, and when the stage lights brightened for a moment, he could see the smoky haze around him like a musky halo. He felt a breeze, and inhaled more.

He turned around. The steaming hot blonde chick was only two rows above him, blowing a thick plume toward him, and he smiled.

"Look who wants me," he shouted to Marty, who ignored him.

A few songs later, Garit felt a tap on his shoulder. A long-haired hippie sitting behind him handed him a matchbook, thumbed over his shoulder back to the hot blonde. She smiled and wiggled her fingers at him when their eyes met, and Garit waved and grinned back. Inside the match book cover was written "Sandra. 667-4456."

Betty smiled, waiting, but Garit went silent.

"And...?"

"And what?" Garit asked. "We broke up. Didn't work out."

"Details," Betty said, leaning toward him. "I need details."

"You're the mystery savant," Garit said. "What could possibly go wrong when you follow a bunch of arrogant young rich idiots in a one-hit wonder band around the country just to be next to a hot chick?"

"I wouldn't know," Betty replied, checking her watch. "I can imagine, and, well, I'm interested. But it's time to get back to work. You'll tell me when you're ready."

"Me too," Garit said, happy to end his story before details emerged.

"It's my first city council meeting tonight," he said. "Know anything I should pay attention to?"

"Tonight's just some procedural stuff, the last rubber stamps on some permissions and permits for the new farmer store," she said. "Should be pretty mild. If you get a chance, you should introduce yourself to Coney Dogues, the head of the farmer group. Great guy."

"His name is Coney Dogs?"

"Spelled D-O-G-U-E-S," she said. "Apparently he set a record in high school for eating more hot dogs than anyone else on the football team. And since his real name is Cornelius, the nickname Coney seemed like a natural."

As he walked to the meeting, Garit fidgeted, double- and triple-checked for his reporter's notebook and pen, and double-checked that his phone was charged enough to last the whole meeting. He opened the audio recorder application so he'd be ready when the time came.

The only real official public meetings he'd attended in his life were press conferences for the Acrid Reins, and they were consistently, predictably ludicrous and shallow. Those guys were arrogant self-promoters, and moronic fans hung on every stupid thing they said. Tony Finn, in particular, was an idiot who got lucky with one catchy tune. And Garit has been the idiot who promoted his fame. He did it well, too. Maybe too well. The band's vapid, meaningless fame landed a new girl in the musician's beds every night. They thought they had made it. They were living the dream. Bu then, suddenly, Garit's dream was over. The Acrid Reins were still on tour, with the world by the tail, according to most people who followed them, bought their albums, and hung on their every note. And here he was in a small-town council meeting, writing about potatoes that looked like Oprah. Really changing the world now, Garit, boy. Only 23 years old, and already finding the popular world to be meaningless? How does that happen? Why him? Why did he have to question everything?

He pulled open the door to the Jovial City Fire Barn, and took the edge off his nerves by remembering he had a friendly contact here.

Mayor Macintosh Benz III had come into the *World* office to buy a legal ad earlier that day, and when Wally introduced him to Garit, the mayor gripped his hand warmly.

"Nice to see a fresh face covering the city council," he said. "It helps us all get out of our rut when we get a new point of view. You're at the grassroots level now, son. This is where government really has an impact on people. A critical impact. I'll help you any time I can. You just ask."

As Garit now moved past the fire trucks into the City Hall meeting room, the Mayor, whose crooked smile leaned the same direction as his old football injury, nodded at him and smiled.

The city council meeting room was small and tidy, with an opulently high ceiling and beige acoustic tiles lining the walls. Garit stood in the nearly empty room's center and looked around. He felt a hand on his shoulder.

"This entire building was paid for by a grant secured by city grant writer Jim Deadfrick," the Mayor said. "This room has been made so soundproof that it's like a mystery spot." He pointed toward the front of the room. "Up there, that podium in front of our council desk is where citizens—the grassroots folks I've been telling you about—give formal presentations to the council."

The other council members came in, and the Mayor patted Garit on the back. Garit moved to the back row. Even there, he had an unimpeded view of a long, curved walnut desk where city councilmen and women were seated. It was clearly the most expensive item in the room, with a large raised wood carving of the city seal attached to the center of the desk's front.

Mayor Benz pounded the gavel hard, just once, and called the meeting to order. He stood to signal the Pledge of Allegiance recitation, after which Councilman Sam Richardson mumbled a brief guttural prayer for guidance and wisdom.

"Old business!" shouted the Mayor. "We have seven ordinances up for final approval. Motion to dispense final reading?"

"So moved," said someone.

"Then we'll vote," the Mayor said. "All in favor of City Ordinances ten-sixteen through ten-twenty-two say aye?" They all said aye.

"Passed," the Mayor shouted, and banged the gavel.

The five people in the crowd other than Garit paid little attention, but he wrote down the numbers. Maybe Betty would help him understand them. "Next up? Public comment," the mayor said.

To the podium microphone in front of the councilman's table stepped a painfully thin man with pale white complexion. He wore a dirty white tank top with a peace sign on the front, worn Bermuda shorts, and sandals on his bare feet. His hair was thinning on top, mostly ungrayed and reddish-blonde. From the sides it had grown long and was tied back into a pony tail, but dozens of wild strays stood out parallel to his narrow shoulders like whiskers on a cat. His voice broke a little, so he cleared his throat and began with formalities.

"Dan Pinckney, 7800 Dublin Way Court." The council members leaned back in their stuffed leather chairs as if they expected a long speech from Mr. Pinckney. Garit tried to remember where he'd heard that name before.

"Once again I feel duty-bound to come before this council with grave concerns about what you have just allowed within the fair city of Jovial." His voice was steady as he leaned awkwardly toward the microphone, which suddenly picked up the sound of his knees cracking. He steadied himself.

"By condoning, and yes, even advocating and publicly promoting the establishment of the farmers' store, you so-called city leaders are unwittingly contributing to the demise of this nation, like pawns in a giant chess game." He stood a little straighter. His knees cracked again. Mayor Benz leaned forward.

"The new store is undermining this nation, Pinkey?" The Mayor asked. One of three men in the crowd snorted and shifted as the mayor held back a smirk.

"Please don't try to intimidate me, Mac," Pinckney said, smoothing and stroking his pony tail as if it were a security blanket. After each stroke, the wild hairs jumped back out straight. "This is a real concern," he whined. "I've just uncovered the fact that the farmers of this town and nation are causing the downfall of the social security system."

The only woman on the council, Mary Gudebeck, leaned forward. "This is a new one," she said, looking at her fellow council members in feigned anticipation. "Please, Dan, expound your latest theory."

"This is no theory, Mary. The logic is irrefutable. Fact: The average lifespan of people in the United States has increased dramatically in the last twenty years, to where people commonly live into their eighties. Fact: all these people living longer means more social security money must be paid out, bankrupting the system. Fact: It is the food, laced with hormones and antibiotics and preservatives and who knows what else, that's causing this longer life, just like a Twinkie's shelf life is hundreds of years due to all the preservatives. Therefore, the food we eat is bankrupting Social Security. And this council, by allowing this union—that's what it is, in essence, a union—of farmers to open their own store, is contributing to the demise of social security and the bankrupting of this nation. Not that I have anything against unions. But there are good unions and bad unions. I happen to head up the teacher's union, a good one. The farmers union is a bad one. But I digress. You must stop this trend by taking a stand here and now. Somebody's got to draw a line in the sand, and it must be this council!"

Mayor Benz spoke again.

"Now Dan, wasn't it just last month that you stood in this same place and said it was a fact that the 'factory farm food' "—he motioned air quotes—"was killing us all? How is it now that we're all living as long as a Twinkie?"

"You're distorting my words," Pinckney said. "You people here that are so fond of praying before meetings can't seem to understand clear, godless, irrefutable logic when it stares you in the face. You don't even reason as well as your children. They get this stuff. Why can't you? The food produces a grand deception, like the devil all you people think is real. It appears to keep us healthy, but it's just like that barren farm soil around this town. It's only good for holding up the plant. The chemicals in that toxic soil provide all the nutrients, but they're just placebos. Sure, we live longer, but we're sicker all our lives, so our lives are miserable."

"Misery is a choice, Dan," said a man sitting near the front of the room dressed in a long-sleeved dress shirt with the sleeves rolled up to mid-forearm. Garit watched him as he continually flexed his hands, which were swollen and red.

Benz banged his gavel so loudly Garit jumped, startled, but he was enthralled at the authority in this audience member's voice. It was as different from Pinckney's demeanor as a sprout is different from a fully developed plant.

"Save it for your turn, Coney," Benz said. The man nodded and continued watching. Pinckney continued.

"You mark my words, Mayor. This town will all take to their sick beds if the farmers' store is allowed to open. It's all poison, I tell you. Then you'll all come running to the organic co-op store begging us to bail you out. But I'll just laugh."

"You'll laugh if everyone in town gets poisoned?" Mayor Benz intoned.

"Not a ha-ha, funny laugh, but an I-told-you-so laugh," Pinckney said. "Of course, we at the co-op, particularly myself and the owner, would never laugh at human animal suffering anymore than we'd condone non-human animal suffering. All I'm saying is that when the unregulated and raw product from corporations starts being ingested by our people, then you'll understand that I was right all along. Their products are poisoned with all kinds of nasty chemicals, and their animals are crammed into little sheds and kept alive with drugs. It's all quite immoral, as I've stated before—on the record, if you'll remember! These cows and chickens are ripped from their mothers as infants just like slaves. They never see the sun, and believe me, they hate their lives. They long for better lives. They aspire to better lives, but their pleas fall on deaf ears of corporate greed mongers whose god is money. I'm just trying to save the citizens of Jovial from poisoning themselves for the profits of people like that."

"Haven't most of the people in Jovial been eating local farm produce for years, without any ill effects except maybe for the gas money they've spent driving clear over to Sventon?" asked Mayor Benz. "I don't see them all dying because they didn't eat your veggie burgers."

"Our food is sustainable, wholesome, organic, and natural."

"I'm sure it's fine for your clientele," the mayor said, calmly. "But this council decided two years ago that competition would best serve the people of Jovial, and you've done nothing but second-guess us from the start. Face it, Dan, we're not going to reverse course just because you say so, especially when you come up with ridiculous allegations like you did here tonight. I mean, come on, Dan. Each conspiracy theory you bring here is more ridiculous than the last. You've got your proposal on the ballot. What more do you want? Now. Can we move on?"

There ensued an awkward silence, and Garit was scribbling furiously. He checked his phone battery again, because he didn't want to miss this. It was good stuff.

"Anything more, Dan?" The mayor asked.

"No. You won't listen to reason and logic anyway, Mac. But I will say this: I've become privy to some pretty damning photographic evidence that Coney Dogues here ..." He pointed across the room to the audience member Garit had been watching, "gets his jollies torturing cows." Dogues laughed heartily and shook his head, as if he'd heard this all before.

The mayor gestured with his hand as if shooing a fly, and Pinckney retreated to his seat in the front row.

"Coney?" The mayor asked. "Next on the agenda is a progress report from you."

The man who seemed so authoritative moments earlier rose from his seat. His broad shoulders tapered down to a solid chest, and a slight belly was all that betrayed that he might be entering middle age. He walked to the mic, dressed in Dockers, and his dress shirt held a tie that was loosened down to his third button. He adjusted the microphone upward to meet his voice.

"I'll ignore that most recent rant and lie," he said. "I just wish that Mr. Pinckney would be a little more objective when it comes to farming. Last I'd heard, Dan does not hold any type of degree or expertise in soil science. Propaganda against farmers might fly in the big city, where he's from, but not here," he said. "But on to reality. We're right on track to open the Farmer's Own Store within eighty days at the outside," he said. "Oh, sorry. Cornelius Dogues—or just Coney—president of the

Jovial Area Farmers Association." Mayor Benz leaned back in his comfy Mayor's chair.

"And have you ordered the poison you're going to sell?" the mayor asked, getting a raucous laugh from the council. He glared at Pinckney, who glared back. Coney snickered.

"For the record, I'm afraid we won't be selling poison, Mayor. If you need some, though, I hear the co-op has a special coming up."

"Ha, Ha!" Pinckney responded. "We don't sell poison. We sell only organic crop protection products!" The council members snorted as Coney grinned.

"I would respectfully respond to Dan's comments by saying I don't believe we're a risk to the Social Security system, either," Coney said.

"Anyway, our coolers are set to arrive next week—custom-made in the United States—and our contract with Noah Brenner for the milk is all but signed. We've gotten agreements from every farmer in the association, and a few backup handshake agreements from other sources; and I feel comfortable saying that ninety to ninety-five percent of the food we'll sell will be sourced from farmers in a one-hundred-mile radius. The rest, you know, bananas and other tropical items, we have to find where we can, especially in the winter. But we're dedicated to top-quality produce that I think will match up favorably to Dan's Co-op offerings."

Pinckney snorted derisively, bringing a quick and loud bang from Mayor Benz's gavel.

"I for one will be very happy when you open," interjected Councilwoman Mary Gudebeck. "I'll be happy to not have to drive to Sventon to buy my groceries, and I'll be even happier knowing the people who raised the food I'm eating. And I think most of the citizens of Jovial would agree with me."

Pinckney snorted again. "I'm right here, and our store sells food too," he snided.

"Thanks for the vote of confidence, Mary," Coney said, ignoring Pinckney. "The farmers in the association won't let you down. You know that."

That sounded like a promise, and probably the lead sentence for Garit's story. He wrote it, underlined it, circled it and glanced at the recorder. He wrote the numbers he saw in the display, reference points in the recording.

Coney returned to his chair, and Garit again noticed his hands. Coney's fingers were thick and looked to be the texture of old cracked cheap leather, and they didn't quite seem to fit his much more youthful speech.

Mayor Benz snapped the gavel again.

"Any more new business?" Silence.

"Call to adjourn?"

"I'll make the motion," said a councilman at the far right, whose nameplate Garit couldn't see.

"Second," said Mary.

"All in favor?" Ayes mumbled out.

"Against?" Silence.

"We're done," the mayor said, banging his gavel.

12

Unsatisfied with what he didn't understand, Garit waited for the city council members to finish their post-meeting conversations, then walked up to Mayor Benz, who greeted him again with a handshake. He'd wanted to speak with Mr. Pinckney, but he had bolted quickly out the door just as the last gavel strike sounded.

"Well, what's your first impression about Jovial government?" Benz asked.

"I don't really know what to think, Mr. Benz. I know I didn't expect such an abrupt end to the meeting. I felt like I missed something, some ceremony or a trumpet blast or something."

The Mayor laughed as Garit continued. "Everything happened so fast. I don't even know what to write about. Do I just write a story about the rantings of some old hippie?"

"That old hippie is the superintendent of schools, Garit."

"Really? He doesn't seem to fit the part. I'm sorry. I didn't mean to offend you or him."

"No problem. Dan is an unusual character for a school administrator, but I guess that's why the kids seem to relate to him. He's always against the status quo."

"Well," said Garit, "maybe I can do a larger story on the new store, but I'm sure Wally's probably already taken care of it. How long have these two been fighting?"

"Since Pinckney first got here from San Francisco. We were all just kids back then. Their little disagreements are just par for the course. I'm sure Wally's written about it, but it's not a big deal. The store is. Wouldn't hurt to give people an update. So, Garit, how are things working out with Wally? You two getting along OK?"

"Well, it's kind of hard to tell," Garit replied. "One thing about Wally. He doesn't interfere with my job much. On the downside, he doesn't contribute much, either. When he has, it's been last-minute rushes, and it always involves something tedious like double-checking a quote with someone who can't be reached. He loves to pick nits. When I see that look in his eyes, I try to avoid him, especially the last few hours before the paper goes to the printer."

"Well, you just hang in there. I like your writing, Garit. You have real style. Do more of those features you do. You know, some investigative stuff. You seem to have a flair for that. And don't let Wally get to you. Sometimes he can be inattentive, but he's just trying to run a business, and sometimes the stress gets to everyone. I got to get going, Garit. Anything else?"

"You think you can explain to me what passed so fast with those city ordinances?"

"Oh, that's just boilerplate stuff, things that were in the works for a long time. Mostly just boring stuff like approving budget money to refurbish drains and manhole covers, that sort of thing."

The mayor tapped Garit on the shoulder. "I'll see you soon, Garit," he said, and escorted Garit out of the meeting room. The mayor pulled the door shut and checked that it was locked, and once outside the fire barn, walked the opposite way of Garit's apartment. Garit checked his phone clock. It was a lot earlier than he thought it would be. Wally and Aspen had both told him the meeting would last until at least nine or nine-thirty. It was barely past eight o'clock.

Garit thought about stopping at the Pump House Bar, but he didn't want to spend the money. His last paycheck had nearly all gone for kitchen utensils, thanks to Aspen.

"I'm waiting for a special occasion," he told Aspen when she asked if he'd used the plates and pots and pans yet. "I don't want to get them dirty just for me. Maybe I can cook dinner for you some night."

She giggled. "How do I know you can cook?"

"You don't, and neither do I," he said. "At least not a real meal. I can melt cheese, and boil water in an emergency, but that's about it."

She giggled again, and gently touched his arm and lingered over the eye contact between them. He broke the gaze first and thought of Sandra, wondered what she was doing now besides coke.

He stopped at the Jovial Knights Party Store for dinner.

As he reached for a white-bread turkey sandwich from a cooler, he was suddenly thirsty, so he walked to the beer cooler and pulled out a six-pack of Bud Lite bottles. He would have preferred a locally-grown craft beer, but there were surprisingly few offerings, and none that he recognized.

He walked home past the Brite and Jovial Cleaners store, the Jovial Carpet and Flooring Emporium, and the Pump House, which was empty except for one man sitting at the bar staring out the window. Monday nights in Jovial weren't exactly big party nights. He made his way down an alley that led between the *World* office building and an accounting firm and came out behind the *World* and its cement loading dock. He looked at his Jeep, which hadn't been started for two days, and went up the *World's* dock steps to a side door.

He fished his key from his pocket and stepped into the print shop, then opened a door without a lock that led into the newsroom and the half-wall that led to his apartment stairs. As he walked across the newsroom, he heard muffled voices. He checked his phone. 8:32. No one should be in the office.

He paused to listen. A male voice that could have been Wally's was making guttural sounds, like a robber grunting instructions. Not really a conversation, but maybe his office walls were muffling too much.

Suddenly, he heard a female voice, but it too was muffled. Then the male voice seemed to be getting agitated, though Garit still couldn't make out any words.

Garit held his breath as the sounds receded, then rose again, then receded. Then silence. He took a couple steps up his stairs, but his view was still blocked by the half-wall.

Suddenly, he heard a crash. It was unmistakable, like knowing the sound of a car wreck when you hear it. He froze, wanting desperately to back out of the room and forget what he was hearing. But maybe he should just keep going up the stairs, and they wouldn't see him. But then Aspen did.

She shouted: "Wally! Stop!" Garit reflexively turned to see, just behind the glass in Wally's office, a hairy male butt, perched atop skinny hairy legs like a weather-worn pink lawn flamingo that had developed mounds of algae. The buns were wobbling like two halves of a hairy Jello coconut being hit by a mallet. Wrapped around his hairy back were a pair of very nice, long and smooth legs, kicking as if in protest. Aspen's arms pushed Wally's still-shirted top half away from her.

Wally turned to see Garit putting his hand up to blind his vision as he bounded up the remaining stairs two at a time. He immediately locked the apartment's hallway door after he'd clumsily fumbled with his keys to unlock it from the *World* side.

Breathing heavily from the short sprint, he grabbed a beer from his six-pack, stuffed the rest into the noisy fridge and stepped out to his porch. He slugged the beer and gulped down the sandwich. He didn't know which would linger in his gut longer, the scene he'd witnessed or the starchy, dry, manufactured sandwich.

He fidgeted in his chair, downed one beer and went in to get another. He picked up his cell phone on the table, scrolled down to Doug's number and pressed send. Doug answered after four rings.

"Hey, man, how's it going?" Garit asked, trying to sound upbeat.

"Same old. What's up?"

"Any jobs in the produce warehouse?"

"Already? Why, dude? Too cold up there?"

"It's a little too hot, actually," Garit said, twisting the beer open. He sat in his lounge chair on the porch. "I just called to keep in touch, and to tell you my new boss is a total jackass." He told Doug what he'd just witnessed. Doug was impressed.

"Let me ask you something, Doug. How can a girl as gorgeous and talented as this Aspen chick fall for an idiot stick like Wally? I have more writing talent in my big toe than he has in both hands. He can't write worth a darn and he's an even worse human being. He has to be old enough to be Aspen's father, And he's married!"

"What about her?" Doug asked. "She was participating, sounds like."

"I don't know. I never saw this coming. She'd made enough eye contact with me to make me think maybe someday I might just make a move. But I never did. I'm still snake bit from Sandra, probably. I guess I have to put all that out of my mind now. She's just a whore and my boss is a major hypocrite. What a great, empty place I've come to."

"If you want to come back, I can see what we have open," Doug replied.

"Let me think about it. I'll be in touch."

"You better," Doug said. "Look at you. Gone a month and already you run into a story to tell."

Garit said his goodbyes, drained his beer, and heard the *World's* loading dock door slam shut beneath his porch. He pressed his back to the plain painted wood of the outside of his apartment and patiently waited until he saw Aspen walk left and Wally walk right.

When they were out of sight, he took an empty beer bottle firmly in his right hand, the bottom in his palm, and pitched it so hard his shoulder emitted a snap and ached dully for a few seconds. The bottle flew above the city parking lot and smashed loudly, scattering glass into the street. He stood and listened as silence returned, interrupted only by the ding of bells at the gas station.

"Augh!" He screeched, and listened as it echoed across the downtown area. He leaned forward, took his face in his hands and wept for the first time since he'd gotten the call from his parents' attorney, Tom Saxe.

"Garit?" he had begun. "Your parents are gone. ..."

13

Fulton had just finished greasing a field
disc and washing his hands in Orange Goo when his phone rang. He
picked up only because it was Coney.

"Hey," Coney said. "You got time to help me look for 405? Ernesto
took the morning off to bring his boy for a doctor's appointment, and
she's missing."

"What's up with that?"

"I don't know. She didn't come up from pasture with the rest of the
herd."

"Is she pregnant?"

"No, she freshened a couple months ago, so she couldn't have
wandered off by herself when labor started. I'm starting to think the
worst here."

"What, wolves?"

"No, worse. She's one of the strongest cows, and a wolf would go
after smaller, weaker prey, like a newborn calf. Still, I sure would like
to take a rifle with me. What might be worse is if it's a bunch of animal
rights people. I wish one of those wackos would spend one day on a farm
working hard with animals. That would cure them."

"Maybe you better take a rifle in case it's them, too," Fulton said.
"You know they aren't above killing an animal to make their point,
whatever that is."

"I'm just about done milking. How soon can you get here?"

"Might be awhile. I just got the disc greased, and I have to get this new bunch of workers going. The field down by the creek is ready to go."

"OK. I'm heading back to check the pasture."

Coney finished milking, then drove down the pasture lane to look for 405. Scully and Mulder saw the pickup take off, and ran from behind and pulled ahead of him.

"Go get 'em, Homeland Security!" He shouted as they ran past him. "Go get those animal rights wackos!"

It had been only one week ago when a police officer had come to his farm, just before the evening milking.

"What's in that back barn, anyway? Deputy John Mead asked.

"That's the hospital and separation barn," he said. "You know, cows who had been treated with antibiotics and whose milk can't be put in the tank until it's out of their system. And your assorted injured or sick animals who needed a safe place to recover without competition from the rest of the herd," Coney answered. Mead grunted.

"What's this all about?" Coney asked as he led the deputy to the barn.

"Complaints of animal abuse," said the deputy.

"John we've known each other since middle school," Coney said. "Who called this bull in?"

"Can't say. It's my duty to follow up on all complaints."

"Even from crackpots?"

"Yep."

"And I don't even have a right to know my accuser's name? Someone who obviously trespassed if he's been in my nurse barn?"

"The law's the law."

"Well, the law's got to be changed."

"I don't make the rules. I just follow orders."

"That's the problem with your policies," Coney said. "Hide behind your orders. Ever consider using your own noggin?"

"That's against regulations," Mead said. Coney grunted. "But it's okay for someone to put a board of nails in my dry cow lane and trip wires?"

"I don't know anything about that," Mead said.

Coney showed officer Mead around the barn, and laughed when he tiptoed between cow piles. "I thought you were a country boy, John," he said. "You look like some Nancy-boy tippy-toeing around here." Mead ignored the comment.

"Just be aware that these whack jobs are watching you for some reason," Mead said as he left the barn, using all his feet now. "Call the department if anything seems out of place." They walked back toward the house. "Tell you one thing, though," the deputy said. "I'd like to know how they'd get to this barn past the dogs."

"I'd like to know that too," Coney muttered.

Coney continued to drive toward the pasture, watching Mulder and Scully for signs of something. "Lord," he prayed, "Give me the strength—your strength—to be clear-headed and calm if I find that something horrible happened to 405."

He drove around the pasture fence perimeter, but needed to cut a corner near the very back of the thirty-acre section of open, well-maintained pasture and woods. It was only two days ago when he and Fulton had fenced this section. He emerged from a small wooded part of the last portion of lane and into the open pasture, thick with new grass. There were Scully and Mulder, waiting for him as he parked the truck.

He walked behind a swail in the new area and saw Number 405's head. Fearing the worst, he ran to her, but she was alive.

"Thank you Lord," he muttered. But as he neared, he could see nothing more than her head. He rushed up. She had sunk into some mud, up to her chest and back knees, but was calm as Coney approached her.

"Hey, girl, you're in some mess, aren't you?" He spoke to her calmly and patted her neck. He walked around her, continuing to speak calmly. "How'd you get into this mess? He said. "You just stay calm and I'll be back. Scully, you stay here with her." The female dog immediately sat, then laid down with her face to the cow, alert to her duties.

Coney ran to the truck and sped back to the barn. How long had 405 been struggling to get out of her predicament? Was she calm now because her strength to fight was already sapped? He had to work fast, because wolves wouldn't stay away long if they got wind of a wounded cow. Mulder and Scully would keep them at bay, but not forever.

He grabbed a shovel, as much rope as he could find, a halter and a couple chains, and went back to her on the loader tractor. Illegally, he put his 30.06 rifle in the bucket too. If he couldn't get her out, he'd have only one bitter option.

Once on his way, he called Fulton's cell phone, but got the voice mailbox.

"Fulton, 405's stuck in a rut of mud in that new area we fenced. I'm going back to try to pull her out. Come over as soon as you can." He hung up.

"Lord, give me help," he said. "Give 405 help, strength and a will to live. Give me your wisdom to get her out of this mess without hurting her any more. Forgive me for fencing in the area, but man, I thought there was no way it was still this soft. I've given the cows you gave me access to this little five-acre corner every spring for years, and I never had a problem like this. It's almost like a spring burst from the ground and turned this whole corner into muck and mush. Didn't see that coming, Lord. Guess you got your reasons."

He backed the tractor to 405's head, knowing it would frighten her, but he had no choices. When the back wheels began to sink, he wondered if he had enough rope. She was weaker already. She had laid her head on the ground, and as he forced her head up to apply the halter, she looked as if she had given up. Luckily, he saw no signs of wolves, but it wouldn't be long. Scully was alertly staring into the woods. Mulder patrolled the perimeter, nose to the ground.

Coney put the halter on 405's head, then tied the other end of the halter to a shorter length of rope and tied it to the tractor draw bar. He took a longer length and threw it behind her and jumped into the mud with her. She had sunk even deeper during the fifteen minutes it took him to get back to her, and her tail rested on the ground above the mud, nearly straight out.

"Thank you, Lord, that I remembered a shovel," Coney said.

He worked up a sweat getting out of the pit with effort that drained strength from his legs. The mud made a sucking sound with every inch. He grabbed the shovel and jumped back in, frantically moving mud and creating an even louder sucking sound with every shovel full.

The pit was cold and wet, and every shovel of mud required force that strained Coney's well-used muscles. The mud was heavy and smelly, but he worked through his sweat, which further slimed things up when mixed with the black mud on the shovel handle. As he worked, it became difficult for him to see which was mud and which was 405's leg.

He shoveled carefully when near her, fearing he might spear her leg. Once, when she flinched, he'd thought he had scraped a little fur from her, but he couldn't tell until, as the hole opened to him, he spotted a faint sight of blood. But it wasn't bad, he thought. No gushers, and she hadn't protested much. But she was very weak. He had to work fast.

Finally, he could see her back knees again, and he grabbed the rope and pushed it into the mud, right above her knees so it would pull against only the fleshy parts of her thighs, and not on any joints that could cripple her. He tied one end of the rope to the tractor draw bar and tightened it against 405, but it was too short for the other end to reach the tow bar. He grabbed the chain, the only length of anything he had left, and pulled the rope away from her. He packed the chain against her back legs, as the rope had been before, and tied it to the end of the rope.

"Lord, make this rope strong enough to hold the chain and 405's weight without breaking," he said.

Finally having secured the rope, he fired up the tractor and inched it forward, slowly until the ropes and chains were taut. 405's head was upright only because the halter kept it that way, and Coney knew this probably hurt her, but there was no other way.

"A little pain is better than dying in a mud hole, girl," he cried.

After both the halter rope and chain rope were taut, he opened the tractor throttle to get full power and eased off the clutch. With a sucking sound he could hear even over the tractor's roar, 405 came out of the mud and laid on solid ground.

Coney quickly backed the tractor up to loosen the tension and removed the halter, then the rope and chain. 405 laid on her side for a moment, breathing heavily. Coney patted her neck and shoved mud from her flanks with his hands, inspecting for more shovel wounds, but found just the one. It was deeper than he'd thought, but the blood was clotting. Finally, she sighed deeply and rose laboriously to her feet. Although caked in mud, she started walking toward the barn without a look toward Coney.

He gathered the ropes and chain, and looked into the hole, which was already filling with water.

"Lord, I thought this was absolutely dry enough," he prayed. "Forgive my mistake. May I always remember this, learn from it. We'll fence it back off today. I probably got impatient, Lord. You know that's something I've been working on. But I thought it was dry enough. Give my memory a boost if I get all in a yank again next spring."

He loaded all the ropes and chains and the shovel into the loader bucket and passed 405 in the lane to the barn. He moved a gate so she would be directed to the nurse barn. She was walking slowly, but appeared no worse for wear.

Coney only then noticed that he was caked in mud from top to bottom.

When 405 was in the barn in a stall, he hosed the mud off her and found the shovel mark he'd made. It would in no way hinder her recovery, but after he gently hosed her down, he coated the cut with a thick layer of bag balm anyway, just to keep infection at bay and flies off the open wound. He moved the portable milking machine compressor near the milking stall in the nurse barn, and milked her, then led her to a deeply bedded stall, where she sighed heavily again and laid down.

"Thank you Lord," Coney whispered as he watched her relax. "She's a good cow."

14

A month after he'd driven into Jovial,
Garit awoke with an unfamiliar stiffness in his back. He patted his air
mattress, and it gave way sloppily under his hand. He pulled back all
the coverings he owned. Just two thin blankets on top of a loosely fitted
sheet he'd bought without Aspen's help. It was made for a king-sized
bed, but it tucked nicely underneath the air mattress and stayed in place.
He lay flat on the bare mattress, and finally discovered a slow leak.

He marked the leak with a pen as best he could and walked the
mattress down the stairs, past the empty newsroom and the *World*
parking lot, and on down to Phil's Philling Station. It was a Saturday,
and Wally was likely out fishing on his new bass boat and cursing the
heat that kept the fish near the bottom of the lake.

Garit walked past the unoccupied front desk of the gas station
toward voices in the back. A young man about his age was in the far
corner of the three-stall garage, working on a tire. Sounds of power
tools came from another bay on the other side of a cement block wall.
Garit rested his mattress against the wall and waited. The tire worker
wore a blue uniform shirt with "Sam" written in neat cursive over his
left front shirt pocket.

Sam was speaking with a man Garit assumed was the tire owner.
Another man, apparently also waiting for Sam's services, leaned against
a far wall, sipping something steaming from a Styrofoam cup.

"... All in all, it only took us about fifteen, twenty minutes max," Sam was saying, and he giggled. "I almost got caught, too, but I slipped out of my shirt. Schoen is way too slow to catch me! I had a pretty good buzz on. I didn't think it was that big a deal, but then when the paper came out ..." Both Sam and the tire customer burst out laughing, and they looked beyond Garit as if he wasn't there. He spun and saw the photo he'd taken of the deputy scrubbing paint off the statue. Someone had cut it out of the *World* and mounted it crudely with Scotch tape to a metal tool chest door behind him.

"... When I saw it in the paper," Sam resumed, "I just about busted a gut. Silly statue gets painted all the time, and now all of a sudden it's big enough to be on the front page of the paper?" The customer grunted. "Darned if Fulton didn't finally get one right," Sam said. "The cops sure were quick to clean it off this time, too. I remember a couple years ago, it took them three months to get it cleaned up."

"Guess it all depends on how close we are to Founder's Day," the customer opined. "Can't have old man Jovial wearing tighty whiteys with all these people coming into town." Both he and Sam laughed. "It's all about image, after all."

Sam finished with an air hose, then picked the repaired tire off the machine, dropped it to the cement floor and caught it when it bounced back up.

"Ten bucks, Joe," he said, and Joe handed him the cash. Sam stuffed it in his front pocket.

Sam looked to Garit, ignoring the other man sipping from the cup.

"He was here first," Garit said. The other customer looked at him.

"I'm waiting for my car in the other bay," he said.

"Well, Sam, is it?" Sam nodded. "I have a leak here in this mattress. Can you patch it?"

"No problem," Sam said. "A good old-fashioned bike tire patch kit will do the trick."

He took the mattress back to the tire fixing area, searched around in a metal cupboard above the work bench, and pulled out a small square of rubber and some sort of liquid cement.

"Ain't never seen you around," he said as he scraped with a tool that looked like a cheese grater around the tiny leak.

"I'm Garit West, the new *World* reporter," Garit said, holding out his hand. Sam took it firmly and shook it.

"Sam Perkins," he said. "New *World* reporter, huh? Did you take that picture?" He pointed to the photo on the tool chest.

"Yep, I took it. It was the first one in this job. Hadn't been here more than an hour or two. And the cops weren't very happy about it." He knew how to carry through on a common theme in conversation. It was part of what made him a good reporter, although he didn't really recognize it yet. Sam looked up from his work and grinned.

"I don't imagine they were," he said. "Great picture. Everybody was talking about it."

"Thanks. The guy doing the scrubbing there?" He pointed to a spot on the photo. "He smashed the camera when I was leaving, but Wally East managed to find the card. Amazing that it still worked."

Sam shook his head. "I don't know nothin' about them cameras," he said. He pressed the rubber patch on top of the rubber cement.

"Let me ask you something," Garit said, looking back at the man standing behind them. He turned Sam to one side to hide their conversation.

"Why does no one seem to even notice that a cop threatened me just for doing my job? You didn't even look up when I told you he smashed the camera. He stuck a gun in my face, too!"

"Was it Schoen?"

"That's what Wally told me."

"He's a jackass," Sam said. "Has been ever since he was a kid. Used to be the biggest bully in school, or so they say. He was a few years ahead of me, in my oldest sister's class."

"Then why is he a cop if everyone knows about him?"

"You kiddin'?" Sam asked. "What makes a better cop than a bully? They ain't nothing more than playground bullies, every single one of them."

"Good to know. And now I'm on their watch list because of that picture."

"Did you get a new camera yet?"

"Well, one I can use, yeah."

"You might just get another chance to take a picture that makes

Schoen look like an idiot. Every time you got the guts to put one like that on the front page of the *World*, you're a hero to a lot of people."

"Are you giving me a hot tip of some kind? Because I don't think Wally has the guts to print another one like that. Schoen came in and chewed us both out pretty good. Said I had one-and-a-half strikes."

"I'm just sayin'. Keep your eyes open. Never know when something else might happen." He filled the mattress with air and pushed it toward Garit as he looked at the man standing with his cup. "Just be careful," he whispered.

"Here you go," he said as Garit reached for his wallet. "What do I owe you?"

"Special today for the new guy in town," Sam said. "No charge. Welcome to Jovial."

Three days later, Sam whistled as he locked up the gas station for the evening. He locked the front door, checked all the bay doors and turned the lights down to night mode. As he shut and locked the back door and went to his car, he felt something cold and hard jam harshly onto his lower spine.

"Sam Perkins, you're under arrest for destruction of city property, conspiracy, vandalism and gang activity," he heard a voice say as he was slammed headfirst into the gravel parking lot, driving stones into his face. His arms made a cracking sound as they were yanked brutally behind him, and plastic strips bit into his wrists.

Suddenly, he was jerked to his feet, and he collapsed when the back of his knees were bashed by something wooden and swift. He heard it whoosh! again through the air before he dropped painfully to his knees. He was picked up and thrown headfirst into the back of a police car. He wondered what the horrible smell was as he was taken to the Jovial County Jail, where he was pitched onto the floor of a cell.

15

On the two-month anniversary of his arrival in Jovial, Garit heard shouting as he opened the door between his apartment and the newsroom.

"... So just get off your high horse and do your job!" Wally shouted.

"High horse!" It was Aspen. "How dare you! Just because I won't do you anymore you give me the crud work and then throw me under the bus? You bastard! You're nothing but a no-talent hack. I've been carrying you and this whole paper for two years now, and you dare lay this stuff on me? What you're doing is wrong, Wally, and I won't do it. I can't do it!"

Garit cleared his throat loudly as he clunked his old, comfortable black shoes down the stairs. He saw Wally's face, red and turning to crimson, and Aspen was breathing so hard that her whole body was heaving back and forth. They each turned and saw him, and hastily went into the darkroom and spun the door shut.

Garit looked at the two Debbies, who for the first time he could remember, were not working. Their backs were to their computers. Garit gave them a crooked smile, and they each shrugged, first Debbie, then Debbie.

Garit sat at his desk and tried to begin writing a feature story. But the sounds of arguing and cursing continued from the darkroom. Finally, Aspen opened the darkroom door.

"Screw you, Wally. I quit!" she shrieked tearfully. The two Debbies looked up, smirked at each other, and went back to work.

Aspen disappeared and returned soon with an empty paper box, and stood in front of her desk. Tears carved rivers into her high cheeks and dripped onto her sleeveless orange blouse as she went through her desk drawers, pulled things out and put them roughly into the box. Finally, she held out a small box, unopened.

"Here, Garit," she said. "I'd forgotten all about this camera. I bought it a year ago, and never used it. Can't even remember why I never did, but you might as well have a new one." She handed it to Garit.

"Thanks," he said, awkwardly. Their eyes met, and she lingered before breaking the gaze.

"Sorry that you kind of got put into the middle of all this," she said. "I know it's been a little tense around here since, well, you know."

"I know."

"I had hoped we all could just move on from it," she said, "but I guess not. I should have known better than to trust a total jerk like Wally." She spat a large white blob toward his office door, and it stuck on the window like a tree frog.

"So, what are you going to do?" Garit asked.

"Don't know and right now I don't care," she retorted. "I just know I have to get out of here before I suffocate or take a gun to Wally's fat head."

Garit opened the camera box and pulled out the innards. It was a point-and-shoot Kodak, one of the last of its kind. He found the owner's manual and began reading as Aspen continued her packing and weeping. Finally, the box was full, and Aspen sighed.

"Now it's up to you," she said to Garit.

"What's up to me?"

"Well, I suppose it's only right to give you a little time to decide what you're going to do," she said. "See you around, Garit," she grumbled. Then she turned and walked out the back of the office.

"What did she mean by that?" Garit asked one of the Debbies.

"Sounded to me like she expects you to quit too," she said.

"Really?" He asked. "You got *that* out of *that*? Why would she expect something like that?" Debbie shrugged.

A few minutes later, Wally opened the darkroom door and emerged, his head held high. He stood in the middle of the newsroom, his arms crossed, saying nothing.

"Well?" He shouted finally, looking at no one. "Any of you got anything to say?" Garit and the Debbies shook their heads.

"Good," he said. "I'll expect this to be the last mention of the name Aspen Kemp in this office. Understood? What happens in this office stays in this office, and I mean it. Now get back to work, all of you." Garit and the Debbies nodded. Wally walked back into his office and slammed the door, rattling the glass windows. Aspen's spit wad remained stuck firmly.

Aspen dropped the box of her office stuff on the off-white sofa that had come with her apartment, but she wouldn't settle down. Anger kept her spinning. She paced around the tiny kitchen, whirling, wondering how she let this happen. She had always been the one in control. She had always been too good for this kind of thing. It was supposed to be a reporter's job to expose corruption, not support it.

She looked out her window and didn't see a Jeep she hoped to see in the apartment complex parking lot. What a fool she was for expecting anything. She dialed her cell phone.

"Mom? Aspen."

"Hello, dear. What's wrong?"

"Does something have to be wrong?"

"You tell me. You never call unless there is something wrong, so I just assumed–"

"Don't give me that guilt trip again, Mom," she said. "Aren't moms supposed to be there for their kids?"

"Most moms, I suppose. What time is it?"

"It's like 10:30 in the morning, Mom. Have you been drinking already?"

"What, you called to give me a lecture?"

"No, just to update you. I just quit my job."

"Well don't expect to come back here."

"I wouldn't dream of it. Will you just listen a minute?" Aspen heard a heavy sigh, or maybe her mom had just lit a smoke. They sounded so similar. "OK. What is it?"

"It's just that sometimes, I just don't know how men think at all, Mom. I'd like to spend a day as a man just once, so I could act stupid like a man, get angry about being fired instead of crying like a woman. Maybe even throw a punch or two. But no. This whole world is run by dip sticks like Wally East. I could out-write that moron even if I were drunk! No-talent hack. How dare he do this to me? He'll be sorry someday."

"So why did he fire you, dear?"

"He didn't fire me, I quit." she shouted into the phone.

"That's not what you said a minute ago."

"That's exactly what I said, Mom. Whatever. And on top of that, this um, boyfriend of mine wouldn't even support me at all. At the very least he should have come running up behind me, trying to be some jerk of a knight in shining armor or something. But no. Nothing out of him at all. Wally wouldn't have treated me this way if I were a man, or if we hadn't been—well, let's just leave it at that. All men are insensitive jerks."

"Don't I know it."

Aspen paced about the room as she talked. Finally, she sat on the couch and opened the lid of her box. She pulled out a framed photo of her parents, taken years before the divorce. It had been so buried on her desk that she'd forgotten it was there.

"Look," said her mother. "You made your decision, or you did something bad that got you fired. Either way, it doesn't matter. It's just a part of your life. Everybody does stupid things. You've been there before, right? Just let yourself be hurt by this for a little while. Cry it out, and you'll be fine. Then do something nice for yourself."

"I have a good work record here, Mom. I know you've never believed in me, but I was practically running this newspaper. Besides that, I have another editor interested in me. But what really hacks me off is that I worked so hard to build my skills here, and I was the top reporter. Two years shot. I don't know what to do, Mom!" Tears streamed down her jaw and onto the couch.

"Maybe I was fooling myself. Maybe I was just a better hack than the rest of all these hacks that have rolled through this place. I've seen half a dozen reporters come and go at the *World*, and they were all hacks. Maybe it's time to start fresh, Mom. Maybe I have to find another profession.

"Well you can't move back in here with me."

"I have no intention of intruding on you and what's-his-name."

"Malik."

"Whatever."

"Well what about this other editor you were bragging about?"

"I wasn't bragging, Mom. Just stating a fact. He's the owner of the Sventon paper, in the next town over."

"Don't expect me to help you move."

"You're two time zones away, Mom. Why would I expect that?"

"Don't you get all snotty with me!"

"Sorry to have intruded on your busy life, Mom," Aspen snapped. "How stupid of me to think you might be interested in my life."

"You're the one who moved away, dear."

"I'll call you back when I'm on my feet, OK?"

"That's fine. Don't call so early in the morning."

"Bye, Mom." Aspen hung up. She tossed the framed picture of her parents back into the box and punched up another number on her cell phone.

"Hello?"

"Hi, Sheila. It's Aspen."

"Hi, Aspen. Just a minute, I'll get your dad."

"No, Sheila. Actually, I wanted to talk to you."

"Really? What about?"

Aspen poured out her story, including the affair with Wally.

"You know, if all this had happened just a few months ago, I might have just left it all behind and gone to Botsdorf on a moment's notice, but today—and suddenly I regret it—I wonder if I should just chuck it all and start over. Maybe real estate. Maybe money would be the cure I need."

"Something must have changed in the last few months," her step-mom said. "There's something you're not telling me, Aspen.

"Alright. It's that bastard Garit."

"The new reporter? Oh. He's keeping you there!"

"Don't say it like that, Sheila. Maybe I think he's cute and everything, and he is a good writer, after all, but he didn't even have the guts to come after me, or quit and walk out the door right behind me, like a real man would do. God knows I left him enough hints."

"Men are notoriously bad at picking up on our subtleties," Sheila said.

"There was nothing sexual between us, Sheila, but there was a real connection. At least I thought so. But what do I know? What do I know about making the right choices? I've ruined my career by sleeping with the boss. And why? For the life of me, Sheila, I don't know why I did it. Was it some subconscious need to rob him of his power? To gain some of my own? Or was it just raw animal lust? What kind of bimbo does that, anyway?" She stopped to sob and dab at new tears. "Maybe I was just trying to be a big fish in a really small bowl. I'm only 26, Sheila. Am I already that big a failure?"

"You're not a failure, Aspen. Just go out and do that investigative story you told me about. Give it your best shot. I'll bet it will lead to a new job before you know it, and you'll be able to put this all behind you. What's this story about?"

"I'm so glad you asked, because it's really pretty cool," Aspen said. "It's like something you see in the movies. I'm all undercover, infiltrating this animal rights wacko group. I bought a blonde wig and dull brown contact lenses."

"That's smart, Aspen. Your baby blues are too distinctive. Anyone would spot you in a minute."

"Thanks, Sheila. I got a tiny microphone that I tape inside this sports bra. Makes me flatter. I have this inflatable underwear that makes my butt and thighs look bigger. I don't think even Garit or Wally would recognize me. Maybe I should try it someday. I wonder what Wally would do if he knew I'd started this assignment for his competition while I still worked at the *World*? I hope he finds out when he reads the front page of his competition. A pub so high-class he couldn't even touch it. I'd love to rub his nose in it."

"That may come with time, Aspen," Sheila said. "A fringe benefit.

But to be good, you have to have the right motivation. Do it because you're a great reporter and writer, not for revenge. Revenge won't get you a good story. Following your God-given talent will. Only He can help you forgive yourself."

"You're right, Sheila," Aspen sighed, ignoring the God comments her dad's new wife always seemed to wedge into their conversations. "I've already spent too much time being self-absorbed and feeling sorry for myself. And I do have a meeting to go to tonight for that story. I'll worry about all this other stuff later."

"That's the spirit." There was an awkward pause.

"Thanks for listening to me blubber, Sheila. You're really easy to talk to."

"Glad I could help. Don't you hesitate to call me again, now. Either way. I won't judge you, you know that."

"Thank you for that, Sheila. It was nice finally having a talk with you."

"I feel the same way. Want to talk to your dad?"

"Maybe next time."

"That's fine. Go get 'em, girl. God bless you. I know you'll knock 'em dead."

"Thanks, Sheila. Bye."

16

At about 2:30 a.m., Mulder and Scully patrolled along the back fence line of a thirty-acre pasture, their noses low to the ground. On a 400-yard stretch on the southernmost fence line, a dirt two-track road ran parallel to the barbed wire before it veered off to meet with another gravel road that led ultimately to Brenner Road.

Just inside the fence, the dogs discovered two cold McDonald's hamburgers on the ground. They growled at each other briefly over the first one, and Mulder won. Scully quickly found the other and gobbled it down, pills and all. They each sniffed around for more, but quickly gave up and finished their patrol around the fence line.

They were back in the house snoring, unnaturally still and dreamless when three people, guided by a single cell-phone flashlight, walked the two-track road to where they'd tossed the burgers.

"Don't touch the fence," one of them said. "It's electrified."

"Figures that a slaver would want to give their animals an electric shock," said a young woman as she slipped warily and carefully under the fence, careful to protect the camera hanging from her neck. The young man with the flashlight crouched to go under it next, but the last young man, dressed in a dark sport coat and black shirt, hesitated.

"I want to check it out," he said. "If we're going to know what we're talking about, we need experience. Shine the light over here a minute, man."

The man with the flashlight was dressed sloppily in torn jeans and a worn flannel shirt, and he sported several earrings, tattoos, and a nose piercing. He shined the light toward the well-dressed man, who grabbed hold of the fence, wrapping his fist firmly around it.

"Yeoww!" He screamed when the electric pulse went through his body. He leaped back and shook his arm as if every muscle had cramped.

"Wow," he said finally. "I'll be able to testify in any court in the land now, for sure. That is sheer torture."

"Dare you to pee on it," said the tattooed man. The well-dressed man laughed. "That's the type of punishment the slavers should get, man," he said. "Electric shocks to their pee-pees." He giggled, reached out and grabbed the fence again, and waited for the pulse.

"Yowza!" He cried, and began laughing, again trying to shake the pins and needles rushing through his fingers. "This is just wrong!"

"Come on you guys," complained the girl. "We have work to do. You guys are so immature. You been hanging around this Hicksville flyover town way too long."

The tattooed man handed the flashlight to the well-dressed man, and reached for a McDonald's bag on the ground. He picked it up and crouched to get under the fence.

"Why do you have to carry that smelly meat around?" The girl said.

"Duh. Did you forget about the dogs?" he said.

"Well, just keep that dead carcass away from me."

They walked in silence the rest of the way to the Dogues' hospital barn, dodging cow pies with aid of the flashlight.

The well-dressed young man quickly found an unlocked screen door into the Dogue's Farm hospital barn. He opened the door slowly, and it creaked only a little. He hesitated a moment, listening for barking. Finally he motioned for the others to enter. The flashlight scanned the room.

"Must have been an office or something, back in the day," he said. "Maybe the room where they kept the milk tank? Either way, a structure of oppression and cruelty." He looked to the girl for approval, but she gave him none.

The room was lined with shelves and cupboards. Against the only wall with a window was a large locked cupboard with a caution sticker on the door. The drug box. The well-dressed man pointed the flashlight on it, and the tattooed youth tried unsuccessfully to open the box silently. It was padlocked shut.

The well-dressed man shrugged and waved the flashlight around until its beam landed on another door, a solid wooden slider. He pulled it open.

Once through the door into the hospital barn, the well-dressed young man found a switch and turned on a light.

"Oh, look at the poor abused animals," moaned the girl, putting the camera to her eye. "How could anyone eat you, my babies? Don't worry, I'll protect you. Don't you know I love all animals? Well, except humans." Her companions grunted.

The hospital barn contained twelve large box stalls fifteen-feet by fifteen-feet square on one side and a row of fifteen free stalls on the other, with a large stack of straw bales and sawdust beside each other in an open space. Two cows lay side-by-side in the free stalls, and they stood as the strangers entered.

"Ooh, don't get up babies," cooed the girl. "You need your strength. Look where they keep you, crammed in that little space." She looked at the well-dressed young man. "What is this, anyway? Is this their torture chamber or something? Look at this! It's horrible. They must be doing some kind of morbid experiments or something!" She moved quickly and jerkily, waving her arms between shutter clicks.

As the two cows backed out of the free stalls and moved away from her antics, the three activists looked behind them to a barred, deeply bedded stall, where lay a cow in the midst of delivering a calf. She was lying calmly on her side, and her udder, bulging with milk, protruded. The calf's front two feet showed, but the cow tried to get up when the girl rushed behind her and gasped.

"What have they done to you, Mr. Cow?" She shrieked, holding the camera out to see what was in its screen. "What kind of torture leaves you in such pain? Did the farmer beat you?" She began snapping photos.

"I wish we could free all these poor slaves," she said as she made her way along the box stalls. Only one other box stall was occupied, and in it, with her face to the wall, was another cow, number 230, in the hospital barn after a difficult delivery. Afterbirth still clung from her and stretched across the stall toward the walkway.

"Look at this!" The girl stage-shouted as she took several pictures. All the cows in the barn flinched at that, and the ones in the free stalls hurried to the far corner of the barn.

"It's just disgusting!" The girl said. "How did this cow's guts get forced out of his butt?" She grunted and pinched her nose with the index finger and thumb of her left hand, the other three fingers pointing in the air. "This whole place is rancid! How can they force animals to live like this? There ought to be a law! Who allows this to go on?"

"All the slave owners," said the well-dressed young man. "But you're exposing this, Bambi. You're going to make a difference. Your anger is totally justified, and your courage is totally, like, commendable. Plus, you're a very talented photographer."

"I wouldn't even have to be here if you guys had any idea how to take a photo," she said. "I think I'm going to throw up. " She rushed away toward the door, holding her nose.

"You get what you need?" asked the well-dressed young man when she came back into the barn.

"I think so," she said, coughing. She kept shooting, though, taking photos of every animal in the barn. "But if I didn't, we always have Photo Shop."

The well-dressed young man closed the sliding door behind him, turned out the barn lights and lit the floor with the flashlight for his companions. It was nearly 3:30 a.m. when they left the barn and followed the pasture fence line back where they began. They crawled under the electric fence and walked the two-track road to a pickup truck. It was jacked up on over-sized tires and carried a rebel flag in the rear window. It roared to life as the well-dressed man fired it up. It crept slowly down the two-track road, and disappeared.

Mulder and Scully got up groggily when Coney punched the clock radio and awakened to milk at 4:10 a.m.

"What's the matter, kids?" he asked them as he walked out the door and onto the large farmhouse porch. "You seem a little lethargic. Probably the heat and humidity, huh?" He made a mental note to watch them, maybe call the vet if they didn't perk up, and thanked God that they had these two wonderful dogs.

Mulder and Scully, absent their usual enthusiasm, followed the thirty-acre pasture fence line, their noses to the ground all the way to the two-track road a half mile away. As they began feeling better, they trotted back to the barn when the scent disappeared and truck tire tracks began.

17

Garit was at his desk writing briefs for the Upcoming Events page when he heard Wally shout from his office.

"West! Get in here." Garit stood in Wally's office doorway.

"Who was doing the statue vandalism stories, you or Aspen?"

"I was," Garit said. "Don't you remember? It was my first story, and the photo you picked put the entire police force against me. Still don't know how you got a photo off that mangled old memory card." *Placate the bully*, Garit thought. *It's worked before.*

"Oh, yeah," Wally said, absentmindedly. "I got it off your phone. Well, there's been an arrest in the case. I want you to go to the jail and interview the perp."

"Perp?"

"Perpetrator, West. Jeez, don't you ever watch TV crime shows?"

"Not really."

"Wally sent him a look of incredulity and shook his head. "Just get down to the jail. The kid has apparently lawyered up, but I want you to see if they'll let you talk to him."

"What's his name?"

"Don't ask stupid questions. How should I know? Just get down there. Jeez, it's always a battle with you, isn't it?" Garit shrugged. He'd always thought himself easy to work with.

"I thought the name Aspen was never to be mentioned in this office again," Garit said, saying what he wished he'd only thought.

Wally stared. "I make the rules, and I can darn well break them, West. Don't be such a wise acre. Just get down to the jail!"

Garit walked through the front door of the Jovial Police Department and stood before the front desk. An obese dispatcher spoke into an ancient silver microphone perched in front of her like an obedient parrot.

"You just sit tight," she said into it. "Detective Meyer is on his way." She turned to look at Garit.

"May I help you?"

"Is Chief Dulogski in?"

She looked at Garit and scanned him from top to waist. "Just a moment." She pressed a button on her right. "Chief? Someone here to see you." She looked back at Garit. "Hold tight, hon," she said.

In a moment, Chief Dulogski opened a door to Garit's left that had a "Authorized Personnel Only" sign on it.

"Oh, West," he said, and sighed. "Come on back. I told Wally I'd be cooperative." He held the door open and led Garit to a tiny office piled with papers in one corner. Clutter was everywhere except on the chief's desk, which was clean and polished, sporting only a desktop computer, wireless mouse and keyboard. He pointed to a chair and sat behind his desk as Garit sat.

"What do you want, West? I'm very busy."

"Wally said I might be able to interview the person you arrested for painting the statue," Garit said.

"What makes him think we'd allow that?" Dulogski said. Garit shrugged. "I don't know. He just sent me down here." Dulogski put his hand on his chin and leaned forward on his desk.

"I guess this is your lucky day," he said, after an uncomfortable pause. "His lawyer is in with him now, and I can have you join him only if the lawyer is there, OK?"

"Thanks, Chief. Any comment you'd like to make on the record about this arrest?"

The chief thought momentarily, as if trying to remember the rehearsed first line that would bring his entire speech back to the front of his mind.

"I would just say that it's a tribute to our detective work and persistence that we caught one of the gang members who continually desecrate our town founder's good name," Dulogski said. "We intend to prosecute this gang banger and all of his gang members to the fullest extent of the law. Gangs and all other forms of organized crime have no place in Jovial, and my police department intends to send them all packing. We might even give them a little boot on the butt just for good measure. There. You have a little color for the story now, too."

"Thanks, Chief," Garit said. "One other thing. I hope there's no hard feelings left about that picture of the statue. I didn't pick it out, you know. Wally made that decision."

"Is that a fact?" The chief said. "I'll take that into consideration, but let me tell you something. I don't like snitches. Never have. Never will."

He picked up a land-line phone receiver that rested on clutter behind him. "Officer Schoen?" he asked. "Can you come up and bring young Mr. West here back to the interrogation room?" He hung up.

"Officer Schoen?" Garit asked.

"Yes," Dulogski replied. "Is that a problem?"

"I think it is," Garit replied. "That first day I met you at the park, after you left, he smashed my camera and threatened me at gunpoint." Dulogski stared at him.

"First of all," he said at last, "I don't believe it. Second, that was what, four months ago?"

"It's barely been two months," Garit argued.

"The story I got directly from one of my best deputies is that you were all up in his face, asking stupid questions and challenging his authority like some punk," Dulogski said. "He even told me he warned you, gave you one strike. So why are you telling me this now, if it's true at all?"

"Wally told me to let it drop, too, but since then, I've heard stories from other people who say he's well-known for physical and verbal abuse all around town."

"Strike Two!" The chief shouted, and jumped out of his chair. "And to think I was almost willing to cancel out your first strike. I almost believed your story about the picture for a minute there." He paused and stared at Garit. "You lying piece of work," he spat. "I'll be darned if I let you have the interview now. You will not slander the good name of one of the top deputies in this county. Now get out of my office!" He pointed to the door, and Garit backed out, unsure whether he could trust the Chief any more than he could a teeth-displaying dog. As he took a step back, he felt a hard boot smash into the back of his left ankle, and he fell on the floor, hard on his back. The Kodak in his back pocket smashed and its guts spilled out. Garit looked up and saw Officer Schoen standing over him, and he gave that same ankle another violent kick.

"Jeez, kid, you OK?" The deputy asked and offered a hand to pull Garit off the floor. Garit refused it. "Watch where you're going from now on!" The deputy said.

Garit stood, rubbed his lower back and looked back at Chief Dulogski, who stood expressionless in his office doorway. "Can I at least get the police report on the arrest?" Garit asked.

"That's public information," the chief said. "Ask Zoe at the front desk. And tell Wally we're now charging a buck a page for copies."

Garit turned and walked out.

Wally stood over Garit's shoulder, a habit Garit didn't like, but to which he was becoming accustomed.

"I thought I told you to get an interview," Wally sneered. "This could have been done from a police report."

"It was," Garit replied. "Chief wouldn't let me do an interview, and Schoen kicked me when I was walking out. Twice. I think he may have cracked a bone in my ankle." Wally sighed.

"Sure, West," he said. "You certainly are a major martyr, aren't you?

Why don't you just give it up? No one will believe you, even if it's true. You should have insisted on getting that interview!"

"I don't think that would have worked," Garit said. "The chief was already teed off because I told him that Schoen had pointed his gun at me."

"You did what? West, didn't I tell you to let that drop? Now I have more fences to mend with Dulogski." He shook his head as he looked at Garit's computer screen.

"You sure this is all confirmable?"

"Directly from the police report."

"Why didn't you give the perp's name?"

"It was redacted on the report."

"Let me see the report."

Uncharacteristically, Wally read the report carefully, when suddenly a spark seemed to jump from his eyes.

"Good job, Garit. My editor's column is going to be on this very subject." Wally directed Garit out of his office and picked up a desk phone.

"Chief? Wally," he said. "What's the name of the statue vandal, anyway?" Pause. "I know it was blocked out in the report, but that was my rookie reporter. This is me, Chief." Pause, longer this time. "Look, he's not going to spread that around anywhere. Besides, how does holding back news help you protect your department—or me?" Another long pause. "Look chief, we're all in this thing together, you and me. If we're going to get anything done—er, for the good of the town—I have to sway some public opinion our way. Who knows what will happen when Botsdorf gets his hands on it? We have to get ahead of him, Chief, and you know it." Longer pause. Wally nodded a few times. "Sam? Sam Perkins? Great. Thanks, Chief. We'll get this done."

Wally pecked loudly at his computer keyboard for much of the next two hours, and finally, he shouted. "West, get in here!" Garit stood in the doorway to his office.

"Come on around here so you can see my screen," he said. "I'm going to teach you a little something about writing editorials that sway public opinion."

"Is that what editorials are supposed to do?"

"Just listen and learn, J-school boy," Wally said. He began to read aloud from his screen.

> "The arrest of a young hoodlum named Sam Perkins for desecrating the city's statue of town founder Alan Jovial in the park was announced recently by Jovial Police Chief James Dulogski." He started, then paused. "Oh, that's good," he muttered. "That will really grab them. Desecrating. A great word. Almost as good as hoodlums." Garit grunted.

"How do we know he's a hoodlum?" he asked. "Maybe he's just a kid playing a prank."

"This kid will be what I say he is," Wally retorted, and smiled. "Don't second-guess me, West. I get to flex my muscle as the only editor in town. People expect it. The trick is how to use it with power and subtlety, so the sheep don't even know they're being led. Power like that can only be wielded at the right time. The trick is knowing the right time when it comes along." He continued reading to Garit.

> "As regular readers know, the editor and owner of the *World* has made it his practice to not name youthful miscreants, instead choosing to give them a chance to straighten out their lives without the intense public scrutiny that goes automatically with having your name disparagingly mentioned in an influential community newspaper. That policy holds.
>
> However, the young gangster in question has so steadfastly refused to reveal his co-conspirators or cooperate with the police in any way, that this town leader cannot help but wonder if the conspiracy once known as the Jocular Society has once again reared its ugly head. If that is indeed the case, one can reasonably assume that the arrestee is following a code of silence for fear of his life. No doubt this young man has been browbeaten or worse, brainwashed into his

uncooperative ways, because he's certainly much too dull to have taken on a project to desecrate the hallowed name of Alan Jovial on his own. He's lawyered up, to capture a phrase. No mastermind here."

"Wow. This seems like fiction to me, not an opinion piece," Garit said. "It borders on libel. How do you know he's a gangster, whatever that is? And now there's a gang? And what is the Jocular Society, anyway? Chief told me about it once, but I thought it was little more than an urban legend."

"Look, I'm trying to teach you something about writing here, West. Stop nit- picking and pay attention." Wally continued reading.

"This Jocular Society gang was wiped out once, and it should be again. That's a fact. But who is the mastermind behind the graffiti and the gang? What could possess an evil mastermind to do such a thing? A gang initiation ceremony? Fortunately, due to the forward thinking of our city fathers, they, nary two months ago, voted to crack down on gang activity. And while the rabble rousers forced it onto the ballot instead of rightly letting the council decide what laws to pass, I'm not saying we have a gang problem like big cities, but I am saying that the prosecution is prepared to rub these activities out faster than our crack deputies can clean up the desecrated tribute to our town founder. Our laws demand it.

Citizens of Jovial, I urge you to keep your eyes and ears open, and report suspicious activities around the park immediately to the police. They're busy enough these days with their normal duties without having to track down a misguided agenda of mischief, or even worse, gang violence."

Garit groaned. Wally glared at him, but continued reading.

"And a personal note to the nameless mastermind behind the mischief: Rest assured, you will be caught, and prosecuted, and sent away, after a fair trial, where you can't slander the name of Alan Jovial ever, ever again. And if there is a Jocular Society revival; and if that organized crime group has once again reappeared, I will speak for the God-fearing citizens of Jovial when I say get out of my town!"

Garit rolled his eyes. "Yep. Good stuff, Wally. You're Clint Eastwood and Walter Cronkite all rolled up into one."

"Shut up for once and learn," Wally said. "You're too young to know good writing when you see it. It's almost quitting time. Go home."

Garit went to his desk and finished the brief he was working on, then went upstairs to his apartment.

Wally saved his opinion piece, copied it, pasted it into an email addressed to deadfr@jovialfood.com. In the message box he wrote: "FYI," and pressed send.

Two days later, Garit, along with every other subscriber to the *Jovial World*, could read a column on page two with the headline "Stamp Out the Gang Bankers." Garit's story on the arrest did not appear, but the typo was priceless. So priceless, in fact, that Garit had to share it. There was no one else who would understand. He looked through his phone contacts, hoping he hadn't deleted Aspen's number the night he caught her and Wally together. It was there.

He texted: "Check out Wally's type-o. Gang bankers? Thought you could use the laugh."

18

Coney and Fulton finished milking one
morning in mid-June. The grand opening of the Farmers Only Store
was racing hard toward a pre-Independence Day event, and Jovial was
experiencing the hottest stretch of spring and early summer weather in
recorded history.

On top of the long string of unusually hot, humid days, heavy rain
had put all the area farmers behind normal planting schedules. Almost
all the vegetable acreage around Jovial was tiled, but it still took a while
for the black, heavy muck to dry enough to plant or harvest. Coney had
just pressed the button that sent liquid sanitizer surging through the
milk pipeline like a series of tiny waves when his cell phone rang.

"Hi, Frank," Coney said. "Can you hold on just a minute? I need
to catch up on one thing." Coney pressed the phone to his chest and
waved his hand at Fulton.

"Are you gonna cut that north forty today?" he asked. Fulton
nodded. "I got to get Carlos going on planting third-crop celery over
at the old Pruse farm first. By then it should be dry enough. Haybine
all greased up?"

"Yep. I'll get out to plant sweet corn at the Williams field at some
point, depending on how long it takes with Frank here. Everything
involving Frank takes longer than it should."

"How's old man Williams doing, anyway?"

"Not bad for eighty-four. I'm sure he'll want to talk awhile when I get there."

"Good luck with Frank."

Coney smiled and nodded and took the phone away from his chest. He remembered the meeting of the Jovial Area Farmers Association (JAFA) when they hired Frank last winter. Coney's was the only strong voice in opposition.

"Listen, Coney." Frank Gladding said now as the cell phone connection wavered between clarity and brokenness. "I'm afraid I'm going to need you to step in here with Noah. He just won't listen to me, and I'm afraid we're going to lose our milk supplier at the last minute. I don't think I can put together another deal on such short notice, Coney, and I could use a little help here. I didn't buy into this kind of hostility. Not for a measly forty-five grand a year."

"What's the problem, Frank?" Coney said, looking at a few of the painful new cracks in the skin around his right thumbnail. "Didn't we hire you to take care of things like this?"

"But Noah won't listen to me, Coney. He's going to pull out of his contract." Coney held his phone away from his ear and sighed. Most people in town had trouble understanding Noah Brenner, and for a newcomer to town like Frank, it was nearly impossible unless you put in the time to get to know him.

"No one's going to pull out of anything, Frank. Is Noah there with you?"

"No, but he's coming right now to do something with his signs. Can you meet him here? He'll listen to you."

"Look, Frank. This problem is not new," Coney said. "It's high time you get it resolved, once and for all. Why are we re-plowing old ground here? This is going to take up most of my morning if I have to come down."

"Please, Coney?" Frank whined.

Coney changed into a clean pair of jeans and a light green T-shirt when Jenn asked what was going on.

"I got to cover Frank's butt again, which means I won't get to planting corn at Williams' until at least this afternoon," he said. "Maybe we need to start thinking about adding another hired hand if I have to drop everything for this store. Think we can afford it?"

"Can't afford it to let the store go untended," Jenn said. "We have way too much sunk into it for that, just like all the association members."

"Something to think about," Coney said as he walked out the door. "I'll be back as soon as I can calm down Noah and Frank."

"Say a thankful prayer on your way. I'll be at the farmers market, trying to sell the last of the maple syrup. If I can, we'll only end up losing about a thousand bucks on the deal."

"Great news," Coney said, grinning.

Coney had known and liked Noah Brenner and his family since the third grade, when their teacher at Jovial Elementary, Miss Cooper, assigned Coney to help the new kid with his reading.

"Your dad bought the old Webster farm, right?" Coney had asked, parroting what the grownups were saying.

"Yep, and we're gonna have the best dairy herd in the state there someday," Noah had said. He was true to his word.

Coney admired Noah for what he'd overcome. He developed a knack for the dairy business in spite of his struggle with the written word. Coney had been unsuccessful in getting Noah up to the third-grade reading level, and to this day, Noah didn't read well. He could get by, even grasp a context if someone read something to him, but words on a page never seemed to come easy for him. As a kid he was obviously frustrated by it, especially when classmates bullied him, labeling him stupid. But for some reason, Noah read figures and spread sheets just fine. He could remember statistics and fractions and analyze data better and quicker than anyone Coney had ever known. Noah's dairy was today more computerized than any of the other dairymen in the area. He had accomplished more than any of his teachers ever would have imagined.

Coney remembered with sadness—back then it was bitterness and unforgiveness—when sadistic teachers made Noah read aloud, even when they knew it would embarrass him. Coney was to this day convinced they did it on purpose, because Noah was called on as much in May as he was in September. It was painful to watch, but unpopular to defend Noah.

Things were different today. Coney credited his faith, his desire to make his life follow Jesus's example, for his mostly unpopular commitment to upholding the dignity of odd-looking and strange-acting people in the face of societal bullies; and for the courage to do it. Though the phrase was way out of fashion, Coney didn't really have to ask what Jesus would do. He knew. Jesus would treat Noah the same as the Governor. Coney had decided long ago that if he were to commit to following Jesus, he'd do the same. Not because he had to, but because he wanted to. A genuinely changed heart would do it naturally.

The biggest struggle to defend Noah was at the Jovial Area Farmers Association meeting a little more than a month ago.

"We've boiled it down to three milk suppliers, and I say we can't go wrong with Noah." Coney told the executive board.

"The guy's kind of stupid, isn't he?" asked executive board member and fish farmer Harvey Birch. "The man can't even read."

"Let me tell you something about Noah," Coney began. "Reading well or not does not predict intelligence, and Noah is far from stupid. My dad used to call him a cattle judging savant. He could score cattle, especially dairy cattle, on a par with the finest college animal science post-grads. When he dropped out of of high school and went full time managing his dad's herd, he brought giant leaps in the farm's animal quality, almost overnight. And you all know his milk quality can't be beat."

"How do we know that?" asked fruit farmer Harry Smuthers.

"Look at his pedigree," Coney replied. "He's bred dairy genetic champions and high-priced, trophy-winning bulls. He has a history of milk quality awards going back three decades."

"I've heard he keeps his feeding mixture a big secret," said Birch. "What does he have to hide?"

"Wouldn't you?" Coney said. "He's registered for a patent on it, and though I hate to admit it—and won't admit it too loudly—Brenner's milk just tastes better than what I and the rest of our local dairymen send. Look at his farm. It's a showplace, from its manicured entrances to its manure handling system. Take a visit sometime. The Brenners have never tolerated so much as two days worth of manure buildup in calf pens, and they're meticulous with milking equipment maintenance and herd health. Even the shop floor on the farm shines. Mud from the tires gets scraped off before the tractor even gets worked on. There is no one who will give us fewer food safety concerns or recalls. It's as clean as you'll find anywhere on the planet."

Frank Gladding spoke up. It had been his first JAFA board meeting.

"I'm sure Noah is a fine dairyman," he whined. "But what concerns me is this whole BST thing. What's that about, Coney?"

"Time for a little history lesson, Frank?" Coney replied. "OK. It was back in the early 1980s when some drug company—I don't remember which one, they've all consolidated so much—introduced recombinant Bovine Somatotropin–what we call rBST–to increase milk production. Me and Noah, and a lot of others, did our homework. We and most of the members of this very association went to a whole bunch of meetings to hear some high-paid city boy in a tailored suit and tasseled shoes give us all the big sales pitch. And they convinced us—most of us— that it was safe for both the cows and the milk supply when managed properly, so Noah could easily handle that. But there was something about it that unsettled him, and I took that to heart. He learned from tough embarrassments in the classroom that if he didn't feel peace about something, he wouldn't do it. So he never used BST. Neither did I, and neither did a lot of folks. But we didn't look down on people who did use it. We just decided to use genetics and nutritional advances to increase production. Slow and steady. Personally, I didn't think it made any sense to introduce a milk production booster into a market already saturated with milk. Increase production in a glut market? Seemed like short-term profits were being pushed at the sacrifice of long-term, steady, although slower, growth. And besides, the public didn't want it. But the drug company had invested millions into it, and was not about to back down. So it was aggressively marketed all across the United States. Noah and I talked about this a lot back then," Coney continued. "Neither one of us ever learned to think of cows as just units of production who should be injected to squeeze a little more out of them. We both suspected that, in the long term, the cows' lives would be shorter for it, so at best, using BST seemed to be a wash. Noah proved it to me with a computer projection that he designed. Again, we never had a quarrel with the few farmers who chose to use BST. In fact, we kept pretty close tabs on how it performed in the cows. It was simply a management decision, neither one being right or wrong. But somewhere along the line, for Noah and his family, it all got personal."

"That's when he stared his own bottling plant?" asked Birch.

"You were on the board that approved backing his loan, Harvey," Coney replied.

"It was a major financial risk," Coney told the executive board, of which he was president. "Not a one of us sitting here ever had the guts to do what he did. He invested five million dollars into his own bottling plant. He developed his own brand name, bought a few trucks and started delivering Brenner's Best fresh milk door-to-door in real glass bottles; and started a retail store on the farm. He's established, he's local, and he'll deliver quality milk. We'll get plastic bottles in the store just to keep his delivery business separated by its own brand. He's the best choice to be the Farmers Own Store milk supplier, hands down."

"We all know the rest of the story," Birch said. "Brenner's Best is a thriving business. The farmer's association has been paid back with interest, and Brenner products have won quality awards for flavor, packaging and customer service. Besides that, he's been a good example in this town. Just stop in for breakfast some morning at the Auction House Cafe. Everyone's happy to see what Brenner's built. It gives everyone in there hope about how to make a living in this world. But there's still that one thing that bothers them, and it's the only reason I hesitate here, Coney," Birch said. "It's those gaudy signs." He held up a picture of one of Brenner's delivery trucks. In bright, harsh colors, assaulting the senses with their gaudiness, were the words: "Brenner's Best contains no pesticides, no antibiotics and no BST."

Birch paused.

"I'm concerned about mentioning BST in our store, because it sounds so much like some kind of chemical compound. It will scare people off," he said.

"Tell you what," Coney said. "I can't tell Noah how to advertise at his farm store or on his trucks. But I can get him to tone it down for what we'll sell."

"If you can make BST a non-issue, Coney, I'll support Noah 100 percent," Birch said. The rest of the board members nodded their agreement.

When Coney entered the store, Noah was standing on a ladder leaning onto one of the "Brenner's Best" placards above the store's empty dairy cases. His long, thick frame stretched out, and he held a ratchet wrench in his left hand.

"I'm telling you these signs go up or you don't get the milk," Noah was spouting to Frank as Coney walked up.

"Oh boy!" Said Frank, raising his right hand as if in half a surrender. "Now Coney's here. Maybe you'll listen to him. Lord knows I can't get through to you." He sulked off, mumbling and twisting a toothpick in his hands.

Coney walked up, reached up to shake Noah's hand.

"This again, Noah?" he said.

"Look, I don't want to be the bad guy here, Coney, but I think I have to insist that these signs go up. It's important to my business that we market things consistent-like, and people expect to see that their milk is clean. It's the only thing that gives us an edge."

"You been listening to your cousin, the marketing student in Ann Arbor again, haven't you? Coney asked. "I keep telling you, Noah, Ann Arbor is a good world or two removed from the real world of Jovial."

"He's the expert."

"But Noah, you have the exclusive contract to supply this store's milk. We won't buy from anyone else as long as you can meet demand. That makes you a supplier, not a marketer. Isn't it up to us to market it? Isn't that why we hired Frank?"

"My signs have to be the same here as on my trucks."

"Look, Noah," Coney said. "We've gone over this. I thought we had an agreement. The video screen is going up—when Frank, this week still?"—Frank nodded from his perch within a safe hearing distance. "Later this week you'll be able to see the promo video about your farm and your milk—your Brenner's Best quality brand milk. Your message is still consistent. The video will run on a non-stop loop the entire time the store is open. We've started the marketing campaign that says we offer only the highest quality, best-tasting milk—Brenner's Best. You stand to make a significant profit and latch onto a market for years, Noah. Do we have to have signs, too, and signs that lie?"

Noah started down from the ladder.

"Sorry, Noah, but I'm tired," Coney said. "It's high time plain English was spoken. I owe you that, man. You trust me, don't you?" Noah nodded.

"I trust you because you trust Jesus, just like me," he said, stepping off the ladder. He glared down into Coney's eyes.

"So you think Jesus wants you to market your milk with lies?"

"All the things we say are true," Noah said.

"True and very deceptive, Noah," Coney said, meeting his stare. It was obvious that Noah was not able to justify those two concepts at the same time.

"True, your milk has no pesticides," Coney said, determined to convince Noah with logic. It had worked before. It would just take some time. "But there also is not a single drop of milk sold in this country that has pesticides," Coney said. "True, your milk contains no antibiotics. Zero milk in this country is allowed to be sold if it has antibiotics. It's dumped and the farmer is fined and won't ship milk for a very long while, if ever. You know that as well as anybody."

Noah broke his stare and looked down at the ground. "And as for saying it has no BST," Coney continued, "well, that's a blatant lie. Every cow's milk contains BST naturally, so don't go getting all righteous on me, Noah. We as a board can't stop you from using that kind of advertising on your farm or on your trucks or even in the newspaper, but we can stop it here, and we intend to. You signed the agreement, Noah. I thought you were a man of your word."

Noah looked up again, but would not meet Coney's eyes. "For

heaven's sake, Noah, can't you see it's to your advantage? We provided the market, and we offered you the contract because we believe in your product. It's certainly no lie that you produce the best-quality milk in this state, shoot, maybe several states, but we don't have to believe in your marketing, and that's all there is to it. Now, can we finally put this behind us and get this store off the ground? Let's not screw all this up, Noah. There are a lot of people besides you and me that depend on this."

Noah finally looked into Coney's eyes.

"I'm a businessman first," he said as his gaze drifted across Coney's. He shrugged reluctantly, then began to pack up his ladder and banner.

"I thought you'd be on my side at the end of the day, Coney" he said. "You ain't never used BST neither."

"But I don't find it immoral for others to use it."

"I never said it was immoral. I'm just tryin' to sell my milk."

"But wouldn't you feel better selling it for all it's excellent qualities, rather than cast aspersions on the competition?"

"I don't know what a 'spersion is, but my cousin knows marketing, and he says that's how it's done."

"I guess I never thought you were one to go along with the crowd, Noah."

"I ain't goin' along with nuthin. I'm just usin' the best way to sell my milk that I know how, and I ain't lyin'!"

"You're betting on a technicality there, Noah. Do you think the ends justify the means?"

"Yes."

"Really? Who told you that?"

"Jim Deadfrick."

"Really! He said the ends justify the means?"

"Not exactly. But he said God rewards good people with money. Said it's in the Bible. Said it just last Sunday after church."

Coney groaned and rolled his eyes and neck. "He didn't happen to give you chapter and verse, did he?"

"I dunno. He told me the parable about the three guys who'd been given money, and two of them did what God wanted and made more money. It doesn't say how they made more money, just that they did. The only one of the three guys God was mad at was the guy who buried his money. So God wants people to make money. How we do it is up to us."

"I think how we do it is of great concern to God," Coney said, and began helping Noah with the ladder and signs. When they'd packed the last into Noah's truck, Coney reached out his hand.

"Are we all OK here now, Noah? I mean, is this finally over, no matter what your idiot cousin says?

Noah cracked a reluctant smile and accepted the handshake. "I don't really like him neither," he said. "But he's supposed to be the expert."

"The expert in Ann Arbor, Noah, not Jovial. Two different worlds, man."

"We'll wait and see." Noah said.

19

On the dark backside of the Sventon
Village government building, just ten miles away from Jovial, was an
unmarked door that led into a dingy room with a low-sloping, dirty-
white ceiling.

Aspen Kemp, known to this circle as a thick-thighed, flat-chested
blonde named Cindy, smiled at some of the people mulling around as
if they were at a cocktail party.

An older, heavy woman holding a little dog dressed in a red knit
hat and sweater, panting as if it was in heat distress, approached and
smiled at Aspen/Cindy.

"Good turnout tonight?" she said.

"I just wish we could find another place to meet," Cindy replied. "It's
too dim in here. And what's up with this old red carpet with these awful
swirls? This pattern couldn't have come from the mind of a sane person."

The lady laughed. "I'm going to get a vegan cookie, and one for my
little goober here," she said, kissing the dog on the nostrils. She walked
away, her nose squeezed against the dog's snarly snout.

Folding chairs were set up in short sections, with two aisles between
them, like a tiny church with no budget.

Aspen as Cindy pushed her way farther into the room, and stepped
beside the only person she felt any sort of comfort with, a thick, nice-
looking middle-aged man with a bushy white beard and cowboy hat. He

nodded to her and smiled as she felt a presence behind her, like shadowy fear lurking in a dark alley.

"Glad you could make it, Cindy," Dan Pinckney said, putting his arm around her shoulders a bit too warmly. "Welcome again to JAAR. I think you're really going to be inspired tonight." He was dressed in a black robe, but his skinny legs and bony ankles protruded, revealing dark, calloused feet in old sandals. He moved on to schmooze with other people. Aspen as Cindy looked to the cowboy.

"I hope he doesn't show some of that disgusting video again," she said.

"We were all disgusted last week," the man said. "And now we find out it was all staged, a fraud."

"Really? I hadn't heard that."

"Yeah. These guys out in San Francisco pay homeless people from the city to sneak on farms and hurt animals, just so they can film them. Now that's disgusting."

"But if it exposes a real problem, then it's still good, right?" she baited.

"You mean the ends justify the means?"

"Well, don't they? I mean, isn't that what being an animal rights and environmental activist is all about? You have to fight fire with fire." The man shrugged.

"I didn't always think this way, like these people," she said. "But when I thought about it, read their literature, watched their videos and listened to their songs, it made sense. I still don't buy completely that animals are just like people or are equal with people. I'm not sure if animals are on an equal footing with humans at all. Intellectually, anyway. Some say they carry the same emotions, desires and intelligence as we do, and I can't really argue that, but, I would have thought by now, even if man hadn't messed with nature so badly, they would have gained more equal footing. But you have to factor in human animal's insistence that they own slaves. And slavery is wrong. Always. When animal rights supporters rally peacefully to end animal slavery and suffering, it seems like a worthy enough mission to me. They say that a society can be judged by how it treats its animals."

"Who told you that?" the man asked.

"Isn't it in the Bible?" Cindy asked. The man shrugged again. "I think it was Gandhi."

Someone banged something on a table in front of the room, and mulling people began to find seats. Aspen as Cindy sat in the back row in the far right corner, along with the cowboy.

Dan Pinckney made his way slowly to the front of the room like a priest sauntering to the baptismal, and motioned for the people—Aspen counted fourteen—to be seated. He paused, pressing his hands together as if in prayer, and looked upward for a long moment. Finally, with a long, loud sigh, he looked solemnly at the people gathered.

"Now some of you have expressed concerns to me about some of the more popular animal rights song lyrics you've heard lately," he started. "They may be a bit radical for some of you to swallow at this point." He spoke softly, kindly. "To tell the truth, I'd rather listen to Deep Purple myself, but that's just my taste. Believe me, at one time I thought ending animal cruelty and slavery could be accomplished through nice, soft, convincing words, you know, work within the existing system? But I've seen the light now, in a way blind rabbits and dogs and cats can't do anymore after being tied down and tortured by aerosol poisons. You saw the footage last week from the cosmetics lab. It wasn't easy to watch, but changing the world is never easy. It requires a first-hand experience if it is to be credible. These animals have no voice. Who will support them and give them a voice, if not us?

"I've visited factory farms across this part of the state—under cover, of course, because they keep their evil and brutal industrial torture facilities well-guarded and hidden. And after seeing thousands of videos from our brothers and sisters in some of our more advanced chapters, I understand now what I didn't before. We're in a war, people." He stepped from the podium and strolled around the front of the room, vigor in his step.

"The enemy is all around us," he continued. "Fools are all around us. Fools who are blind to the enslavement and cruel treatment of farm animals. Oh yes! Just as certainly as people were blind to the slave trade before the Civil War. They fall back on the crutch of their religion, citing asinine Bible verses to justify their cruelty, and, as the Bible says:

"none are so blind as those who will not see." He paused dramatically. He was about to pick up the tempo.

"See what I did there?" He smiled. "I used their own Bible against them, and you can too."

Aspen looked around. Heads nodded in the crowd. One well-dressed young man blurted out his approval. "Yes," said the dumpy lady eating her store-bought cookie as she fidgeted with her embarrassed, panting lap dog. Aspen as Cindy leaned over to the cowboy.

"What is it about this guy?" She whispered. "I've never seen this kind of charisma. Reminds me of the old footage of KFJ!" The man raised his eyebrows. "You mean JFK. And no, he's not anywhere near JFK's league. KFC, maybe."

"I urge you today to stop the inhumanity," Pinckney said, his tone rising with emotion. "If you must, fight violence with violence, if that's the only thing these animal slave owners understand. Our cause is just. Our cause will win in the end. We must get onto every street corner, knock on every door, spare no expense in spreading the truth that—unfortunately—far too many blind, ignorant people won't want to hear. The truth is hard to hear for some people, and some will refuse you, maybe even verbally assault you. They might even treat you like you're some kind of flipped out religious zealot, like a Jehovah's Witness, but don't be discouraged. Our cause is just, and"—his voice softened to a whisper as he leaned over the podium—"we may have to endure a little pain. But extremism for the cause of liberty is no vice." He tried to make eye contact with everyone in the room, but Cindy wouldn't do it.

Pinckney nodded slowly, each nod bringing his head lower. Finally, he raised it again. He looked each parishioner in the eyes, lingered on each pair and paused until people began to squirm. "But nothing worth doing is without cost, is it?" He said, finally. His voice began to build again to a crescendo. "Take courage from the example of your fellow soldiers in the fight who have gone before you," he said, his voice softening again. "In fact, we have one really battle-tested warrior in town this week, a soldier from a PETA offshoot in San Francisco. Sorry I can't introduce her to you tonight, but we can't risk the slavers finding out she's here. They have a hit out for her, a fatwa. Believe you me. The truth still isn't easy, people, but because people like her spilled blood, it's easier for you today. She's been brought in as an adviser only, for her own safety." He was in full voice. "We're not to her level yet. She's been brought in as a consultant for the election and the carcass store issue, because we still hope to accomplish this noble endeavor peacefully. Some people will listen to your voices. Yes, and if they will not listen to your voices, if they will not listen, they will listen when we shout louder!" He was shouting now. "And if they still will not listen, we may, nay, we must, be willing to take the next step! Have any of you spilled your blood? Have you gone that far in defense of the defenseless non-human animals? Will you?" Three young men shouted "amen!"

"You are right!" Pinckney screeched. "They are wrong!" The crowd was loud now. "Open their eyes! Never look back! Our animal brothers and sisters need you today! Fight! Fight! Fight!"

"We will," shouted five men in unison as Pinckney led their rhythm with his fist, banging on the podium. The women soon chimed in, and the tiny room shook with the chant: "Stop the slavers! Stop the slavers!"

Pinckney stepped away from the front of the room when the uproar died, and began passing sheets of paper among the faithful, shaking hands with everyone he encountered. Aspen was reaching for one when he pulled back the stack.

"Are you with us, Cindy?" He spoke as gently as a lamb.

"What do you mean? I'm here, aren't I?"

"I mean, are you going to be with us next week to protest the new dead carcass market?"

"The farmer's store in Jovial?" Pinckney nodded.

"Well, I don't know," she said. "I guess I don't see anything wrong with the farmers having their own store. I mean, doesn't it just mean fresher, healthier food?"

"It's about the farm animals, Cindy. They're still going to serve non-human animal carcasses there. Dead flesh. It's all so gross and disgusting and immoral."

"But won't they also sell nice, fresh locally grown fruits and vegetables? Isn't that something we know is best for us?"

"That's a ruse, a marketing gimmick to make their immoral practices seem better than they are," Pinckney snapped. "Their overriding agenda is to torture and kill non-human animals. Poisoning fruit and vegetables with their chemicals is just a bonus to them. If we can stop those chemicals from getting into our bodies, it's our first step to letting them know we won't stand for their cruelty with animals, either."

"Why would they want to torture their animals?"

"Because farmers are evil, Cindy. Cattle are like widgets to them, just inanimate chunks of metal or plastic. The only thing these farmers understand is cold, heartless profit. It's their only motivation. Here, Cindy," he said, pointing to his papers. "These are plans for the demonstration, but I'm afraid I can't let you see them unless you're committed. There's no room for sitting on the fence in this fight. We must be strong and never doubt that our cause is the only right thing. Do you believe that, Cindy?" His voice was as gentle as at first.

She was caught. She had only one answer if she wanted a story, if she wanted to be employed.

"I believe," she said softly, looking into Pinckney's suddenly hypnotic eyes.

"Excellent," Pinckney beamed, his smile as peaceful as anything Aspen had ever seen in a human.

Pinckney returned to the front of the room without handing her a paper.

"My final instructions before the rally?" He asked loudly. "To spread the word to vote Yes on Proposition 1. That's top priority, and we'll really hit that hard after the demonstration at the slaver's store. Go on home. Your cause is just!"

People began mulling out. Aspen/Cindy turned to the cowboy.

"I guess I never knew until this moment how Pinckney kept his job as school superintendent with his view about these things," she said. "He's just a good teacher, and an even better motivator. Maybe even a little hypnotic, like those gurus of some whacked-out religion that order their followers to drink the Kool-Aid." The cowboy gave no reply.

Cindy joined the crowd filing out, and Pinckney, standing at the door, handed her a flier and patted her tenderly on the back once, then stroked his hand up and down her spine. "I guess you are ready to join us," he said. "But you have to put aside all doubts. The flier has locations for gathering before the protest, a list of items the group will need. There are suggested slogans to be painted on signs, and a time to get together in two days to prepare future strategy and paint those signs and banners. We'll all be busy."

"I'll be there," she said. "Do you think there will be a need for weapons?

"Whoa, Whoa, Whoa, let's just wait and see on that," Pinckney said, holding a cautious gaze on her. He tucked the papers under his arm, squeezed her arm with one hand and raised his other arm, as if in protest. "I'm not sure this group is quite ready for that yet," he said, softly smiling. "We want to be a peaceable band until the time for revolution is ripe. Be patient, young beauty. Perhaps our time will come to create martyrs for our cause, but first we have an election, and before that, we have a protest. So be patient. Store up your pent-up frustration for the proper opportunity. Timing is everything."

He raised his voice for the remaining people to hear. "Remember this is not cheap, either, people. We need funds, so play on guilt. If people refuse to join our cause, they can at least save one poor abused fellow animal with a twenty-dollar bill. Make them feel guilty, as they should, about animal suffering. Guilt is a wonderful wallet opener. And fear is a wonderful vote getter!"

Aspen stepped out the door, and joined the cowboy walking to the parking lot.

"I wondered how much a cow really costs," she said. "Now I know. Twenty bucks."

"At least," the cowboy said.

20

"I can't believe I just blurted out the weapons thing," Aspen told Botsdorf. She was out of her Cindy disguise, and the tiny recorder she used at the JAAR meeting was plugged into a desktop computer in Botsdorf's plain but comfortable office in Sventon. "I might as well have just come out and asked him if he's a violent wing nut."

"He already knows he's a violent wing nut," Botsdorf said, smiling. The bags and wrinkles around his eyes framed them like green marbles in a clean fish bowl. "But it doesn't sound like he got too suspicious. And he probably won't, as long as he thinks there's a chance he can sleep with you."

"That's just creepy, Bots," replied Aspen, shuddering. "But I shouldn't be surprised. I've never met a man who didn't want to sleep with me. All men are dogs. Except you." Botsdorf ignored the comment.

"Well, he's a creepy guy with a huge ego. But you have to push him more. You've got a good start here, but you have to push harder." He scrolled back in the recording, and found a spot he'd marked.

"Right here," he said, pressing a button on the computer keyboard. "When you said you didn't see anything wrong with the farmers store?" He replayed the short section. "Did you pick that up?" Botsdorf asked, then played the short section again. "Did you hear how he talked like his teeth were clenched together? Very subtle, but he must know he's doing it, because he stopped doing it pretty quickly. That's a sign he's trying to hide something. Questioning him makes him angry. He thinks his authority is supreme, and he despises anyone who dares question him. I've seen it before, and it's more than just that inherent teacher's ego. He will go over the edge. The only thing we can't predict is when."

"How do you know all this?" Aspen asked. "Are you a psychiatrist besides a lawyer and a writer?"

"Let's just say I've seen it before."

"You talk like you've seen it a hundred times before."

"When you've been with a genuine wacko, you never forget," he replied.

"You've got to tell me this story," she insisted.

"It's a very long story, and it happened long before you were born," he said.

"Come on. I bet it's a great story."

"It was a great story, but it's long past. Just trust me, will you? Pinckney's following the same pattern as a lot of other wackos."

"Please? Maybe it will help me figure out Pinckney's breaking point." She touched his arm. Botsdorf sighed.

"It was my first undercover investigative assignment," he began. "I joined this group of religious nuts that called themselves Charles' Chosen Ones."

"A cult?"

"A rather typical cult, as it turned out. Some vague moral principles they call 'values' get manipulated to the point that the promoter of those principles demands total devotion. They frame it in the general cover of values because it's a cover phrase, a catch-all. Their values are never really defined, but people think if someone uses the word, they must know what they're talking about. The less thinking the better. Too much logic is not really tolerated, kind of the way Pinckney runs the school system. Of course, the followers, who aren't usually given to critical thinking anyway, get involved by giving everything to the cause, which in my case ended up being just one man—Charles Chalby. He started kind of like Pinckney. Good intentions, at least in his own mind, but then he started slowly turning insane. I don't know if he just got drunk with power, or if he had serious mental illness, but either way, he was a master manipulator. He had the wild, crazy eyes too, and believe me, Pinckney's will get crazier. You have to be careful, though, because he's probably trying to hypnotize the entire group. I don't know if he can do it, but better to be safe. So never stare into his eyes if you can help it." Aspen suddenly realized her eyes were fixed on Botsdorf's, and they broke the connection at the exact same time.

"So what happened to that Charles guy?"

"He ended up convincing everyone to kill themselves as a sacrifice. They thought their loyalty to him was insurance—that when they ended their lives for him, they'd awaken in a new dimension where they ruled along with him. They would be equals with him. A very lofty goal, you know. He promised Nirvana. Quoted scripture to give it some authority, even though he most often just made things up. People weren't allowed to have Bibles in his compound. Eventually he killed himself too."

"You witnessed all this?"

"Most of it. I wasn't there when his followers drank the poison, but I watched him go completely off the deep end when he realized he had no more followers to serve him and write him checks. I was labeled a heretic for questioning him, and was tossed out of the group two days before they all did it. I questioned him too much, especially on his Bible quotes, and he didn't know the answers. No one had ever challenged him before. He had that strong a personality. Anyway, when he saw all his followers dead, he drank about a gallon of the poison that killed them, mixed with cheap whiskey, but he didn't die. He ended up slitting one wrist with a broken glass, and hanged himself with a clothesline. I found him. The autopsy said he had enough poison in him to kill about a dozen people. He was like Rasputin."

"Who?"

"Look him up. He was a Russian priest with crazy hypnotic eyes. The only one who could control the prince's hemophilia. Fascinating dude. The good ones, the real manipulators? They're all fascinating. But they have fragile egos. They can be pushed only so far, and they push back."

"You pushed your guy?"

"Relentlessly. My editor was threatening to pull me out if I didn't get a story soon, so I started challenging Charles. Looking back now,

I wonder why he didn't have me killed. Any one of his followers would have done it if he'd just ordered them to. Guess he chose to kill all those thirty-five people instead. And sometimes I still wonder if I didn't push him there."

"Wow. When did this all happen?"

"It was 1989."

Aspen paused and looked at Botsdorf's rugged face, worn by wind and sun and rumored hard living.

"If you don't mind me saying so, you don't look that old, Bots. How old are you, anyway?"

"What do you think?" he smiled. She paused and looked at him.

"I would guess late forties or early fifties, knowing that date," she said, and smiled. "I've got you pegged, Bots. Remember you're my father figure, so I have a right to profile you."

"I would expect nothing less from my protege'."

"You're old enough to have a few distinguishing wrinkle lines on your face, but still young enough to attract women," Aspen began. "I've heard the stories—how you charm all the old gals with this easy, honest way of yours, that quiet confidence. Very disarming. Maybe you're the real cult leader." Botsdorf grinned.

"I suppose it takes an older woman to understand that, huh?" she asked.

"One other thing." Botsdorf blurted, trying to change the subject.

"Pinckney has one thing my guy didn't have, and it makes him even more dangerous."

"What's that?"

"He has another master manipulator pulling strings behind him."

"Who's that?"

"Don't you know? You've been undercover here for what, three months?"

"Deadfrick?" Botsdorf put his right index finger to his nose.

"I know he seems crazy, but isn't he a religious nut? A real churchgoer? As boring a man as ever tied shoes?"

"That's just his cover. He loves to pull Pinckney's strings. That way he doesn't have to do the dirty work himself. An even more masterful manipulator."

"Spooky," she said. "I sure wish I had your wisdom, Bots."

"It's not wisdom. Just experience."

"Well, whatever it is, it suits you," she said. "And you've always treated me with respect, like an equal, and I appreciate that, because I know I'm not your equal."

"You can be as good as I ever was," Botsdorf said. "When you first came into my office, what, four-five months ago, looking for a job, I didn't decide to mentor you because you're pretty. Pretty is a dime a dozen. But talent and character, they're rare. Especially when they're put in one person at the same time."

"How can you see it?"

"You watch, observe, and be patient," he said. "That's how you've got to handle Pinckney, but you have to push him too. His world, even though he thinks differently, is fragile. It seems like he trusts you at this point."

"But he really repels me," she said. "Way too much to let him get too close. I'm afraid I won't be able to keep it together. And what if he grabs my butt and gets a handful of air pillow or accidentally pulls my wig down?"

"Yep, he won't like being lied to. It would add to his enormous persecution complex. Right now I don't think it would change anything he's doing except maybe to kick you out of his group. He can never know that Cindy is Aspen. He's paranoid, but not stupid. He'll get stupid later, like white tail bucks during the rut. Eventually he won't be able to control himself. He's following a pattern most sociopaths follow, and it won't take much to make him crack."

"I don't know. He seems pretty much under control to me. What I don't understand is the connection to Proposal 1. What does an organic food law have to do with animal rights?"

"Making people believe—or not even question—his logic is the sign of a good cult leader. Believe me, he's unstable. His thoughts don't connect with each other like most people's. He's closer to the edge than you think, so you have to be more careful than ever. School's out now, so he has the whole summer to simmer in his bitterness and manipulation. At the same time, Deadfrick wants a monopoly on food. For him it's just greed. Run-of-the-mill top-three motivation: power, sex, money. Now, what do you have to do for the rally at the farmers' store?"

"Four or five of us have to write anonymous, veiled threatening letters to the editor for the television and radio stations, and the *World*, but maybe I should do that from here, you think?"

"You write them and I'll send them from a public computer," said Botsdorf. "But change your writing style. We don't need him even thinking you're a *World* reporter, or working for the *Sasser*. But how could he know that? Wally does a pretty good job of making sure our publication hasn't been seen much in Jovial."

"OK." She started, then stopped. She looked into Botsdorf's eyes.

"We've never had any secrets between us, right?"

The silence became awkward as Botsdorf waited. Finally, he blurted: "C'mon, girl, spit it out."

"The truth is, Pinckney might know soon that I—Aspen—am not a *World* reporter, the way things travel around town. He kind of liked me, I think, because I always gave his side equal treatment when it came to some of the ridiculous philosophies he's promoted to the school kids. I don't know if he will trust Garit the same way. I don't know if he trusts Wally. If he has any sanity left, he won't. But all that aside, I have to tell you, I quit the *World*, and I'm trying real hard here to keep from begging you for a job."

"So that's why you've been kissing my butt!" Botsdorf cried. "What a relief!"

"What do you mean?"

"Lord, girl, I thought you were hitting on me!"

Aspen blushed and giggled as she turned away. "Really? Well, I'm glad we straightened that out. You must think I'm quite some kind of whore, coming to look for a job like that."

"No, I didn't think that. What I thought was that you quitting had something to do with that new reporter. Garit is his name?"

"Not really. Oh, he's an insensitive jerk and everything, and I confess I had a little crush on him, but I didn't quit because of him. I quit because of Wally."

"Not surprising, but I'll ask anyway. Why's that?"

"Besides the fact that he's a no-talent hack with a marketing degree, not a journalism degree; who's so impressed with his own byline that he can't think of anything besides himself?"

"Yes, besides that." Botsdorf grinned.

"Look," she said. "You know what I can do. You know my writing. It's what the universe destined me to do, and I think I could start to, you know, fulfill my destiny working for you. Wally can't teach me anything anymore."

"So you want me to be your stepping stone?"

"I've never looked at any job that way. All I want to do is be a reporter, Bots, and write for a living. If something else comes up that's right for me, I'm not going to lie to you. I'd probably take it. But for now, I need a job, and I'll give it everything I have."

"Tell you what," Botsdorf said. "Concentrate on this animal rights wacko group, and write a nice long, detailed and fact-checked piece, and I'll give you a steady job on the *Sasser* staff. You got enough cash to tide you over?"

Garit told Wally he was going to the

library to get ahead on his Yesteryears columns, but he really needed to milk Betty for some information.

"Hi, Betty," he said as he approached her desk. "How's my oldest friend in Jovial?"

"Just peachy," she said, too loudly. "And I'm not that old! SHHHH!"

"I didn't mean it that way," Garit stage-whispered, defensively, then stopped. She was grinning. "Ya got me, Betty. Lunch later?"

"Sure."

"Hey, where can I find background on the farmer's store? The grand opening is tomorrow and I have to cover it."

"You're in luck. I just archived last year's *World*, and I think Aspen did a story on the property's history somewhere. I don't remember when, but I'm pretty sure it was last fall when they broke ground."

Garit quickly found the new *World* microfilm box in the library closet, loaded it on the machine and scrolled. Eventually he found the headline: "Vacant Downtown Lot to Feature Grocery Store," and began to read under the byline Aspen Kemp:

> "Ground was broken last week for a new enterprise on an
> old and storied piece of property in Jovial's downtown.

The Farmers' Own Store, to be owned and operated by 57 members of the Jovial Area Farmers' Association (JAFA), will sit on a large lot on the western edge of the Jovial business district when completed, JAFA officials said.

The space at one time held a movie theatre and bowling alley combination, but it went out of business in the 1970s."

Just like Aspen, Garit thought. Using the British spelling of theatre.

"The last movie ever shown in the 250-seat theatre was Kingpin, but only about 40 people attended the grand closing, which was not without bitterness. Owner Joe Franklin, in an interview with the *Jovial World* in 1972, said he thought the irony of the bowling-flick choice would attract people.

"I guess I underestimated the public's apathy and ignorance," he said. He left town soon after.

The bowling alley was later sold and converted into a bar, but the owners reportedly struggled to get the sheen and oil out of the old bowling alley wood. Patrons complained to the *World* that they could never find good footing in the place.

"It was like walking on smooth ice with plastic bags on your feet," one customer was quoted as saying. Eventually, the surface allegedly started emitting toxins when harsh disinfectant cleaners ate through the oily layers, and the owners struggled through a long court battle with the Environmental Protection Agency.

When the bar went bankrupt in 1983, the liquor license remained unclaimed until a New York investor bought it in the late 1990s. That investor, Peter Mopes, also financed the Weyer Winery, a bed-and- breakfast facility on the former John Weyer vineyard that overlooks stunning, grassed bluffs on Lake Michigan's picturesque shore. And there's the connection. The Farmers Own Store is expected to feature award-winning local Weyer wine at anywhere from $5 to $14 a bottle, depending on the vintage, JAFA officials said.

Soon after the downtown Jovial bar closed, and after the property had changed hands twice more, the entire two-faceted building burned under mysterious circumstances in 2004. Though police suspected foul play, an arsonist was never caught, and the trail has long been cold and forgotten, not only by local police, but by state and federal officers as well."

Didn't need the 'as well' there, Aspen.

"The building's rubble was eventually hauled away to a landfill, and the lot sat empty, growing weeds and broken bottles until local farmers formed the Jovial Area Farmers' Association in 2007, and eventually purchased it about a year ago from what some city officials referred to as an investment group called the Jim Dandy Corp. That group disbanded five years ago. None of its stockholders of record are still alive.

The new store building is expected to be built to exceed the latest required specifications, right down to the bushy evergreen shrubs that block the view of the loading docks. The store's front, according to what was agreed to by the City Council, will be set back off the road 85 feet, farther than city ordinances require. Ample parking, according to the architect's drawing, will be available along both sides.

The store is expected to open about mid-summer."

Garit left the microfilm, remembering something. He went to the recent newspaper stacks and found another story Aspen had written, exactly one week before she quit. The headline read: Farmers Adjust Plans for Store Grand Opening

"Public relations and a make-lemonade-from-lemons attitude prevailed last week at the monthly Jovial Area Farmers' Association (JAFA) meeting.

With less than a month to go before the scheduled grand opening of a second grocery store in Jovial, a snag in the plans threatened to delay that event, but the farmers turned innovative.

"What happened," said store manager Frank Gladding, "was that in the front of the store, where parking originally had been planned, the pavers had a catastrophic equipment failure, and told the JAFA executive committee that they could not complete the job on time."

The farmers, expanding on an idea Gladding first brought forward at the previous JAFA board of directors' meeting, shipped in rich soil, seeded the area with a pasture mix common to local farmers and fenced an area about 50-feet deep by 50-feet wide.

"The idea was for the grand opening to have sheep and maybe a cow or horse grazing there for the day," Gladding said. "It would be a nice way to show people who don't know better that the Jovial farmers really care for their animals. Besides that, it's a great chance for moms to bring their kids and pet a little lamb and make a connection with their food."

Dairy farmer Noah Brenner, who will supply most of the milk the store will sell, argued that farmers shouldn't expose children to the realities of food production.

"Do you honestly want to tell them that the cute little lamb they were just petting would someday have its throat cut and its skin peeled off and its carcass cut into chops?" he asked.

Brenner's concerns were allayed by JAFA's hired public relations firm Lyon and Sack, of Petosky, which convinced the JAFA executive board that it's better to "put a face on the food," since so few people make the connection between a live animal and their entrees. Brenner's objection was voted down and the little pasture construction began."

Garit's concentration was shaken loose by the smell of pizza. He walked upstairs to see Betty putting paper plates in the alcove reading area. A large pizza sat on the table in a cardboard box.

"Thanks, Betty," Garit said as he walked in. "I would have bought lunch."

"It was my turn," she said, tearing paper towels off a half-consumed roll.

"So how ya doing, kid?" She asked after putting a slice on each plate. "Any big mysteries solved yet?"

"Did I tell you about Deputy Schoen kicking me in the ankle? Twice?"

"No. When?"

"I was trying to get an interview with the guy they arrested for painting the statue. Schoen just came up behind me and slammed his boot into me. I think he cracked a bone."

"He's such a jerk. I didn't know they arrested somebody for the statue painting."

"I wrote a story for the issue that's coming out today, but Wally didn't run it. Instead he wrote an opinion piece about it, and it was awful."

"I never read his editorials. He never makes any sense."

They each sipped from glasses of warm, dark soda on the tables.

"So that's the only mystery I have going now. Hey, maybe you can tell me. Why underwear? I've been told that people have been painting stuff on that statue for years. Why not just paint your name on the water tower or something? What's the big joke?"

"I don't pretend to understand everything that happened, and I'm not old enough to remember it, contrary to what you seem to think," Betty said, grinning again. "But I know what they taught us in school. Old man Jovial's son Alan-the-Second had started this textile company, back in the 1930s or something. He hit it big making long underwear for the military. Most of the wool was supplied by local sheep farmers. It was big business back in the day. Outside of the farmers, it was the biggest employer in town. Probably a hundred jobs, which was huge back then. And it was all started because Alan-the-Second lobbied for and got a major tax abatement, which has been renewed by a wide margin in every election for decades.

"But later, when Alan's grandson Trip took control of the company and changed it to specialize in jockstraps about 1967, that was really just a cover story. Trip had been production manager for a long time, and he'd already been producing risque' lingerie, though nobody knew it."

"How could people not know it?"

"The workers had to swear they'd never tell or they'd get fired. They didn't want to jeopardize their jobs. The lingerie business was far more lucrative than athletic supporters, although jockstraps remained the business cover story. The *Jovial World* actually broke the story of the lingerie. It was a big scandal in the late sixties, early seventies. Not that they were making frilly underwear, but that it had been covered up—so to speak. Soon after that, a group of drunk high school seniors without prom dates started painting underwear, jockstraps, thongs, stuff like that on the statue. That turned into a tradition for years. But these days, it doesn't happen all the time like before. When I was a kid, there was almost always a jock or a thong painted on old Alan. People just came to expect it. But when you think about it, I guess it was an insult to the man, and maybe he deserved it. He must have been a real jerk if he commissioned a statue of himself. Kind of a political statement to paint underwear on him, although a little obscure if you didn't know all the history."

"So what happened to Trip and the factory?"

"Trip—short for triple—was a pretty fair athlete at Jovial High in the mid-1960s, but his minor league baseball career ended with his draft notice. He went to Vietnam, and with only six weeks left in his tour of duty, he stepped on a land mine."

"Ouch!"

"Yeah, ouch. Shrapnel shot up directly into his crotch. The concussion severed his penis and testicles from his body. He nearly bled to death, but when he recovered and came home, he became a coach for nearly every sport that needed one, and he dove into community service. The story goes that all fourteen pieces of what had been left of Trip's genitalia had been eaten by dogs and rodents in Vietnam as he laid there bleeding, watching them."

"There's a detail I could have lived without." Betty ignored the comment.

"The family business called, of course, and Trip half-heartedly managed it until the opportunity came along to sell it. By then, even his best idea—the lingerie—was becoming unprofitable. He couldn't keep up with modern times if not for the tax breaks. Wool underwear couldn't compete with the new synthetics, and his heart wasn't really in it. He made a bundle on the sale, and went to work for the company he sold to. He even modeled their brand of jockstraps in the company catalog. Having no junk, he was safely asexual. Perfect for attracting discreet, embarrassed and sheepish buyers."

"Who did he sell to?"

"I don't know, but it's changed hands probably six or seven times since those days. Now, Deadfrick owns half of it. Uses it for storage and a business incubator. And he enjoys the tax abatement even though his business has nothing to do with keeping jobs or producing the iconic organic underwear."

"Organic underwear?"

"Yep. Still made from itchy old wool. Doesn't make much sense, but it's a great marketing angle for people with more money than brains."

"So when did they start cracking down on the statue painters?"

"Your guess is as good as mine. For all I know, it's just this year. I mean, I've never heard of anyone being arrested for it before."

"Is it illegal?"

"Of course it's illegal to vandalize city property, but it's never been enforced around here. Like jaywalking. Who cares?"

"So why now?"

"Last winter the city council discussed some new ordinance to make it a police department priority, but I don't think it passed. It was never reported in the *World*, anyway. The police pushed to have it put on the ballot, but hid it under this gang activity proposal. Rumor is that if it passes, the city is in prime position to get a big grant that can be used for just about anything, since there is really no gang activity here."

"How do they know they can get a grant?"

"It's just about a shoo-in. Deadfrick is a master grant writer. He's been doing it since he was in high school, and I don't think he's ever been turned away. He knows how to dot the i's and cross the t's."

"You know," Garit recalled, "at my first city council meeting, they passed a bunch of things, but they never discussed them. They just read the numbers and voted. No one objected. I was told they were just boilerplate. Could some new law pass that way?"

"This city council would not be above that. At least that's my opinion. You're the hotshot reporter, kid. Dig into it. You might find a mystery yet."

Garit walked down the sidewalk to the

Farmers Own Store grand opening. His newest point-and-shoot camera, taken from the drawer in Wally's office, was in one back pocket. A digital voice recorder and his phone were in the other, and a short legal pad and pen were in his hand. Ahead he could see the portable electric sign that he'd seen when he drove into Jovial his first day.

In bright, bold letters the sign now proclaimed:

"The Farmers' Own Store opens TODAY! Come on in! Biggest deals, highest quality!"

The sign buzzed like a hummingbird caught behind a window as Garit walked past it. A large crowd milled about the parking lot. The fenced-in area was green and empty, though lush, and a hose led from a faucet outside the store, across the parking lot to a water tank in the far corner of the long grass.

Mid-morning humidity hung in the air like wet blankets on a clothesline, but Garit could feel the excitement, thick as a football Saturday on a Big Ten campus.

As Garit walked across the parking lot, his legs heavy in the humidity and Dockers, the milling crowd fidgeted, disorganized as a flock of turkey vultures fighting over a 'possum carcass.

Between the store front and the pasture area, some people carried signs tacked onto sticks, but Garit couldn't see what was written on them. He walked over and took out his camera. At picnic tables set up around the parking lot's western perimeter, under some tall cottonwood trees, people were painting signs, and others were tacking sticks to the signs.

Garit knelt down and pressed the shutter behind a blonde with a rather large posterior tacking sticks onto signs with a hammer that seemed way too small for the task. She heard the shutter click, looked over her shoulder at Garit and quickly turned, got up and walked away.

"Hey," Garit shouted after her. "Can I ask what your signs are for?" She kept walking.

An older woman holding a small, bug-eyed dog with a thick collar studded with brass rivets answered: "We're protesting the store," she said, kindly as a librarian reading to children. "We think farmers are bad, the way they treat their animals."

"How do they treat them?" Garit asked.

"Terribly," the woman replied. "They don't allow them to live with their mommies and daddies. They don't even name them. They give them numbers instead. Just like prisoners or slaves. Then they underfeed them and keep them alive with drugs until they kill them, taking as long as possible like some sadistic ritual. Then they send that poisoned meat into the food chain."

The little dog squirmed, and she tightened her grip. Her tiny forearm bulged slightly with the effort. "Thor! Stop it or else," she scolded.

"How interesting," Garit patronized, and moved on. He took a few more shots of the protesters and headed toward the store entrance. Standing there were two intimidating, large-muscled guards, wearing tight red T-shirts that said "Michigan Security Incorporated" across the chest.

"Is it just me, or do some of the faces in that crowd seem angry?" Garit asked one of them, pointing to the people with signs. "This is a celebration, right?"

"We're trained to interpret crowd dynamics, son," one guard said, even though he was not much older than Garit. "We're on top of things."

Suddenly, from the back entry onto the property, two ultra-clean white-and-red vans fitted with small satellite dishes on top sped into the parking lot and squawked to a jerky halt. One had a giant NewsCenter 14 logo on the side, the other a NewsTeam 5 logo.

From behind the crowd, Garit heard Dan Pinckney instructing the people with signs.

"Let's set up in the green area," he shouted though a wholly unnecessary voice amplifier. "They can't make us stand on this hot tar all day!" The bullhorn squeaked as he shut it off. His followers, some of them holding their hands to their ears as they passed him, began to climb over the two-tiered wooden fence as the TV cameramen pulled gear from the vans, eyeing each other with suspicion.

As they worked on their equipment, a pickup truck pulling a fifth-wheel livestock trailer rolled slowly past Garit and the guards. A woman driving the truck stared at the little pasture over her sunglasses. She backed up the trailer within about ten feet of the little pasture and walked to the fence. She approached cautiously, but confidently.

"Excuse me," she said to no one in particular. "Are you folks supposed to be in there?"

From the middle of the pack stepped Dan Pinckney, shouting.

"This is public property, Molly. We have a right to be here!" His alarmed outcry brought the TV cameramen running across the parking lot, each with one eye to the viewfinder.

"I have no intention of stepping on anyone's rights, Dan," Molly said, calmly. "It's just that we had arranged this, planted it and everything, so we could put a few sheep in there today." A sheep bleated from her trailer, as if on cue.

Frank Gladding padded heavy-footed past Garit and the guards as they walked toward the scene. He ran femininely, with his left hand flailing back and forth and his right hand holding his pens and pocket protector in place. The guards giggled and pointed at him.

"What's going on, Molly? Mr. Pinckney, why are you in there?" Frank asked, breathing heavily.

"It's public property here, isn't it?" Pinckney accused.

"Well, technically—"

"We have every right to be here, safe from the unsafe traffic you allow in this parking lot," Pinckney shouted toward a camera. "You have to provide us a safe place to protest! That's our right! Are you animal slavers trying to violate our rights?"

"Technically, this is private property," Frank said. "We planned this as a very important part of our grand opening, and we have sheep that need to go in there. Can't you protest on the sidewalk, the real public property?" He took three steps backward.

"The people's rights are more important than sheep!" Pinckney cried. He raised his right hand in a Black Panther-style pose and assaulted the bullhorn. "Human rights are animal rights too, because we're all equal, and we all have rights!" He flapped his arms to get his followers riled up. "We have rights!" he shouted, and the protesters joined him. "We have rights!" they chanted. "We have rights!"

"Look, Frank," Molly said, pulling Frank by the arm to turn away from the cameras. "I don't want to make a big scene here. Just let them be."

"That would probably create the least hassle," Frank said. He turned back to Pinckney.

"OK, Dan, have your little protest. But don't ruin that sod." He turned and walked back to the store. Pinckney flapped his arms up and down again, palms up, urging his followers to raise their signs. Molly got back in her truck and drove out the driveway behind the store, and Pinckney had the full attention of the TV cameras.

"Do you see what these factory farmers have done to repress any peaceful opposition to their brutality?" He shouted. "They lock us in behind a fence, just like they shackle their animals, cramming them in little crates like this, with barely enough room to turn around. Take a good shot of this, boys." He kicked the earth as he turned and gestured to his followers. The followers squeezed tightly together, some also kicking up sod. They created the illusion of a cramped space for the cameras, and several clods of sod spit out onto a TV reporter's shoes.

"What are they afraid of?" Pinckney shouted. "I'll tell you. They know what they do is wrong, so they try to put down all of us who tell the truth! What are you afraid of, Frank?" Frank was already inside the store. The crowd in the fence began to chant: "Hey, hey, hi, ho, Vee-gan is the way to go!" That eventually melded into "Meat ain't no fun, vote yes on prop. 1."

"Well now they're just getting silly," Garit said to the guards who were standing, motionless, halfway between the store entrance and the protesters.

The two TV cameras were intently pointing at Pinckney, and a newly arrived third cameramen urged on the crowd like a frat boy chanting for faster beer chugging.

"Louder," he yelled. "If you're gonna stop animal cruelty and stuff, you gotta yell louder!"

Garit walked behind the cameramen and took about fifteen shots of the protesters, then walked back to the store entry, where the guards had resumed their ominous presence.

"I have an appointment with Mr. Dogues," Garit said. The guards nodded and stepped aside.

Coney was engaged with a local radio reporter, so Garit turned away and walked up and down the store aisles. He wanted to get a feel for the place, find something that he could use to pull people into the story.

"You Garit?" said a voice behind him, friendly as a familiar dog. Garit turned and nodded.

"Fulton Gray," the young man said, and reached to shake Garit's hand. "I'm one of the owners of the store."

"Nice to meet you," Garit said. "I'm Garit West, from the *World*. Do you know Sam, the guy who works at the Shell station?"

"I know him. Do you know him?"

"No, not really, but I was there at the station about a week ago. He patched an air mattress for me. For free. And I heard him talking with a buddy. He said something about Fulton getting one right. Your name is unusual, and I guess it stuck with me."

"So what do you think of the store?" Fulton diverted as they slowly walked down another aisle.

"Well, I don't know much about these things, but I'd have to say that it's without a doubt the nicest store I've ever seen. It's well-lit with wide aisles, and really clean. The vegetable coolers are filled with all kinds of beautiful stuff. Look! Fresh asparagus! The meat case is full of red cuts with very little fat around the edges, and what, you can have a butcher custom-cut portions while you wait? That's all pretty cool."

"So is it different from what you expected?"

"I don't know," replied Garit. "It's just like a regular grocery store to me, I guess. I mean, I didn't expect cows in the aisle, but then, I didn't expect it to be some mom-and-pop place where old white-haired codgers watch kids over top of their glasses, either. Ever notice how they're always on the end of their noses?"

"Fulton laughed. "I know the type. Maybe I'll be there myself some day." He paused as if he'd never thought of that eventuality before. "What a great aspiration." He giggled. "After hours I can sit on my front porch, shake my fist and yell 'darn kids. Get off my lawn.'"

"Can I interview you for the *World*, Fulton?"

"Coney's the president of the farmer's association, but I can give you some background."

"Cool. But can I quote you?"

"I wish you'd just quote him, but you're the reporter."

"I don't want to be a pushy, obnoxious reporter, though, so I won't quote you at all if you give me the straight poop, something that will help me ask halfway intelligent questions when I get to Mr. Dogues."

"He'll ask you to call him Coney. Nothing but the poop? I can respect that," Fulton said. "Fair enough. Ask away." Fulton swept his arms across his body and out like an exaggerated stage motion, and then waved them like a game show hostess. "The full resources of the Farmer's Own Store are at your disposal, on one condition."

"What's that?"

"Tell me what you know about Sam."

"I know he's been arrested."

"For what?"

"Vandalism, I guess. Nobody knows. The cops won't let anybody see him. Especially me. Deputy Schoen kicked me in the ankle twice when I tried to interview Sam."

"What did they say he vandalized?"

"The statue," Garit replied. "You were in on it, right?"

Fulton grinned. "You're not going to report this, right?"

"No way. I'm like a lawyer or a priest. Confidentiality."

"That's cool. Maybe there will be a story someday, and I'll give it to you first if you treat me fairly. It's all steeped in political games, and it wouldn't do to go off half-cocked."

"I appreciate that, and I understand your caution," Garit said, even though he didn't understand at all.

"So what's the big deal about a store opening?" Garit asked. "How'd you get involved?"

"Good idea. Change the subject," Fulton grinned.

"I'm just a farmer, in partnership with Coney, but I've got a stake in this store, just like most of the farmers in this county," Fulton said. "The big deal is that there's no middleman involved to skim the profits off the top, and we can deliver fruits, vegetables and meat so fast there's nobody can get them fresher. I'll grow vegetables to sell here mostly. It's a steadier market, and prices are set by farmers. All my other prices are set by retailers and marketers and brokers. This is our first market where we're price setters, not takers. So it's a good thing for my veggies, and I can also send along some beef and turkey."

"Free-range turkey?"

Fulton laughed warmly. "No, not free-range. If they ranged free they'd be wild, wouldn't they?" Garit blushed.

"Don't be embarrassed, dude," Fulton reassured, tapping Garit's shoulder. "Most people don't know the first thing about their food. Why should you be any different? No, my turkeys are raised in a well-ventilated barn where they can run around and be both social and safe. If they could get outside, they'd be in danger of all kinds of crazy diseases, not to mention the risk of them running off and getting killed on the road or eaten alive by wild animals. See, turkeys are really stupid birds, with brains the size of a pea. They'd drown from looking up into the rain, wondering what it was."

Garit laughed.

"It's true, man. For sanitation, health, and economics, indoors is the best way. Where'd you get the idea for free-range anyway?"

Garit pointed through the store's gigantic front window, where the small and motley group of people stood inside the pasture fence with their picket signs now held high. One of them read "Free-range birds or tortured slaves?"

"Hey," Garit said. "Do you know that chick out there, the blonde with the puffy behind and small chest?" Fulton looked.

"I see which one you mean, I think, but I don't recognize her,"

Fulton replied. "What, you think she's hot, don't you?" He was grinning, teasing.

"Pretty face, but her butt's too big," Garit replied. "She just kind of reminds me of someone, that's all. So what's the protester's problem?"

"Oh, I don't know. I have theories. Still off the record?" Garit nodded. "I guess I've always looked at them as if they're religious zealots," Fulton began, "but they're really and truly just uneducated, misguided people who need to find something to complain about because their stomachs are always so full. They're like Crusaders. You know, convert to Christianity or I'll kill you? Only these guys want everyone to convert to their veganism or else they'll make life miserable for everyone else. It's like they want everyone to be as miserable and angry as they are. They don't seem to understand that this country is based on the right of everyone to make their own decisions, and they certainly don't understand the agricultural heritage that made this country what it is today. Mostly, I think they're just a bunch of trust fund babies looking for something to provide meaning for their lives, and they've chosen to jump on the first emotional line guys like Pinckney preach at them—like a religion—in school. He's the real dangerous one in that group."

"Why would people with money and leisure time come up here?"

"You kidding?" Fulton replied. "Have you looked around? This place is beautiful. Lots of woods and lakes and rivers, close to the Big Lake, and property is cheap compared to other places, like Ohio."

"Illinois," Garit replied. Fulton looked at him, knowing nothing about why that comment was made.

The radio reporter walked past Fulton, and the two made eye contact and smiled competitively. Coney greeted Garit with a big smile and a hard-gripped handshake.

"Glad to meet you, Garit," he said. "I think I've seen you at a city council meeting or two, right?" Garit nodded.

Suddenly a roar came from outside.

The protesters, TV cameras still trained on them, shouted a new chant. The three cameramen bounced around the protesters in the fence like puppies bouncing around an older dog.

The fenced people cried:

"Factory farms have got to go, hey hey, ho ho!"

The protesters, including Pinckney, locked arms and formed a line that stretched and turned in the small pasture area. Every second person bobbed up and down in tandem, in beat with the chant, like a whack-a-mole game at a carnival. Great scene for television.

Pinckney beamed into the cameras, and finally broke his arm link to give a camera a one-on-one interview.

Garit looked back at Fulton and Coney, who were laughing. "What do you bet those wing nuts will be the lead story at six tonight," Fulton said.

In an instant, like a deer jumping in front of a car, three Jovial City Police cars—the exact number of cars in the city's fleet—bounded from the street where Molly had exited with her trailer. Their old-style flashers revolved like feathers in a tiny tornado. They slid and skidded from the street into the parking lot, sirens blaring.

The crowd watching the protests scattered, and Pinckney's protesters leaped over the short fence and dived behind light poles and other people.

"Look at those wackos run!" smirked Fulton. Garit and Coney looked and laughed as two young men, one dressed neatly and the other unkempt, greasy and pierced, ran like bobcats after rabbits and disappeared into the neighborhood.

The police cars squealed to a stop in front of the store's front door.

Garit saw Pinckney step boldly toward a TV camera. He made an exaggerated movement to link arms again, but his human chain consisted of only himself and the older woman with the tiny dog.

"We will not be moved!" Pinckney yelled toward the cameraman, who had already turned to film the police. He raised the bullhorn to his lips. "I said, we will not be moved!" he shouted, but the cameras ignored him.

Garit pointed his point-and-shoot camera through the store window, zoomed in and snapped several stills of Pinckney stomping his feet. He did the same with his phone. He felt something behind him, and turned to see a big pale white cop who looked like a German weightlifter, who pushed him to the ground harshly. He also turned and shoved Coney, but couldn't knock him down. Another officer grabbed Fulton by the collar, spun him around and body-slammed him to the floor with a loud, dull grunt and thud. Garit shot photo after photo of Fulton's face as they twisted his arms behind him and cranked his palms up between his shoulder blades.

"Take it easy, fellas," said Coney as he stepped toward the police, only to be blocked by the big white cop. "What's this all about?"

"We're arresting this pervert for criminal sexual activity," the blocking deputy said.

"Sexual activity!" What are you talking about?" Fulton cried. Garit sat on the floor, shooting frame after frame.

"You painted a filthy graffiti on the statue in the park, pervert!" shouted the cop who had body slammed Fulton.

"What's that got to do with sex?" asked Fulton between gasping breaths.

"Shut up, ya perv. All I do is arrest 'em. I don't file the charges." The officer growled as he and another lifted Fulton from the floor. Coney took a step forward, ready to put up a fight, but Fulton squirmed and cried: "Don't, Coney. Don't get yourself in trouble. You got a store to open. Just call Botsdorf." Fulton yelped in pain as the smaller of the cops twisted his arm harshly toward his shoulder blade again. Garit stood and continued to take photographs when he heard Coney shout "Watch out, Garit!"

Garit looked up from his camera as Deputy Schoen rushed him like a linebacker salivating for a quarterback. He bashed his shoulder into Garit's stomach and gripped him behind the legs. He lifted him slightly and slammed his back into the floor, his shoulder driving into his stomach again. The camera flipped out of Garit's hands and crashed behind him.

Schoen stood up and smashed it several times with his boot heel. He roughly kicked Garit onto his stomach and pulled his hands violently behind his back. He handcuffed him tightly and jerked him to his feet. On their way out, Garit saw that Coney was being restrained by the big

Aryan cop. The police led Garit and Fulton to their cars and put them in separate back seats as the television cameras imposed themselves.

Coney made a cell phone call when the big Aryan let him loose. "Botsdorf?" he said into the phone, "I need you to bail out Fulton and another kid, OK? ASAP? Call me back if you need to. Appreciate it." He punched his phone off. He watched the police cars leave and shouted to the people milling about in the parking lot.

"Excitement's over, folks. How was that for a grand opening? Great, fresh food and a show besides!" He smiled broadly. "C'mon in, folks. The Jovial Farmers' Own Store is officially open!"

Customers entered the store as Coney stood by the doors and greeted each person with a smile and a handshake.

Pinckney stood alone, finally, in the grassy pasture area, glaring at the store. He spun around. Several discarded protest signs had been thrown near his feet, and he stomped one of them repeatedly. Finally, he stopped, glaring down as if in a trance. Then, angry that he alone was left for the grunt duty, he picked up the signs, put them into the back of a one-ton pickup truck and drove off, muttering. Before he was out of the new store's parking lot, Pinckney was on his cell phone.

"Jovial Organic Foods," a voice answered. "This is Mr. Deadfrick."

"Jim. Dan. I think it's time we take this thing to another level."

"How's that?"

"Let's talk. There are none so blind as those who will not see."

"That's from the Bible, you know."

"I don't give a rat's behind where it's from, you stupid jerk. There are lives at stake here, and I'll be darned if I'll be anybody's fool."

"Come out to the house this afternoon."

23

Pinckney arrived at Jim Deadfrick's house and walked in without ringing the doorbell. He slinked down the stairs to the basement. Deadfrick didn't get up from his couch, where he was sitting with a very attractive young woman with entrancing brown eyes, short-cropped brown hair and a perpetual scowl that couldn't hide her head-turning genetic combination of oriental mom and European dad. She wore tight jeans despite the heat, and a pink golf shirt with an HSUS logo on it. Her only makeup was black eye liner and black lipstick, a throwback to her Goth teenage days. Deadfrick greeted Pinckney with a grunt.

"Hi, Bambi," Pinckney said. "I thought you had a flight out today."

"Later tonight," she said. Pinckney grabbed the remote from Deadfrick's hand and changed the channel from a baseball game to the local news. The massive 72-inch TV was the focal point of the room, alone in the center of the widest paneled wall.

"So what's got your pony tail all in a knot?" Deadfrick said after he watched Pinckney help himself to a stiff drink from the small bar to the side of the couch.

"You'll see. The local news will probably get this all wrong."

"You never know," Deadfrick responded, calmly.

Deadfrick's square jaw and broad shoulders were hidden by minor middle-aged fat, but he was far from obese. His hair was cut short in a flat-top on his round head, and it emphasized his round jaw like a carpenter's square put up to a tree. He carried his head high and his shoulders back, his only legacy from a brief high school wrestling career. Three walls of Deadfrick's basement were covered with white-grain paneling that held various crucifixes, each one signed on the horizontal cross-piece by a sports figure. Interspersed among the crucifixes were autographed pictures of disgraced baseball stars such as Daryl Strawberry, Denny McClain and Chad Curtis. The bar was adorned behind with Coke and Pepsi memorabilia. At the very center was a painting of an old man praying over a loaf of bread.

Deadfrick turned to the TV when the 5 p.m. pseudo-news cycle began. NewsCenter 14 opened with this dramatic teaser: "Porn bust boggles best bargains. We were there and got it all on camera."

"You see that?" Pinckney shouted. "Do you see anything about our protest? No! Not one word. If anything, the slavers' store will get *more* publicity out of this. And where's my message? Where's the outrage about these factory farmers ruining the planet with their ugly, useless, cows and pigs? That bastard Dogues probably rigged this whole thing!"

"Just calm down, Dan, and let's try to figure out how we can profit from this," Bambi said, patronizingly. Deadfrick nodded his approval. "Nobody pays attention to television news anymore anyway," he said. "Most everybody knows it's all a pack of lies. Who got busted for porn?"

"Oh, one of the farmers. Dogues's nephew, I think. They took in that new *World* reporter too, but I don't know why."

"They probably arrested him for being a reporter," Deadfrick deadpanned. "Isn't that crime enough?" Pinckney nodded. "Who cares? We're not going to win this election. Then where will we be?"

"I got a feeling the election just fell into our hands, Dan. What God-fearing person in Jovial would buy groceries from a porn-sicko pervert?"

"You know it's not true," Pinckney whined.

"The truth should never get in the way of opportunity," Deadfrick said, leaning over and grabbing the remote from Pinckney's hand.

"Or a good story," Bambi said.

"You and I have never been ones to waste a crisis, have we?" Deadfrick asked Pinckney as he turned up the TV volume. "Play up the pervert angle to your kids at the high school. Let them put pressure on their parents, and maybe they'll boycott the new store and vote for Prop. One just to make themselves feel better."

Pinckney sighed deeply. "That won't be easy, since we're in the middle of summer vacation, duh! But you're right about one thing. People really are that stupid, aren't they?"

"You bet they are," Bambi said. "From my experience all around this country, I think they'll believe whatever we tell them, as long as we tell it right. So here's what we should do. We'll get a full-page ad into the *World* by Saturday morning, some B.S. about how Jovial Organic Foods is run by families with real, old-fashioned family values *and* a real concern for the earth. Imply that the factory farmers don't have the same ethics. Play up the planet. That will resonate with all these rich suburban transplants around here. Make it a real and intense P.R. campaign. Jim, you haul out that old picture of you and Mary and the kids before the divorce, and Dan? Find one with you smiling in a crowd of adoring high school kids. Think you can get that picture before Saturday?"

"No problem. If I get a few of my little boot licks out of summer school, they'll eat my crap and call it a fudge sickle."

"That's the spirit," Deadfrick said, suddenly animated. "We'll announce a family values weekend sale, put Mexican grapes or some other crud on sale below cost and get them in the store to buy all the other stuff at regular profit. We'll get our money back out of this investment yet."

"We were on our way until these stupid farmers decided they were smart enough to be retailers," Pinckney spat. "And you let them, Jim. You're the one who couldn't get a city ordinance passed to stop them." He pounded his fist on the edge of the bar, but Deadfrick was unfazed.

"Hey, the past is the past," he said. "Besides, a little competition can be a good thing, Dan. Don't worry so much. We've beaten odds greater than this before, haven't we? C'mon, man. You didn't think you'd get your insurance money out of the theatre fire either, did you? And what was it that bought you your house addition?"

"Insurance money," muttered Pinckney, looking down at his shoes.

"That's right. Insurance money," Deadfrick mocked. "You keep forgetting, probably because you're an atheist, that all things work together for good."

"What did I tell you about spouting asinine Bible verses to me?"

"I'm just saying ..." Pinckney hushed him. The news story was coming on.

The segment began with an establishing shot of the storefront, then a wide, panning shot of the protesters as a talking head voiced over the video.

"See that?" said Pinckney. "What did I tell you?" Deadfrick raised his hand to hush him as he watched his friend's snarling face grow bigger on the screen.

"We know for a fact that factory farms are horribly cruel and stores like this only promote further exploitation, and poison, and murder, and all for the sake of profits. Nothing but profits," Pinckney said to the camera. His face was quickly cut off, replaced by shots of smiling people stacking their grocery carts with luscious cuts of beef and pork and lamb, and loading large heads of lettuce and fresh vegetables on top. The vegetables were richly colored, bright and moist.

Pinckney slapped his hand to his forehead. "How do they sell that stuff so cheap?" he screeched. "Our veggies look like garbage compared to what they have there, and our prices are a lot higher. Look! On top of that, they're passing out free publicity! Get that camera off the produce!" he shouted toward the TV.

Just then the reporter's voice raised two octaves, and the camera spun. The rest of the report showed Fulton's and Garit's violent arrest, and finished with the reporter pretending to fill the role of serious journalist.

".. and that's why police believe they've caught the leader of the gang of vandals who desecrated the statue of town founder Alan Jovial." The camera shot faded, and the reporter sent the signal back to the studio. "Where was the porn?" Deadfrick asked.

A sidebar story was introduced by the anchor girl.

"Check her out, Dan," Deadfrick said. "Her name's Mindy, a home-town girl just back from college. You had her in school, I think. I recognize her, or is it her mamma I'm thinking about?"

"Apart from the excitement over the arrest," the pretty young anchor said, "there was further controversy at the Farmers' Own store."

"Stop saying their name!" Pinckney growled. Mindy resumed: "Early this morning, NewsCenter 14's cameras caught a near-fight over where the protesters could gather, and whether they would be allowed to gather at all."

The screen cut away to silent footage of Mindy speaking with Pinckney, then cut to Frank's pathetic attempt to run.

"The controversy began when the protesters commandeered an area that had been reserved for a display of cute little sheep and lambs and ewes and rams," Mindy sing-songed. "But in the end, it all worked out with a happy compromise, and the protesters won the day, along with the right to be in the grassed area."

The picture on the screen zoomed in on Pinckney's angry face. "The people are more important than sheep!" he cried, bug-eyed into every living room that had Channel 14 tuned in.

Pinckney looked closer at the screen and waved his arms wildly. "I didn't say that! How did they make me say that? What kind of bull are they pulling? I've been misquoted. It's out of context!" The anchor's face reappeared.

"She's a real looker," Deadfrick said. "What's her last name?"

"I can't remember every little beauty pageant slut that runs through that hole of a school," he said, pacing with the drink in his hand.

"I know!" Deadfrick exclaimed toward the TV. "She's Janie VanderBroek's oldest! I should have known. She has that same turned up nose. Relentless little bitch. Ambitious. I helped her get a couple scholarship applications done. Not much worry about morals or ethics, if I recall. I like that in a woman. I wonder if this little hottie's anything like Momma?"

"Funny," Pinckney snarled. "That total lack of morals was what I liked about you when I was in my first year teaching. Even back then, you didn't seem to have a conscience. That was what made you such a go-getter." Deadfrick frowned. He could easily have gotten where he was today without Pinckney's lame help.

"That was Jovial Schools superintendent Dan Pinckney," Mindy said. "Mr. Pinckney is a known animal rights advocate, who has taught in his classrooms, before he became Superintendent, the idea that animals are on an equal footing with humans and deserve the same rights." She tapped her stack of papers on the desk. "I guess Mr. Pinckney has changed his view on that position, right Carl?" she said, smiling. The camera cut to Carl.

"I guess so, Charlotte," he giggled. "It's Mindy," she said, but the anchorman ignored her and introduced the weatherman.

Pinckney clicked off the TV and stood silently, shaking.

"See, Jim? They set me up. They twisted my words." He spun, pounded his fist on the bar and cursed. "I'm telling you, we're going to lose this election! And your whole plan is that we put an ad in the *World* and try to smear the farmers? What if we still lose the election? And what about me? How am I supposed to defend myself from my own words? Did you see how they twisted my words? Who's going to stand up for me?"

"Luckily, we have Bambi here to consult," Deadfrick said. "We'll take the necessary steps to protect both our interests." He turned to the girl. "OK, Bambi. You've been paid well. What are your recommendations?"

"First thing," she said. "My money?"

"No, no," Deadfrick said, wagging his right index finger. "Our agreement was your evaluation and a meeting here, half the money, then a written report."

"I remember," Bambi said. "First off, this TV report doesn't surprise me. Your whole effort, from what I've seen, is a disaster. Mishandled from the start. You've had no media training or strategy, no real effective plan to get Proposal One passed. It's why you have to start with the ads, maybe get the papers and TV stations to give their endorsement."

"Don't worry about the media," Deadfrick said. "I have this handled."

"How so?" Bambi asked.

"Let's just say the owner of the *World* owes me a favor," Deadfrick said.

"What about social media?"

"That's a lost cause until we get some kind of reliable internet service," Pinckney said.

"Well, you should get something started as best you can," Bambi said. "Start with the gross photos I shot the other night. Make accusations.

Keep making them. The key is repetition. Say something enough times and people will believe it. It's a proven tactic."

"OK," Deadfrick said. "What else?"

"If I were handling this like I did in California, I'd have started a lot earlier than this, and that's why your campaign has to be intense here in the next, what, five weeks? Oh, and get rid of those two morons you hired, Pinkey."

"I got them straight from PETA," Pinckney said. "They must be credible. They came highly recommended as guys who do the dirty work and never leave any traces. Our hands have to stay clean here, after all."

Deadfrick put up his hand.

"I agree with Bambi to a point," he said. "They already botched one of their stupid plans."

"That's right," Bambi said. "Those idiots didn't have to kill that cow. I mean, if they had set it up right and actually taken at least one decent photo, we could have used it. But they didn't, and the farmer cleaned up their mess, collected insurance money. As far as I know, the police didn't even investigate. The only redeeming quality about it at all was that one poor abused animal was put out of its misery."

"The cops are too busy trying to get Proposal Two passed," Deadfrick said. "We need that, too. If we can get an anti-gang ordinance passed, I can write grants that will take care of our store's financial trouble and keep the money flowing. That should be our top priority, after all."

"If that's the top priority, I should never have come here," Bambi said. "I was told that this could be the start of ending animal slavery and cruelty in this part of the world, but if money trumps that, well, just pay me now and I'll get out."

"Calm down, Bambi. What's your recommendation?" Deadfrick asked. "How do we win this election and stop the Farmers Own Store from eating our lunch?"

"My recommendation," she said, sternly, "is that you rethink your priorities. Step back and get the big picture in focus. Sometimes it's easy to lose sight of the end game when you have morons running around, too impatient to use political action, you know, working within the system—instead of violence. We're in this for the long haul. People won't stop eating meat overnight. It will take time to eradicate animal agriculture across the country, but we can start here."

Deadfrick took out his phone, tapped a few times.

"Give me your account password," he said. Bambi took out her phone and showed him a code. They both pressed buttons.

"While we wait, I'll tell you the best strategy you can have, in my opinion," Bambi said. "The best way to go is in stages. Start with political action. You're already on your way, getting the organic proposal on the ballot. Work within the system. It's the only way to retain mainstream credibility. Use social media, regular media and public opinion. Turn it your way with these gross pictures. Then use the courts. File charges against the animal slavers. Even if you have no truth or evidence, you can keep them tied up in court for years, spending money and time that farmers don't have. Bankrupt them. There's no shortage of lawyers who will do it. Only if that won't work should you take physical action."

"And when do you recommend we begin taking action," Pinckney asked, excitedly.

"I don't recommend that you take action at all," she said. "Violence hurts the overall cause. Keep the big picture in mind. We're here to end animal agriculture, not make a couple people rich." Bambi's phone chimed. The bank transaction was complete.

"As we agreed, I'll send you all this in a written report," she said, standing. "Look, I'm an independent consultant. This is just my opinion. But I've been on the fringe. This movement, at least in its corporate side, is filled with hate. It doesn't win converts. Courts. That's the best way. Why do you think HSUS is filled with lawyers and P.R. people? And even they encourage and fund some of the others. They're terrorists."

"Extremism in the cause of freedom is no vice," muttered Pinckney.

"Any last things before you catch your flight?" Deadfrick asked.

"Just one. Fire those two idiots. More than likely they're involved with a group that's even crazier than PETA, like Kill them with Kindness, or some fringe radical anarchists like that. You'll never win over the public with violence, and the things they like to do could easily be prosecuted as terrorism. If that happens, your grant money for gangs will be gone overnight. Get rid of them as fast as you can. They're dangerous, and even worse, they're stupid." Bambi shook hands with both men and walked up the stairs.

"So what do you think?" Deadfrick asked Pinckney.

"I think we don't have the time for some idealistic cold feet from a little girl," Pinckney spat. "We'll both be bankrupt soon after the election if we lose."

"I tend to agree with her tactics," Deadfrick said. "At least before the election. We'll see what happens after that. And I also agree with her about those two morons you brought in. Violence and threats are not going to force farmers out of business. Not in this political climate, anyway. And it doesn't fly well in the court of public opinion. We need that public opinion for the election, Dan."

"Duh!" Pinckney sulked. "I'll keep them stoned and drunk and happy for the time being, if that's what you want. They'll do what I tell them, even if it's to lay low for awhile."

"How will you do that?"

"You forget my profession," Pinckney said. "I've spent my whole professional career manipulating dangerous, stupid kids."

24

Garit held his throbbing temple with one hand while massaging a knot in his lower back with the other. A quickly swelling and discoloring eye impaired his vision, and it hurt to try to force his eyelid open.

Fulton pressed his bare hand against a laceration in his jaw, but blood still dripped onto the floor. They sat, perspiring, on a sticky metal bench in a single cell at the Jovial County Jail, stripped of all clothing except their underwear.

"Get some cool air pumped into this place," Botsdorf shouted over his shoulder when he walked through the cell door, held open by a young deputy.

"Well, Fulton," he said cheerfully. "What, did they find a joint on you or something? And who's this that Coney told me to bail out?" He held out his hand to Garit.

"Garit West," he said, shaking Botsdorf's hand.

"The new *World* reporter?"

"I'm not so new."

"Believe me, son, you're new." He smiled at Garit, and the tension eased just a bit. "But how exciting, huh? To be arrested for your first time for being a reporter? I'm envious of the novelty, Garit. Every reporter worth his salt should be arrested at least once. So what did they pop you for? Interference with a police activity, some BS like that?"

"Don't know. No one ever told me."

"How about you, Fulton? What are the charges?"

"They said something about criminal sexual activity, but that's total crap," Fulton retorted. "It has to be for painting the statue. Apparently somebody thinks underwear on a statue is pornographic. They busted Sam Perkins a few days ago. I heard they didn't give him any water for two days. I haven't seen him since I heard about it."

"Who gave you the pounding?"

"It was officer Schoen for me," Garit interceded. "He's assaulted me three times now, but no one seems to care."

Botsdorf nodded and looked back at Fulton. "I don't know his name, but he was intent on hurting me," Fulton said. "Punched me several times. Made sure his ring ripped my face open."

"Did you paint the statue?" Botsdorf asked.

"Yeah."

"Why?"

"Why not? Didn't you?"

"Of course I did. I did it once with a bunch of people that included your mom. Everybody did it. But that was back in the day."

"So what's the difference?"

"The difference is we never got caught," he said. "And we never got caught this close to an election where the cops need to make a public splash."

"I stand by the political statement," Fulton said. "Somebody has to pull down the pants of this city's B.S."

"Well," Botsdorf said, calmly, "the first thing we have to do is get you some medical treatment, then your clothes, then get you out of here. This shouldn't take too long." He walked out of the cell as the deputy opened the door.

"Who is that guy?" Garit asked Fulton.

"Botsdorf, our attorney. Your attorney if you have a lick of sense. The only honest attorney in Jovial County, if there is such a thing. You should be glad he's helping you."

"What does he charge?"

"Hadn't thought about it. I've never had to use him for anything like this before."

"I sure can't pay him. Wally hasn't paid me in nearly a month."

"He'll be cool about it. Unlike every other lawyer in the world, Botsdorf doesn't practice law for the money. He's more into his publications."

"He has publications? Where?"

"Right up the road in Sventon. He owns the *Sasser* and some other things. Does it mostly by himself. You haven't seen it?"

"Nope. Never even heard of it."

"Oh, Wally makes sure people here in Jovial don't see much of it. I've heard he even goes out to newsstands and buys them all up before people know they're there."

"Sounds like something Wally would do."

"Maybe you should hook up with Bots. He's a great writer, even better reporter. And he likes to mentor young reporters. He was even nominated for a Pulitzer back in the day. Exposed some wacko's cult murder or something like that."

Garit jerked his head up, sending a throb of pain from his aching back through to the top of his head. "Now that sounds interesting," he said cautiously.

"Oh, he's a great guy. And a friend of my family."

"So you trust him?"

"Absolutely. He's one of the few real, genuine Christians you'll ever know."

"How do you know the difference between real and fake?"

"I don't know how most people tell, but for me, it's about his peace. Did you see how he didn't get all excited and berate or threaten the cops for this? He just walks in, and they jump."

"He did seem to have an air of authority and confidence about him, not like Wally or the cops or the town council. How did you ever hook up?"

"Oh, he did all my legal work when my parents were killed. Mostly probate stuff, wills, estates, stuff like that. But I never had to worry about it. He handled it all well."

"Your parents were killed?"

"Nearly two years now." He said it so matter-of-factly that Garit marveled. Could his own pain be two years away from subsiding? Could healing ever be as complete as Fulton's seemed?

"How?" he asked Fulton.

Fulton was about to answer when, from the hallway, entered Zoe, the dispatcher, with a small plastic first aid kit. Fulton pressed for silence with his index finger to his mouth, and Garit didn't press for an answer, even though he wanted one even more intently than he wanted an end to the throbbing in his back and head.

Silently, Zoe donned latex gloves and pulled out a disinfectant wipe from the kit. She roughly cleaned Fulton's jaw, drawing a little more blood, then applied a large bandage to the cut. She tore open a small sample package and gave Fulton two pills. She waddled out the cell door, down the hall and returned with a funnel-shaped paper cup of water.

"It's Ibuprofen," she said, and handed Fulton the water. "You might want to get a couple stitches in that." He took the pills. Zoe looked at Garit.

"What about you?" she demanded as her eyes scanned him toe to head. "Any bleeding?"

"My head and my back hurt like crazy," he said. She nodded and walked out the cell door, shouting. "Get somebody in here to clean up this blood on the floor."

Botsdorf returned before the cleanup began with a different deputy who carried their clothes, folded neatly, with their shoes on top.

"You both are bailed out," Botsdorf said. "Mr. West, I'll come and see you and Wally as soon as I can. Fulton, we have some talking to do. Come on, get dressed. I'll give both of you a ride home."

When they had begun their ride, Botsdorf turned to Fulton.

"They're saying they got you for vandalism, but more charges could follow," he said. "Something about a new ordinance about gangs. You know anything about that?"

"The city council must have passed the anti-gang ordinance without telling anyone," Fulton responded. "That can't be legal."

"I'll check into it. They can pass any ordinance on third reading just by proclaiming its legal number," he said. Do you know if they had three readings?"

"I know they argued it once, because I remember Coney saying what a stupid idea it was," Fulton said. "That's all I know."

"Well, I wouldn't worry much. It's a pretty big stretch to say you're a gang. Besides, it's on the ballot coming up. Why would they pass an ordinance and then keep it on the ballot? Maybe they're just over-confident they'll win the election."

"They passed a bunch of things a month or so ago, without discussion," Garit said. "It was my first meeting, and I asked the mayor about it. He told me not to worry about it, it was just boilerplate, technical stuff that readers didn't care about."

"Interesting," Botsdorf said. "We'll cross that bridge later. Fulton, anyone else with you when you painted the statue?"

"There were four of us, altogether."

"Still seems like a stretch to say it's a gang. I wouldn't worry too much. Once they all calm down, it should be a minor fine if you admit to it. Maybe a couple hundred bucks, max." He made eye contact with Garit in the rear-view mirror.

"And Garit? They got nothing on you. They want to say obstruction of justice, but you were on the job as a reporter, right?"

"Right."

"So I don't even have to see Wally. Just tell him I'll take care of it, and I'll talk to him tomorrow. The charges will probably be dropped within a week. And put some ice on that eye. You're going to have a nice shiner."

25

Garit's battered left eye had turned a healthy healing purple a few days later when Wally called him into his office.

"I need you to do a story about the election coming up, West," he said. "It's only a couple weeks away, and it's dividing this town right down the middle. That's how I want your story to be. Right down the middle, perfectly fair and balanced. None of this taking sides stuff that landed you in jail."

"I never took any sides," Garit retorted. "You talked to Botsdorf. You know what happened and you know Deputy Schoen. You're the one who took sides when you didn't do anything about it."

"Stop trying to cover your butt," Wally snapped. "You've already lost me two cameras, and all in all, if you weren't a capable writer, you'd be more bother than you're worth. But I have to put up with you since we're short-handed."

"Yeah," Garit said. "That reminds me. When are we going to get another reporter?"

"Just mind your own business."

"I think it is my business when my work load doubles and I still haven't been paid for darn near a month."

"You agreed that we'd change the payroll system from weekly to bi-weekly," Wally said. "Your last weekly check will clear just fine. Then you're going to have to wait for the system to catch up. This kind of paperwork has to be done. I don't like it either, but it'll save money on accounting services in the long run. Besides, I had to pay your bail and legal fees. I ought to deduct that right off the top."

"How much was that, anyway?"

"None of your business."

"I think it is my business. I'm the one who was arrested. I was the one who got assaulted three times now by the police. I would think that's a newsworthy event, but you refuse to even consider a story. You've already saved a couple months worth of Aspen's salary and you still can't cover your bills? I think I understand just fine," Garit said. "This place is in deep trouble, isn't it?"

"You want to keep your job or not?"

"What good is a job if I don't get paid?"

"I told you, those checks will be covered." Wally stared. "And it's none of your business how I run mine. We've been doing just fine without Aspen, and we'll keep doing it as long as you do what you're told. My workload is twice as heavy as yours, plus I have to be the business manager and sales manager on top of that."

"Don't go complaining to me about it. You're the owner. You made your own bed." Wally glared at Garit again. Garit stared back.

"Why can't you just admit that you can't handle both jobs?" Garit asked. He stared into Wally's eyes defiantly until Wally turned away. The little victory emboldened him.

"If advertisers aren't paying you, it's probably because we're short a reporter and can't cover the news that should be covered. Without Aspen, the quality of our editorial content has turned to crap. I'm beginning to think she was running the editorial show here, because you sure don't seem to be able to handle it. Maybe it's time you stopped blaming Aspen for all the stuff you've gotten yourself into and face up to some facts."

"You think you know the facts?"

"I know one. I haven't been paid. That's all that matters to me."

"Ah, there's the problem," Wally said. "You're just a selfish punk kid who doesn't know his butt from a mole in the ground. I have more to worry about, like the future of this entire town. But I'm too busy to explain it to you right now. Just get me a story on the election, starting with Prop. One, and make it a good one for a change."

"And if I don't?"

"Then you'll have to find yourself someplace else to work."

"Again, Wally, that threat isn't all that great when you haven't paid me in nearly a month."

"I gave you a roof over your head, didn't I? Got you out of that armpit town in Ohio? If you want to stay here, you'll shut up and do as you're told."

"You're right, Wally," Garit said, sarcastically. "You have me by the short hairs. I can't leave because I don't have any money. And since you owe me, I'm stuck. I'll do what you want. What else is there to do in this boring little town?"

"Just do your job. That's all I want," Wally said. "You got one thing right. I own you." He paused for effect and to reestablish his moral high ground. "I need the story in two days, so you better get moving. Start with Jim Deadfrick about Prop. One, but watch him. He can be slippery."

Garit went to the Jovial Public Library.

"Betty," he said. "What do I need to know about this election coming up? I can't seem to get the straight poop, and Wally wants an unbiased story. How do you do that when everyone seems to have a bias?"

"What do you want to know? Prop One, Two, or Three? All you need is over there, in our political reading section." Betty pointed to a dark corner of the library Garit had never visited before. Under a 1950s-era light hanging from the ceiling was a round table and four overstuffed chairs. On the table, Garit found a stack of papers, on which were printed sample ballots for the election.

The ballot language read:

Proposal 1:

"To ensure the safest and healthiest food supply possible
for its citizens, and because of the danger of an epidemic
of obesity and disease caused by unhealthy industrialized
food, the people of the city of Jovial hereby propose to
establish the Jovial Wholesome Food Commission and
assess food producers a one-time establishment fee to be
determined by the Commission. The Commission will
be established as a four-member authority to oversee the
food supply sold in the city, inspect it for wholesomeness
and quality, and prohibit all said food from sale if it were
not produced within 200 miles of Jovial, and if it were
not organically produced and humanely treated until
slaughter. Should this commission become established
as an amendment to the city charter?"

Garit carried a copy back to Betty's desk.

"Seems simple enough, although a little strange and overreaching,"
he said. "What's behind it all?"

Betty escorted Garit to the alcove where they'd had lunch so many
times already. She lifted the top *World* newspaper from the stack neatly
arranged on a shelf.

"Maybe it's time you read your own paper," she said. She opened the
paper from the back and folded the pages. She pointed to a full-page ad
that featured pictures of both Jim Deadfrick and Dan Pinckney above
copy that said:

"A YES vote for Proposal 1 is a win-win for our children."

Beneath that header was smaller type. Below Deadfrick's picture,
in which he held a black book that looked like a Bible, was a description
of himself and a reference to his credibility.

"Jim Deadfrick has been a respected member of Jovial
all his life, and a member of the Church of Christ
Church since his baptism at age 13. He's been active
in the church all his adult life, and he secured the first

of many government grants to help the city through its dying tree crisis when he was in high school.

The principal stockholder and owner of the Jovial Organic Foods and Farmers' Elevator (JOFFE), he also cares about all our children's nutrition and future. He's even started a new business incubator in the south half of the Jovial Organic Underwear building. He's also been a respected member of the school board."

Below that, in bold letters inside a word bubble that pointed to his head, Garit read: "I support Proposal 1 because I care about the future of Jovial."

"This is all such tripe," Garit said to Betty. "Obviously, Wally wrote this. No real information there. I guess I'm going to have to interview this Deadfrick."

"Be careful," she said. "Don't ever trust him. And before you do it, read up on organics. He'll try to buffalo you with a bunch of his own hand-picked facts. Be armed, Garit. That's your best defense."

The smell of the Jovial Organic Foods store was insanely stereotypical, and as he coughed when he inhaled the smell of various scented candles and incense, Garit's mind drifted back to the days of being driven from Decatur to Bloomington for his parents' weekly food shopping trip. His parents had dragged him there every Sunday for most of his teenage years.

When he opened the store's door, a bell that hung from a flat piece of silver jingled, but no one was on the floor. He walked around the aisles, every step reminding him of those boring Sunday afternoons. Finally, Jim Deadfrick appeared from a back room and approached Garit.

"You the new *World* reporter?" he demanded, smiling.

"Garit West." Garit offered his hand, but Deadfrick ignored it. "So what do you think of our little slice of Heaven?"

"Funny you ask," Garit said. "Are you part of a chain of organic stores or something?"

"No, West, we're completely independent. Why?"

"It's just that this layout is almost identical to the organic store my parents shopped at in Illinois."

"How so?"

"Oh, you know. An older, classic building with a false storefront facade. This one seems quaint. The one I remember was kind of tacky. You know, a kind of sixties feel. And it cried out for modernization."

"Well, we have an image to maintain for our clients. They really don't go in for modern fads."

"Some people would say organic is a modern fad."

Deadfrick's face changed for a moment. Garit regretted going right on the attack, but the store owner's anger seemed to fade as he condescendingly and quickly turned serious.

"Organics is the way farming used to be from the beginning of time," he said. "And it's still the best way. It's not a fad. It's the only food choice that will endure. Regular farming is unsustainable."

"What does that mean? Seems to me that our food supply in the United States has been sustainable, and even abundant, for at least six generations."

"And we're about to reach the tipping point," Deadfrick said.

Deadfrick led Garit around the store. The dull hardwood floors creaked under their feet.

"I'll have to do more research about that," Garit said as they walked past a large assortment of dull-colored hanging peppers and onions. "I can't get that whole big picture in one story. I have to narrow it down. That's why I came to you first for this Proposition One story. I need to be educated before I can write about it."

Deadfrick nodded, and Garit thought he'd eased the tension, at least a little.

"As I said on the phone," Garit said, "The goal of interviewing you is so you can tell me why people should vote for it."

"Well, because it's in their best interests," Deadfrick said, smiling as he cocked his head slightly to the right. Garit turned on his recorder and held it up, resting his elbow on the wrist of his left arm, locked against his midsection as if he were afraid of being punched in the belly.

"But why?"

"You've seen all the food recalls lately, right?"

"Well, not really..." Garit said, but Deadfrick wasn't listening.

"Local food can be much more easily traced back to the farm where it was contaminated, and people can be held accountable," Deadfrick said.

"So Proposal One is about assessing blame when something goes wrong?"

"Blame is different than accountability," Deadfrick said. "Recalls are reactive. Proposal One is proactive and protective of our people. When food travels twenty-five thousand miles, how can you tell where it's been?"

"Aren't there required origin labels?"

"Not always. Think about this, Gary," Deadfrick said warmly. "You're an intelligent guy. Coming from Ohio, you have to know by now that our food system is killing us. If not chemically, then socially and economically. It's all controlled by Big Ag. The evidence is overwhelming. It's all these chemicals and genetic engineering. It's obscene."

"So is the Farmers Own Store a part of big ag? I thought this was a completely local effort."

"I can't speak for them, but they obviously buy their poisons from big ag, you know. Monsanto? The major killers in the world."

"It doesn't make sense to me," Garit said. "I thought we were the healthiest people on the planet. Look at us as a society. We're taller, stronger, and our life spans are longer than they ever were. Where's the evidence of poison? And why would any business want to poison their customers?"

"Like I said, look at all the diabetes and obesity. They're in cahoots with big pharm. One poisons people and the other sells drugs to cure it. Luckily there are some government controls to stop the massive number of food recalls."

"Massive? I only hear of one every now and then. Have there been food recalls around here?" Garit asked.

"No, but there could be. That's the proactive part. I want to be sure people don't get sick from their food." He looked down at Garit's recorder, and added "Uh, because I care about the people of Jovial."

"Aren't there FDA and USDA inspectors who test both your store and the Farmer's Own Store? I mean, even in the largest, worst national food recalls, only ten to fifteen people died. That's a pretty low percentage for a country of 350 million."

"I don't care about them," Deadfrick said. "Don't write that down. That's off the record. I do care."

"Back on the record?"

"Sure. I care about all God's children in the world, including the non-human animals. I mean, in the eyes of the Lord we're all beasts, when it comes right down to it." Garit recognized the line from a Jimmy Buffet song. His parents had been middle-of-the-road Parrot Heads.

"That's what distinguishes organics from the factory farmers," Deadfrick continued. "Organic farmers care about the earth and their animals. Factory farmers care only about money, and they'll even abuse their animals for their greed."

"How do they abuse them?" Garit interrupted.

"Do your own research, Gary," Deadfrick said. "Visit any farm around here, and see how horrid the conditions are. Babies ripped from their mamas and tied in solitary confinement crates where they can't even turn around. Voters will try to get us as a society above that. I'm already above that, and so are the loyal customers of our products. Proposal One is above that, too. First and foremost in my thoughts and prayers have to be the people of Jovial. They need to see what I saw about our food supply when I started this store so many years ago. That's why I said I don't care. I do care, but compared to my passion for the good people of Jovial, compared to my deep-seated Godly love that I pour out onto the people of this town, it's as if the other people didn't matter. That's how much I love them, Gary. And the only way I can care about them that much is because of the love God has given me. I see Godliness and care for the planet—and that means the human animal body too—as the same thing. If people don't start eating wholesome foods, they're going to be as obese as the rest of the country. The whole country could look like a bunch of Godless Chinese Sumo wrestlers. See, I'm trying to make a difference where I am, Gary. Because if I try to tackle the whole world, well, I'd have to be president or something. The only way to eat an elephant is one bite at a time. Maybe that should be off the record. Change it to this: God put us here so we could put our own marks on the world. That's been my passion ever since high school. To leave my mark on the world."

"I understand," Garit said. "But how would the commission work if the proposal passes?"

"It would be appointed by the mayor with the city council's approval."

Deadfrick waved Garit into his office to have a seat on an old couch covered by an off-white Afghan.

"Who do you think would be best suited for the job?" Garit asked. "Would you want it?"

"I can't name names, Gary, uh—What was your name again?"

"West. Garit West."

"How long since you left Ohio, West?"

"Illinois. And about two months ago. Why do you ask?"

"Well, I think it's important for a civic leader like me to be careful that our local issues aren't distorted by an outsider who may not understand them. Nothing against you, Gary, but you're from Ohio, and that's a long way from Jovial, Michigan. Let me ask you a question, professional to professional. What are you going to put in your story?"

"I won't know until I understand the issue and sit down to write."

"Do you think you understand?"

"That's why I'm here. To learn."

"Well, understand this, Gary. We have a tight-knit community, and we watch out for each other, at least the Christians do. And if you try to twist my words for some liberal agenda, you'll have a higher power than me to answer to, do you understand?"

"What's that supposed to mean?" retorted Garit, immediately offended. "Are you threatening me?"

"Heavens, no, Gary," Deadfrick soothed, touching Garit's shoulder gently. "I apologize if it came off that way. I'm guilty of being excitable. Extremism in defense of a right cause is no vice. Because I'm passionate about making a mark, I want to help you write a factual story that's not slanted in any way, and to make sure it's a positive piece. Besides,

I don't have to threaten anyone. The Lord is on my side, and He will repay treachery."

"I have no treachery in my mind at all, Mr. Deadfrick, I'll tell you that right now. I'm just trying to get the facts and write a balanced story that will help people decide how they want to vote."

"If they have any sense of decency and morality, they'll vote the right way." Garit quickly scribbled down that quote as the recorder kept doing its job.

"And that way is your way?"

"Yes, it is."

"And your way is the only moral way when it comes to food choices."

"Yes. The Lord is on my side—our side. The organic side."

"Fair enough. Now, I've heard other people say this is a very deceptive proposal, full of double meaning; and it's nothing more than a power grab. How would you respond to that?"

"I'll simply stand on my record as a long-time member of the Jovial Community Church of Christ Church, as an elder, and as a leader in the community since I was in high school. People trust me because I obey the golden rule."

"What does trusting you have to do with the ballot proposal?"

"I've endorsed it, so that connects me to it."

"Sounds like more of a beauty pageant than an election when you put it that way. What if voters turn it down?"

"That's their mistake, and it would be a sad day for Jovial. And it's not a beauty pageant. This has serious implications for the future of Jovial."

"I guess I still don't understand how limiting food choices is good for the community. I mean, farmers can't grow oranges in this climate, so in winter, you'd deny them citrus fruit from Florida or California?"

"There you go, distorting my words," Deadfrick said, smiling as if the phrase held no animosity at all.

"I'm just asking a question."

"So it's your job to ask these gotcha questions designed to trick me?"

"It's my job to ask questions, but I believe you're far too clever for me to trick you."

"What's that supposed to mean?"

"It means I don't think I could trick you, Mr. Deadfrick. Nor would I want to. But you haven't answered my question. Would you deny proper nutrition to the people if their food couldn't be grown locally or organically, for whatever reason?"

"Let me tell you why you're so wrong, Gary," Deadfrick said with a lilt in his voice, as if he were about to praise Garit for something. "I and the people who care about their food would deny Jovial's citizens nothing. In fact, we want them to be as healthy as possible. That can be Jovial's mark on the world. That's why we offer strictly organic food in our shop. If we would deny people anything, it would be the dangers of the chemicals used by factory farmers."

"But how is their food worse than yours? They have chemicals that they call crop protection products, and you have different kinds of crop protection products, like sulfur and copper. They're not exactly good for you, either, and they have to be applied a lot more often. Which one is worse?"

"Just do a little reading on your own, Gary. You're an investigative reporter, right? Do a little digging on the right websites and you'll find that our food is killing us."

"I guess I'll have to do more digging on that," Garit conceded. "I don't want to get too far off subject. Let's talk about the ballot initiative that you're throwing your support behind."

"Here's the best thing about passing this proposal," Deadfrick said. "Not only will it keep us all healthier, it could put Jovial on the map."

"How's that?"

"A new commission to oversee food would create the safest local food supply on the planet, and that, my young friend, would be national news." They talked for a few more moments, and Garit stood up to leave. He noticed a picture above where he'd been sitting.

"I've seen this picture before somewhere," he said, turning back toward Deadfrick. "What is it?"

Deadfrick reached across Garit and took the photo from the wall.

"This is my start to the path of making my mark in life," he said, beaming. "This is me with my first successful grant. I was just a senior in high school, and I wrote this $10,000 grant to help beautify Jovial. Here I am with Dan Pinckney, who was my teacher and soon-to-be friend. He's the school superintendent now. He really helped me along, encouraged me. Some people would call him a mentor, but all I know is that he really cared about me. He gave me the encouragement I needed to go ahead and try for the grant to begin with, and it opened a lot of doors for me. It got me started in a career in business, and it made Jovial into a Tree City back in the 1980s. Gave us a nice little hand up for federal funds, and they saw this city through some very tough times. Since then, I've written a total of ninety-four successful grant applications, each and every one a benefit to the city of Jovial and the surrounding area." He placed he photo back on the wall and straightened it. "Why are you so interested in it?"

"I don't know. Trying to learn about Jovial's history, that's all. It just seems like there's something about the picture that's out of place. It's like I've seen it somewhere before, but I can't quite figure where."

26

When Dan Pinckney walked into the next
planned meeting of the Jovialites Advocating for Animal Rights
(JAAR), he discovered a copy of the *Jovial World* on his podium, with
certain headlines, stories and passages circled in red ink. He fingered
his way to two stories that immediately added heat to his boiling anger.

"Tame protest!" He shrieked to one of his followers. "Tame! They
call this writing? There's no way we were tame at the dead carcass
store! You guys were standouts. The way we commandeered the green
space? The way we protested? We made a difference. We made people
think!" He checked the byline. "This is why I get all my news from the
internet," he said.

"Newspapers are dying because of this kind of biased crap. This
West guy is a no-talent hack, a paid mouthpiece for the slavers and
poison brokers. I didn't trust him from the day I first laid eyes on him,
carcass-eating bastard."

Aspen, dressed as Cindy, stood with her spine against the back
wall of the room and tried to recognize familiar faces as her heart sent
a wave of adrenaline from her lower back through her neck. Placing the
marked-up paper on the podium as a way of 'turning up the heat' might
not have been such a great idea after all. But now she knew what she'd
suspected: Pinckney's fuse was very short.

Two young men in the room popped breath mints and went back

to staring at a laptop computer. One of them, neatly groomed, was overdressed for this crowd in a white shirt, sport coat and new blue jeans. The other wore long, straight, greasy hair, leather and a variety of tattoos and piercings.

As casually as she could, hoping no one else could hear her heart beating, she sidled behind them and saw poorly composed photographs on the computer screen. One showed a large cut that oozed a little blood from some animal's hind leg.

"You can just look at them, even in a picture, and know they're unhappy," a girl, also new to the JAAR group, said to the two young men.

Aspen settled into a seat at the edge of the back row, next to the man she always sat next to, the one with the beard and the cowboy hat.

As she surveyed the crowd, she saw most of the usual suspects, including the woman with the embarrassed dog on her lap, panting heavily in the heat and its wool sweater. There were three women and four men who seemed scared all the time. Mostly familiar faces.

"I see we have some new blood here tonight," she whispered to the cowboy. He shrugged.

"Let's get started," Pinckney began. "I want to call your attention to these headlines. I don't know why I'm surprised, after all these years, that reporters are paid shills in the pockets of the slavers. Put those photos on the screen and scroll through them," he said, and the long-haired young man plugged a projector into a computer.

"As you can see," Pinckney said after a brief wait, "here we have indisputable evidence of non-human animals brutalized and exploited for nothing more than money, and what gets the headlines? Arresting some dopey farm kid for vandalism and porn! And what does our message—our just cause—get us? We're ignored by the press. Or called tame. Tame! That's the word they use to make their slave trading more acceptable. We're the victim of propaganda from the people who love the status quo and refuse to see the moral high ground." He slammed the paper down to the table.

"They think we're tame, huh? Tame like the cows and pigs and chickens they cram into tiny sheds so tight that they can't even turn around? Tame like the dogs they beat into docile dolts instead of wild, wonderful, free creatures? Tame like the fat-bottomed little plump farm wives who keep clogging their family's arteries with saturated fat from their animal carcasses? Well, we'll show them tame!"

"Darn right we will," shouted one of the young men, the one with tattoos and piercings."What should we do?" he asked, as if on cue.

"You'll do what I tell you, when I tell you," he glared at the young men as they lowered their eyes to break his stare. Finally, Pinckney collected himself like a windstorm's brief lull.

"First things first." he said, stationary again behind the podium. "You all trust me, right? You all know that our cause is just?" A few heads nodded. "Are you the kind of people who just let this stuff go on? I'm not. You know that. You wouldn't be here if that's the kind of people you were. But let's target our passion to the right places at the right time. The election is only three weeks away, and we've got to pass Proposal One. That's Job One. What do the polls say?"

"We're way behind," said one of two ladies with a rat dog in her lap. "I don't see how we can win when we get this kind of negative press all the time."

"And whose fault is that negative press?" snapped Pinckney. "Maybe we'd better take care of some of these reporters first, make them see things the right way. But I would ever condone violence at this time." He winked at the two young men.

"I happen to know West hangs out at the Pump House," said the young man dressed in tattoos, black and leather.

"Yeah," said the clean-shaven young man with short hair. "I've seen him eating burgers and other rotting flesh in there. We could take him out no problem."

"I didn't hear you say that," Pinckney said, once again calm, but he smiled. "Consider this. He's just the symptom, a mere mouthpiece for the slavers. No, we've got to go to the source if we want to change the world. And in fact, a means of getting to the source is already in motion. But, again, first things first. We can win this election. Everything needs to be on the up-and-up so no one can accuse me—er, us—of not trying to go through proper channels. Let's be rational, go through the proper bureaucracy. We have nearly three whole weeks to get the young people to vote, and I think they might just put us over the top. I'll work the influencers within the school community, you folks work the rest of town. It might be helpful if you all would show up at the Jovial City Council meeting next week. I intend to deliver a rousing polemic on logic, and a large crowd of supporters might sway some opinions, unless this West character continues his wrong thinking and terrible writing. Remember, the first rule in guerrilla warfare is to get the people on your side, and we can do that door-to-door."

Aspen leaned toward the cowboy.

"How can he so quickly calm down and appear rational when only moments before he was so angry?" she asked. "All these people seem to be so afraid of him. Why do they follow someone they fear?" The cowboy shrugged.

Two weeks before Fulton's court hearing,

Botsdorf arrived at the Dogues farm a little past noon. Mulder and Scully announced his arrival with barks and bounces.

He opened the light screen door and stepped aside as the two white dogs romped into the house ahead of him.

Jenn placed platters of sliced carrots, cucumbers, celery, broccoli and cauliflower on the table along with a pitcher of lemonade filled with ice.

"Dig in, Bots," she said. "Most of the vegetables came from Fulton's farm. Second crop already. You can't get veggies any fresher even if you took them out of your own garden. This was all harvested less than a half-hour ago. And the lemonade was made from lemons picked from my miniature tree."

"The one you had in college?"

"The same. I'm shocked that you remember that." She set out another platter of small sandwiches with lettuce and tomatoes surrounding mildly seasoned venison sausage patties.

Botsdorf nodded easily at the three farmers, poured himself some lemonade and sat down at the table.

"How you holding up, Fulton?"

"Ain't been much to it so far. Just going crazy waiting."

"Well, let me tell you what's going to happen. That'll help a little. But remember they're going to try to make an example out of you."

"An example of what?"

"They want to show the whole county that they're going to crack down on painting the statue. The prosecutor has been getting a lot of pressure from the police. The deputies are sick of scrubbing paint off old Alan's buns every summer, and they're bound and determined to see you get the worst punishment possible. That picture on the front page of the *World* didn't help much. It embarrassed the department. They're on some election-year high horse over there, saying only a pervert would be so interested in painting a statue's crotch. But don't worry. I don't think they have the guts to even try that one. There's no evidence of it, not even a suggestion, no matter what Channel 14 reported in their news teaser."

"So then what?" asked Coney. "That leaves them with a little graffiti charge. What else they got?"

"That depends on how we plead. For some reason I haven't figured out yet, they want to charge Fulton and his buddies with conspiracy to destroy public property on top of malicious destruction of property. If it was after the election and the gang prevention ordinance passed, I could see it. But right now it seems a little silly."

"Malicious destruction!" burst Coney. "What's malicious all of a sudden about painting underwear on old Alan? Kids have been doing it for generations. It's like painting 'Coney loves Jenn' on the water tower inside a big heart. It's expected! A fine, maybe, sure, I mean, there have to be consequences after all, but conspiracy? Wow."

Fulton gobbled up a handful of the cool, raw vegetables and munched, drumming the fingers of his other hand on the table.

"These charges don't even sound real," he said, finally. "This all has to have something to do with them passing that gang ordinance, if they even passed it."

"I still haven't had the chance to check that out," Botsdorf said. "Even if they did, it seems like a stretch to get it to trial. But they might be able to convince a judge that there was a conspiracy."

"What could I get for all this?" Fulton asked.

"The worst they can do is two years in jail."

"What?"

"Don't worry. They'll never get that through. These charges are all trumped up, like I said, to make an example of you. I'm going to do my best to get it down to a fine, maybe community service. They don't put people in jail for graffiti!" He smiled, drained his glass of lemonade and wiped the sweat off his brow.

"Can they even prove I did it? What if we just plead not guilty? Isn't the burden of proof on the prosecution?"

"Yes, but they have a witness—Sam—who already confessed that you were the ringleader of this little gang. That's how they'll put it, too. They'll use the word gang. It's part of the P.R. campaign to get Proposal Two passed. And I've already been told—off the record—that if we plead not guilty, they have a surprise witness. Some chickie in the bar who saw that you had paint on your arm that night. I think it's better just to plead to as low a charge as we can, say petty vandalism, pay a $250 fine and get it over with."

Fulton and Coney nodded their agreement.

"I thought that's what we'd have done to begin with," Fulton muttered. "Sure takes the court a long time to do anything."

Botsdorf thanked Jenn for the wonderful veggies and lemonade, and rose to leave. Mulder and Scully stayed on the cool kitchen floor until Coney and Fulton rose too. The last thing Botsdorf said as they parted was: "Try not to lose any sleep over this, Fulton. Unless they have some real surprises, this won't take long. Remember that all things work together for good for those who love the Lord."

As he drove out, Coney put his arm around Fulton's shoulders and squeezed like a vice.

"So, who's this chick you thought you could trust?"

Fulton shook his head. "I have no idea, man. How many women does a good-lookin' single guy talk to in a bar in a night?"

"Ah, the question that's eluded scientists for centuries," Coney said. "But how many does a guy who looks like *you* talk to?" Coney punched Fulton lightly on the shoulder. "I know why you don't want to tell me. It was Melissa Hawthorn, wasn't it?"

"I ain't sayin'."

"Well, then, get back to work. Those veggies don't harvest themselves. I've got to cut some more hay."

28

The Dogues' driveway was lined with mature oak and maple trees. Their leaves formed a canopy that darkened the driveway and cooled the asphalt as naturally as a watermelon in a rapids.

Garit drove the company Kia slowly through the tunnel, and smiled as two big white furry dogs greeted him, barking but nonthreatening. He remembered his unsuccessful attempt, at age nine or ten, to convince his parents that the family needed a dog.

"Dogs tie you down too much," his father Harold had said. "Life is about being free, son. Free to pick up and drive off to wine country on a weekend, just because you feel like it. The fewer the responsibilities, the better. You'll learn that someday."

Idiots. It was their lack of responsibility that got them where they were today.

Scully jogged alongside Garit's driver's side as he slowed and pulled up in front of a detached garage. Mulder trotted along the other side, and by the time Garit got out of the car, they both stood between him and the porch.

"You guys are just gorgeous," he said as he walked boldly toward them. They wagged their tails and panted lightly.

It was a big, beautiful dog, a St. Bernard, owned by a fan who somehow secured rare backstage passes, that started a major argument with Sandra. They were traveling somewhere in Kansas, following the Acrid Reins bus in Sandra's Chevy van. Truth be told, it was her dad's, and he had no idea what she was doing with it.

"You don't like dogs?" Garit asked, astonished. "How can you not like dogs?"

"I don't know," she answered. "They all just seem to try too hard, you know? They always have this happy attitude, but it just seems so fake to me, like a beauty pageant queen or something. I'm always worried that they'll turn on me, being descended from wolves and all. And don't even get me started on why humans choose to enslave them and then pretend they're part of their families."

"Well," Garit had said, "I admire dogs. There's something about a good looking, healthy, happy, well-trained dog that has always given me a belief in something. It's almost as if dogs possess something that some vague, mystical creator couldn't trust humans with. They almost make a case for God, a proof of some kind. I know this isn't logical, but dogs have always given me a sense that there's something out there that makes me free, yet I'm still under some kind of blanket of protection at the same time. It's their loyalty, their unconditional love, if animals can love like humans. It's like authority without pride. Like celebrity without conceit. Accomplishment without money. Just like that beautiful Saint that you were so afraid of."

"I wasn't afraid of him." Garit couldn't help but poke.

"You were terrified. Admit it. Now don't take this wrong, but you're just like a dog. You possess something that's beyond your looks. You'd be a beautiful dog, for sure. In a way, that Saint, and all good dogs, for that matter, know they're attractive, but it doesn't impress them the way it does people who were born with good looks and became conceited about it."

"You're saying I'm conceited?"

"I'm trying not to say that, because I don't think you're conceited. But you do follow Tony Finn around like a puppy." That had been the wrong thing to say.

As Garit stepped onto the porch and began scratching behind dog ears, he heard a voice call behind him. Coney walked up. He slapped the dust out of an old and tattered Detroit Tigers baseball cap against his leg. It was so worn that Garit could barely see the Olde English D.

"Hi, Garit," Coney said, reaching out to shake hands. "Welcome to our home."

"Good to see you again, Mr. Dogues."

"Call me Coney."

"Will do."

"Have a seat on the porch, here, Garit. I'm going to go hose off. I'll be right back."

Garit took a seat at a medium-sized picnic table under shade on the sprawling, wrap-around porch. He petted the dogs as Coney stripped off his shirt and walked to the side of the garage. He was solid across his broad shoulders, and showed a slight belly when he bent. He turned on a faucet and pulled out an ordinary garden hose from a coil attached to the garage. Bending at the waist, he put the hose over his head and rubbed his hair with his other hand. When done, he shook his head as a dog might, wiped his wet shoulders, upper back and chest with the shirt, which he'd turned inside out, and shut off the water. As he came back onto the porch, he snagged a clean shirt from a shelf attached to the deck near a window.

"Sorry about that. Just came off the chopper, and it got a little windy. Can I offer you something to drink? My wife Jenn makes the best fresh-squeezed lemonade in the world."

"That would really hit the spot."

Coney came back with lemonade on ice in two tall, slim glasses, handed one to Garit and sat down.

"How have you been, Garit? Your eye's all healed, I see. So how are you doing with the city council? Got it figured out yet?"

"Before that, I'm curious about one thing," Garit said. "You're a helicopter pilot? What, for crop dusting?"

Coney laughed. "No. Sorry I wasn't more clear. You're an urbanite, aren't you? How could you know? I was on the hay chopper."

Garit's stare explained his continuing ignorance.

"A hay chopper chops the alfalfa, in this case, into small pieces and blows it into a wagon, and we take that and put it in the silo." He turned and pointed to a large cement structure, where a hired hand was driving a very large tractor up and down a pile of green.

"Julio there is packing the haylage, getting the air pockets out of it so it will ferment without rotting."

"Then the cows eat it?" Garit asked.

"Yep."

"Thanks. Sorry for my ignorance. I've been given the farm beat now, and anything I can learn would be helpful."

"Anything you want to know, just ask," Coney said. "Glad to help."

"Well, let's see. The city council," Garit said. "I've been to five meetings now, and aside from that wacko Pinckney guy who complains about everything, not much has happened. Is that what you mean?"

"No, I just wondered if you've gotten comfortable yet. I know that even small-town government can get confusing, and it's tough to know the issues when you come in right in the middle like you did."

"That's for sure. And there are some really fascinating personalities interacting there. I mean, even you and Pinckney seem to have your— how can I say this?—Differences of opinion?"

Coney laughed heartily, throwing his head back as if if was still dripping from the hose. "Yep. We do have our differences, me and Pinkey. By the way, try not to call him Pinkey if you can help it. He doesn't like that. He's the kind of guy my dad used to say that it was a good thing Jesus loved him, because it was darn near impossible for anybody else."

Garit laughed. "That's off the record, of course," Coney quickly added.

"No problem. We haven't been on the record."

"I've heard it said that if you're talking to a reporter, you're always on the record."

"There were a few people in college who insisted on that, but it always seemed too all-consuming to me. You can't be a reporter twenty-four hours a day, and how do you establish trust if that's your attitude? But you're right about stepping in the middle of something. That's why I'm here. I've interviewed Mr. Deadfrick for his side of Prop. One, and I was told by several people that you're the best person to talk to for the side that wants a no vote."

"Well, they only say that because I just happen to be taking my turn as president of the Jovial Area Farmers Association, and our new store is at the center of the controversy," Coney said. "When it comes right down to it, there never would have been a Proposal One if we hadn't started that store."

"Alright," said Garit, sitting up a bit straighter. "This is what I've been waiting for. Background. That will help clear things up. I understand the connection between establishing a wholesome food commission and food sold in your store. Kind of like they're trying to set up a regulatory agency. But I guess I don't understand why it's needed. Your store, from what I understand, already sells mostly locally grown products. And I'm certain that it's certified by some sort of state inspector, so it's guaranteed not to poison you, right?"

Coney laughed. "Not if you ask Pinckney, But you're right. This law isn't needed. It's nothing more than a power grab that would add an extra layer of bureaucracy to the local food supply, and probably raise prices. You can quote me on that. We'd have to pay the food commissioners, after all. A percentage of sales. That's in the fine print that Pinkey and Deadfrick don't want anyone to read. And what do you call the tax they propose? I call it protection money. Only the farmers will pay it. Besides, if people really are worried about their food, they should have a little faith in the food safety laws already on the books. Either that or grow their own. And another thing I'm sure you've already figured out, if you've interviewed Deadfrick. There's a major sticking point in the proposal. The little word 'organic.' By prohibiting non-organically-grown food, you force people to buy at the organic food store or drive to Sventon. Eventually we will have organic products in our store too, but right now, before we increase organic acreage, most of the organics go to Deadfrick's store, on contract. And the two-hundred-mile provision? How you gonna get oranges in Michigan in January from less than 200 miles away?"

Garit smirked. "And organic oranges at that?"

"Exactly," smirked Coney right back at him.

"So let's say it passes," Garit started.

"I'd rather not," laughed Coney. "But go on,"

"How would it be enforced? And couldn't you farmers just start growing organically?"

Coney took a long draught of his lemonade.

"Yep," he replied at last, exhaling a throaty breath after drinking. "Yep, we could all go totally organic. But passing a law to force us to go organic is basically restraint of trade. It would never stand up in court. Never. Besides that, if we put all our eggs in one basket, one major pest outbreak could ruin the whole year's production."

"But are you against growing organically?"

"Not at all. Fulton has quite a bit of organic ground, and it does well, even though it's more work, more expense and more risk. But it doesn't make business sense for everybody. Take Noah Brenner, the guy who supplies all the milk for the farmers store. He's not organic, but he has himself a nice niche. He produces fantastic milk, but being organic or not means nothing. It's just a method of raising things. Noah is an amazing manager and an incessant clean freak. That's why his milk is so good. But guess what else? His costs are higher than everyone else's. Vegetable organic production costs are even higher than that. Sometimes the market pays for the extra cost, and sometimes it doesn't. Just like every other market for every other consumable product. Every method is a gamble. You find your niche and hope you can survive. One isn't better than another. Just different. And don't even get me started about environmental impact or carbon footprints or nutritional value, because there's no difference in nutrition from one system to the next. Worry about quality, not a method of production. The greenies don't seem to understand that organic methods increase carbon compared to other ways of doing things. And if this law passes, it would be like banning Charolais beef and allowing only Angus. It's just a breed. No significant difference if the two animals were raised on the same rations in the same conditions."

Garit wanted to ask what those two breed words meant, but decided to keep on subject.

"Then why do people like Pinckney and Deadfrick seem so convinced that everything but organics is going to kill us?"

"Well, Garit, you have to understand a few things about those two, off the record. Pinckney isn't just the passionate vegan he plays in public. He's an animal rights wacko, er, activist. Not only that, he's on the edge of something that he doesn't even understand. He's becoming blinded by his own passion and his own visions of grandeur. He came here from San Francisco, that bastion of common sense, for reasons he's never told anybody. Rumor is that he was involved in some HSUS sex scandal years ago. He always went back there during summer break, up until a few years ago. But that allegation has never been confirmed. The way he acts makes me think he's trying to prove something to the animal rights muckity-mucks out there. His mission in this vote is to get a foot in the door to controlling the food supply. If he can do that, he thinks eventually he can ban meat from menus in the whole county. If he can do that, he'll be the hero of the animal rights radicals. He believes a man has no more value than a rat or an ant. And as for Deadfrick, he just wants to control everything, and he's ruthless. Be careful of him."

"From what I've seen," said Garit, "that's probably good advice. And you're the third person to warn me about him."

"Take that advice to heart, Garit. I hate to cut down anyone personally, but I'd have it on my conscience if I didn't tell you straight up. You cannot trust either of those two."

Mulder got up from his post on the lawn and came to the porch. He laid his head on Coney's lap.

"Those are the two most gorgeous dogs I've ever seen in my life," Garit said. "What are their names?"

"This is Mulder, and that one is Scully."

"Very unusual names," Garit said. "How did you come up with them?"

"You've obviously never seen the X-files," Coney said.

"Never heard of them."

"Not them. It. A TV show. About aliens and stuff. The two FBI agents who were the main characters were Mulder, the man, and Scully, the woman."

"Must be you were a big fan."

Me and Jenn both. Jenn's my wife."

"Well, I can't think of anything more to ask about this," Garit said. "Seems pretty black and white. Not much middle ground in this proposal."

"What about you, Garit? What's your story? Where you from?"

"Illinois. Decatur."

"Really?" Everyone said you're from Ohio. What else? Got any family?"

A lump began to form in Garit's throat, and for the first time since he arrived in Jovial, he felt his guard dropping.

"Well, I think Fulton and I have something in common," he said. "I heard that his parents were killed. So were mine."

"Yep," replied Coney. "My sister and her husband were on a motorcycle trip out West. Killed in a head-on collision. Oddly reminiscent of my own parents, killed in a train accident many years ago."

Garit looked at Coney as he felt the tears that seemed so odd, so absent of the rage that always seemed to accompany his memories of his idiot parents.

"How long has it been?" Garit asked.

"My parents?" 15 years this year," Coney said. "My sister was only about two years ago. How about yours?"

"Nearly four months, now," Garit said, regaining his composure.

"Emotions still pretty raw," Coney said, thoughtfully. "If you ever want to talk, just come over. Jenn's parents were killed too, but it's been twenty years for her. But we all understand what you're going through. It helps to know someone has been through the same thing you have."

"My parents weren't the victim of an accident, though," Garit said, then stopped himself. "They were victims of their own attitudes."

"Well, If you need anything, just call me," Coney said, and gave him his business card with his cell phone number, e-mail address and website. "The subject matter doesn't make a bit of difference, Garit. We can talk about newspaper stories or Jovial or your parents. We'd like to be able to help you. Fulton, too. I have a feeling you and he made a connection. You're both about the same age, and you both lost your parents. You can help each other. You should help each other. And you know what? Because you're new in town, I'll have Jenn cook up a nice dinner for you sometime soon. We'll have a regular party. You and Fulton can reminisce about your time together in the slammer."

"Sounds good," grinned Garit, forcing it. He patted Mulder on his rump as he rose to leave.

"Thanks for making me feel so welcome," he said. "It's been kind of a tough adjustment for me here so far, you know, being arrested and beat up and all. Which reminds me. No one will tell me how Deputy Schoen gets away with all the stuff he pulls. Will you? Off the record."

"Not much to say," Coney said. "He's just a bully, and the Chief lets him get away with it. And no one dares file suit, because, well, I don't know why, other than knowing that in a town this size, the police can be playground bullies all they want, and they can make life miserable for anybody. Ask Botsdorf if you see him."

"I will. He sure got me out of jail fast."

"What about the charges?"

"They were dropped. Even faster."

"He's a good lawyer. And a good man," Coney said. "We're blessed to have him on our side."

29

Garit weaved his way among a murmuring pride of milling people eating free cookies and drinking free coffee or water. It was by far the largest crowd he'd ever seen at a city council meeting. Fourteen maybe fifteen people in all, besides the council members.

He thought about his failed attempt to be a running back in high school as he dodged and jibed toward the front of the City Council meeting room. He sat next to Coney.

"What's going on?" Garit asked. "Something big on the agenda?"

"Not that I'm aware of," Coney said. Garit looked around the room.

"Hey Coney," he said, nudging the farmer gently. "See that girl over there?" He pointed, but kept his arm close to his abdomen. "The blonde with the big hips. Do you know who she is?"

"Can't say I do," Coney replied. "Got a little thing for her, Garit?" he smiled.

"Naw, I just think I've seen her before, or she reminds me of someone. Was she at the store's grand opening?"

"Who can say?" Coney replied. "There were a lot of people there that day, a lot of them newer people from the Turner Lake housing development. But most of the attention was on you and Fulton, you glory hogs." He nudged Garit playfully with an elbow to the ribs.

Mayor Benz banged his gavel and commanded the throng to settle and stand for the Pledge of Allegiance. Then he told them to sit, which they did, loudly.

"Since I know Mr. Pinckney would be offended, I move that we dispense with the prayer tonight," a councilman said.

"We have a motion," Benz said. "Second?" There was none.

"Motion failed," Benz said. "Sam, would you give the invocation?"

As Councilman Richardson began his prayer, Pinckney began coughing loudly, drowning out the invocation. A few other coughers joined in, but Richardson plowed through. When he said "amen," the coughing miraculously ceased.

The clerk read minutes from the last meeting, and the council went through some minor procedural matters before it moved to the obligatory public comments period.

Dan Pinckney stepped to the microphone, dressed in cutoff jeans, sandals and a 'Meat is Murder' T-shirt, and lowered the mic to his level.

"Members of the Jovial City Council, I come before you tonight with yet another plea that has persistently fallen on deaf ears. Maybe I should have made those pleas demands, but I'm a peaceful man. I've been a pacifist since my college days at Berkeley, where I learned the power of community action. But tonight? Tonight this council cannot lean on your special interests and cater to your biases. Because tonight? Tonight the supporters of right and morality and compassion are here, and if you turn a deaf ear and blind eye to me yet again, you cannot quench their collective voice. We—" he swooped his arm outward toward his supporters–"We are the members of the Jovialites Advocating Animal Rights, or JAAR, a group of right-minded people who hold the upper moral ground in the fight for Proposition One!" The crowd erupted in a surprisingly brief cheer, like a false start at a swimming meet.

"But JAAR has been given a new, unexpected mission," he said softly into the microphone. "Tonight, we are a group that has been pulled into the fight against the immoral actions of one of the Farmers Own Store owners." A low murmur ran across the audience. Mayor Benz leaned forward.

"I submit to you—" Pinckney's emotional voice was building— "that in light of the evidence of moral corruption on the part of Fulton Gray, a co-owner of the carcass shop, that the Farmers Own Store be immediately shut down. And not only for the obvious health concerns. His lewd actions are an affront to the values we hold dear here. Values of family and tolerance and values. Let's not wait for Proposal One to pass." His supporters put up a medium-volume cheer at that. "Let's force these immoral factory farmers out of business before someone else gets hurt!" Pinckney shouted over their cacophony. Then came the bigger roar.

"My, don't self-interests speak loudly. And just who has been hurt here, Dan?" Asked Mayor Benz when silence was regained by his gavel. "I know you don't like competition, being a socialist. What are you afraid of? Afraid you can't compete? Well, you're in mainstream America now, a country that is what it is because of competition. That's historical fact, even though I know you don't like teaching history in your schools."

"History is fine, but not your white supremacist history," Pinckney retorted.

"If you were really a proponent of the people, you'd want to do what's right for them, right, Dan?" Benz said. "Competition lowers prices, and we've already seen that since the Farmers Own Store opened only a few weeks ago. How is that bad for the people? Or do you simply want to keep the grocery monopoly you've enjoyed for the last ten years?"

"This entire community's health has been irreparably damaged by the introduction of factory farm food into Jovial," Pinckney retorted. "Any time the animals in a society suffer, it shows that society itself has lost its way. That's from the Bible."

"That's not in the Bible at all," Benz said. "But I suppose you're going to tell us all over again just how the animals are suffering?"

"Open your eyes, Mayor. They're crammed into little sheds, ripped away from their mothers right after birth, the very time babies need to connect with their mothers. They're forced under threat of violence to give up their milk into a scary-looking machine. Some of these so-called farmers even have robot milkers. That's proof they're nothing more than factories. Then these poor animals—disposable widgets to be used up and thrown away—are force-fed meager rations and drugs —just enough to keep them alive for the sake of profits, the dirtiest word in the English language—all the while being denied their right to enjoy the sunshine and the green grass under their feet." The crowd murmured its approval.

Benz banged his gavel and glared to keep the nascent uproar in check.

"Look, Dan," he began. "We've been through all this before, you and me, both publicly and privately. We'll never agree on this. And from what I'm hearing tonight, you still haven't taken my advice and gone out to visit one of these so-called factory farms. Because if you had, you'd know just how far off-base your descriptions really are. You're the superintendent of schools, for crying out loud. You'd think you'd want to set a good example of rational, critical thinking instead of jumping to conclusions without knowing the facts. Now get to the point."

Pinckney stared at Benz, but the mayor had his head down, unknowing. The silence was as uncomfortable as the little sweater-laden dogs held tightly by two of the older women in the crowd.

"My point is, Mayor, that until this council shuts down the Farmers Own Store, my followers—er—my fellow warriors in the just cause of animal rights—will be there day and night, protesting and disrupting business. And we'll take our cause to the people of Jovial by ringing their doorbells and making sure they get to the polls and vote to approve the good food commission, a commission that is sorely needed during this time of unhealthy so-called food that's dragging all but the true vegans down the path of disease and death and, yes, moral corruption." The crowd of followers cheered again. "I represent the school here, the children, the future of Jovial's society. How can I stand by and let crimes go unpunished? I will not!" He banged his hand on the small podium, and his pace frenzied. "Doesn't it bother you that one of the carcass store's owners is guilty of lewd behavior—criminal sexual conduct— toward our town founder, the revered Alan Jovial?"

"Tell it, brother!" someone shouted. Another answered: "Amen!"

"We must stand for what's right, and we will be heard!" Pinckney said when Mayor Benz slammed his gavel.

"Yadda, yadda, yadda," Benz said. "This is all old stuff, Dan. We've all heard it before. There is no evidence of your claims. You'd know that if you'd just open your mind a little. And making unfounded accusations against an individual who has not yet even been charged with a crime is proof positive that your mind is closed. You won't ever let yourself be confused by the facts, will you, Dan?"

"It's you so-called Christians—hypocrites—who have closed minds!" Pinckney shouted. "You think your Lilly-white manifest destiny gives you license to brutalize innocent animals. Just be forewarned that this group that represents the majority of the right-thinking people in this town is prepared to take action. And we will take whatever action is necessary to rid this town of brutality and poisoned food!"

"Once again, we're getting nowhere. Let's move on!" The Mayor said, banging his gavel.

Pinckney stared at the mayor but could not stare him down. So he turned to walk down the center aisle. He raised his fist high in the air and walked out, his followers applauding and filing out behind him. Garit took a few pictures of their backsides.

"Meat is murder!" they chanted in unison as they walked out.

30

The room in the Jovial County District
Court was modern, with sparse vestiges of opulence which seemed
to apologize for the courthouse's old, ornate exterior. Outside the
courtroom, in a long hall that smelled of disinfectant, was an unadorned
folding table, at which sat a lone, frowning, obese middle-aged woman
with headphones on, speaking into a black, foam-covered microphone.
A banner taped to the outer edge of the table hung down to hide her
legs. It said, in letters made to resemble flames, that she worked for
WJCR, and under the call letters was emblazoned: "Jovial County
Rocks."

As Garit walked past, the girl removed her headphones and seemed
bored.

"How 'bout playing a little Acrid Reins?" He asked. She smiled, or
at least it appeared to be a smile. It was hard to tell, because her face
seemed to be in a permanent frown.

Garit had hoped he'd be assigned to cover this trial, or hearing, or
whatever it was. Now he hoped he still had a job when the day was done.
Wally had called him into his office that morning.

"West, you're going to cover that vandals trial," he said. "I think
there's a big story there, so I want you to keep an eye on things, and
be sure you don't screw everything up. There could be a lot at stake for
this town in that trial."

"You sound like you expect me to screw up. Like you screwed up the sales department?" Wally glared. "I didn't screw up anything," he snarled.

"Two salespeople quit on the same day?" Sounds like something's screwed up."

"You got your check," Wally replied, surly.

"Yeah, but you still owe me two," Garit said. "How long can you keep going with page counts down so far?"

"Times are tough, boy. Are you trying to tell me about business? What does a punk like you know?"

"I know that the *Sventon Sasser* seems to be doing OK, but you can't pay your staff."

"Just let me handle the business, boy. You were hired for one thing only. So just shut up and do your job," Wally replied. "Hearing starts at ten."

Garit took a seat at the back of the courtroom. Judge Eric Meade, a square-headed man who Garit thought must have been a marine at some point in his life, walked in from a door behind the bench and took his seat.

Suddenly, from a side door, appeared Botsdorf, who walked over and stood before the judge with Fulton Gray, dressed in a well-fitting black suit, white shirt and conservative dark green tie.

Garit pulled out a reporter's notepad and flipped a switch on his small digital recorder just as Judge Meade asked Botsdorf to tell his story.

"Story, your honor?"

"Yes, Bots, your client's story. I can't ask the defendant directly, since this is a hearing and not a trial, so I'm asking you for the real scoop. Why are you here?" Meade stared down at Fulton over flat glasses perched on the end of his nose.

"Your honor," interrupted a whiny voice. A bone-thin, hollow-cheeked attorney rose quickly, almost jumping from his seat, and introduced himself.

"Stewart Corrunna for the people, your honor. If it please the court, this is highly unusual. This boy should be instructed to enter a plea at this time, not be coddled by a court with obvious conflicts of interest with Mr. Botsdorf."

"I'll handle the instructions in my courtroom, Mr. Corrunna," said the judge.

"Your honor, studies have proven a correlation between deviant behavior and lurid interest in certain body parts with future anti-social behavior."

"Save it for a trial, if I don't throw the whole mess out before it gets that far," the judge growled. "This is a cause hearing, nothing more. Bailiff, read the charges."

A small, stout, uniformed man with a sidearm that was pushed almost horizontal by his rolls of side fat, stood.

"The people of the city of Jovial and Jovial County vs. Fulton Gray, a citizen," he began. "Mr. Fulton Gray is charged with one count each of destruction of city property, conspiracy to destroy city property, criminal sexual conduct, gang activity and conspiracy to engage in gang-related activity."

"Gang activity!" Shouted Botsdorf, rising gracefully and theatrically from his chair. "CSC? Where did that come from? Your honor, I was not informed that these charges would be so onerous. I should have been informed of these malicious and outrageous accusations, and I wasn't. This constitutes a breach of ethics at the least, and I demand that they be thrown out immediately. Gangs! In Jovial? You have to be joking, Stew."

"Gang activity is no laughing matter," Corrunna replied, snottily.

"Since these are obviously fabricated charges, and since the prosecution decided to illegally keep them hidden and secret from the defense, I'll have to advise my client to remain silent against these ridiculous charges, your honor," Botsdorf said. "Mr. Gray was arrested based on the coerced confession of a single companion who had water withheld from him for most of two days, obviously with the consent of Mr. Corrunna and the entire prosecutor's office. That makes them no better than torturers. What none of them seems to understand is that the arrest of Mr. Gray was made based on allegations of vandalism of city property. I know you know that, your honor. You signed the arrest warrant. And then there's this sex charge! Again, the prosecution withheld that intention from me, and it's absolutely without basis, and absurdly ridiculous! How a sex crime was fabricated at this late date is beyond all reasoning, and undoubtedly a ploy to get more publicity for the case. And gang activity is simply preposterous."

"Your honor," whined Corrunna, "Using spray paint in an act of vandalism is the very definition of gang activity as cited in City Code ten-dash-seventeen. This was clearly premeditated. Mr. Gray is a danger to society as surely as if he'd been a drunk driver or a drug kingpin."

Botsdorf rolled his head dramatically. "That's the silliest thread of logic I've ever heard," he cried. "And don't you dare attach the word drug to the lies about gangs, Stew. Stop trying to add subliminal remarks meant to sway a judge. Mr. Meade has already seen through it."

Botsdorf turned back to the judge. "Mr. Gray is accused of painting underwear on a statue, your honor, a childish prank, and nothing more. And it's in keeping with a tradition that goes back nearly eighty years in this town. And the fact that he's alleged to have produced a stencil, if true, is to be commended, not condemned. If anything, he took extra precautions not to damage any more property than he is alleged to have damaged. And, your honor, you must admit that this long-standing joke about Jovial's history and government should be considered a free speech issue, and as such, a protected right."

"That's ridiculous," said Corrunna, jumping to his feet, exposing a thick vein in his skinny neck. "This is vandalism and conspiracy at the very least, your honor. Free speech? The defense is grasping at straws. Besides that, we have a witness that will attest to the CSC."

"Again, your honor, this is the first I've been informed of this," Botsdorf said. "Who is this witness and what do you allege?"

"We have a young lady that will testify that she saw paint smeared on Mr. Gray's arm the very night in question, when he engaged in conspiracy to engage in gang activity and destroy city property. To get a paint smear on his arm, this man would have had to have reached between the legs of the statue of Alan Jovial in order to apply the stencil that the police will produce at trial as Exhibit One, and that proves a lurid ongoing interest in a male body part, a certain precursor to sexual crimes. CSC!"

The judge frowned and sighed.

"You're both trying the patience of this court," he said, then leaned forward over the bench. "Mr. Corrunna, it's apparent to me that you've fabricated at least a few charges here, and now you've messed up my chance to hear what really happened in a setting less formal than a trial." He paused and glared at Corrunna.

"Mr. Corrunna, I will allow this to go to trial only on gang activity and vandalism charges, because after reading the briefs, it's obvious to me that the criminal sexual conduct allegations are unwarranted, if not blatantly contrived by your office in order to sensationalize this case. Further, I warn your office not to invent things like this ever again in the future. Are you willing to drop them?"

"Yes, your honor," Corrunna said sheepishly.

"And Mr. Botsdorf, are you willing to take this to trial?

"Your honor, I have pleaded with the prosecutor's office several times before to reduce these charges to a simple misdemeanor and stop wasting the court's time, but Stew has refused. In fact, I believe Mr. Corrunna's failure to inform me of the charges should earn him a reprimand."

"Noted," said the judge. "Mr. Corrunna, would you accept a plea deal and get this off my docket?"

"No your honor. The city believes it has a strong case that demands prosecution and wishes to go to trial on all charges. After all, gang activity may start with vandalism, but it leads to drugs and violence."

"Very well," said the judge, turning to look at Botsdorf. " I will not allow the CSC charges, but will go to trial on the rest. I urge you to make your defense carefully, because these are serious charges."

"Yes, your honor. But your honor? Seriously. Gang activity? Where did this come from?"

"Dispute it at trial, Mr. Botsdorf," the judge said. "Hearing adjourned. Mr. Gray, you're released on your own recognizance. Trial will be scheduled." Before either of the attorneys could object, the judge banged his gavel and called for his next case.

31

Garit walked out of the court room, past the radio worker he'd passed coming in.

"Great timing," she said, looking Garit up and down carefully as if he were a package of burger with a hole in the packaging. He'd experienced the look before. "The studio's playing your request!" she turned up a speaker on her table. *'It's All the Same'* was playing.

"I was kidding, Garit replied. "Who wants to hear that overplayed one-hit-wonder?"

"It's all they let us play," she said. "Acrid Reins has other stuff that's pretty good. And Tony Finn! Ooh-La-la!"

"Huh!" Garit grunted. If these people only knew.

"How is it that I can see it so clearly, and you can't?" He'd asked Sandra one night, soon before it all ended.

"How can you say they're shallow?" she asked, argumentatively. "That's not how you used to think! This band is brilliant. Look how they poke holes in society's hypocrisy!"

"Bull!" Garit argued. "Can't you see it's all been done before? 'Ooh. Look at us, the way we press the edge of scandal,'" he mocked. "It's all just shock value. Let's refer to the devil and God as if they were the same thing. Let's just confuse people. Let's never offer a solution. Let's never think about consequences. It's all the same as a million other bands."

"Do you see what you're saying?" Sandra said. "Listen to yourself. You use the title of their biggest hit, *'It's All the Same'* to tell me it has no value? It's obviously stuck in your thick head!"

"I'm not like those sheep who committed suicide, Sandra. Seventeen Acrid Reins fans in the United States during the forty-three days the song was number one on the charts. How's that helping anyone live their life? How's that helping people think?"

"It's not about normal life," Sandra sighed. "It's about going beyond normal. Abnormal is good. No one can help you do it. It's within yourself. You just don't understand."

"No, *you* don't! What do you think? That all these blind followers in every city are trying to improve themselves by digging into the minds of musicians? No, they're just here for the party, for what they can get for themselves. You think there's inherent value in Tony Finn's head just because he got lucky with a catchy tune and struck it rich? I don't think so. It's time to face the fact that there's no inherent value at all in some people, no matter how much money they have. And most of the time, it isn't worth the time to try to dig it out or assume otherwise. Sometimes it's easier just to let empty heads be empty."

"Are you calling me empty-headed?"

Garit walked away and went back on the tour bus. He picked up the only reading material there, a *Rolling Stone* magazine with his cover story from a couple months before. He slumped into a cushioned seat, but it offered little rest.

Four months before, he'd thought—convinced by Sandra—that it was the only print publication in existence that didn't bend to the government or corporate America, the very institutions that bred society's shallowness. But it couldn't hold him anymore, even after his cover story had gotten major kudos. He had been on the verge of becoming a star in the entertainment world. The story got him invitations to drug parties and other various and licentious events, but each one was the same as the one before. Vapid. Different people, no difference in attitude. No depth anywhere, no purpose, no end goal. Not even a thought about goals unless it was better-quality highs. Only he seemed to realize that rock stars riding their temporary wave of fame could offer the highest-quality substances and flesh, but it wouldn't last all that long.

He was tossing his copy to the floor as Sandra followed him into the bus.

"You're not empty-headed, you're just not digging deep enough," he started. "It's all drivel, Sandra. Have you ever really talked to Finn? Who ever decided that a life where you just get stoned all day and never have to dive into the deep end of anything is the key to happiness? Shallowness is replacing depth in this society like a plastic bag, stretched thin and long until it's at the breaking point, and will never be useful for anything again. And we're just a part of that shallowness. We think we're above it all, promoting young, angry airheads whose only depth is pointing out the world's hypocrisies? We're nothing more than bandwagon jumpers. It's been done to death! Do they ever offer any solutions? Do they ever take us beyond the accusations? Oh forgive me, I forgot. Their solution is easy. Get high, get laid, get drunk, get shallower. Serve yourself because no one else will."

Sandra sighed and shrugged and tapped out a long line of cocaine from a pill bottle onto a small, round mirror on the bus table. She snorted it, half into each nostril. She closed her eyes for a long moment, then blinked them open.

"Want some?" she asked.

"No thanks." Garit went back to Sandra's dad's van and crawled inside his pungent sleeping bag.

As Garit walked back to the *World* office, a pickup truck pulled up to the curb and stopped beside him.

"Garit!" It was Coney, from the pickup's driver's seat, leaning over Fulton in the passenger seat. Garit had already tossed his suit coat aside, and the tie hung loosely mid-chest. Can you make it tonight? We're going to have a big dinner and drink a few beers!" Garit stabilized himself. "Sure. I'll be there!"

"About seven or so," said Fulton.

"What's to celebrate?" Garit asked.

"It's the little things," Fulton replied, grinning. "I'm not in jail, we have hired help doing the milking in the morning, God's alive and it's Friday night in the summer. Need any other reasons?"

When Garit drove into the tunnel of trees lining the the Dogues's farm driveway, he looked through beginning shadows toward large hardwood trees in the distance. The place looked so much different, so much more peaceful than it did when he interviewed Coney. He felt as if his eyes had been opened as he saw young cattle grazing lazily on wide, rolling hills of green.

The driveway emerged from the trees into an open, graveled area that held diesel and gasoline pumps on metal stilts of angle iron; and an old well under a lattice-designed, well-maintained, working windmill. Behind them was a single, traditional red barn with the top parts of three silos rising behind them, two cement stave silos of equal height and one taller blue silo. Beside them was a bunker silo, nearly overflowing with green stuff that Garit now knew as haylage. Flanking the red barn were two longer, pole-type barns. The longer one was interrupted by another well-kept, red wooden shed, the calf barn and hospital barn combined. The shorter barn was half-concealed by a white block building nearer the center of the pole barns, the milking parlor. Two pickup trucks were parked in front of the parlor.

Coney appeared in his Power Wagon from behind the barns, dust following him, and parked his truck under a tree by the garage. Garit saw Fulton get out and run off toward the parlor. "I'll see if Dutch needs any help finishing up," he hollered. "Take the night off, Coney." One of the beautiful pure white dogs bounced from somewhere to catch up to Fulton and nuzzled his hand, to which Fulton responded by pushing her gently, starting a brief, playful tussle.

"You should do the morning milking too, you know, just because you've been such a bother," Coney called behind him. At his voice, the other pure white dog ambled up, and Coney rubbed him behind the ears. Sufficiently scratched, the dog walked to Garit as he stepped out of his Jeep, and he smiled broadly as Mulder wagged his tail and leaned into his scratches.

"What are their names again?" Garit asked.

"The one chasing Fulton is Scully, and this is Mulder," Coney instructed."C'mon in and meet the Missus."

Through a light screen door and onto the porch came a striking woman, large-framed but fit, proportioned precisely and pleasantly for a middle-aged woman. She was dressed in jeans cut off and frayed just above the knee and a loose-fitting t-shirt that displayed a cartoon fish and the words: Sventon Carp Festival. She wore the clothes elegantly, as if her indifference to fashion would never go out of style.

She wiped her hands with a towel. Her blonde-orange hair was tied in a ponytail, and she offered her hand as Coney introduced them.

"Jenn, this is Garit," he said. "Garit, my wife, the lovely and talented Jennifer."

"It's just Jenn," she said. Her voice was like a singing sword, pleasing but edgy, and her blue eyes seemed to throw off sparks as she spoke. The wrinkles around them were just deep enough to reveal unusually graceful aging and character, a thoughtfulness and depth of life that Garit hadn't noticed in anyone before.

Coney excused himself after bidding Garit to sit in a padded porch chair, worn but comfortable. He came back out holding a beer, and handed it to Garit.

"As promised," he said. "You just relax, Garit. I'm going to help finish milking."

The beer was ice cold, and Garit appreciated its temperature more than its taste.

"This is really good beer," he enthused, not knowing what else to say. "It's pleasant, but not too light. Kind of a mix between a low-calorie and something heavier, like a Heineken."

"Describe it to me," Jenn said.

"What? I don't know what you mean."

"You're a writer," Jenn said. "How would a professional writer describe this beer's taste?"

"I'm hardly a professional," Garit said. "I just got out of school less than a year ago. This is my first real job."

"But you're paid. You write for a living. Lots of people think they can write, but you're doing it. You're pursuing your gift, and that takes a certain level of commitment to your calling."

"I guess so," Garit replied. "I hadn't really thought of it that way before. I'm too busy with the trees to worry about the forest, I guess. I've only just gotten started, but so far Fulton's case is holding my attention. The election holds a certain mystery too. There's an awful lot to learn."

"I would imagine so," she said. "You've already been bruised and beaten by the police and arrested. I've heard that's a real badge of honor for a journalist."

"Again, I guess I never thought of it that way."

"Anyway, it's a far cry from my first few months on the farm. No excitement at all around here."

"You say that like it's bad?"

"No, I didn't mean it that way. A farm has it's own kind of excitement, and I guess there aren't too many people alive anymore who are cut out to do it, so we think of ourselves as a special breed, even if we're boring to most people. Most farmers won't admit it because they don't like to be prideful, but we're elite, chosen people, farmers. That's not pride, that's fact. We know who we are. Not that we're better than anyone, it's just that we're a pretty small minority these days. We're called to be farmers just like you were called to be a writer."

"How do you know if you're called to do something?" It was a question he'd never asked himself before.

"I don't know if I fully understand it myself," she said. "And I can't judge anyone else's motivations. But from what I've learned from life is that a calling is just something you can't get away from. It's not from anything inside you, either. Its from the outside. From God. It's like you aren't happy until you find it and follow it. And people who are doing what they're called to do show a certain passion that makes them stand out. I've seen your stories, Garit. Your features stand out. There's a real passion there."

"You may be right," Garit said. "I've always felt a little restless if I wasn't writing something. I've even been told I had a calling, but the way everyone else said it was too much like religion, you know? I've never heard a voice or anything like that tell me to write, so I never really understood what other people seemed to see in me. And I've been told, by a close friend back in Decatur, that I lacked passion when I was traveling around with the Acrid Reins. And to tell you the truth, I haven't felt much passion here so far. I'm just kind of existing, like I'm still in a fog."

"You followed the Acrid Reins?"

"Yep. I was their road publicist for almost six months. My first published story was about their rise to fame. Cover of the *Rolling Stone*."

"I'll spare you my flat singing voice, but I love the song. Dr. Hook, right? What made you leave?

"Lots of things." Garit hesitated, took a long slug of beer. Could he really trust this woman? A voice somewhere told him yes.

"There was a girl..."

"Now we're getting somewhere," Jenn cooed. "Were you in love or lust?"

A few weeks after they'd met, with Sandra as Garit's constant companion and lover, Acrid Reins spoke to Garit in the same kind of smoky, hazy, shoulder-to-shoulder way Sandra did their first night together.

"Doesn't Tony Finn, like, really capture the essence of what's wrong and corrupt with American society?" Sandra had asked Garit one cold, fateful night in a campus club. "How dare people—or should I say hypocrites—judge them by their look? It's just an image, like a trademark or something. People shouldn't judge by appearances anyway. Acrid Reins captures the emotion I can't express, you know? They're so deep! Their music just really speaks to me, you know? Especially when I'm stoned. Then I can really concentrate on the lyrics, you know? It's like they're exposing every bit of the hypocrisy in politics and culture and college and parents. I don't think anyone's ever had balls big enough to do that, you know?"

"Well, let's see," Garit said. "Let's start with the bands who had much bigger balls, starting way back in my parent's album collection. How about the Beatles, then Dylan..." She was impassioned and stoned and not listening, and she ended his thought process when she leaned over and kissed him.

The thought struck him now that she did that quite often, likely just to shut him up.

"Come with us, Garit," she'd said, holding her gaze intently in his eyes. "Come on tour with the band. I'll pay your way. Wouldn't you like to see the Southwest and get away from winter before it hits? I'll talk to Tony, and you can write promo pieces for upcoming concerts. C'mon, Garit. Christmas in Los Angeles? How can you turn that down?" She put her hand on his bicep, kissed his ear, then whispered into it, her hot breath reaching instantly into his crotch. "I'd really love you to go."

"Just let me go home this weekend and tell my parents," he sighed.

"Yippee!" She squealed and jumped from the table. "Oh, Garit, it's going to be the best time of your life! And the best part?" She pressed her arms around his neck from behind and whispered in his ear again. "We'll be together all the time."

"Lust," Garit told Jenn, admitting it to himself for the first time. "Mostly, though, I was sick of the band's lifestyle. After awhile, living on the road, doing the same stupid things day after day just got old."

"Well, dissatisfaction can be a good thing, Garit. A lot of people just live with it all the time. They fall into a pattern that becomes comfortable. It's like they lack the courage to change. It can't be easy to pack up and move into a place where you don't know anybody." She leaned forward. "Do you know how much courage it takes to do that?" She shook her head twice. "It's crazy. Very few people would even consider it. To just shift gears in mid-stream and leave everything behind? That's passion. That's a calling, whether you heard a voice or not. What did your parents think?"

"I'd rather talk about farming," Garit said. "I want to learn more about the farming conflict. You know, the myth and the fact. It's a fascinating industry, farming. Filled with fascinating characters. But they don't excite most people. You're right there. There's one thing exciting, at least to me. Here I sit, on a real farmer's porch. The thought of being here never crossed my mind, ever in my life. It's like I got an exclusive interview with the last of the Mohicans. I've never known any real farmers before." He paused reflectively. "But without farmers, what would life in America be like?" He asked Jenn.

"Am I being interviewed?" she asked.

"No, Jeez, no," Garit stammered. "I'm sorry if it feels that way. I meant, just to be here. Imagine the great story someone will have someday, interviewing the last farmer." Jenn smiled and tilted her head back, contemplating. "That's good," she said finally. "I don't want to be interviewed by a journalist tonight. I just want to have a pleasant evening with family and a new friend. I knew what you meant. But the words you used betrayed that passion you're not convinced you have. You think in terms of stories. You're called, man, plain as day."

"And you're called to be a farmer. That, unlike mine, is a huge calling. You have responsibilities to feed the whole country!"

"We can't be worried about the whole country," Jenn said. "Our first obligation is Jovial. We can feed the town well enough, at least during the growing season, and maybe a little beyond that with greenhouses and hydroponics and controlled atmosphere storage; but both Coney and I worry about what will happen if these animal rights folks and Greenies ever get their way."

"What's up with them anyway? They seem so angry all the time." He knew a little something about anger.

"My opinion is that it's just a reflection on their leaders," Jenn said. "They're like a football team that takes on the personality of their coach. I don't know the folks at the national level, but locally, Dan Pinckney isn't exactly a happy-go-lucky guy. Coney and he have had their run-ins over the years."

"What about?"

"About nearly everything. Every time Coney or any of the other farmers get anything accomplished, Dan wants to tear it apart. He's been against the store from the beginning, I don't know why. He's just against farming, I suppose."

"How can anyone be against farming? Doesn't he know where his food comes from?"

"I guess not. So few people do these days. Everyone takes it for granted. The grocery store is most people's closest connection to their food. That's one of the reasons Coney and all the farmers around here got together to build the new store. They cut out the middle man and keep a little more of their money. They thought they could use it as an opportunity to educate people about agriculture, too. Only time will tell if it works." She gazed toward the horizon, as if pausing to ponder her own words, then turned, smiling, back to Garit.

"I'll let you talk farming with Coney and Fulton," she said. "You're the new kid in town. Tell me about yourself. I want to hear more about your calling."

"I don't know any more than you," Garit said. "All I know is, writing is all I've ever wanted to do." Jenn looked at him as if there was something to see under his skin, and Garit was warmed by her stare.

"That's because God was calling you to it," she said. "Do you believe in God?"

Garit sighed deeply and took a long slug of his beer.

"You know, I've asked myself that question so many times I can't count them, especially since my parents died." Jenn looked into Garit's eyes, confused by their instantly guarded hue, as if they'd suddenly changed colors and gone cold. But she leaned in, encouraging him to continue.

"How long ago did they pass?" she asked.

"Pushing five months now. Sometimes I want to stop arguing with myself and say no, I can't believe in a god who would abandon me and kill my parents. They didn't do anything to anybody. And I was at a point when I needed parental guidance the most, you know?" He paused. His anger was building again, and perhaps he had, at long last, a way to vent it. But he wasn't ready. He pushed it back down.

"But still, sometimes I get mad at God, if he's real, and sometimes I rage and just have to throw something. But it's just some self-inherent human catharsis, you know? A way to sort things through in your own mind even when you didn't really want to. Especially if God isn't there. That's the only logical reason a god they say is love would allow these awful things to happen. And not just my situation. Look at all the wars and murders and rapes. No benevolent god would allow it, so a loving god must not exist. His existence just doesn't make any sense. But at the same time, I always seem to question myself. I could be wrong. Maybe that makes me an agnostic, I don't know."

"What did your parents teach you about God?" Jenn asked.

"My dad told me religion was a conspiracy to control society, and his opinion shaped most of mine to this point, I suppose. He quoted Marx—you know, the opiate of the people and all that? But I have an advantage if I ever want to reevaluate that opinion. I've stopped believing in anything my father ever said. He and my mom seemed to be always searching for something. And then, when they thought they'd finally found it, it was all a fraud. I just haven't had time yet to reevaluate my thoughts about God. He's not exactly my top priority right now." He paused, and Jenn left the silence alone. "I guess that's a mighty long way to say I don't know." he said, finally.

"I know how it is," Jenn replied. "I was unsure myself until I'd spent a couple years on the farm. Something about spring, about a calf being born, about the seasons changing and the skies opening up with rain just when a crop needs it—that's what convinced me. I think it's very difficult to be an atheist on a farm. There's too much consistency. What looks random to most people becomes clearly structured on a farm. That implies a plan, not just chance."

Garit stared toward the pasture, trying to hold back his emotion.

"So there's this big cosmic connection," he said, mockingly, as his eyes hardened. "Maybe you and me and all the other people who've wrestled with the deity question are part of one big restless spirit, and some spaceship will take us all home if we measure up and give some guru all our money. Don't take this the wrong way, Jenn," he said bitterly, "but I have a hard time right now believing in any religion. In fact, I have at this moment deep-seated hate for everything religious. Religion killed my parents. Not God, because he doesn't exist. It just doesn't make any sense that any kind of god is real. My old man's life— and death—convinced me of that."

"What was your dad like?" Jenn asked, gently.

"Oh, he was full of problems," Garit replied, softening a bit. "Excuse

me if I'm a little critical of him right now, but my eyes were opened a lot
in the last few weeks before I came to Jovial. My dad was too politically
correct all his life. He was too quick to compromise, and found it too
difficult to stand up for anything, even himself. A real man of extremes,
with no middle ground, but yet he compromised his ideals so much that
he was always in the middle."

"I guess I wouldn't understand that unless I'd met him."

"Yeah, maybe. Don't get me wrong, he played the rebel in college.
I heard the stories about sit-ins on campus and even some LSD use
along with lots of reefer. But even then, he'd been fooling himself. He
was letting himself be conformed to an expectation, and from what he
said, he hated that. But he let it happen. My dad never changed after
he left college. He hung around liberals because they were easy to find
in the state's social services department. Essentially, from that point
on, he never had to take a stand on anything. He just drifted around,
trying to make peace with all sides when peace is totally unattainable.
I've learned that already. How could he have grown to be almost sixty
and never learned it? My dad never had to personally take a child from
his inept mother in his job as a social worker. They had tough guys to
do that. He just pushed paper back and forth from the field agents to
the upper managers. And outside work, he was habitually lukewarm."
Garit paused.

"What else?" Jenn encouraged. Garit took a deep breath.

"He was an agnostic humanist with deference toward eastern
religion and European socialism, living in a Christian community."

"Wow. That sounded rehearsed," Jenn said, but it didn't seem
accusatory.

"It's a definition I've been working on, like the perfect nut graph,"
Garit said, smiling. "My old man, for all his wishy-washiness, never
could accept the religious practices of churchy people, even when they
were in the majority. He'd never even considered that there might be
someone other than government in control of things. He refused to
consider it. His mind closed down and turned to mush. He had no
foundations. He just drifted through life, thinking it was a random
time span that didn't matter much, and without a foundation, he floated
with every new philosophy that made him feel good or important or

confirmed, no matter how temporary it was. Randomness was the only thing he ever got right. Anyway, I will not follow his path. He was an idiot to fall for what he did. But there's one thing even more wrong. He dragged my mother along on his ridiculous journey through life without a compass or GPS map. And so far, my legacy is the same as theirs. I was never called to Jovial. I drifted here the same way my two idiot parents would have thirty years ago."

"No bitterness there, huh? It doesn't matter how you got here, hon," Jenn said, touching the back of Garit's hand gently. "Even a drifter has to drop anchor sometime, and you can drop it here if you want or if you need. Sooner or later you'll find that it's better to have that anchor than not."

Coney and Fulton were coming out of the barn. "Excuse me, will you? I've got to get our feast going. We're here to celebrate!"

She slipped into the house as Garit finished the last gulp of his beer.

"Let's knock back a few more of those Indians," said Coney as he bounded onto the porch. "Give me a hand, Garit." He led Garit into the garage and told him to grab a handle on a large galvanized steel tub filled with ice and beer. Indian Head beer. They carried it to the porch.

"How do you like it?"

"Pretty good. Never heard of it before."

"It's produced locally," he said. "Our farmer's association members grow some of the hops and barley and such, and we own stock in the brewery, so we kind of feel obligated to kill a few Indians from time to time."

Coney's warm grin told Garit he was unaware of the racism he'd just uttered.

"That's an interesting turn of a phrase," Garit said.

"How so?"

"Well," Garit laughed, "What you said made me flash back to my dad. He would have called you a racist—but not to your face—for saying 'kill a few Indians.' But then, he was a social worker, you know, sensitive to things like that. He would have sneered, maybe even coughed, at you.

It was part of his passive aggressiveness. But he never would have said anything. He'd just give the old stink eye and hope someone noticed that he was above such things."

"I take it you and your dad didn't get along?"

"Oh, that's not it," said Garit, who was happy to see Fulton striding with his graceful glide to the porch.

Coney tossed Fulton a beer, and they all popped their tops and sat in comfy lounge chairs, all facing the west woods and a long, clear, gorgeous nascent sunset. The two farmers smelled of cattle and milk and manure, but it wasn't a bad combination. Garit inhaled deeply, and the three silently watched the cattle graze.

"This beer is really good," Garit said, after a time. "Not only do you produce most of the food in Jovial, you have beer and wool and organic underwear. Is there anything around here the farmers aren't involved with?"

"Not much," said Fulton. "For a long time, the farmers even produced the animal hides for the jockstraps, but that was well before our time."

"Yours, maybe," said Coney. "When I was a little kid, my dad used to sell a few hides over there, but that was when the factory was making exotic underwear, before they went to specialize in jockstraps and boxer shorts. That's really what hurt their business. That and the toxins from the tannery. When the EPA was formed by Dick Nixon, one of its first real aggressive actions was right here in Jovial. They saw the chemicals the tannery was putting into the river and just about peed their pants."

"So what's in that big building north of town, then?"

"They use that as a warehouse for different businesses now," Coney said. "They have it divided up into offices, and there's a guy who makes his grandmother's jam out of one space, but nothing's really manufactured there anymore. On the other side, they still make their specialty—you pegged it—organic boxer shorts. Small market for gullible people, but they survive. Not like in the heyday of the underwear market. Jovial was at one time the underwear capitol of the upper Midwest. But these days, without a tax break renewal every few years, they'd be gone. They still directly employ about a hundred people, not to mention the ancillary services, you know, wool producers, truckers, waste haulers. So paying an extra ten bucks a year in taxes for them doesn't seem like a bad deal. That's why I'll vote yes on Proposal Three again."

"So what took them down besides the EPA?"

"Markets, mostly, and a bad business plan that didn't respond to its customers," said Coney.

"And one big fraud," said Fulton.

"You don't know that," said Coney.

"Yes, I do. I don't have any proof, if that's what you mean, but I'd bet a year's income that it was him who took the money and ran."

"Who are you talking about?" asked Garit.

As with one voice, the two said "Jim Deadfrick."

"That's enough swearing for one night," said Jenn through the screen door, grinning just enough to show she was incapable of carrying true animosity toward anyone. She placed four large whole potatoes, wrapped in foil, on the grill at the other end of the porch, and opened a beer before sitting closely next to Coney on the swinging lounge chair.

"I've met him," Garit said. "Something about him I just don't trust."

"Good instincts," Fulton said. "The jockstrap factory was probably one of his first large-scale scams. My mom used to say he was so crooked they'd have to screw him into the ground when he dies."

"So how did he ruin the underwear factory?"

"If we knew that, or if the police knew that, he'd be in jail," Coney said.

"Let's just say that mysterious fires and big insurance policies always seem to go along with businesses he's involved with," Fulton said. "He's even beat the EPA on a cleanup bill for the old tannery after he bought the back half. He's always been able to step waist-deep in manure and come out smelling like the first crocus of spring."

"Because the church bails him out." Jenn said.

"What does the church have to do with it?" asked Garit.

"He's the biggest, greatest, most church-going, most faithful, most pious, most pure-hearted Christian ever to walk this part of the earth. Just ask him," said Fulton.

The conversation continued, and soon, Jenn rose gracefully and disappeared into the house again, then came out with four thick steaks, and put them on the grill. She tended them carefully, and by the time the three men finished their beers, she announced that dinner was ready. She steered them into the house, where four place settings were at a huge round oak table with only three matching chairs. She sat at an oddball chair after she'd set out a wooden bowl of salad so fresh Garit didn't know what it was at first.

"All of the things you'll eat here tonight came from this farm and Fulton's," she said.

The three ate slowly, and Coney offered a post-meal prayer:

"Father," he said, "Thank you for filling us with your spirit and your gifts, and bless this fabulous food—and the cook—well beyond our feeble human expectations. And thank you for bringing us a new friend, Garit West. May his path lead him to your favor and glory. Amen." Jenn and Fulton repeated: "Amen."

"Well, Coney said. "We have beer to drink."

Garit and his friends settled back on the porch.

"So what do you think of Jovial so far?" Fulton asked.

"This has been my best evening since I got here," Garit said. "The salad was amazing. Better than any salad I ever had. I'd never had a salad make my mouth water before. The best. So was the milk, the butter for the rolls, the baked potatoes and the thick, moist steaks. Best I ever had, by far."

"Jenn's cooking has spoiled me for life, that's for sure," Coney said. "Wow," he exclaimed. "The peepers are really loud tonight. Must be a rain coming."

The group became silent, listening.

"That's what you call that noise? Peepers?" Garit said finally.

"What did you think they were?" Fulton asked.

"Guess I never really thought about it," he said. "Maybe I never even noticed."

"Well, now you know," Coney said.

"What a gorgeous night," Jenn said. "How about it, Garit? Anything here worth writing about?"

"I don't know about that, but you know, for the first time in a long time, I really feel at home," he said. "It's kind of odd, actually, but nice. I don't need to put on an act here, and I appreciate it. I don't have to play the journalist or the band publicist. I feel like I've known you people all my life. You've just really made me feel welcome."

"And you're welcome to stay and sleep on our sofa bed," Jenn said. "In fact, I insist."

"Oh, I can drive home," Garit said.

"Not after this next beer," she said as she handed him another. "Why take the chance? The cops around here look for any reason to pull someone over, especially with out-of-state plates."

"Well I guess you're right," Garit said, trying his best to appear resistant.

"Well, then, we can kill another Indian or two," said Coney.

Jenn excused herself, and the three men knocked back a few more beers.

"My life's taken a real turn here tonight," Garit said as the last of the beer drained into his stomach. "I want to thank you guys. Right now I have new friends who have the potential to be old friends."

"Glad you're not a mean drunk," Coney and Fulton laughed as they guided Garit onto the sofa bed, just feet away behind a screen door in the living room. Fulton walked to his house a stone's throw away, and Coney went up the stairs, carefully and silently.

As Garit settled in to sleep, one of the two pure white Great Pyrenees dogs—he thought it was Scully—jumped on his bed to sleep. He patted her on the rump and rolled over, and slept soundly until morning.

32

The deadline for the election story was
pressing hard on Garit, and he was struggling to find an objective source
to quote as balance to the rival sides.

"I think I know the facts, if you interpret the ballot language at
face value," he told Betty at the Jovial Public Library. "I've done more
research than this is probably worth, knowing Wally will probably hack
it to pieces."

"So what's your opinion?"

"I don't care about the underwear factory tax break, and neither does
anyone else, apparently," he answered. "Seems a given that it will pass.
Proposal Two, the gang ordinance, doesn't seem to be needed. I've never
seen any evidence of gang activity here, and neither has anyone else I've
talked to, even Chief Dulogski, although he made sure that our whole
conversation was off the record."

"What about Proposal One?"

"Seems like a scare tactic, but I don't understand why," he said. "Most
food-borne illnesses aren't even serious enough to be reported. And for
all the play these food scares get in the media, the number of people
who were made ill was insignificant, statistically. How many people
every day suffer a little discomfort after eating, but chalk it down to part
of life, part of the risks people take every day? I mean, isn't it obvious
that the benefits of food far outweigh the risks? Ninety-nine-point-nine

percent of the time. And—you'll love this, Betty—buried beneath the scare tactics, most food-borne illnesses occur because of poor sanitation at the home kitchen counter. It's the people's own fault! Those are the incidents that are rarely if ever reported. Must have something to do with admitting that humans make errors."

"Or that they lack someone to sue," Betty said.

"Exactly!" Garit agreed. "Overall, my research shows that the food supply in the United States is safer than anywhere in the world. Food costs less here than anywhere in the world. Lots less. A dozen apples for a couple, three bucks? That's mighty cheap eating, if you really think about it. So why all the fuss? What do the animal rights folks have to gain by these scare tactics? Why do vegans care what people eat? Why does everyone have to make mountains from all the little molehills that people step on every day?"

"The enviros and animal rightists have motives that are unclear at best and lies at worst," Betty said.

"And I've noticed they all seemed to have liberal leanings, which is even more confusing," Garit said. "My whole life, my dad told me being liberal was about letting people live the way they wanted. Tolerance. Acceptance. Those were the pillars of liberality. That's not how these folks act. These animal rights groups seem to want to control people's lives more than anything else, and I'm sorry, but that is not a liberal way of thinking. At least not the way my ultra-liberal parents brought me up. They won't even agree that there's any middle ground anywhere in the food debates, and no one seems to be looking for it." He paused, reflecting.

"I wish Aspen were here to tackle this," he said, finally.

"She's still stuck in your mind, huh?" Betty asked. "Got a little thing about her that you can't shake?"

Garit was weary, and his guard was down. He was tired of hiding things.

"I guess I do," he said. "I texted her a couple times, but no response. It would be nice to know what she's doing and who she's doing it with."

"There's only one way to find out," she said. "Go see her. No texts or emails. Get some flowers or something and go!"

"I'm not sure she even lives in the same apartment."

"Only one way to find out," Betty repeated. "Aspen is a good girl. Talented, pretty and determined."

"Don't you go making a play for her," Garit joked.

"I told you, I'm committed," she said.

"I'll consider it," he said. "First things first."

Garit wrote the story about Proposal One. No passion, no opinion. Facts came directly from the ballot language. He put in a few quotes from Deadfrick and Coney. It was short for such a complicated issue, but okay. He'd done his job.

He went to Aspen's apartment building. He didn't see her car in the parking lot, but he checked the address on the bank of mail boxes by the entry to the covered parking area. Her name was still there, so he went to her door.

As he knocked, he felt suddenly lonely. Maybe even lonelier than he felt driving to Jovial after having left everything in his old life behind except the Jeep and a bunch of pending bills. The family attorney would take care of that. Things in his old life were being handled. Even if they weren't, he had no control over any of it.

After a few minutes of knocking, he gave up and decided that his stomach flutter was the sub sandwich he'd eaten.

He stepped out the apartment building's front entrance door and noticed two young men, maybe a bit younger than him, coming up the front sidewalk. One was dressed all in black and had a few facial rings, ear rings and half-hidden tattoos. The other was more clean-cut, and wore a sport coat over a T-shirt with jeans. Garit looked at them and nodded as they passed, just to be friendly, when the clean-cut one called out derisively.

"Are you Garit West, the hack reporter?"

"I guess so," he said. He stopped and turned around as his stomach did belly flops.

The two moved close to Garit. The clean-cut one stood face to face with him, and the taller, black-clothed man put his arm around Garit's shoulder.

"What's up?" Garit asked, working the facade of nonchalance as fiercely as he knew. If anything, Garit was the taller of the three, and the tattooed guy was rather slightly built. He thought he could take them—one of them, at least—if it came to that.

"You're up," said the black-dressed one. "You're even the problem, I think. You seen a chick named Cindy around here?"

"No man, I don't know any chick named Cindy."

"You were up at her apartment, I think," said the clean-cut one.

"No, man, you got the wrong info."

"I don't think so. We watched you go to her door, dude."

"What, you got a crush on me?" He swatted away the tattooed one's arm. "You stalking me? Why would you care what door I knock on?"

"Because Cindy is one of us, and you been slammin' us in your newspaper."

"Who's us?"

"JAAR, dude."

"Never heard of her. Unless you mean Jar Jar Binks, and then you got the wrong movie." He liked this rebellious side of himself. Show no fear. That's the way movie heroes did it.

"Not her, dufus. Jovialites Advocating Animal Rights."

"Still never heard of you."

"Well, you're going to hear us now, jerk!" said the tattooed one, putting his arm around his shoulder again, but tighter this time. "You're going to give us some headlines, or else!" he spat.

"Wow, you're really threatening me? I don't know if I should be flattered or scared, dudes. I'll choose flattered. You've made my day! Come on, threaten me again, but let me get my recorder going first."

The tattooed man punched Garit in the stomach, hard enough to make him utter a woof and bend with the strike.

"We don't threaten, we act," said the clean-cut one. "And if we don't see some headlines about JAAR pretty soon—favorable headlines—you'll understand."

"And if I don't write about JARV?"

"Not JARV, smart-boy," said the well-dressed one, punching him sharply on the chest with an open palm, pushing him back upright.

JAAR. J-A-A-R. You best learn to respect it or you'll find yourself flat on your face on this sidewalk."

"And we'll keep kicking your behind until you get the message," said the tattooed one.

"I write news, not propaganda," Garit said, gasping. He hoped his bravado was counting for something here, because the splash in his stomach was now pounding hot adrenaline into his spine. "What have you done that's newsworthy aside from threatening a reporter? Maybe that's the real story of J – E – R- K!"

"Shut up," said the well-dressed one, smacking Garit's chest again, a little harder. "It's JAAR, and we'll make the news. You just better report it."

"That's my job," Garit said, hoping to cut off this conversation before he really did get beaten by these goons.

"And stay away from Cindy," said the clean-cut one. He motioned to the tattooed one, who released his grip on Garit. The two began to walk away.

"Who's Cindy?" called Garit as they moved toward a hopped-up pickup truck.

"Shut up," yelled the tattooed one, who took a step back toward Garit, but the clean-cut one stopped him.

Garit went back to the library, but Betty had left for the day. He went downstairs, telling the desk clerk he was doing more Yesteryears, but first he checked the Internet.

He could find no references to JAAR on the web, although he found a lot about animal rights groups. The information made him uneasy, but it wasn't specific enough. He went to look at more recent *World* archives.

He found something just as he was about to finish in defeat. Tucked away near the classified ads in an issue from two years before was a small, bold-lettered business card-sized ad, that simply said:

> Love animals? Want to protect them? Join Jovialites Advocating Animal Rights (JAAR), organizational meeting at 7 p.m., April 11 at the Jovial City Hall, meeting room B. Meet like-minded people and help the poor creatures that can't help themselves.

33

A couple days later, Garit walked into the Jovial Public Library, grinning and holding the latest copy of the *World*.

"You gotta read Wally's opinion piece, Betty," Garit said, and handed it up to her. "Good thing he owns the paper, because this stuff couldn't pass Journalism 101."

She snapped open the paper to the opinion page and read:

> I wish I had a five-cent nickel for every time I heard someone at a City Council meeting say that they moved into Jovial to get away from something or other in the big city. That sentiment doesn't always set well with the old-timers around here, but it's important to know.
>
> If we're ever going to attract new people, new taxpaying citizens to Jovial that will move the town forward and make it grow, we must maintain that small-town character, that flavor, if you will. And that starts with crime fighting.
>
> And that's why we should all be proud and thank our local police for pro-actively reacting to potential problems by nipping a potential big- city problem in the bud.

I'm talking, of course, about gang activity.

Our city law enforcers are about to bring one Fulton Gray, a young man with questionable heritage, to trial, and it's very clear from the evidence they're going to present that this Gray is guilty on all charges. Gray is a ringleader of a gang just as surely as if he were some Hispanic or African American gang-banker with tattoos, chains and pins on his body and drugs and sex on his mind.

Betty looked at Garit. "Gang bankers?" she smiled. Garit laughed. "That's the second time he's missed that error. I already texted in to Aspen. She'll love it." Betty continued reading.

Oh, you may think a gang in Jovial would have to be mild by big-city standards, but this gang has a rich and sordid history right here in our quiet but bustling city.

This gang is known to many old-timers as the Jocular Society. I know that doesn't sound as threatening as the Hoods or the Jets, but this gang is a real threat.

Many of you learned in school about this local gang, which in the past, historically was known for nothing more than drunkenness. But occasionally throughout past history, this gang has retorted to violence, and that's just what was done by this latest gang member, Fulton Gray and his co-conspirators.

One of the first characteristics of a gang, the Jovial prosecutor will show at trial, is tagging, better known in polite society as graffiti.

And if that sounds tame to you, think of where it leads. Many a young juvenile has started with a simple act like breaking a window, but it always invariably leads to worst behavior. Graffiti drawing is a gateway. A gateway to greater crime. And if we have greater crime, our city will not grow. And if we do not grow, we're falling behind. We can't maintain our small town character and grow bigger if we have organized crime running rampart in our streets.

When I learned how aggressively the prosecutor's office intended to get on this crime, I had to applaud with both hands. And now I stand up for Jovial and implore the citizens of Jovial to support the persecution to the full extent of the law, and drive gangs out of Jovial once and for all. When we do that, we will thrive. We'll get more government aid, more effective law enforcement and perhaps even more police presence to keep these ganks out of Jovial forever.

Once that happens, we can all spread the word. Jovial is a great place to live. With that kind of reputation, it's even better than a great big sign outside of town that would say: Gang bankers, You're not welcome!

Betty rolled her eyes. Garit looked at her and they both started laughing way too loud for a library.

"I don't know whether to mock him or feel sorry for him," Betty said. "This is just awful, and he must have worked so hard at it, poor thing. But gang bankers? And twice!" The two laughed heartily again. "I wish I were a cartoonist," Betty said. "I'd love to draw the dreaded gang bankers in their full glory. What, would they wear money clips rolled up in their T-shirt sleeves?"

34

Exactly one week before the Jovial
election, Deputy Schoen drove onto the Dogues farm. Mulder and
Scully stood at attention on the porch, together, blocking the door that
led into the kitchen. They barked and growled deeply from their throats
as the deputy got out of his car, and their tails were straight out behind
them, unwagging.

The deputy hesitated and stayed close to the police car. His hand
was on his gun when Jenn came out of the house.

"Good morning, Miz Dogues," said the deputy, touching his index
and middle fingers to the edge of his hat. "Is Mr. Dogues here?"

"What's this all about?"

"I have a summons here, ma'am," the deputy deadpanned, grinning
as if he had a secret. "He's being charged with animal cruelty."

"Again? Stay where you are," she sighed, and went into the house.
"Stay, kids!" The dogs immediately sat, side by side, their heads held
high and alert, facing the deputy. Mulder throated guttural sounds,
highlighted by an occasional "woof" while Scully just stared. The deputy
was frozen in place until Jenn came out of the house with a cell phone
to her ear.

"I don't know anything at all, Coney," she said. "But we got Deputy
Schoen standing here waiting to take you in." She listened a moment,
then touched the phone off. "He's on his way."

Coney parked the Power Wagon and approached Schoen. Neither of them extended a hand to shake.

"I'm just doing my duty, Coney," Schoen said. "You've got to come down to the courthouse, or I have instructions to bring you by force."

"Well, at least I'll know it's coming, right? Not like that low blow to the new *World* reporter."

"That kid deserved it," spat Schoen. "Let's get going. And keep those dogs away from me!"

Coney grinned as Jenn came out of the house with keys to their 1996 Buick. "We'll follow you down," she called to Schoen. "Mulder! Scully! Stay and guard the place."

The dogs perked their ears and remained on the porch as Coney and Jenn followed the deputy out of the driveway.

They walked into a small meeting room in the courthouse where, at an oval white table surrounded by leather rolling chairs, sat Judge Eric Meade, prosecutor Stewart Corrunna and Schools Superintendent Dan Pinckney.

They all got up and offered to shake Coney's hand, but he accepted only the judge's.

"I'll get right to this, Mr. Dogues," said the judge. "Mr. Pinckney here says he has photographic proof that you or someone in your employ is torturing animals."

"You actually file charges against me based on Pinckney's word? And right before an election he's got a major stake in? You're wasting my time! I have work to do," Coney said, impatiently.

"Animal cruelty is a serious charge," said Corrunna. "Any allegations are taken very seriously."

"And you're a very serious kind of guy, aren't you, Stew? Alright, then, let's see the proof Pinkey says he has." Coney sighed and looked back and Jenn, who rolled her eyes.

"Pinckney has tried this kind of stuff before," Jenn said as she rose. "Don't you know by now that this is all just his twisted little plan to proselytize everyone into his vegan religion? This has all been debunked before, several times. These are frivolous complaints. How does it all suddenly come before a judge?"

"We never had photographic evidence before," growled Pinckney, but he was interrupted by the judge.

"I wanted to settle this privately," Judge Meade said. "There are no real formal charges, and I thought, since charges like this have been brought before, there would be no use embarrassing any of the parties involved here."

Pinckney grunted as he pushed photographs, one at a time, across the table. "There's torture in every one of these images," he said. "If he did this to a dog, he'd be in jail. But because they're called livestock, he can be as cruel as he wants."

"All of these are way out of focus and blurry," Coney said. "Judge, how could you even look at these and make me come in here?"

"I saved the worst for last," Pinckney said. "This," he cried "is proof positive of torture. A wound of this kind cannot have been accidental. It was obviously an intentional blow against this helpless animal."

Coney picked up the picture and examined it. He tossed it back down on the table and laughed.

"This picture is of Number 405, a cow I rescued from the mud earlier this spring." He picked up the next photo. "And this is her, later that morning, or sometime later, lying in the hospital barn pen, contentedly chewing her cud. The wound is from the shovel I used to dig her out. She would have died if I hadn't been there to shovel enough mud to get her out. Once, I got a little too close and nicked her."

"Likely story," Pinckney said. "And quite creative for something you just made up!"

"You let this idiot call me out of prime haying weather for this?" Coney said to the judge, shaking his head. "This so-called intentional wound is minimal, and 405 here is healed completely and back in the milking line, no worse for wear," Coney said.

"Oh, that's all you care about, is your widget, your unit of production," swelled Pinckney. "Greed, greed, greed."

"And what were you doing trespassing in my barns, anyway?" Coney said, leaning toward Pinckney. Schoen took a step forward from his post just inside the door.

"I was never there," Pinckney said, smugly. "These photos came into my hand serendipitously."

"Your honor," sighed Coney. "Can I go? I've had enough of this. And way too much of Pinkey's serendipity!"

The judge lowered his head toward the table for a moment, then pulled the pile of pictures toward him and looked them over quickly, tossing each one back toward Pinckney as if he were dealing cards.

Finally he sighed deeply. "Yes, Mr. Dogues, you can go, and I apologize to both you and your wife for these spurious allegations. You're fortunate that I worked summers in college on my grand uncle's dairy farm and understand a little about what you do. I would suggest that you investigate filing for relief under Michigan's Right-to-Farm Act, which would hopefully put an end to frivolous complaints." He turned to Pinckney.

"As for you, Mr. Pinckney, you are warned to first, stop ordering your goons to illegally trespass on farms. And second, I warn you to learn a little more about farming before you try these tactics again. These photographs you say are evidence of abuse are in reality evidence of kindness, of care and of concern for the well-being of these animals. Don't you ever waste my time with anything like this again or I'll have you arrested for contempt of court. I wish I could have you arrested just for stupidity alone, but I can't. Now get out. Stew, the same goes for you."

35

Aspen, dressed as Cindy, walked into
the next meeting of Jovialites Advocating Animal Rights and
immediately looked for her nameless cowboy friend. But as she looked
fruitlessly, she felt smooth hands grab her arms from behind and pin
them close to her body.

Two faithful members of the JAAR group, a well-dressed young
man and the other wearing leather and tattoos and several piercings,
escorted her roughly against a wall.

"What are you DOING?" she cried, jerking her arms free, but the
clean-cut well-dressed one said "relax, we just want to know more about
you, Cindy."

"What if I don't want to tell you?"

She was backed in a corner now, and the clean-cut young man's nose
was uncomfortably close.

"We already know some things about you, Cindy," he spat. "But we
want to know more about your boyfriend, the *World* reporter."

"What, are you looking to find your gay BFF?" she snarled.

"Shut up. We know he's your pal. We saw him at your apartment.
What we don't get is your connection to him."

"I don't know what you're talking about."

"Then let's clear things up. We're talking about that *World* reporter.
West? Have you been talking to him? Giving away JAAR secrets?"

"I don't know any *World* reporters, and I didn't know JAAR had any secrets."

"Then why does he show up at your apartment?"

"How do you even know where I live?"

"I'm asking the questions," said the clean-cut one. "We know where you live and we know you used to live with a reporter who was fired from the *World*. Maybe you still do."

She pushed him away from her face and straightened her shirt. She could feel the microphone pressing against her breast, still in place.

"If you're talking about Aspen, she's moved out, back home to her mama."

"And what about Garit West?"

"Who?"

"Your reporter boyfriend?"

"If I knew who that even was, who cares? He's got nothing to do with me."

"Look bitch, I know you're lying," spat the tattooed young man, leaning in to get his face and liquor breath way too close. "But I don't care. Your sex life is up to you. Just make sure that little pissant writes good things about JAAR." Aspen turned her face, waved her hand in front of her nose.

"I can't do anything for you, dogie breath," she said, sneering. "Now let me go!" She tried to push her way past the two, but they blocked her. Just then, Pinckney stepped between them and pushed them aside as if he were separating schoolyard squabblers.

"Time to take your seats," he said. His eyes met Cindy's, and she turned away quickly. "We have a guest speaker tonight."

The gathered faithful chose their seats and sat as Pinckney stood behind the table in the low-ceiling room. No sign of her cowboy friend, so Cindy took a seat in the back, on the opposite side of the room from the two bullies, who sat next to a young black-haired girl dressed in an extremely tight black T-shirt, baggy jeans and work boots. She hadn't seen her here before. Recruits came and went, Aspen supposed, wishing the cowboy were here.

Behind Pinckney, seated in a chair like everyone else's except for a cushion, was Jim Deadfrick.

"Now as you may or may not have heard," Pinckney started, "the corrupt court system in Jovial has once again sided with the abusers and slavers. So now we have a judge to add to our distinguished list of enemies. Judge Eric Meade.

"Within the last few days, indisputable photographic evidence of intentional non-human animal cruelty and abuse, bravely taken by members of this very group, were tossed out by Judge Eric Meade, which shows you where his loyalties lie. Before I go on, I'd like to thank the group of animal freedom fighters for their bravery in securing the evidence. I won't reveal their names because I won't take the chance and jeopardize their future, noble work. They had to break the law to get these photos, but it was right that they did. But even with clear-cut evidence, Judge Meade, the paid abuser-lover, let one of the chief slavers, Cornelius Dogues, off Scott-free. It was his farm where our freedom fighters took the indisputable photographic evidence of cruelty." He paused, as was his normal routine before working up a lather.

"Now, I don't know much about the justice system in Jovial County," he started slowly, softly. "But I know injustice when I see it." He lifted his head, and as his voice raised he seemed to get taller and more confident.

"I know, when I see a photograph of a horrible gash in a cow's leg, that it isn't normal! I know abuse when I see it! And I know ... I know! That people who turn their heads and let it go on are just as evil as the people who took the rusty, dull, infection-laden knife to that cow's leg. And why? What possible purpose could there be other than cruelty? These sick bastards. Cows' legs don't just get cut! These pictures are evidence of a sick need to control prescient beings that they think are inferior to the almighty human! They'll do anything to hang onto their control. Anything! Intimidation, abuse and even cutting an animal's leg just for fun!" He paused and looked at each face in the crowd until the silence became uncomfortable.

"This has to stop, people, and it will stop." Pinckney said at last, softly, readying for his big buildup.

"I'm putting out an ultimatum, right here and right now. This is what I'll call my three strikes ultimatum, and strike one has already been called. Strike one was a judge who probably took money from Dogues to keep the slaver and sick abuser doing business as usual. Strike two will happen if we lose this election, and"—his pace and volume were building again—"and, then we must be prepared to take strike three to them. Are you with me?" He shouted.

"Strike three is our cue to strike hard and bitterly! Those who will not see must be shown! A judge may be able to keep evidence of abuse from the public, but we can end the cover-up with one quick, decisive strike that opens the eyes of everyone in this county, maybe even to the ends of the earth!"

A cheer went up immediately from the two young men who had cornered Aspen, and the others soon joined. In the small room, it became a roar.

"Yes!" shouted Pinckney. He pointed to someone in the back who dimmed lights to reveal, projected on the wall, the grainy picture of Coney's muddy cow, lying peacefully in her stall, the gash on her leg barely visible.

"This is your motivation!" Pinckney shouted. "This poor guy can't fight for himself. He's just like you! He has no voice in this society. All the fight has been bred out of him in some insanely cruel conspiracy. Guys like this have endured generations of perverse genetic manipulation. This so-called science has produced milk and meat, sure, but it's killing us all. The whole dead carcass industry in the United States is nothing more than a corrupt system that keeps filthy-rich farmers in power along with the Republicans! Greed always overcomes the good of the people, but we are the patriots that will restore power to the human animals and take it from the abusers and slavers!" The crowd became even louder than before.

Pinckney held up his hands and quelled the uproar, but the grin on his face was as unmistakably smug as it was rare.

"Now, friends, speaking of the election, I've asked my good friend and business partner, Jim Deadfrick, to give us a polling update. Jim?"

He stepped aside and stood as a smattering of applause frittered through the crowd.

"Now many of you may not know me, but as Dan said, I'm Mr. Deadfrick, a businessman who's solidly in favor of Proposition One," Deadfrick started. "I'm co-owner of the organic store, have considerable stock in the organic underwear factory, and I run the Jovial elevator. But my chief job is as a grant writer for the city, and let me tell you, folks, this town needs a commission to safeguard our food. If we have it in place, a whole world of new federal grants opens up, and that means money to spend on the good things in life, like pure, organic food, like maybe a pool for your kids and, best of all, the more grants we get, the less taxes we all have to pay. I don't know about you, but I would welcome lower taxes." He paused, and received a smattering of applause.

"But unfortunately, I have bad news," Deadfrick continued. "This proposal is in danger of being defeated." Boos came from the two young men.

"We just don't have the budget to go at this full-scale. Dan and I have done our part. We've paid out of our own pockets for full-page ads in the *World*, and we've put our positions as influencers solidly into the public mind. Now that's on the practical, business side. But I won't sugar-coat this. We need money. Everyone knows it, so enough said. You know what to do. Give until it hurts. That's the right thing to do.

"Remember that we have the moral high ground. I think we all strive for the moral high ground, because we're all moral people. We wouldn't be here if we weren't. Amoral people don't care enough to fight for what's right. That's why I—we, if we both agree on the morality of this issue, can be so righteously indignant about Judge Meade's wrongful decision Dan spoke so eloquently about. Now Dan and I disagree on some things, but remain friends. And so I cannot agree with him about tactics sometimes, but I certainly defer to his expertise. He's more well-versed in political activism than I. But there's one thing we agree on. It is not wrong to disobey unjust laws. It is always right to defend the proper moral position, regardless of law. Defending lives—human or animal—is always the right thing to do, and people who disobey human law to perform on a higher moral plain are in the right, just like all those people in prison right now for protesting animal abuse.

"So while I will never advocate breaking the law," Deadfrick went on, "I know in my heart—my moral, bleeding heart, bleeding for the lives of these animals—that it is right for people to fight for the lives of animals, even if that is against the law. Are you with me?"

Pinckney nearly leaped out of his sandals as he bounced from his seat. He led a rousing round of applause, then grabbed Deadfrick's hand, pumped it in exaggerated fashion, and shouted above the cacophony: "Don't forget to vote, people! You are right. They are wrong. See you in two weeks!"

Aspen heard a commotion across the room as the applause died down. She turned to see the two young men and the girl gathered around a laptop computer on a small table pushed to the back of the room.

As the people stood and the low rumble of beginning conversations masked her movements, Aspen moved behind the trio. She saw a confusing window of some kind of system, maybe heating or cooling, or some kind of diagnostics on the computer screen. The black-haired girl saw Cindy and stared at her. Aspen turned away. As she did, she heard the well-dressed man say "See? I'm the baddest! I can hack into any system ever made!"

36

This item appeared on the front page of
the *Jovial World* the day after the election, authored by Garit, though
there was no byline, by choice of the editor:

Two of Three Ballot Proposals Fail

Proposals 1 and 2 failed to gather enough votes to create
a local commission on food or prescribe penalties for
gang activity in yesterday's annual Jovial City elections.

On an election day that saw light turnout for the
issues on this year's ballot, voters turned away Proposal
1 by a vote of 3,988 to 2,765. Less than half the eligible
voters turned out.

Proposal 1 would have created a city commission
responsible for ensuring that food sold in any retail
grocery establishment within the Jovial city limits be
"organic, locally grown and wholesome." The proposed
ordinance did not define wholesomeness, but city
officials said if the proposal had passed, details would
have been worked out later, in the rule-making process.

Proposal 2, which voters turned away 4,097 to
2,003, would have imposed mandatory sentences of two

years in jail for anyone convicted of gang activity within the city limits, although gang activity was not defined in the proposal.

Jovial Schools Superintendent and animal rights activist Dan Pinckney said in a formal statement that he was disappointed in the Proposal 1 vote.

"Food is the most important thing in life when it comes to the health and well-being of our children," he said. "I am disappointed that people don't understand that factory food, raised after being doused with poisonous chemicals, is killing them. But they'll understand sooner or later, when they're sick or dead because of their own appetites and bad choices."

Proposal 1 opponents said common sense won the day.

"It didn't take long for the people of this community to understand that Proposition 1 was an overreaching grab for power," said Coney Dogues, a farmer and president of the Jovial Area Farmer's Association (JAFA). "The people gave a loud-and-clear message that the government should have no business deciding what they can and cannot eat or the methods by which their food is raised. That's how they voted."

Other reasons for voting against the proposal, cited during informal exit interviews at the polls, indicated that some people saw it as an attempt to ensure a business monopoly for the Jovial Organic Store, a cooperative that specializes in organically grown and raw foods.

Proposal 2 was turned away, said Jovial Mayor Mackintosh Benz III, because voters apparently didn't see any evidence of gang activity, even though the county prosecutor, Stewart Corrunna, is preparing to level gang charges against four local men, charged with vandalizing the statue of town founder Alan Jovial.

Proposition 3, which extended the Jovial Organic Underwear factory's tax-exempt status for three more years, passed overwhelmingly, and will continue to cause a $10 per year surcharge to be added to citizen tax bills.

Conspiracies danced dirges through his head. Dan Pinckney paced.

"It's not possible," he muttered. "Blind idiots. How could they not understand? Why won't anyone listen to me?" He dialed Deadfrick's phone.

"Hi, Dan."

"So what do we do now, Jim?" Pinckney spat into the phone. "We've been betrayed. My legacy is down the crapper and so is yours. I'm supposed to be an educator. Educators don't fail. Educators have the answers. People look to me for answers. If I've lost credibility and they won't listen to me, how will I lead them into a better future? When are they ever going to learn? How long are they going to allow this brutality to continue? How long are they going to let themselves be poisoned by an immoral, corrupt industry like big agriculture? Why won't they listen to me?"

Deadfrick had planned for this eventuality, and he was well-prepared.

"It's not you, Dan. It's these blind people. They're the problem. They have no vision like we do. And that's nothing against them. That's just the way God made them. You should pity them, not be angry." Pinckney grunted.

"And sometimes God raises prophets to make them see the light," Deadfrick said. Pinckney hesitated, then smiled sarcastically as his anger became more intense.

"And I suppose you're the prophet? Don't tell me. I don't want to know your plans," Pinckney said. "I'm going to make plans of my own."

"What, you're going to throw another little hissy-fit protest?"

"I don't know what I'm going to do, but it's going to make an impact, I can tell you that!"

"No way!" shouted Deadfrick. "Once again, you're jumping the gun, Pinkey. You need to learn a little patience. We'll get this on the ballot again next year, which gives us twelve months to get our organic message out there. And money should be no problem after I get some gang prevention grants."

"That proposal failed too, you know."

"Not a problem. We still have city ordinance seven-dash-seventeen, or whatever its number is, and I think that may be enough. All we really need is one gang-related conviction, and those grants will go through like crap through a goose. So what if there's no mandatory prison time? We'll still have the money. Maybe not as much as we could have had if the proposal passed, but enough. Remember, I know what I'm doing. We'll all be sitting pretty with the grant money, as long as we can funnel it back to us, which we can. Just like always."

"I still think we need to take action right now," Pinckney said. "The public has to be on our side for you to win your little political battles."

"And what action do you propose?" Deadfrick asked. "All your hippie sit-ins put together don't amount to a piece of donkey doo. What kind of a warrior are you anyway? You call yourself an animal rights defender, and you won't fight? What would the folks in San Francisco think? You're weak, Dan. And cowardly if you don't grow a pair right now and take the next step. I know how to work the system and you don't. Let me worry about the government, and you start working on the people. The idiots who voted against Prop. One, and more importantly, the people who were actively against it, have to be made to see the light. That's where you, as an educator, come in. God demands that his people open their eyes or pay for their sins. This won't hit home with them until it touches them personally. And I think I know how to kill two or more of those birds with one stone."

"Shut up," Pinckney stage-whispered through clenched teeth. "I'm sick of listening to you. Whatever you're going to do, I don't want to know about it. You blew the election." He slammed the ancient land line receiver back down.

"You're right about one thing, Jimmy boy," Pinckney muttered to himself. "Someone will have to pay for this. Maybe I can't fight the whole swarm of mosquitoes alone, but if I kill one, it's better than nothing."

37

Garit scanned through the 25 year-old *Jovial World* pages on the library computer. He was a few weeks ahead by now, and Betty apparently trusted him enough to let him remove and refile the microfilm.

He was nearly ready to end his work when a glimpse of a familiar photo caught his eye. He wound the machine in reverse and found it. The photograph showed a smiling high school senior, Jim Deadfrick, with Dan Pinckney. They were holding hands in a classic grip-and-grin shot, with Deadfrick accepting a grant check. The young teacher Pinckney wore a wide grin that Garit had never seen in person, and his long, brown hair and sparse beard couldn't hide an earring studded into each ear. No wonder kids way back then responded to him, Garit thought. His rebellious image caught their attention, as if he were one of them.

The photo stared at Garit as if it were begging him to find the flaw, like a double-framed cartoon that asks readers to find six differences between the two. Garit stared back. Something was wrong. Didn't the photo in Deadfrick's office show the check as ten thousand dollars? Didn't Deadfrick himself say his first grant was for ten thousand? Yet this photo in the *World* showed a check for one-thousand dollars.

Garit printed a screen shot of the photo and caption. After quickly rewinding the microfilm and removing it from the old, loud machine, he took the stairs two at a time to see Betty.

"Betty," he said, excited. "Tell me how I can find the city's records back twenty-five years ago?"

Betty sighed. By now Garit knew her sighs were not irritation. It was just her way. But he understood how she could put people off.

"Well, you'd have to go into the city offices basement and dig up old paper files," she said. "They only computerized things back to 2000."

"And who do I see to let me in there?"

"Nobody, because you're going to need a FOIA to get in. They don't like people messing up their files at city hall. They'll probably even deny that they have them, but I know better. I've been archiving records slowly for about five years now."

"I've never filed a Freedom of Information Act before," said Garit. "What do I do?"

"Can't help you there, cowboy. Never done one myself."

"But you have access to records?"

"Why?"

"Just digging, that's all," Garit replied, still unable to shed himself of caution when dealing with Betty. "You told me there were no mysteries to uncover here. What about this for starters? The picture hanging in Deadfrick's office shows a check for ten-thousand dollars, but the one in the *World* archives shows only a thousand." He showed her the screen shot. "I want to know which one is right. But the only place I can think to find the truth is in the city records."

"Sounds like a job for a FOIA to me," Betty said. "Seems like the best place to start, legally." She grinned, betraying some sort of mischievousness.

"I'd look up how to do it online, but all the systems are down. Good luck getting an internet connection up here."

Coney was wrapping up a conversation with Botsdorf and Fulton on the farm porch when his phone rang.

"Hi, Garit," he said.

"Hi, Coney. Say, do you know anyone who can help me with a Freedom of Information Act thing?"

"Wow, are you in luck," Coney said. "I have an attorney-slash newspaper man sitting right here beside me." He looked at Botsdorf, his hand cupped over the phone's bottom half.

"Bots, help this kid out, will you? Garit West. Needs some legal advice."

Botsdorf took the phone. "This is Botsdorf, Garit. I hope I don't have to bail you out of jail again." He winked at Coney.

"Shouldn't have had to in the first place," Garit said, hoping a bit of retained bitterness would endear him to Botsdorf. "But I do appreciate it. Wally would have let me sit there for the night."

"So what can I do for you?"

"I need to know how to file a Freedom of Information Act request to the city. I want to check out why a town leader has two different photos of the same event. One of them has to be doctored."

"What leader?"

"Jim Deadfrick." Botsdorf twitched his neck sharply at Coney, then smiled.

"And what has Mr. Deadfrick done to arouse your curiosity, Garit? Confidentially, of course." Now, Coney smiled.

"The photo of his first grant way back twenty-five years ago. In the paper it's one grand. On his office wall, it's ten grand."

"And what makes you think anyone will care what happened twenty-five years ago?"

"I don't know if they'll care, but if this guy scammed nine grand from a city the size of Jovial twenty-five years ago, it had to hurt. I want to know if it was really a scam or just an accounting error. But even if it was just an error, why do two photos of the same event have two different amounts written on the check? Were there two checks or did someone Photo Shop the photo?"

"Wasn't anybody around here proficient in Photo Shop twenty-five years ago, but I like your curiosity," Botsdorf said. "Tell you what, Garit. I'll scratch your back if you scratch mine. I'll file your FOIA, but you have to promise me you'll do some work for me."

"What's that?"

"I want you to look deeper. Not just into the photo, but into the grant, and into every grant Jim Deadfrick has ever written. I'll make it worth your while."

"Do I still get to break a story if I find something interesting?"

"Absolutely, Garit. This is your byline. It would be about time the *Jovial World* had a good story that Wally hasn't mishandled."

Garit saw an opening. He'd be a fool to ignore it.

"You got a deal. And while I have you, what's going on with Fulton Gray's trial?"

Botsdorf smiled again, cupped the phone and whispered to Coney: "This kid reminds me of myself a few years ago. No wonder I like him." He spoke back into the phone.

"Come to the trial and see."

A week later, Wally screeched from his office: "West, get your butt in here." He held up a piece of paper.

"What do you think you're doing, going behind my back?"

"What are you talking about?"

"I'm talking about you filing a FOIA in my name without telling me about it!"

"I didn't file it, Wally," Garit protested. "I asked Botsdorf to help me, and I guess he filed it under your name for some reason. Maybe because you're the editor of the paper?"

"Don't get smart with me, boy," Wally snarled. "What are you looking for, anyway?" Garit told him about the discrepancy in the two photos.

"And you really think anyone will care what happened twenty-five years ago?" Wally snapped.

"I would think you'd care, Wally, since you have me do a column every week about what happened back then."

"That's just a light feature, you dummy," Wally said. "It's meant for entertainment, not some dead-end investigative piece. Besides, there's nothing there. I was here twenty-five years ago, and that grant

Deadfrick got was a good thing for the city, no matter how much it was for. Why do you want to nitpick it to death?"

"What if it turns out he stole nine grand from the city? Isn't that news no matter how long ago it happened? Who knows how much he's really scammed from grant applications over the years?"

"Look, you're not going to find anything there," Wally spat. "And you're not Woodward *or* Bernstein. Besides that, Deadfrick is a well-respected official of this town who's brought in enough grant money over the years to more than make up for a piddly-squat nine grand ten times over."

"Corruption is corruption," Garit insisted.

"Whatever you say," Wally barked. "It doesn't matter anyway, because the city doesn't have any records to prove anything. Look!"

He tossed the paper toward Garit. On official City of Jovial stationary, the letter read:

> "Dear Mr. East:
> Re your request dated July 21 under the Freedom of Information Act regarding records detailing a grant awarded by the federal government in 1993 to the city of Jovial; be advised that no such records exist, and your request cannot be fulfilled."

It was signed by the FOIA information officer for the City of Jovial, James R. Deadfrick.

Garit folded the letter and stuffed it in his pocket.

He went to the library and showed it to Betty.

"What did I tell you?" she said. She read it again, just to be sure. "I didn't know Deadfrick was FOIA officer. How convenient."

"So is this it, then? The end of the trail?"

"Only if you want it to be," Betty said. "I can get you into the archives to look at the files, but we have to do it quick. Deadfrick knows someone's digging into it now, and there's only two ways he'll respond. If he hasn't destroyed them already, he'll either try to destroy them fast or he'll be so arrogant that he'll just do nothing. He's been bulletproof at every step in the past, so why should he be worried now?"

"Which way will he go?" Garit asked.

"I would bet on the arrogance, but we can't take any chances. Meet me here at five o'clock and we'll get those records, just to be sure."

Garit showed up at the library promptly at five o'clock, and the doors were still open. He walked in and waited as Betty calmly worked behind the desk, sorting books.

"So what's up?" Garit asked when the last patron left.

"We can't just rush into city hall at closing time," she said. "It's better to give the office workers time to pack up and get out."

At 5:15, as Garit fruitlessly tried to find grant listings for Jovial on Google, Betty came from behind her desk carrying an empty box and motioned to Garit.

"Here's the deal if someone challenges us," she said as she locked the library's front door. "You're with me only to carry boxes. That's all you know."

The warning was unnecessary. They approached the back door to City Hall and Betty produced a key. They walked through a hallway lined with cleaning supplies, pails and mops, and descended a dimly lit, short staircase.

Betty flipped a switch and a bank of florescent lights blinked on.

"I'm going to get some stuff I need to archive and put it in a box for you to carry," Betty said. "1993 is over there."

She pointed to a dark wall lined with file cabinets. Garit rushed over and found 1993 quickly. He looked for a folder called Grants, but there was nothing. He fingered through the files, looking for something that would be vaguely familiar.

"This is a real shotgun approach I'm taking," he said to Betty. "How can I narrow this down?"

"Did you look for a folder called Grants?"

"Yes, there's nothing."

"How about under F for federal grants?"

He fingered backward in the drawer. "Nothing marked Federal," he said.

"D for Deadfrick?"

"Nothing."

"I for Income?"

"Nothing.

"Accounts receivable or payable?"

"No."

Betty loudly dropped an armful of files into the box and rushed over. She pushed Garit aside and fingered through the drawer herself.

"I was wrong about Deadfrick's arrogance, I guess," she said. "He must have gotten to this. Too bad you had to tip him off with a FOIA."

"I didn't know what else to do," he said. "I told you I'd never done one before. Besides, it was Botsdorf who filed it, and in Wally's name."

"I thought he was smarter than that," she said. "There's only one option, and that's if Deadfrick didn't think about the backups."

She sidestepped left along the banks of file cabinets. Finally, on the very bottom layer, she found a drawer that was labeled only with a C. She opened it.

"Jackpot," she said, excited. "C is for carbon copy. Go nuts." She walked back to her box as Garit pulled file folders and stacked them on the floor. He found one with a G at the top and opened it.

"This is it!" he cried. "Grants. And not just for 93. All the way through to 1999!"

"SHH! Someone's coming," Betty whispered. "Bring them all over!"

Garit pulled a thick pile from the file drawers and rushed over. Betty lifted the pile of files in her box, and Garit shoved his stack into the bottom.

"Someone down there?" a voice called.

"It's just me. Betty." Betty cried back, cheerfully. Mayor Benz appeared in the doorway.

"Oh, Hi, Betty," he said. "Anything I can help you find?"

"No, just getting some files to catch up on putting the archives onto the computer."

"Great," Benz said. "How far have you gotten?" He stepped forward and stuck his hand into the box.

"1997," Betty said quickly.

Benz lifted a top folder and looked at the date, then looked at Garit.

"You know you're not supposed to bring anyone down here, Betty," he said. "What's he doing here?"

"I'm just here to carry boxes," Garit said.

"I could have helped you with that," Benz said, turning to Betty.

"Garit just happened to be at the library, and I thought he could use the exercise," Betty said. "He's looking a little out of shape to me." She winked. "Must be all that locally-produced cheese."

Benz looked at Garit, then back at Betty.

"Oh, I see," he said, and winked back at Betty. "OK, well, you two carry on." He smirked and turned. "Don't strain yourself, Garit." He giggled over his shoulder.

Betty pulled a few more folders and put them on top of the pile in the box, then slid a lid on it.

"What was that all about?" Garit asked.

"Oh, nothing," Betty said. "Just be prepared that before long a rumor will be around town that you and I are having an affair. Let's go."

She lifted the box, put another one on top. She handed the two to Garit and led him up the stairs and out the door.

"When we get back to the library, take your files into the basement and put them into the microfilm closet," she said. "They'll be safe there, and you can look at them when you can."

The treasure trove awaited.

38

Botsdorf was working late into the
evening preparing his defense for Fulton's trial when he heard a soft
knock on the wooden door frame outside his office.

"Hi, Bots." squeaked the meek figure before him. Botsdorf did a
double take. "Wally?" He said. "Come in. You don't look real good.
Having health problems?"

"Naw, I feel fine, Bots." He said, standing a little straighter. Then
he just stared as Botsdorf waited.

"What can I do for you, Wally?" Botsdorf said at last.

"Well, Bots, I, uh, hate to even ask, since I'm already in debt to
you, but, well, I need to extend my loan. I can't go to the bank, because
I'm tapped out. I thought you might understand 'cause you're in the
newspaper business too. I got a lot of people who owe me money, but
until they pay, I need something to meet expenses. You know how it is,
as a businessman yourself."

"But Wally, legally I already could take possession of your place
just because you haven't paid me back for the last loan. You're deeply in
arrears. Why should I continue to help my competitor in the newspaper
business?"

"We're not really competitors, are we, Bots? I mean, we're in two
separate towns. Besides, what's the difference between now and six
months ago when I got the fifty grand from you?"

"We're in the same county, both fighting over a measly thirty thousand readers and about 500 advertisers—" interrupted Botsdorf.

"But if we each keep our territories, at least we're pushing each other, don't you think?" Said Wally. "I mean, don't you think Jovial should be able to support a paper the same as Sventon does?"

"Why doesn't it?" Wally didn't answer.

"What do you need, Wally?" Botsdorf said after another awkward pause.

"Just twenty grand, to get this month's bills paid," Wally said. "I'll show you the books. I got at least thirty grand owed to me." Botsdorf paused again.

"How can I believe that?" he asked. "Odds are good that you have two sets of books, maybe three, depending on who's doing the auditing. You know, ever since we were kids, I've had this feeling that I could tell you were lying just by looking at you, and I think you're lying now. But maybe you're just desperate. I heard you lost Aspen Kemp."

Wally fidgeted. "She quit on me."

"Too bad. She was a good writer. How about this new kid. West? How's he working out?"

"He's doing fine," Wally said, warily. "A little too cocky for my taste."

"A good writer, from what I've read."

"He's OK. I've seen better. You were better."

"Tell you what, Wally. If you'll stop kissing my hiney for a minute, I'll loan you twenty grand, at five percent interest, for ninety days, with a ten percent rate every ten days beyond that, added onto the thirty grand you still owe me. Seem OK?"

"Sure. I'll have you paid back long before ninety days. Thanks a lot, Bots. I really appreciate it. It's good when two businessmen can work together for the public good, and I do think having two papers is for the public good."

"I'll send over the legal papers tomorrow."

"Thanks, again, sir," said Wally as he backed out of Botsdorf's office.

"He called you sir?" said Aspen as she peeked out of the office Botsdorf had set up for her, just down the hall from his office. "Wally must be desperate." Botsdorf smiled. "I think he's very desperate. And I have him over a barrel. Hey, let's listen to your tape of the last JAAR meeting."

Aspen went back into her office and returned with her small digital recorder, and set it up on the computer on Botsdorf's desk.

The recording came around to the part where Deadfrick talked about his ads.

"I saw those ads. They were five percent for the proposal and ninety-five percent promotion for the organic store," she said. They listened in silence until after Pinckney's rant about his righteousness.

"You know, that got to me," Aspen said, stopping the playback. "I'm beginning to wonder if he isn't right. I mean, what's the point of killing animals just so we can eat them? We could eat other things."

"We could," Botsdorf said, "but it's against our nature. We are carnivores. Omnivores, really, but meat is a part of that. It's not immoral to eat meat. It may be distasteful for people who have to watch it be butchered, but they don't have to watch. Besides, there isn't enough land in the whole country suitable to raise all the vegetables we'd need to feed everyone if we had no protein from meat. Cattle in particular are very efficient at turning grasses that humans can't digest into protein. Livestock agriculture, as decades of credible data shows, is the best, most efficient use of the land."

"But what if Pinckney and all those other people like him are right? What if the whole meat industry in the United States is just a scam, just a way to keep wealthy farmers in power along with the Republicans? What if the government really does know that meat is killing us, but chooses to take the money from the rich farmers and ignore the facts? Wouldn't be the first time greed overcame the good of the people."

"You think farmers are wealthy?"

"That's what Pinckney believes."

"Pinckney's brain is addled, girl," Botsdorf said. "He's never been one to think straight on anything. He sees conspiracy in everything, and he's paranoid. He's fallen into an easy trap. He's interpreting data with preconceived notions, and he refuses to see another angle. Maybe it's time to push him a little harder, see if you can make him snap. Then we can get his real agenda out in the open before he goes completely off the trolley and hurts someone."

"He's never seemed all that violent."

"It's coming, Aspen. I can hear it in these recordings. It's classic mental confusion and inability to think straight. He's very unpredictable. But don't let that intimidate you. If you can break this story, show the town what a wing nut he really is, well, maybe we can expose this whole animal rights wacko stuff for what it really is."

"What is it?"

"It's the opposite of what they'd have you believe," Botsdorf said. "The overriding object is money. They use the paranoid ravings of mad men and a bunch of morons who follow them in exchange for a nice flow of cash from people who think with their emotions rather than with truth. It's anarchists and misfits and old hippies desperate to cling to the unrealistic ideals they had in college. They're angry because they abandoned their ideals to corporate ladder-climbing. They're sell-outs, Aspen. Hypocrites trying to salve their guilt for giving up on themselves. They're just empty-headed protesters who need something to cover up their guilt, so they latch onto the first little conspiracy theory they can find. They're just drifting, deceived. They have no real purpose in mind. They're just looking at the past, living in the past, and they don't even know it."

"But what about all the young people who are anti-factory farm and meat?"

"More drifters. They're almost sadder than the old folks. They've been indoctrinated, and it was easy for guys like Pinckney to do, because this generation was raised without any moral standards, without any real belief in anything. It's what they're taught in school. They can be manipulated so easily, it's not even funny. You know what they say: 'If you don't stand for something, you'll fall for anything'. That's the animal rights movement in a nutshell."

"But these people really do seem to believe their cause is right."

"You watch," he replied. "Cut off the head and the body dies. It's a sure sign of a false religion. If we take down Pinckney, the whole JAAR movement will crumble. And that is a wholly worthy goal."

39

"West, get in here," shouted Wally from his office. Garit walked in.

"What time does the vandal trial start?" he demanded.

"Ten o'clock."

"OK. See you there."

"I thought I was covering it."

"You are, and so am I. I've heard on the street that you and this Fulton Gray punk are becoming friends. I have to be there to be sure there's some objective reporting going on."

"Why don't you just come out and say you don't trust me?" Garit said. "What have I done to betray your trust? Name one thing."

"I don't have to name anything. You're just too green to be covering a trial of this much importance to the town."

"I must be green, Wally, because I don't have any idea why someone on trial for spraying paint on a statue is like the trial of the century. What aren't you telling me?"

"It's complicated politics, and you wouldn't understand," Wally said. "For right now, you're better off not knowing. That way maybe you can write part of the story without letting your friendship with the defendant get in the way."

"Don't worry. You'll get objectivity."

"Take a camera. And if you wreck this one, it's coming out of your pay."

"My guess is it will probably cost me exactly the two weeks wages that you owe me?"

"Shut up and get down to the courthouse."

Fulton walked into the courtroom from a side door, dressed in a new black suit that complemented his tall athletic frame. Botsdorf wore a light gray suit that appeared to have been tailored to taper his upper body from shoulder to waist.

Garit, turning to look at the crowd filtering in slowly, noticed Wally take his position two rows behind him.

Fulton turned, once seated at the defendant's table, and gave Garit the thumbs-up. He seemed peaceful as a cat purring on its owner's lap.

Garit wrote in his reporter's pad:

> What does FG have inside him that makes him so serene on what must be the most stressful day of his life? How can anyone be calm with a storm raging around your future? The world is a giant messy desk, but Fulton acts like everything's neat and clean and in its place. How does he do that?

Judge Eric Meade walked in robed in black, and as he instructed the crowd to be seated, he nodded toward the team of three prosecutors led by Stewart Corrunna, each one's hair greasier than the one before him.

The Bailiff stood.

"The defendant, Fulton James Gray, is hereby charged with one count each of gang-related vandalism to city property, malicious destruction of city property done while engaging in gang activity, and one count of conspiracy to engage in gang activity," he read loudly. Garit scribbled in his reporter's notebook: 'Gangs? How did Botsdorf allow them to keep a charge like that'?

Botsdorf rose slowly from his chair and with a hand gesture that appeared magnanimous and genuine, said "Your honor, my client pleads not guilty to these ridiculous charges."

"As expected," said the judge. "Let's proceed. Mr. Corrunna?" He pointed to the prosecutor's desk.

"The people will prove," said Corrunna, rising slowly and with great feigned effort, "that Mr. Gray was not only engaged in gang activity on the night of April 26, but that he is indeed the grand master—the pimp, you might say—of the gang that operates out of Jovial with the expressed goal of bringing down the city government through ridicule and a practice known in gang circles as tagging. And once that has been proved, the people will demand that Mr. Gray be sentenced under Jovial city ordinance seven-dash- seventeen, which provides specific parameters for defining engagement in gang activity within the city limits."

He returned to his seat, smirking like a teenager who had successfully bested his math teacher. Garit scribbled down the ordinance number, which didn't seem to match with what he'd remembered from the city records.

Botsdorf stood, silently. Once he was balanced and his tie straightened, he began to chuckle. That grew into a laugh, then a guffaw. Garit was impressed with his showmanship.

"I'm sorry, your honor, but the more I think about these charges, the funnier they become. I giggled at them the first time they were presented a few weeks ago, but now that I hear them spoken, well, they're hilarious. And did you hear? He called Mr. Gray a pimp." He giggled again, then paused for dramatic effect, and it worked. Garit fidgeted.

"But enough of the insanity," he finally said, his voice clear and baritone, with a quality Garit had never heard from him. "We've got business to do, and I believe, your honor, that I can save the good citizens of Jovial and this court a lot of time and trouble by simply requesting that you throw these charges out immediately because they are frivolous, to say the least. The prosecution's case rests solely on the testimony of three drunken companions and a young lady—let's call her a socialite—who was interested in Mr. Gray physically, without any interest in the facts behind these ludicrous charges. The prosecution has no evidence of anything against Mr. Gray, and even less evidence that gang activity exists in Jovial. Furthermore, I will show that the ordinance to which the prosecution refers was designed as a way to deceive the federal government into releasing grant funds. I'll have you out of here by noon, your honor, by which time I will have spoken the truth and defended this young man's right to free speech."

Garit scribbled in his notepad: 'Three arrests? I thought only one. Who's the chick?'

"I'm more interested in justice than time, Mr. Botsdorf," said the judge. Wally was scribbling loudly on a piece of unlined typing paper, pressed against the back of the seat in front of him. His tongue was sticking out the right side as he hurried to keep up.

"Proceed," said the judge.

Stewart Corrunna rose.

"I call Sam Perkins, your honor."

Sam took the stand, dressed in an ill-fitting sport jacket and an out-of-date wide tie with a ferocious bear painted on it.

"Now Mr. Perkins," started the prosecutor. "We've already learned from your confession that you are guilty of helping defame the dignity of Alan Jovial, and that Fulton Gray was the mastermind behind the plot. You're not on trial here, however, but you are under oath. Were you and your gang drinking that night?"

"Yes."

"And did you indeed partake in activities involving marijuana?"

"Yes."

"And did your little gang have a name?"

"Objection to the term, your honor," Botsdorf said.

"Overruled," the judge said.

"It wasn't a real name," Sam said.

"We have your confession transcribed if you'd like to refresh your memory," the prosecutor sneered.

"The Jocular Society," Sam said. A murmur in the courtroom caused Judge Meade to bang his gavel.

"And who gave your gang this name?"

"Fulton Gray."

"And did Fulton Gray lead your gang to the park that night and paint a lewd sacrilege on the statue that stands in tribute to our glorious town founder Alan Jovial?"

"What's a lewd sacrilege?"

"Did you help Fulton Gray paint the statue?"

"Yes."

It was Botsdorf's turn.

"Just what is the jocular society?" he asked Sam.

"I don't know. Some ancient cult or something."

"Cult. Ancient. How interesting. How do you know about it?"

"Fulton told me."

"You didn't learn about it in school?"

"I must have been sick that day." Rustling and murmurs and chuckles escaped, though muffled, from the small but growing gallery.

"Were there any dues, any initiation ceremonies necessary to be part of the jocular society?"

"I dunno."

"I thought you were a member."

"It wasn't really a club, it's just what Fulton called us once, like the Three Musketeers, only with four of us."

The prosecutor rose. "Objection, your honor. The Three Musketeers aren't on trial here."

The judge glared at him. "Proceed, Mr. Botsdorf."

"Would you call it a gang, Mr. Perkins?"

"You mean, like a big-city gang, like the Bloods and Cryps? Or like the Hell's Angels?"

"Yes."

"Oh, No. Nothing like that. We just hung around together sometimes and partied."

"And what would have made you go out to paint a statue? Certainly not an initiation ceremony?"

"He's leading this witness," shouted Corrunna.

"Overruled. Continue," said the judge.

"I dunno," Sam said. "Wasn't nothing like that, like rushing some college frat or anything. Fulton was always talking about all this political stuff, and saying that only idiots just sit around and do nothing while lies were being told by the government."

"Did you believe that?"

"Yeh, I guess so. Everybody in the government lies. But I don't get all worked up about that stuff. It's boring. It doesn't really make any difference to my life."

"You said Fulton was the leader of this group and made you come with him that night. How did he make you? Did he threaten you?"

"Naw. He just got us all excited about doing something cool, that would, you know, blow the minds of city hall, or something like that. And it *was* kind of cool, sneaking around at night and seeing the picture in the paper."

"Did Mr. Gray explain to you why he wanted to paint the statue?"

"He told us a few times, but like I said, I ain't into government stuff."

"Did he ever tell you that painting the statue made a statement?"

"Now that you mention it, I think he did."

"You think? Yes or no, Sam."

"Yes."

"And what would that statement be?"

"I don't remember."

"Was it a political statement?"

"I suppose. Fulton was always talking about political stuff. A lot of it never made any sense to me. That's probably one of the reasons we ain't friends any more." Sam looked at Fulton, who smiled at him and gave him a thumbs up. Sam immediately appeared to brighten. Garit noted it. Wally didn't.

"But we weren't in any gang, and we didn't do any of those other things they said we did."

"Who said you did?"

"The cops."

"What did they say you did?"

"You know, reach through the statue's legs like we're a bunch of homos. They said we were all involved in homo activity just by being there. They told me they could get the next newspaper headline to say we're all queers."

"And what were the circumstances of them telling you this?"

"I'm sorry?"

"Why were you talking with the police?"

"They arrested me."

"On what charges?"

"Destruction of city property, conspiracy, vandalism and gang activity." He listed them on his fingers.

"Are you guilty of any of those charges?"

"No."

"Then why did you sign a confession?"

"They promised me a drink of water."

"They offered you water for your confession? That doesn't seem like much of a reward."

"I was pretty thirsty."

"Why? Had they denied you water?"

"Yes."

"For how long?"

"About two days."

"What about food?"

"I never got any."

"For two days?"

"Yes."

"Other than withholding food and water, how were you treated?"

"OK, except for once."

"What happened?"

"Officer Schoen bashed my arm with his billy club. Still hurts. I told them I thought it was broke, but they didn't seem to care much."

"To get you to confess to something?"

"I guess."

"I'm done, your honor," Botsdorf said. "And disgusted by this city's police department."

The judge called a ten-minute recess, and when they got back to business, Garit noticed that the courtroom was full, and the gallery contained both Jim Deadfrick and Dan Pinckney, along with the entire city council. Aspen had taken a place standing against a back wall. Garit and she smiled at each other, which surprised them both.

Botsdorf leaned over to whisper in Fulton's ear.

"You ready? Just relax. We got this game in the bag, but you can get the last three outs here. Let's do it."

Fulton took the stand, with Botsdorf waiting patiently for him to get settled.

"Mr. Gray," he said finally, "are you now or have you ever been a member of a gang?"

"No," Fulton said with authority.

"Have you ever heard of the jocular society?"

"Yes, I learned about it in high school history class."

"Are you a member now?"

"How can I be a member of something that doesn't exist?"

"Yes or no answers, Fulton."

"No"

"Have you ever known anyone who was a member?"

"No. I believe the last member died more than fifty years ago."

"So why do you know so much about it?"

"I find it interesting that the town I grew up in had opposition to the original city government. It's true-blue Americans defending themselves. Besides, I like history."

"You like it so much that you revived the Jocular Society?"

"I didn't revive anything. But I did consider that it makes a political statement that much stronger if the name is invoked, because it's such a rich part of Jovial history. If it ever really existed, it was never a formal club or a gang. I've never read anything about bylaws or initiations, and I did a college paper about it. It was just a loose group at first, and it's just kind of used now as a catch-all, a real tie to a longstanding Jovial tradition of civil disobedience and freedom of speech. People have been trying to say something, to make their voices heard with a political statement of some kind ever since the Jocular Society was, as you might say, 'founded' in a bar. It wasn't their fault that people sometimes don't understand satire."

"Satire?"

"Painting underwear on the town founder is classic satire, and it's been used for generations to show the town leaders that someone is paying attention to what they do. I believed that the time was ripe again to have it painted to show how ridiculous it was to have a proposal make it to the ballot box that would ban meat unless inspected by local government and raised according to some arbitrary standards that have nothing to do with practicality and everything to do with animal rights. It deserves a jockstrap. I only painted underwear. A law that wants to outlaw gangs in a town without gangs? That really deserves a jockstrap."

"Did you vandalize city property?"

"I made a political statement."

"Did you maliciously destroy city property?"

"I've destroyed nothing."

"Did you conspire to engage in gang activity?"

Fulton smiled and paused, just as rehearsed. "Gang activity? Like guns and drugs and violence and crime? No. I was exercising my right to freedom of expression."

Botsdorf waved to the judge, indicating he was done. The prosecutor stood to speak.

"So you admit, Mr. Gray, that you painted underwear on the statue of Alan Jovial?"

"As a political statement."

"I'll take that as an admission of guilt. And what was your political statement?"

"I would have thought someone in a political office such as prosecuting attorney would certainly understand satire."

"Patronize me, please, Mr. Gray."

Fulton was unfazed. He sat up straighter and slowly began to explain, as sarcastic as Garit had ever seen him. He suddenly understood how people could think Fulton was an Indian. His straight, short black hair shined, and his sun-darkened skin was the color of polished oak. But there was more. There was a confidence, a way of speaking that showed humility and strength and courage, but not in an arrogant way, as if he didn't know he had these traits within him. But neither was he afraid to let them be used.

"You see," Fulton said. "The statue symbolizes the town, you know, Jovial? And the underwear symbolizes several things. It stands for the status quo—that means how things have always been done—in Jovial, since jockstraps and underwear were the backbone of the economy for years. Now the word economy means that goods and services—"

"Don't patronize me quite that much, Mr. Gray." Murmuring revealed a still growing crowd, one with a keener sense of humor, and a favorable opinion of Fulton Gray.

"Underwear stands for support of the citizens—did you comprehend the pun there, counselor?—It stands for a voice. Painting underwear on the statue not only says 'look at the fancy coverings the city council drapes over itself to cover its own buttocks. They've been exposed.' It says to question authority, as any good thinking American would do. Question them to know for yourself if they're really such wise people as they say they are; if everyone can see their bright white underwear and whatever else might be hidden underneath their agendas. It's a wonderfully rich concept, and, admit it, it's pretty funny."

Corrunna frowned to the gallery. "Humor is not my game," he said as he ran his fingers through his hair. He wiped his hand on his pants and continued.

"And you say this is a tradition, dating all the way back to Alan Jovial himself?"

"All the way back to when he got his fanny painted red by his political adversaries."

"Aha! So you admit you partook in an activity that is a tradition. An initiation!" Shouted Corrunna.

"Nothing like—"

"As clear an initiation ceremony as can ever be seen, your honor," Corrunna interrupted. This Jocular Society meets every definition of a gang."

"There's no—" Fulton was cut off again.

"No more questions, your honor."

The judge looked at Botsdorf.

"It's almost noon," he said. You and Stew, see me in my chambers."

When Botsdorf came into his chambers, the judge barked: "You have ten minutes to tell me about this conspiracy to gain grant funds."

"Thank you, your honor," Botsdorf began. "I won't even take five. I have clear, irrefutable evidence here in my hand"—he held up papers Garit had given him from part of his investigation of city records—"that shows a conspiracy between this city government, the police chief, the city's grant writer and who knows how many others—to defraud this county's legal system, the federal government and to make a scapegoat out of Fulton Gray."

"This is just a diversionary tactic," whined Corrunna. Botsdorf gave the judge the papers.

"On April 3 of this year, your honor, the city council passed Jovial City Ordinance oh-seven-seventeen, the Jovial Gang Prevention Ordinance. With a little help from the local press, I've learned that the ordinance was passed specifically to gain grant money. These papers prove that one Jim Deadfrick, the city's grant writer, cajoled and manipulated the city council into passing this ordinance because passing an ordinance would be a key necessary action to gain more than a hundred thousand dollars in grant money from the federal government. I've also learned that the grant would be more than doubled if the grant writer could show evidence that local law enforcement was actively cracking down on gang activity. I have email records from Mr. Deadfrick to Police Chief Dulogski, encouraging arrests under a ruse of gang activity. These folks didn't need real gang activity. All they needed was evidence of the city's efforts, and evidence would be strongest with a conviction for gang activity. The zeal to get that conviction, which is the only reason Mr. Gray has been targeted by this government, would bring an extra two-hundred-and-fifty thousand dollars to the city, ten percent of which would go directly into the pocket of the grant writer."

"Give me time to look this over," said Judge Meade. "We'll meet back in the courtroom after I make my decision."

When they'd all been seated in the courtroom again, the judge began.

"There's no need for closing statements, because this case is clear-cut," he said. He looked at the prosecutor's table.

"The people of Jovial accuse Mr. Gray of three separate crimes for one act of what you call vandalism. Mr. Corrunna. I will address each separately. I have no doubt that Mr. Gray did indeed apply paint to the statue on the night in question, and I find his admission—even though he was tricked into it—enough. Fifty dollar fine for defacing—so to speak." He waited for a laugh from the gallery, but heard only moans.

"As for malicious destruction of city property, I find no evidence of malice in Mr. Gray. Not guilty."

"Now. Gang activity. On the surface, it seems silly to think there are gangs in the traditional sense of the word operating in Jovial. But I have to go beneath the surface, and I have to abide by the law. I'm a rule-of-law judge, and I consider only the law, not my own feelings. The law that prescribes the parameters for specific activities involving organized crime in this city are very clear as passed by the people's representatives, the city council. Ordinance seven-seventeen specifically mentions, among other things, that using spray paint to deface public property is a gang activity. Therefore, I find Mr. Gray guilty of engaging in gang activity."

The courtroom erupted with voices, and the judge quickly banged his gavel. When it quieted, Wally's heavy-handed scribbling could still be heard.

"I'm not finished," Judge Meade barked. "But because of Mr. Gray's political fervor and youth, and at least in part because of his sense of humor, I suspend any jail time and order a suspended fine of five-hundred dollars, and two years suspended probation. After which, his record will be expunged at the prosecutor's expense, if any." Corrunna's head jerked.

"Thank you, your honor," said Botsdorf.

"And as for the city's role in this deception," proclaimed the judge, "I intend to see to it that the state launch a thorough investigation. We're adjourned," he said, and banged his gavel.

As people filed past Garit, he saw Botsdorf and Fulton shake hands. Coney Dogues was inching closer near the end of the line of people.

"What's it mean?" Garit asked him, standing and stopping him with his hand.

"It's called a compromise," Coney said. "Ask any lawyer, and he'll tell you that the best compromise is one in which neither party is happy. This is the best of both worlds. Fulton doesn't have to go to jail or pay a fine, and the city has a gang-related conviction that will keep federal funds rolling in."

"This is how the courts work? I mean, it's still fraud, but now it's sanctioned by the court? It's all pretty dirty."

"But not illegal," Coney said. "You're in the legal field now, Garit. Right and wrong don't matter. Just the law, even if it's dumb, and even if it's applied unevenly."

"How could all these people just accept such corruption?" Garit snarled. "Is there no integrity left in this nation's court system? This didn't make any sense. I thought a small town would at least have some integrity at the top. This really hacks me off!"

"No sense in letting it do that to you," Coney said. "You can't control it."

Just as he was about the reach for the courthouse door handle, a voice came from behind.

"Mr. West!"

Garit turned to see a middle-aged man with a white beard, cowboy hat and tailored suit heading his way. "Can I speak with you in private?"

The man led Garit to a new Explorer, a massive truck with leather seats, and the man turned on the air conditioning immediately when they got in.

"I'm detective Bill Sheridan from the Sventon office of the state police," he said. He produced a business card and handed it to Garit. "I believe you can help us put away some of the government corruption that's been going on here for the last twenty years."

"I'm just a reporter. I'm not a detective."

"But you've done detective work. You've gotten documentation of grant-writing fraud?

"I don't know about that, but it sure seems like it. I haven't pieced it all together. It seems to all connect to a law they passed kind of secretly, and to my shame, apparently right under my nose during my first city council meeting."

"Look Garit—may I call you Garit?" Garit nodded. "We've known for some time that Jim Deadfrick has been at the root of some very shady deals in Jovial, but we've never had the manpower to put it all together and make it stick. But you've apparently already done a great deal of research for us. If you help us, we'll make it worth your while."

"That's the second time I've heard this. Someone wants to nail Deadfrick to the wall pretty bad. Is he really a criminal or just a stupe?"

"He's definitely not stupid," said the detective. "We think he's behind arson, insurance fraud, and who knows what else."

"And what do you mean when you say you'll make it worth my while? When I get the story done, it will expose stuff for the whole county to see. Might even make statewide news. What can you give me that's better than that?"

"Well, there are certain debts that you owe that might go away, for example, if you play ball and don't run a story until the timing is right."

Garit felt a chill run up his spine.

"So the Michigan State Police know about the debt my parents had saddled me with all the way down in Illinois? What else do you bastards know? Do you know about the cult that brainwashed them into drinking poison? If you did, why didn't you stop it?"

"I can't say any more. Will you consider working with us?"

Garit stared at the detective.

"Give me a few days to think about it," he muttered. The detective tapped on the business card, still in Garit's hand.

"Call me day or night," he said.

Garit stepped out of the truck, and didn't notice the Kodak digital camera fall from his pants pocket. Detective Sheridan backed out, and Garit heard a crunch under his tire. The camera was smashed into little pieces. Garit picked up the memory card and went back to the office.

40

Jim Deadfrick sat in his basement man cave, his legs stretched out, resting on an antique steamer trunk that did double duty as a coffee table. He had his hands cupped behind his head. He was as relaxed as the second day of vacation, but Pinckney was pacing.

"Look, Dan," he said. "There is far more rationality in calm planning than emotional knee-jerk reactions. That's been my policy ever since high school, and it's worked, hasn't it? Why do you think we became friends way back then? Do you remember what you told me? You were impressed that I refused to make such a big fuss about things. And do you know why I can remain calm?"

"Don't spew your phony religion at me again," Pinckney snapped. "Every chance you get, you spout some Bible story. Well, your milksop god can't help us now. We've lost all credibility."

Pinckney paced and took slugs from a bottle of Tequila, shaking as if in a diabetic spike.

"You're overreacting again," Deadfrick said. "This is not the end. Just because some punk farmer isn't in jail doesn't mean a thing. We still got our conviction, the city gets its grant money and I get my commission."

"Well, hurrah for you! This is a lot bigger than you, you stupid arrogant phony. I've endured the two strikes I vowed to avenge. What would JAAR think if I backed off of that? That boy painting the statue doesn't mean anything to me. This is about getting back to basics; to saving non-human animals. I'm trying to be their voice, because they have none. It's about respect and standing, and that's all we have in this life until we're laid in the ground, and don't you dare spout your afterlife bull! My group of animal rights fighters expects me to do something. The whole country's watching. How will I look if I just let these things go? The whole Internet animal rights crowd will turn against me, if they haven't already.

"First we have to take care of that darn judge, who's no doubt in cahoots with the farmers," Pinckney continued. "You know he's on the corporate payroll! He wouldn't even listen to the animal cruelty charges against Dogues. Wouldn't even listen! We had pictures! We had that S.O.B. dead to rights. And then, strike two. The election. And now here we are, looking at strike three and four, maybe on into all three outs, and not a single farmer sits in jail where he belongs. This calls for something deeper, Jim, but I'm not the schemer. I'm a doer. This calls for a scheme. Something that will make the adults of this town listen to reason. I can always indoctrinate the kids, and that's the only right thing to do. But I can't wait until they grow up to stop the animal cruelty. What are we going to do? We have to do something! We'll look weak if we don't do something. We have to react proactively."

"The Bible says God helps those who help themselves," Deadfrick misquoted. "But I'll take it one step further. I'll help you. And I'll help the animals. What we have to do is to make sure people know the danger they put themselves in by voting against Proposal One. We need to shut down the Farmer's Own Store in the process. Then we could control the food supply in Jovial again, for the good of the people and for profit." He smiled his crooked smile.

"And how are we going to do that?" Pinckney asked. "The fools in this town love the farmer's store."

"Just leave it to me, Dan. I'll be praying for you."

"Go to Hell. I'm not going to wait for you or your god. This is a very special time. Scheme all you want, but I'm going to issue a call to action. Action that makes people—the right people—sit up and take notice." He took a long slug of his tequila. "There's an old story about a farmer who was asked why he smacked his mule on the butt with a two-by-four before he hitched him up to the wagon. The punch line was 'if you want him to do what you want, first you have to get his attention'. My daddy told me that story every time he swung his belt toward my back. Made me decide never to be like a mule again, unless I could learn to kick like one."

Garit spent most of the next few days in
the library's basement, attacking every detail of Deadfrick's grant-
writing in City Hall's archives. Every day he discussed his findings
with Betty.

"I have to admit I was intrigued by the detective's offer, but I can't
just trust him, can I?" He asked as Betty listened intently. "Why couldn't
the state police do its own investigation if they were so suspicious
of Deadfrick? What weren't they telling me? When will I finally
understand what's going on?"

"It will all come together at the right time," Betty said. "But you
have to promise me you'll be careful. From what you've told me, there
might be nothing as damaging to Deadfrick than the story you're
going to write. It will expose him, and it's his mask that keeps him
so prominent. He can't give that up. But if it will help you sort it all
through, tell me what you think you know, and more importantly, what
you can document from all those carbon copies."

"Sounds like a plan," Garit said. "Here's what I think the records say:

The mayor, and perhaps the whole city council, have been in cahoots
with Deadfrick for years, making laws based first and foremost on their
ability to influence grant acceptance."

"Is that against the law?" Betty asked.

"Don't know," Garit said. "First things first. This was no small sum, all totaled. The police must have known it too, and somehow benefited. Haven't seen the detailed records of how all the money was spent, just some. Everyone in this city seems to have benefited from a grant proposal of some kind over the years. Police got their radar guns through a grant. Firemen got infrared detectors from a grant. Most of the businesses got development grants or tax breaks. So far I've counted ninety-four grants accepted and paid since 1993. The city—through Deadfrick—had applied for one hundred thirty seven. All the proposals were written by Deadfrick, every one with a stipulation that the grant writer get ten percent—sometimes more—of the total grant for his fee. It was the perfect ultra-fine-print arrangement. The city didn't have to pay Deadfrick a salary, or even name him an employee of the city if he took that commission, and grants poured in. It was a no-brainer to get the grants in exchange for some useless ordinances that no one really paid any attention to anyway. The only business interest in the whole county that didn't get some grant money through Deadfrick was the farmers. I don't know why."

"What about that first thing that got you going on this? You know, the check in the photo?"

"Yeah, that's a funny thing. I think it was just a clerical error, just dumb luck. The grant was supposed to be for a thousand bucks. It was all Deadfrick asked for. And the government sent just that amount. But someone in the city treasurer's office put an extra zero on it. That's it."

"Mistake or not, it's still a crime, though, if he made off with nine grand. But it sounds like you have a great story there even without that," Betty said.

"Yeah, but how do I make the connection with *World* readers? A story about local government seeking grant funds is about as boring as they come. Maybe I should start with a light piece about all the silly laws on the books. That would soft-soap it to start. Maybe that would help me get around Wally's censorship machine. Readers would think it's just a nice feature for the paper to point out silly laws. That's when I reel them in. I'll sneak in a sidebar about why those laws were passed, how much money they involved, and finally, ending with a bang, the exposure of a law meant to bring in money at the expense of a citizen who just happened to do the wrong thing at the wrong time, unaware of the conspiracy against any poor schmuck who would be next in a long line of statue painters."

"It's a great story," Betty said. "Worthy of even a veteran reporter, not to mention a rookie."

"But it really just honks me off," Garit said. "Is this what the world is all about, even in a tiny town like Jovial? Everyone's out for their own interests first, last, and always, and they'll throw anyone and everyone under the train if they have to, and never lose a minute of sleep over it. Someone should teach those people a lesson. But where can I print a story like that? Wally won't print it. Botsdorf? I don't know if I can trust him. Why would he submit my FOIA request in Wally's name? I thought it was supposed to be a secret. Who can I trust, Betty? Best not to trust anyone, I suppose. I trusted my parents, and they turned out to be idiots. I trusted a girl I thought was the one for me, and she turned out to care only about herself."

Sandra was the first person Garit went to see when family attorney Tom Saxe called with the news about his parents.

"I have to leave the tour," he said. Sandra, stoned crispy at 10:30 a.m., stared at him.

"What's going on?"

"It's my parents," he said, as stoically as he knew how. "They've been killed. Or they committed suicide. Not real clear yet."

"Wow, that's a real bummer."

"Will you go home with me?"

"What? Why should I go? I never even met them."

"I thought maybe you'd go because of me." Sandra stared, more blankness in her expression than before.

"How did they do it?"

"Long story short? They joined a cult and drank some poison so they could go to the dark side of Mars or someplace and become immortal."

"That's really stupid."

"Tell me about it. Will you come with me? I could use a little support."

"If I support you, who will support the band?"

"I really don't care. Let the cocaine support the band."

"You don't have to get all snotty about it."

"Snotty? My parents just killed themselves, and you dare call me snotty about it? I'm well past snotty, Sandra. I'm well into anger, and not just because of them. If you put the band ahead of me, then maybe we should just call this whole thing off."

"What thing?"

"What thing? You don't remember you and me, the future, the being together always?"

"Maybe that was in your mind, but not mine. I'm just here for a good time, and you've been trying to kill my buzz for weeks. And now you lay all this parental, family bull on me? I'm not the bad guy here, you know." Garit turned around.

"Goodbye, Sandra," Garit said. "Have a nice life." They were the last words he ever spoke to her.

"Here's who I think I can trust besides you, Betty," Garit said.

"Fulton. For sure. Coney? Probably. His age is his only problem. People in their fifties always have some kind of hypocrisy, just like my parents. Jenn? Same scenario. Botsdorf? I don't know yet. All my instincts say no, but maybe I have to trust him."

"Maybe," said Betty. "I just don't know. That's something you'll have to decide for yourself."

42

Before she walked through the door, Aspen, dressed as Cindy, pressed her hand to her chest, feeling the lump that could betray the tiny microphone taped there. It felt much larger than it was, like a sliver in her index finger. She tugged on her blonde wig to be sure her disguise was not likely to fail, and walked into the meeting of JAAR as if walking on thin ice with gas building up in her colon.

"Any misstep tonight will be very messy," she'd told Botsdorf when she left his office.

"Just be careful," he'd grinned. "But think of it this way. If this works, you'll finally get your story. A big story. Don't be afraid, Aspen," he said. "Just push him as far as you can and get out of there. Then you'll never have to put on this disguise again."

Cindy took her seat next to the nice-looking middle-aged man with a beard and cowboy hat.

"Glad to see you're back," she smiled. He smiled back, but said nothing.

Pinckney wasn't at the table that served as a podium yet. Aspen saw him huddled over a laptop computer at the back of the room, looking over the shoulder of the well-dressed young man and the tattooed, pierced one. They were each grinning as if they'd just gotten away with something.

"Tell me something, will you?" Cindy asked the cowboy. "Isn't it funny how no one has ever introduced those two guys back there? I mean, they've been to every meeting for more than two months now, but no one seems to know who they are." The cowboy shrugged.

Pinckney finally took center stage, walking reverently up the aisle. He stood hunched behind the folding table and, with a motion that could have been a baseball pitcher's windup, threw down the latest edition of the *Jovial World*.

The lead story on the front page was Fulton's conviction—at least that's what Wally had called it—right below the big picture of Fulton and Botsdorf walking from the courtroom.

Pinckney picked it up again and held it high for the crowd.

"Do you see this, people? This is what passes for journalism in this town. Look at the front page picture, taken by one Garit West, pissant reporter. I wouldn't give one of our JHS journalism students a passing grade for this hack job. Not only is it composed very poorly, but even at that, it outshines this piece of crud story below it." He slammed it back to the table and began to pace as the crowd murmured their agreement with him.

"You know this son-of-a-farmer is a slaver, don't you?" he asked. "And he was convicted of conspiracy, yet he walks free. He's a criminal, but his crimes are far worse than painting a statue. He's one of the suppliers of the Farmers' Own Store, and he has no shame. No morals. Just like his uncle, Coney Dogues, they're oh-so-smug when they're quoted in the papers about their big win in the election. Lying bastards, every one." He paused for dramatic effect and paced a little more despite the hubbub of the crowd. Pinckney finally growled for the crowd's murmuring to cease.

"Have any of you been more embarrassed than me by our recent humiliations?" he started softly. "I think this is going to be a fight now," he said. "How can we not be embarrassed? We've been humiliated by the election, by the media and by the slavers, and humiliation can never be forgiven. Strikes three and four have been plenty enough. I have a vow to fulfill.

"The enemy won't give up its grip on corruption and animal cruelty," he said, his pace and volume increasing. "And the blind sheep of this town vote with them. Stopping these criminals will not be a walk in the park, people. No, this will be a battle, because nothing worthwhile ever comes easy. Nothing of great importance ever came about without blood being shed."

"Must be Christianity was pretty important, then, huh?" blurted Cindy, pushing her heart to Richter-scale proportions. Pinckney glared at her.

"I mean," she continued, "Christ died a brutal, bloody death. And look how many bloody wars were fought for Christianity. Must be it's pretty important. At least as important as animal rights." She paused for effect, and noticed at least half the crowd was listening to her. "Oh, but you think animal rights are more important than all of Christianity, don't you, you atheist fraud! Are you kidding me?" She continued, louder. "You're talking bloodshed? Over what? An election that couldn't be won anyway? An offensive line in a newspaper? Give me a break." Her heart pounded like a thumb smashed by a hammer.

Pinckney continued to stare.

"Don't you give me that principal's grand stare down," she shouted. "It may have worked for years on your dullest students, but it ain't gonna work on me!" Pinckney broke eye contact first. He sneered and turned away from her.

"Let's stick to the business at hand," he said, looking back at his faithful followers.

"I speak of course, of metaphorical blood," he said, "although, knowing the carnage of the meat-eaters, there is plenty of literal blood spilled, and that's what's so right about our cause. These enslaved and slaughtered and yes, humiliated creatures are blood relatives to us. We're all beasts, and no beast deserves to have its blood spilled except in judgment for having spilled blood."

Cindy rolled her eyes and sighed, loudly for effect. "What a wimp you are," she said. "Any confrontation and you back down. You got no backbone. You said you were gonna do something for all these poor abused creatures, but it's all talk. Where's the action?"

Pinckney turned red and his right eye started bulging. "I take it, Cindy, that you suddenly are having doubts about my mission."

"Maybe I had doubts from the beginning."

"And maybe you're not worthy to share in my mission," he shouted and slammed his fist on the podium. "Maybe you have that fat behind of yours from eating meat. Is that it? Are you a hypocritical cannibal bitch who eats cow and pig carcasses?"

"Don't forget chickens!" Cindy said, raising her voice as well.

"Then you're not welcome here," Pinckney announced. He straightened his neck and took his voice back to normal levels immediately. "I'll have to ask you to leave, Cindy. We'll purge the cannibalism from our midst. Go eat some raw flesh of something and help destroy the planet."

"Gladly," Cindy said, defiantly, and walked out the door unimpeded. The cowboy was right behind her.

"What do you want?" she snapped at him when the door shut.

"I just wanted you to know I feel the same way you do," he said. "That took guts, standing up to a mad man."

"Yeah, well, so what? I failed."

"Failed?"

"Yeah, look," she said. "I'm a reporter. I was trying to get a story that proves this guy is nuts, but I failed. The story is dead and buried."

"It has to make you feel good that some people agree with you," he said. "Those two kids you were asking about scampered out the back door just before you left. Maybe you got to them."

"And that's another thing I never figured out. Who are those two? They were really creepy, but, I guess my reporter's instincts must be off. After all, I thought I knew Pinckney, but he really surprised me with his self-control."

"He didn't seem all that in control to me," the cowboy said.

"I thought I could push him and get him so angry that he would just lose it, that maybe he'd even take a swing at me," she said. "But he maintained control. And I guess there's no crime in being a wacko in this town, even when you're in charge of people's children. But how does he get away with preaching religion—the vegan religion—in school as blatantly as he does? I thought there was a law against teaching religion in schools."

"Maybe that's your story," the cowboy said, and walked the other way across the street.

Garit answered his phone.

"Hi, Garit, it's Jenn Dogues," the pleasant voice said. "Do you have any plans for tonight? Fulton and Coney are taking the night off, so we're going to kick back a little, drink some Indian Head and thank God for that verdict, or whatever it was."

"I'll be there."

On an impulse he didn't understand, Garit dialed Aspen's cell phone. She answered just as he thought the phone would go to voice mail.

"Hey Aspen," he said. "I was thinking about you since we saw each other at the trial, and I thought maybe you'd like to do something, you know, catch up on what you've been doing."

"What did you have in mind?"

"You want to go to a little party?"

"I was going to move some of my stuff to a new apartment in Sventon, but I guess it can wait. What kind of party?"

"For Fulton Gray's court deal, out at the Dogues farm. You should come. Drink a few beers, have some good conversation? They're great folks. I'm surprised you never met Coney or Fulton."

"I know who they are. They wouldn't mind me crashing?"

"They're very hospitable folks."

"OK. Meet me at my apartment in about an hour."

He took his time grooming himself in his apartment, but still pulled into the apartment parking lot in about half an hour. When he shut off the Jeep's engine, he saw the girl he thought he'd seen somewhere before—the one who vaguely resembled Aspen, only blonde and with a big butt—walking up the stairs toward Aspen's apartment. When she'd disappeared into the top floor out of his sight, a dirty pickup truck with a loud muffler and oversize wheels pulled into the parking lot and blocked the main sidewalk entrance.

Garit couldn't tell at first who was in the truck, but as the chick who reminded him of Aspen came down the stairs with a box in her arms, the two got out of the truck, and Garit knew it was the two thugs who had threatened him a few weeks before.

Adrenaline rushed through him as fast as hot iron burns flesh, and without thought, he leaped from the Jeep and ran toward the situation. He watched with bobbing vision as the two confronted the girl, just as they had him, with an initial friendly demeanor.

He ran full speed, but his legs felt like he was stepping in soupy concrete as the man dressed in stylish black slapped the box from her hands onto the sidewalk. Aspen put her arms in the air.

"What's going on with you idiots? She griped. The short-haired, well-dressed one in the duo reached toward her. Just as Garit saw him tear her shirt sleeve and heard the word "bitch," he leaped, landing with his arms crossed on the chest of the well-dressed one. They fell to the ground, with Garit on top, as Garit screamed to Cindy.

"Run, girl! Get out of here!"

Garit tried his best to get up quickly and take on the man he'd just taken down, but he felt a boot dully whump against his right side, barely missing his lowest rib. It knocked the breath out of him, but he somehow spun and caught the second kick with his hands before it could land. He pulled violently, but the tattooed dude did not tumble as they always did in the movies. Instead, he lost only a portion of his balance, and by then, the well-dressed one had tangled Garit's feet with his own, and with a quick thrust, drove Garit face-first into the dirty area between lawn and sidewalk. He felt two hands on the back of his head holding his face in the dirt as boots struck again and again, this time hitting abdomen and ribs and arms and shoulders. Each boot blow sucked more air from him until, with the pressure off his head, he felt a regular shoe, with softer soles, clip his left eyebrow. He felt a heavier boot come down hard on his right hand, and he thought he heard bones snapping, but he was helpless to defend himself anymore. He heard the two laugh.

"Lyin' sack!" one of them snarled. "You said you didn't even know Cindy, Bee-otch!"

They each kicked him a few more times, but suddenly, they stopped, He heard their footsteps running away and tried to look up, but his eyes wouldn't focus. He heard a voice, mumbling, and felt someone trying to turn him over onto the lawn. Before he passed out, he thought he saw a middle-aged man with a white beard and a cowboy hat kneeling over him.

"Detective?" he asked, unsure if he was still within reality.

"Jesus," the man said. Garit couldn't tell if it was a prayer or an exclamation, but for that brief second of consciousness, he thought he recognized it. He decided it was prayer.

Garit had been stitched up and bandaged, and was dressed and waiting for the doctor's final instructions when Aspen burst into his room at the Jovial County Hospital.

"Garit!" she cried, rushing to his side. "I'm so sorry. Can I touch you?"

"You did that a long time ago," he said, wishing he hadn't, but glad he did. "Just be careful of the ribs," he said as she gently put her arms around him. "I'm so, so, sorry," she whispered in his ear.

"What for?" Garit pushed her back to arms length.

"For getting you beat up, what else?"

"What did you have to do with it? It was the two JAAR goons who did this. And how did you know about it anyway?"

"Because it was all my fault," she sobbed. "You took my beating for me. It was all because of me!" she shrieked, tears flowing. "I'm Cindy!"

Garit's eyebrow twitched, and it pulled against the stitches in his forehead. He shook his head slowly. "Fill me in, Aspen, I'm not up for solving any riddles right now."

She poured out her whole tale. How she'd been working undercover on the story for Botsdorf before she'd quit the *World*, all the way to her pushing Pinckney to the brink.

"They were after me, not you! It was me they were going to beat up!" She shrieked and began to blubber again. "I was trying to push a madman over the edge, but you got caught in the middle!"

He reached out and endured the pain of hugging her.

"Sounds like you got yourself a whale of a story," he said, and she laughed through the sobs. "Let me tell you about mine," he said. "It's not half bad either."

As Garit and Aspen made the connection between their two stories, in walked Coney, Jenn and Fulton.

"Nice way to dodge our party," said Fulton, gripping Garit gently by the shoulder that had no bandage.

"Believe me, I'd rather have been there. Fulton, Coney, Jenn? This is Aspen Kemp."

Coney and Jenn politely said hello, and Fulton reached out his hand to her and gripped it gently.

"Now, when are you getting out of here?" Jenn asked. "We're going to take you to our place tonight, so we can be sure you're OK."

"I can stay at my apartment," he argued.

"No," Jenn insisted. "You come to our house, stay in the extra room. You can really get some good rest there, and you'll be guarded by Mulder and Scully."

"I guess I just got an offer I can't refuse," he said to Aspen.

He got up to leave, and Aspen leaned on him slightly and kissed him on the cheek. "Thanks for taking this for me, Garit. I'll never forget it." Then she left the room.

"Dude, she's smokin' hot," Fulton said when Aspen had gone. "Makes the bruises hurt a little less?"

Garit smiled. "Let's just get going before these pain pills knock me over."

They wheeled Garit out the hospital door when Detective Sheridan arrived. He stopped short and looked at Garit.

"Now you see why you need our help," he said, and handed Garit another business card with nothing on it but a cell phone number hand-written on one side and 'Bill Sheridan' printed on the other.

"Let's talk as soon as you get back on your feet," he said, and walked back toward the parking lot.

"Hey!" Garit shouted after him. "Thanks for being there!" The detective kept walking, and raised his right hand as he went.

44

Garit hobbled off the tractor that pulled a grain cart at the Dogues farm to greet Detective Bill Sheridan, dressed in a gray pinstriped suit. He was clean-shaven, and his straw cowboy hat looked like it had just been dry cleaned.

Garit's face was still swollen, and the cut over his right eye was purple and swelled about twice the size of the left.

"Garit," greeted the detective as he walked away from his Explorer. "How're you doing, son? Getting healed up?"

"I'm still a little sore. I never knew how much ribs could hurt."

"Learning to farm, too?"

"I'm just trying to do what I can. I owe the Dogues' a little helping hand. Besides, all there is to feeding a ration to the heifers is to drive this tractor. The guys who mix the feed do all the hard work."

"Can they spare you for a few minutes?"

Garit pointed to the Dogues porch and followed the detective there.

"You still at the *World*, or working here?"

"I haven't lost that job yet," Garit replied. "I told Wally I had to take care of some stuff with my parent's estate. He'd forgotten they were dead. I have the feeling he thought I was lying. I'm glad I came out here, though. The farm work keeps my muscles limber. But I'm about ready to go back, I guess. Don't know how I'll explain the shiner."

"Yeah, before we're done here, I want pictures of you all beaten up. Maybe we can put those two idiots who did this away for a long time."

"Don't worry. Botsdorf has taken new pictures every day."

The detective laughed. "I should have known a lawyer wouldn't overlook that detail. But I'm here on a more serious note, Garit. Have you written the story about Deadfrick's grant proposals yet?"

"No, but I tell you, it's been calling to me. It wants to be let out of its cell inside my brain. If I hadn't been beaten up, I would have already submitted it for publication. But my hands are still swollen. It hurts to type."

"Well, I guess it's true, then, that God works in mysterious ways," said the detective. "If you had published the story already, sure, we would have nailed Deadfrick to the wall, but all the others would have skated free."

"All the others?"

"Corruption this deep is never accomplished alone," Sheridan said. "By holding off, we have the chance to give everyone involved enough rope to hang themselves."

"So who else is involved?"

The detective hesitated.

"Look," Garit said, suddenly feeling bold. "I took a beating over this whole thing. My hands and fingers still aren't limber enough to type a whole lot, and I've done the police's work for them in the process. I don't think it's too much to ask that I be in the loop."

Sheridan nodded, then began.

"You'll be in the loop soon enough. Judge Meade has convinced a federal judge to convene a grand jury based on the evidence Botsdorf gave him after Fulton's trial. You'll be subpoenaed, more than likely, along with me, to provide evidence against a lot of people, and I intend to give it to them."

"Who?"

"We know Deadfrick, Pinckney, Mayor Benz, Sheriff Dulogski, and maybe officer Schoen are directly involved, and we suspect several others. One of those others is your boss, Wally East."

Garit grinned as if he'd just been told that birds can't fly, and it tugged at his stitches.

"Have you met Wally?" he asked, giggling. "Are you sure he's even smart enough to be involved in a conspiracy?"

"That's what we want to find out."

"So who else?"

The detective hesitated again.

"C'mon, detective. If I'm going to be part of this, I need to see the whole story."

"I can't say until we have more proof. That's where you come in, at least where Wally is concerned."

"Believe me, detective, I'd love to see Wally hang, he's such a jerk. But turning against him isn't exactly in my best interests. I have no other job. I have no other place to stay than his apartment I get as part of my salary. I have nothing to gain and everything to lose by this. You'd mentioned making all of this worth my while. What did you have in mind?"

"You'll find this ironic, Garit, but the state police have a grant to help us pay for cooperative citizens' help in cracking government corruption. I can't promise you lots of money, but it could pay off your parents' bills and leave you with a little left over."

"How much left over?"

"Not much, really. Ten, twenty grand?"

"And what about my job?"

"That's out of my hands. It's a chance you'd have to decide to take or not."

"I don't like the sound of that. In other words, cooperating with you could jeopardize my job. I could be on some blacklist and never write again. I tell you, detective, this all sounds like blackmail, or invasion of privacy. All my choices seem bad. And what are the odds of Wally even running the story?"

"We have ways of applying pressure," the detective said. "A story like this could propel you into a better job somewhere else."

"A story," Garit repeated. "Forgive me for saying it out loud, detective, but it's my only bargaining chip here. And it's not a very good one. What's to keep you from tipping off another reporter and leaving me high and dry?"

"Just my word that I won't. That's it, Garit. It's all I have. You have to trust me."

"I don't like the sound of that, either. No offense, detective, but I haven't gained a whole lot of trust in humanity in the last year or so."

"But you have a real trump card. You have evidence that only you have access to, right? I mean, Botsdorf didn't give the judge original documents, did he?"

Garit hesitated.

"Tell you what. If I cooperate and we sting some of these folks, you don't move until I see this story on the front page of the *Jovial World*."

"I'd like to say I think we can do that, Garit, but I can't control what a grand jury will do."

"Just keep the story away from the TV idiots and my competition."

"Anything else?"

"And help me find a job?"

"Who needs a job?" asked Jenn, appearing through the kitchen door with a large pitcher of iced lemonade and two glasses. "Sorry," she said as Garit and the detective stopped their conversation. "Didn't mean to overhear."

"It's OK, Jenn," said the detective, to Garit's surprise. "Bill and I've known each other since grade school," Jenn was quick to explain.

"I might need a job soon, and a new apartment," said Garit, surprised at how bitter his voice sounded in his own ears. "Wally's already mad at me. I told him I had to take care of some stuff back home, but I think he suspects something else."

"We always need help, if you don't mind working for minimum wage, and Fulton's room is empty," she said. "He's got his own place within walking distance anyway."

"Must be he's getting better after his folks," Sheridan said.

"I think so," Jenn replied. "He never would admit it, but I knew when he stayed here for so long that he probably didn't want to be in that house alone. He's solved those problems, I guess. Took a lot of time and prayer."

"I knew Fulton's parents were killed," Garit said. "I don't know details."

"Almost two years now," Jenny said. "Motorcycle accident. A horrible, horribly brutal accident."

Garit stared, numb. He'd assumed no one else could know his pain, but it was clear that these people responded to their personal tragedy a lot better than he was doing. Tears filled his eyes for Fulton, and he tried to hide them, but his voice gave them away.

"Here I am, a near-total stranger to you people and yet you took me in as if I was your own family," he started. "And all the time you're aching inside as much as me, and you never let on. You gave a total stranger all this support, and didn't even think about your own hurt?" He paused to compose himself. "That's crazy. That's not how things happen in the rest of the world. My folks would never have done something like that. They'd have been too afraid of a scam or something. Sorry. But this is all so foreign to me, now that I see more of the picture. Wow. I've never been given a gift like this before, Jenn." A tear was in her eye.

"What gift?"

"The gift of acceptance. Without strings. It's like, freeing or something. It's like I've been anchored, and there's no tornado in the world strong enough to move me."

"Write that down," Jenn said. "Better yet, read more about the anchor available to you in the Bible."

Garit wiped his eye dry and took a deep drink of his lemonade, and watched as the detective drained his glass in two swallows.

"Alright detective," Garit said when he'd composed himself. "I'm young. I have nothing to lose. I need to take some risks for once in my life. What do you want me to do?"

45

At 2:45 a.m., a well-dressed and groomed young man and his tattooed, pierced partner loitered by the back door of the receiving docks at the Farmers Own Store.

When headlights of a delivery truck hit them, they mashed out their cigarettes, stuffed the butts into their McDonald's soda cups and tossed them and the bags—still pungent from the remains of Big Macs and large fries—into the shrubs that blocked their presence from view. Above the dock's bay doors were three sets of bare wires in three locations. Security cameras had been put on back order.

"Old Dead-dick told me those idiot farmers in the co-op didn't want these shrubs here," said the well-dressed one. "They were afraid it would be perfect cover for vandals and break-ins. But guess what? The law requires the shrubs! Isn't it great when the government is so cooperative?" He laughed hoarsely, then pointed as the truck backed into a loading dock.

"Look at that ridiculous truck," he said. "Brenner Farms. A stupid laughing cow with a little star burst bouncing from his top tooth. What's up with that, anyway? Stupid."

"Yeah, that is pretty stupid," said the tattooed one.

The truck backed into the bay and the two thugs approached the driver. He stepped out of the truck, looked both ways like a conscientious child about to cross a street, and nodded to them. Without a word, the driver walked to the dock, produced a plastic key card, swiped it through the proper slot and opened the back door. The two thugs looked behind them as they hurried to follow him in. No one in sight.

In 30 seconds, a bay door opened, revealing the driver and the thugs, who stood waiting. The driver stepped up and opened the truck door.

"It's all yours, boys, I'll be back in half an hour."

The well-dressed of the two thugs reached out to shake the driver's hand, and slipped him three crisp $100 bills. As he walked away, the tattooed thug began unloading cases of milk. He lined them up in front of the coolers where they were supposed to be inserted, and pulled a small leather satchel, about the size of a legal pad folded in half, from inside a light jacket. He opened the satchel and pulled out one of several syringes, its plunger extended three-quarters of its length.

Behind him, the well-dressed thug pushed in the last of the milk crates and shut the truck door, then the bay door. He came alongside the tattooed thug and pulled out a package of candy wax milk bottles, the ones with syrup in them. He tore open the package and drew out a bottle with green liquid, bit off the top of the bottle and spit it on the floor. He swallowed the syrup, and reached into his pants pocket for a Bic lighter.

The two worked quickly and efficiently. The first thug injected each plastic bottle with a portion of the syringe's contents, careful to sink the needle just above the milk line and just below the plastic ring seal. The tattooed one came right behind, melting wax with the lighter until it dripped onto the injection hole. Then he smoothed it out with his finger.

They had just finished with the last case of milk when the driver came back through the entrance.

"Find what you were looking for, inspectors?" he asked, starting to push the milk into the coolers where they belonged. The two thugs began to help.

"Yes, and we appreciate your cooperation," said the well-dressed thug.

"People like you can really help us catch any food dangers—you know, contamination—before they get started and kill a bunch of people. We hate to do covert surveillance, but anyone can pass an inspection if they know it's coming, right?"

The driver didn't look at the young man, but just kept working.

"I can't argue with the FDA," he said. "I don't know nothin' about nothin.'"

Done with the job, the three walked out the door together. The driver drove off to his next delivery and the thugs drove off in a loud, jacked-up pickup truck with over-sized wheels.

46

Garit had finished feeding calves in cozy individual hutches their evening warm milk when his cell phone rang.

"Hi, Garit. Detective Sheridan here. Say, I've been called in front of that grand jury I told you about, but I've kept your name out of it for now. I just need to know positively that all the stuff you've been sending me is legit. I mean, you have the original documents that you'll cite in your story?"

"Like I've said a thousand times, detective, I have the carbon copies."

"Just being sure. Are they in a secure place?"

"As secure as I can make them. Look Detective, I don't know how many stories I've written in my five months at the *World*, but I'm always thorough. I check my facts. I can knock out a city council meeting story in about an hour if I put my mind to it, but the Jim Deadfrick story is different. It took me nearly a week to write it, and that was after three weeks checking and double-checking the smallest details against the carbon copies. There were stacks and stacks of documents, and it took a whole day just to sort the ones that were relevant to Deadfrick. Another day to make copies of them all, and they're stored in several different places. And there are only two people who know where they are. Losing is not acceptable to me here, detective. The most important story of my life will not just drift around like some sound bite. It has order, consistency, direction and solid ground. No one will be able to poke a hole in it. You've seen what I wrote. Can you?"

"No, Garit, I can't.

"Then this thing has been fact-checked more than any story I've ever written. Botsdorf double-checked the documents too. No allegation in my story can be disproven, and every claim can be documented. No figure has gone unverified."

"Well then I guess we're ready. Go ahead and put things in motion."

Garit approached Wally's office, the story on a zip drive in his pocket.

"Oh, you're finally back," Wally said, then looked up, did a double-take.

"What happened to you?"

"I got mugged at a gas station in Chicago. Didn't I call to tell you that?"

"You called to get a couple more days vacation, but you didn't mention this! Man, you look like you been through a meat grinder!"

"Yeah, thanks, Wally. But I was working on something else while I was in Illinois."

"Why were you in Illinois?"

"My parent's estate?"

"I thought you were from Ohio."

"No, Illinois. Look, Wally, I think I have a major story to break here."

Wally stared at his wounds, but appeared interested in what Garit was about to say.

"Congratulations," he said sarcastically, then looked away. "It's about time. What do you think you have?"

"I've been doing research for weeks into the grant writing operations of Jim Deadfrick." he said. The zip drive stayed in his pocket. "There's documented proof that he's been manipulating these grants for years and writing in provisions for money that goes straight into his pocket."

"Pretty serious charges, if they're true," Wally said, looking at the stitches over Garit's eye again. Garit turned away, afraid that the haunted image in his brain would spill out. When the thought of Wally looking over his shoulder at him, with his pants on the floor and his coconut buns flapping like hairy Jello entered his mind, he had to control his nausea. "Got any proof?" Wally asked.

"It's all in the story, man." He pulled the zip drive from his pocket and handed it to Wally. "Pretty good work, if I do say so myself. This also proves a conspiracy against Fulton Gray in order to improve the chances of another big chunk of grant money coming in to fight gang activity, which everyone knows doesn't exist."

Wally took the zip drive and laid it on the other side of his computer, out of Garit's reach. When his shoulder turned for a second, Garit glanced at the newspaper page layout on Wally's computer screen. He saw part of a headline, something about milk.

"I'll go over it." Wally said. "I'm sure there's something you screwed up. This is usually the kind of thing reserved for the big boys. Ain't no rookie ever broke anything like this. Somebody's probably feeding you a big old lump of coal! Right now can you write me some briefs? I got a few holes to fill."

Garit turned around and went back to his desk to find a few short items to write. If the detective was right, the story would never see the light of day. Not in the *World*, anyway.

47

Drew Seifert, public relations and communications director for the Jovial County Hospital, cursed as he sat at his desk, speaking with Fran MacInerney, his counterpart at the health department. She was a wide but well-proportioned dark-skinned woman with a slow Southern accent that made her appear calmer than the turmoil bubbling within her.

"I know, I should have put out a press release as soon as the first medical reports came in Saturday morning, but I would have had to wait for an OK from the CEO, and he was out of town," Drew said.

"Too late now," Fran said. "It would have been a lot easier to keep this quiet if it hadn't been for Wally East spilling the beans about his so-called food contamination crisis—and quite inaccurately, I might add—in the *Jovial World*. When does that hit the stands, anyway?"

"Tomorrow, I think. I still don't know how the big stupe ever got wind of this. He must know a nurse or something. Just proof that even a blind hog can find a truffle every now and then. I just thank God he hadn't posted it on his website."

"Thank God Wally let us see an advance copy, too," Fran said. Drew laughed. "He's found so few real stories, maybe now, finally, he's learning a thing or two."

"He's incapable of learning," said Fran. "But I was glad the little butt-kisser gave us the heads up on this one, even if it did come on a weekend. He was on it, you have to give him that."

"Doesn't it feel good, even a little, that we finally have something to tackle, though?" Drew, excited, asked Fran. "When was the last chance we had to exercise our crisis skills, to stretch ourselves and put out a fire? It feels good to me, Fran. What's it been? Three years? I was getting rusty. This is thrilling. Everything's in jeopardy. Health, business, food. If we had sex, it would be a slam dunk."

"Doesn't feel all that great to me, Drew. People got sick, you know."

"Yeah, but our basic job is the same as it always was—to tell the public there's no need to panic, assure them that the hospital and the health department has it all under control, and when we discover the source of the malady, we'll tell the public all about it, blah, blah, blah. Then, the hospital board will vote to tell them nothing until it decides what to tell them. Standard PR." He giggled, and it infected Fran.

"Think about it," Drew said when Fran had stopped giggling. "Aren't you tired of the same old crap? Sometimes this job is just too easy in a little place like this. It's up to us to control the important news, and here we have a prime opportunity. The press should only know what the board wants the public to know, when they want it known. A free press is a thing of the past, Fran. There isn't a paper left in the entire country in a town the size of Jovial that can afford to pay a reporter to waste time on investigations. These days, reporters can't take the chance that they'll miss stories about local celebrities kissing babies and local politicians kissing butt. I'm so glad I got out of that business."

"My favorite stories are around any three-day weekend holiday, when pretty boy TV reporters tell people important stuff about single moms in tough economic times." Her voice changed to a sarcastic tone. "'It's tragic! How will the little mommies survive if they have to serve hamburgers on the grill on the Fourth of July instead of steak'!" Fran laughed. Drew loved it.

As the reporters drifted in for the hastily called press conference, Drew, a tall, thin fellow with thick glasses and thin blonde hair, handed

Fran his list. On it were the names of the invited speakers—Coney Dogues, current president of the Jovial Area Farmers' Association, Frank Gladding, Farmers Own Store manager, and Fran. It was important to control what was said, and Drew and Fran were confident they had it under control.

Coney had called Noah Brenner to the press conference as well, and when Fulton walked in with Noah, Drew frowned. "It's too crowded there, Fran. Take charge," he said. "Noah Brenner is a wild card, kind of ignorant. Try not to let him talk."

"A quick warning," Coney told Noah when he walked up, just as Fran was about to step to the microphone. "They're going to try to pin this personally on you," he said. "The media needs a face to blame. I told the health department they were probably wrong, and so far they have no real proof, but I thought you should be here at this dog-and-pony show anyway, if for nothing more than to show you have nothing to hide."

"I don't have anything to hide," he told Coney. "Everybody knows we do things right on my farm."

"I know that, but just let me do the talking," he replied.

When Garit walked into the hospital's media center, he saw three TV cameras and Aspen, who smiled at him and patted a seat beside her in the front row.

"Do you know what's going on?" she asked, touching his arm lightly.

"Not a clue."

Wally kept his distance on the other side of the room, and carried no note pad or recorder.

Fran took the microphone calmly. She smiled and took her time, making eye contact with every reporter in the room and the assorted businessmen.

"Good morning, y'all!" No responses. She cleared her throat and read from a single page in front of her.

"A mysterious illness was first reported by the Jovial Hospital late last Friday or early Saturday morning, with patients each complaining of similar symptoms: Vomiting, headaches, and in one case, a seizure. Patients complaining of these symptoms increased in number over the weekend before tapering off," she read. "The staff at the health

292 | Paul W. Jackson

department became concerned when ten people total were admitted to the hospital, and a subsequent investigation has led health department officials and hospital doctors—who are working in collaboration—to believe the source of the contamination is milk from the Farmers' Own Store. We've directed the store directors—and they were quick to comply—to cease sales of milk from the present source until we can discover exactly what caused the contamination."

As she spoke, Dan Pinckney and Jim Deadfrick noisily clodded into the room. Deadfrick's head was held high and Pinckney's face was crumpled from the brow down like a worn-out tissue. Together, they barged loudly to the front row and sat opposite Garit and Aspen.

Fran let them settle.

"Any questions?" she asked. Pinckney leaped from his seat.

"I represent the concerned citizens of Jovial and JAAR, and we demand that this milk be destroyed immediately and the store be banned from selling any products until the health department can assure us all that there's no risk of death from eating their products," he said. Garit saw Coney whisper in Fulton's ear. Fulton nodded and slipped behind the makeshift backdrop, a cloth draped across a round metal tubing frame. Fran kept her cool.

"There's no reason to believe that any other products from the store are contaminated," she said. "We are confident that it's confined to milk."

"And what's the contamination?" asked a TV reporter.

"We're still running tests to determine that," Fran said.

"What do you think it is?" the reporter asked. "Is it contamination?" Garit and Aspen looked at each other and rolled their eyes.

"I won't speculate until the evidence is conclusive," Fran replied.

"What's the store doing about it?"

Frank Gladding stepped forward.

"We have already decided to voluntarily take all the milk off the shelves and destroy it," he said, with a whiny emphasis on destroy. "We're as concerned about the situation as anyone, maybe more, and we will not sell Brenner's Best milk again until the situation is resolved."

"Does that mean you'll change milk suppliers?" Garit asked.

Coney stepped forward. Noah stood too, despite a harsh look from Coney.

"We have no plans to change milk suppliers," Coney said. "Brenner's Best milk has a long-standing record for quality, and so we believe this is an anomaly, and are confident that Mr. Brenner and his family, if the tests show—and we don't think they will—that milk from his farm caused the illnesses, will resolve it and fast. So we'll just refrain from selling milk until this is resolved, Garit. As owners of the store cooperative, we will stand by the Brenners, and will have Brenner's Best milk back on the shelves as soon as this issue is resolved and when the health department clears the milk."

"Mr. Brenner," yelped a young TV reporter. "What do you think went wrong?"

"Myself and my family have been trying to figure that out from the get-go when we got the news," Noah said. "And for the life of me, I don't know what could have gotten in the milk. We haven't done anything different lately. We haven't even changed soap in the milking machines. We did a total check of every step in the milk production line, and there's nothing possible. The data says beyond a doubt that we're clean. I don't believe my milk could have made anyone sick."

"You keep soap in your milking machines?" a different TV reporter asked. "Why?"

"Enough of these lies," cried Deadfrick, leaping to his feet with Pinckney like a shadow beside him. "There's no sense wasting time assessing blame. The evidence is clear. People have gotten deathly ill. The time is for action, and I believe the most prudent action, the only one in line with God's will, is to shut down the store immediately. We can't take any more risks with our children's health."

The TV reporters nodded and scribbled in notebooks as Fran stepped forward to the microphone.

"Again, we see no need for shutting down the whole store," she drawled. "And because the number of cases per day has decreased, and the fact that we've seen zero new cases for 24 hours, we believe it to be an isolated incident. We also believe that future milk tests, once we know what caused the illnesses, can isolate the problem and resolve it immediately."

"That's not good enough," Pinckney shouted. "This is exactly what I warned you people about before the election, but you wouldn't listen to me. If this stupid city had formed a food quality commission, all this would have been avoided. But here we are, at risk of dying because of sloppy food handling from a bunch of animal abusers and factory farmers."

"This is hardly the time to debate farming methods," said Fran, suddenly appearing in control. "And no one is at risk of dying. There are other stores where you can buy milk, even organic milk that's bottled the exact same way Mr. Brenner's is bottled, so you know it's pure, until the issue is resolved."

"We can never trust the Farmers' Own Store again," Pinckney whined. "How can we? How do we know the factory farmers haven't done something to poison us all, just for the sake of their own profits?" TV reporters nodded again. "This is all great TV," Garit heard one of them tell the other. "Nothing like a good scare to boost viewership."

Garit looked back at the TV reporter. "How does poisoning people increase profits?" he asked. The reporter shrugged noncommittally. Aspen rolled her eyes.

Coney, his lips pursing backward as his eyes narrowed, began to answer Pinckney when Noah stepped in front of him to the microphone.

"Mr. Pinckney, we all know you're a vegan, but that is a horrible, hurtful and false accusation," Noah blurted. "For one thing, you can't even tell me what a factory farm is, but my family's farm is a far cry from what you think it is. We're a small operation, and we've been feeding our children and grandchildren our own products for generations now, so our stake in this matter is just as important as yours!"

"You're not small, you're a cruelty factory!" Pinckney shouted. Noah paused and glared at Pinckney. Coney reached, trying to pull Noah away from the microphone, but Noah pushed back Coney's hand.

"I will tell everyone standing here, and every person in Jovial, that I would rather go out of business than take any risk of hurting anybody who drinks my milk," he said, directly into a camera.

"Then I suggest you get out of the milk business," said Deadfrick, "because it's obvious that your cows caused this epidemic."

"Ten people is an epidemic?" Garit asked.

"There is no epidemic," Fran said. "As I said before, the number of reported cases of illness has already declined to zero, and the people who were ill are well on their way to full recovery, so just a little caution will likely resolve the whole thing. And there is nothing obvious"—she stared at Deadfrick—"about anything yet. We'll know when we collect samples and get the lab results in three to five weeks."

"How long before you know the results?" asked a TV reporter. Fran shot him a look of incredulity.

"Three to five weeks."

"And is there any danger to the public?"

"What have we been talking about all this time? Next question."

Garit was curious.

"Mr. Brenner, how could you go out of business? What would you do?"

"I don't know. Start all over, I guess. But I believe keeping the public safe is more important than any one person or farm."

Pinckney groaned and began to lunge forward, shouting "Lies! He's telling you what you want to hear! How long did you have to coach him, Coney?" Deadfrick held him back.

"I just pray it doesn't come to that," Brenner said.

Garit walked away from the press conference, but Detective Bill Sheridan, dressed in a business suit, clean-shaven and without a cowboy hat, touched his arm from behind.

"A tip," Sheridan whispered. "Follow Frank back to the store with your camera. Keep your eye on Deadfrick and pay close attention to his attitude."

Garit walked into the back room of the Farmers' Own Store to see Frank already pushing a cart full of milk gallons to the back, behind the cooler cases. The floor was open there, with other store products stacked in boxes against the walls. He pulled a drugstore point-and-shoot camera from his pocket and cursed it.

"This is about as unprofessional as anything could be," he'd told Wally when he handed it to him.

"It's all you're going to get," Wally had said. "You already wrecked three cameras, so now, as your reward, you get the cheapest piece of crap I could find. Now take good pictures and maybe you can move up the ladder to a real digital."

"Frank," Garit said as he walked in. "I'm going to take some pics of this."

"If Coney said it was OK," Frank replied.

Garit shot, first with his phone, then with the camera as Frank wheeled the cart over a floor drain behind the milk refrigerator cases and began cutting them open with a short machete. Milk gushed like a dam bursting and rushed quickly down the drain.

When Frank was about half done, Deadfrick burst in and, as Garit took pictures of him, he confronted Frank.

"I'm here to make sure all the adulterated milk is safely gone and that no human can be killed again," he shouted.

As Frank cut the last gallon, Garit heard a shriek behind him. It was Fran.

"What are you doing?" she cried.

"Destroying the milk," Frank said, his face showing puzzlement.

"We haven't even taken samples yet," she moaned. "How are we going to test milk we don't have?"

Deadfrick pointed and looked at Garit.

"There's your story, boy," he said. "What more evidence do you need that the farmers know they're guilty than the fact that they're destroying evidence?"

"I didn't know," whined Frank. "I was just doing what I was told."

"Just like the Nazi war criminals," Deadfrick snarled. "Obeying orders doesn't absolve you from criminal prosecution, and I intend to be sure charges are filed. This boy even has pictures of you destroying evidence! You're dead meat, Frankie boy!"

Fran nodded. "Don't worry, Jim," she said. "The health department will see to the prosecution."

"Can I quote you on that?" Garit asked Fran.

"Absolutely. I intend to get to the bottom of this and see that someone is held accountable."

Fran and Deadfrick stormed out, and Garit walked up to Frank, who appeared dazed.

"Isn't it kind of a waste to destroy this milk when the milk that supposedly made people sick had already been gone from the store and in people's refrigerators?" he asked.

"Yeah, it is," Frank replied. "None of this makes any sense. But sometimes you just do what you're told and cover your butt."

"Bull!" Garit spat. "You should do what's right!"

"Right and wrong don't make much difference if you lose your job," Frank replied. He suddenly reached out and swatted the camera from Garit's hand. It crashed to the hard metal floor covered with milk near the drain, and Frank's heavy brown shoe came down hard, smashing the cheap device into small chips of plastic.

"What is with you people in this town and cameras?" Garit shouted.

"I can't afford to have evidence around," Frank whined. "I'll buy you a new one."

"Yeah, that helps a lot," Garit said, and kicked a piece of plastic camera as he walked out the door.

48

Noah Brenner stood in his farm office,
holding two pieces of paper with graphs and numbers and little else,
facing the milk truck driver in front of him.

"Let's be extra-sure, Luke," he said.

"I've already double-checked the milk samples from this lot, and it's
all right there in your hand," the driver said. "Ain't nothing wrong. And
there's nothing wrong with what you sent to the store last Friday, either.
That's all on the second page. I don't know why you don't just bottle it
across the driveway like you always do."

"I couldn't sell it in the store if I did. It's all shut down for the time
being."

"It won't last too long," Luke replied. "Your milk is too good. At
least you can still sell one last load to the blend market. Whatever it
was that made those people sick, it didn't come from this farm. Period.
I have no doubt at all. Probably just some bug that was going around.
I'll testify in court if you need me to."

"I appreciate that, Luke. My computer program agrees with you,
and it's state-of-the-art. Within five minutes of pouring a sample into
the bowl on top of the computer, it diagnoses trace elements of about
a dozen things. If the problem came from here, it's something that no
one knows how to find. It's supposed to detect stuff at levels ten percent
below the government's standards."

He moved from his office and went outside with Luke, who hopped into the cab of the massive stainless steel tanker truck and waved goodbye.

As the truck roared away, a small, rusty car—a Honda with a State of Michigan magnetic seal logo attached to the driver's door—rolled up. From it stepped a young, well-dressed and groomed young man, wearing an off-white shirt, conservative dull red tie and dress slacks under a white smock he donned on the way across the driveway to Noah's office.

"Where's that milk going?" he cried when he saw Noah waiting for him.

"Traverse City," Noah said. "Who are you?"

The young man reached into his back pocket and pulled out a hard plastic card that read 'State of Michigan Special Investigations' on it. "Do you think it's wise to send out bad milk?"

"Nothing bad about it," Noah said. "Had it all tested and got the OK from the milk inspector just yesterday."

"But," said the young man, "what have you been testing for?"

"Everything."

"Let's see."

Noah directed the young man to follow him into his office. Standing, the young man took the milk analysis printout and pretended to look it over.

"Here's your problem," he said. "There's no test here for what hurt all those people in Jovial."

"You know what it was already? They said it would take three weeks."

"For the hospital and the health department, maybe. But I'm in special investigations. We know what it was, and you'd better sit down. This won't be easy to take."

Noah felt the heat of toxic adrenaline run from his lower back up to his neck as he sat in his office chair. The young man leaned over the desk that separated them.

"I don't know how else to tell you this other than to just come out with it," he said. "Your cows are contaminated with PBB."

"No way," said Noah. "PBB happened fifty years ago. My equipment would have detected it."

"That's the problem," the young man said. "PBB is so old that the state doesn't require a test for it anymore. So the computer programmers—even the private programs—don't test for it at all. But our state labs still can detect it if we ask them to, and they're much more sophisticated and sensitive than your home system here. At best, it will show up on your readout as an undetermined adulterant."

"I was just a baby when PBB made the headlines," Noah said. "A fire retardant was mixed in with animal feed on a dairy 500 miles or more south of here. And there's no way that could have happened again. How could it have gotten into my feed? I blend everything these animals eat right here. And they haven't had any feed grown from off this farm in probably nine months."

"I don't doubt you, Mr. Brenner, but the DNR is still investigating."

"What does natural resources have to do with anything?"

"I meant agriculture department," the young man said. "I'm sorry. I do investigations for both departments. Needless to say, your herd is under immediate quarantine, and we'll have to depopulate your farm."

"Depopulate." Noah repeated as his face turned pale. "I know what that means. It's just government talk for kill them all!" He slumped back into his office chair, the shock of it all beginning to reach him, like a sudden collapse hours after a blow to the head.

"There's more bad news, I'm afraid," the young man said. "Because this is not a naturally occurring disease, there is no indemnification for your herd. We'll haul them away at state expense and have them destroyed, but the cost of the investigation will be your responsibility. And, because PBB is an adulterant, I'm afraid you'll face criminal charges for tampering with the food supply."

"But what about my cows?" Noah asked, his hands beginning to shake.

"I don't know what to tell you," the young man said. "I'm sure you understand the position I'm in. This is a public health situation, and I need to be concerned with the overall consumer here."

"Well," said Noah, his brain beginning to recover from the initial shock, "I'm not doing anything without proof. There is absolutely no way PBB got into my milk. I would have seen symptoms in my cows."

"Wait right here and I'll get the proof," the young man said, and left to walk to his car. He came back with a paper bearing a state seal watermark that looked like a lab test sheet. Noah skipped to the bottom line and read the final analysis: Polybrominated methyl bromide. PBB. A large pit instantly kicked itself into Noah's belly.

The young man still stood on the other side of the desk. "There's the proof. You're in denial, Mr. Brenner. Now, I'm not exactly authorized to do this, but I tell you what," he said. "These results won't get to the health department to be confirmed for some time. But there's really no doubt. It's all here in black and white. If you can get rid of your cattle before they get those results, I won't turn you in. Slaughter the animals. Sell the meat to friends. I don't care as long as I get records of who bought what. For public safety alone, you understand. I just won't stand to see any more adulterated milk from contaminated cows get into the public food chain. But I don't want to see you go broke, either. Get something out of them while you can, and I'll keep this out of the press, too."

"I thought you were most concerned with the consumer," said Noah, bitterness already pulling his face toward the earth.

"That's why I want you to sell your animals privately for meat. There's no problem if it's well-cooked. No questions asked. No harm, no foul."

"And if I decide to fight this?"

"You can fight it all you want, Mr. Brenner, but I can't let another drop of milk leave this farm. Starting now."

"I'm going to need a little time to think about it," Noah said.

"I can give you until morning. I'll call you back at 8 a.m.," said the young man. "I'm sorry, sir. I wish there was something I could do. But if you don't slaughter them yourself, I'll call in some truckers and we'll dispose of all the animals in a few days. Think about my offer. We can keep it all very quiet, you know, out of the papers if you'll do as I suggest."

He turned and walked away. Tears were flowing as Noah watched him turn the car around and drive out. The passenger side did not have the state seal on it. Noah called Coney.

"I think I may have been sabotaged," he blurted. "Do you know who could have fed my cows fire retardant?"

"Fire retardant! You mean like PBB?"

"That's what the state is saying it was. I don't believe it yet, but maybe I'm too stupid to understand."

"Let's go over it," Coney said. "Tell me if I'm off base. You personally oversee the exact ingredients in your feed mix, and every cow is fed an individual, exact ration according to nutritional needs, and you change it on a weekly basis, depending on lactation and production, right?" Coney paused. He knew how meticulous Noah had always been.

"Do you trust the fellas who mix your feed?"

"They're all trusted, long-time employees," Noah said. "Ain't no rookies would be doing that job. Besides, it's all computerized. Other than the heifers and dry cows, no animal is fed the exact same ration. The radio frequency collars allow each and every cow to open the feed chute anytime she wants. Computers read her tag, check the database, choose the feed from whatever bins it's in and delivers the mix through the auger. The only way anyone could slip something in is to hand-feed it."

"And that would have to be a hired hand," Coney said. "Any chance an animal rights wacko slipped in?"

"I trust all my employees. And I have security in place. Put it in right after they opened my spigot a year or so ago. I'd know about it if anyone came into the barns at night. But something slipped in. I have the proof from the state lab right here in my hand!"

"Something sure seems fishy," Coney said.

"What about the Brenner name, Coney? Could I ever show my face around here again? Can I ever face people who drank my milk and got sick? Can I look myself in the mirror if I sold friends and neighbors meat from contaminated cows?"

"What about the cows?" Coney asked. "Have you noticed any health problems in the herd? We both know what PBB does to animals."

"No, there are no symptoms that I've seen. No swollen muscles, no curved up hooves. They're all eating good. Maybe the inspector is right, and testing is more sensitive today than it was in the early 70s. It's the only answer. If my cows had ate PBB, they're looking at a painful, slow death. Torture! I couldn't live with that." There was a long silence on the phone.

"What are my options, Coney? I'll look like a big fat hypocrite, a farmer who's just been faking everybody out all these years, putting on a show as a good, conscientious farmer who, come to find out, didn't even know what was in the feed his animals ate."

"Just don't go beating yourself up over it," Coney said. "You have friends in this community, and they all know how good you are. Do you think we'd have asked you to sell in the store if that wasn't true?"

"Well, I can't take any risks. I'm going to retest all my feed."

"Do what you think is right, Noah. We're all behind you."

Noah gathered several pails and plastic bags. He walked to the feed bins and without a tool, scooped hand fulls of grain and placed them into the bags, which he marked with a permanent marker for tracking, and dropped them into the pails. Luckily, he had all his own computerized analytical equipment. He could find out before the day was out exactly what was in the feed. Maybe he could save the heifers and the dry cows, who weren't fed from the same lot as the milking cows with their special and ever-changing needs.

It was nearly 3 a.m. Saturday, almost time to get up for the morning milking, by the time Noah had gotten through every sample. Nothing at all in the heifer feed or the dry cow feed.

Then, suddenly, an anomaly. It was on the sheet for Number 245, a good-producing cow who was pregnant with her third calf and a solid member of the herd. The computer screen flashed. "Undetermined adulterant," it said.

So that was it. She'd been poisoned. How many others? The computer screen was still working.

Like a low rumble, like an earthquake or distant violent thunder, the dreaded answer came to him. Thirty cows, all pregnant, all on the same feed mix. The only other common thread was that they were all getting extra manganese. But while that element was oddly absent from the printout, each of the 30 animal's feed ration showed "undetermined adulterant" flashing on the screen like the repeated stabs of angry hornets. Noah laid his head on his desk and wept bitterly.

Deadfrick was in Wally's office, sitting

in a side chair that was taller than Wally's comfortable chair.

"If I censor this, I'll need something from you," Wally said. Deadfrick waited, silent.

"Can't you get me half of what you owe me now, and the rest soon?"

"I'll go you one better," Deadfrick said. "You'll get rid of this story and the reporter who wrote it or you'll never get a dime."

"I could sue you, you know. I kept the terms of our contract and printed your ads. I've even gone beyond that. I've done everything you've asked. I've supported your positions on everything in this town, even when I didn't think it was right. I've turned public opinion to your side and run your ads! I'm even going to run your milk contamination story."

"Yeah, and you kept on printing my ads, like a dummy!" Deadfrick said, grinning. "Two years without pay and you keep printing ads? Anybody with any business sense would have cut me off when I didn't pay for three weeks in a row. It's your own fault. Sucks to be you."

"Well, I'll just print this story, then. I know at least some of it's true. Maybe even tell the world about your role in the formaldehyde in the milk. You'll be run out of town on a rail after you're tarred and feathered."

"Oh, please, Wally, do! Please print it, all of it. I'll sue you for libel so fast and keep you in court for so long that even if I were convicted, you'd go bankrupt paying lawyers. So why don't you just give me the story and shut up or go broke? You ever want to get another ad from the school? Isn't the school your biggest source of income? You know as well as I do that I have the power to do that. How about the city's legal ads? Want to lose all that potential income for a measly twenty-five grand? You know I control those purse strings, Wally. I could make all that business go over to the *Sventon Sasser* with one phone call."

Wally glared past Deadfrick and sighed.

"You son-of-a-bitch," he growled. "I hope you burn in hell."

Deadfrick smiled.

"The really cool thing is, Wally, that I won't go to hell. I'm a Christian, and heaven is guaranteed. It's a great little loophole! I found it quite a few years ago. You should try it. It's a great gig. Total forgiveness, period. And all you have to do is go to church, cut them in on a little government grant cake now and then, and recruit a few people here and there."

"Just get out!" Wally spat. "And pay your bloody bill!"

"Now, now," Deadfrick mocked as he rose from his chair. "Cursing is a sin! Watch it, will you, Wally? Oh, and I expect my store ad will run as usual this week. I'd like to see it nearer the front this time."

50

Garit was about to end his work day when the UPS man rang the front desk bell.

"Got a package for you, Garit," he said.

The label read from Tom Saxe, Esq., Attorney at Law, and it was heavier than it looked.

Garit took it to his apartment and opened it. On top of some thick packing material was a hand-written note.

> "Garit: I managed to sneak this out of your parent's house before the court ordered all the inside items sold. I think your dad must have bought it not long ago, and didn't want to give it to the cult leader. He may have been holding it back as a present for you. –Tom."

Garit lifted the packing material. Wrapped tightly was a Canon digital camera EOS 60 with four lenses, all in their boxes, with operating instructions and a booklet that boasted that it could teach anyone to shoot like a pro in thirty minutes. Underneath it all was a hardcover book on digital photography.

Garit wept longer and more bitterly than he had ever wept. Maybe his dad had thought of his son once in awhile after all.

He got up and reached into the back of his refrigerator and hauled out the sack of pot and rolling papers he'd gotten from his parent's house when he left for Jovial. He rolled a large joint and put it between his lips. He picked up the camera equipment and books and took them all outside to his deck.

He sat, looked up at the sky and said: "Dad, you probably didn't know this, but I heard you say once that people learn best when they're high, because it helps them concentrate. I think I understand now what you never did. You learn better because you concentrate more, and you concentrate more because you have to put in extra effort—you're high! You never thought these things through, did you? But I'm going to do this one last thing your way, Dad, as a tribute to you, as a test one last time to see if you had any brains at all; and to thank you for the camera. So I'm going to smoke this and learn this camera inside and out. So here's to you, old man!" He lit the joint and opened the boxes. It was Friday night.

51

When Garit saw the *World's* latest edition on his desk, he felt estranged from it somehow. He flipped through the pages, ignoring the front page story about milk contamination. He folded it under his arm and walked outside to the Jeep. He drove to Sventon, and knocked on the door of Botsdorf's office. Botsdorf motioned for him to come in.

Garit tossed the paper on Botsdorf's desk and slumped into the office side chair.

"Thought you might like to see this," he said. Botsdorf read the front page headline and put the paper down.

"Why does this upset you so much?" he asked. "You learned a long time ago what kind of man Wally was, didn't you?"

"It's more than knowing he's a scumbag, Bots. I just feel like I've lost something in the last few weeks. For a while, right before and right after Aspen left, I'd been part of this newspaper-producing team. I'd done my parts, all of them, from research, to writing, to photography, to layout, to proofing. I'd worked long hours. I'd been an integral part of every aspect of the paper, and it was satisfying in some ways. Maybe even fulfilling, for lack of a better word, but that's all gone now. It started dying when Aspen left, and now, even though I get my share of bylines, my heart isn't in it anymore, you know? It doesn't excite me like it should. I feel like I'm just biding time, waiting for the next awful thing to happen to me. I'm drifting again, just like my parents, discontent with everything but never willing to do anything about it except try to escape it with booze or weed for short bursts. They never found what they were looking for, or maybe they didn't even know what they were looking for. Either way, they never found anything to give them an anchor. Or even an oar. I don't want to end up like them."

"I have a feeling you won't, Garit," Botsdorf said. "Let's deal with the issue in front of us first, OK?" He held up the paper. The front page lead story held Wally's byline. "Milk Drinkers Warned by Health Department," read the headline, in 32-point type.

"Look through it," Garit told Botsdorf. "There's no Deadfrick story. The paper is suddenly ad-heavy, too. It's been sixteen pages max for weeks, but this one was probably a money-maker. Thirty-two pages. I would guess ad percentages are around 52 percent. Who knows, maybe I'll get my back wages now."

Botsdorf's eyebrows twitched, but he said nothing.

"And look at Wally's lead story," Garit said. "It could have been written by Pinckney or Deadfrick. Maybe it was. It has no comments from Noah Brenner, but the accusations from Deadfrick and Pinckney are detailed. The same attitude they used at the press conference, but different words. The only thing that saves it from being a total hack job is the quote from Coney. One lousy quote."

"Even with it, it's pretty biased," Botsdorf agreed.

"But there's something else, and I think Detective Sheridan might want to know about this."

Botsdorf punched some buttons on his phone, and the detective answered.

"Bill? Bots. Garit West is in my office. We're on speaker. He wants to fill you in on something."

"Go ahead, Garit," the detective said.

"Have you seen the latest *World*?"

"Not yet, what's up?"

"Well, two things, at least. First, you were right about Wally. He didn't run the Deadfrick story, but he did write a long piece about the public health issues because of the milk contamination. Make that alleged, because I still don't believe Noah Brenner would have allowed something that nasty into his milk. But the clincher, the smoking gun, is the date on the paper."

"Get to the point, Garit."

"The date of publication makes you think everything's kosher, right? It came out on a Wednesday, and the press conference about the milk was Tuesday, right?"

"So?"

"So the deadline was Monday. That's the day we went to the printer. Wally had this story written the day before anyone outside a few doctors even knew about it. I saw the story on his computer. He knew there would be sick people. I saw the headline on his computer even before that! Maybe two, three days before." The detective was silent for a moment.

"Thanks, Garit, That's very helpful. You know what you have to do. Stick with the plan." He hung up.

Garit stared blankly at Botsdorf, then sighed deeply.

"I may be about as naïve as they come, but I don't get this," he said. "Who's Wally a puppet for, anyway? Deadfrick? Pinckney? Both? I mean, I expected that my Deadfrick story would be suppressed, but deep inside I still held hope that it wouldn't be. I thought Wally was just a coward, wouldn't rock the boat and risk losing advertisers. I thought he was too stupid to be a co-conspirator. I wanted to believe that Wally was still, for all his faults and brainlessness, a credible newspaperman, a businessman. A guy who honored truth above everything else and would fight to the death for the right of every member of society to know it. That was the man I thought he was when he hired me. Look what I got."

"Your only fault was believing in the ideal they taught you in college. So what are you going to do about it?" Botsdorf asked.

"Well, I tell you one thing, I'm not going to stick with the plan! This has to be dealt with now. The Band-Aid has to be pulled off fast!" he said and left Botsdorf's office.

He folded the paper, carried it high to Wally's office, barged in without knocking and threw the paper on Wally's desk. "What have you done?" he demanded. "What is this?" Wally looked up from his desk, calmly but sneering.

"It's a newspaper, duh. Is that all?"

"Where's the story I worked on more than a month to research?"

"Contaminated milk is a much bigger story, Garit. If you knew anything, you'd understand the difference between real news and fabrication."

"You're just lost, aren't you, Wally?" Garit demanded. "You're too stupid to know you're being played!"

"Nobody plays me," Wally looked back down at his desk.

"There's no evidence that the farmer did anything to his milk, Wally! The test results aren't back. You've libeled him in this story. At the very least, you should have waited until the press conference."

"I did," Wally lied. "The conference was Tuesday, and the paper came out Wednesday."

"But there's nothing in here from the press conference," Garit accused. "You don't write that fast! You were ready to go with this before the press conference, and you used partial, biased information. My story at least has documents to back up everything. If you'd even read the story, you'd know that."

"I read it, alright. And let me tell you, boy, that accusations against a prominent member of the community needs to be assessed by more than a stupid kid who wants to be the next Woodward and/or Bernstein, but hasn't gotten past his own ego to see he'll never be even close. This is as good as it gets for a punk like you, Garit. Why don't you just settle in and make a nice living writing about heifer shows and beauty pageants? It's a nice enough life. The stress level is low, and the scenery is beautiful. Lots of pretty girls your age around here too. You could do a lot worse. Don't try to play with the big boys. You'll get burned, sure as I'm sitting here."

"And I suppose you're one of the big boys?"

"Bigger by a far shot than you, boy. Get off your high horse. Deadfrick's word carries more weight than yours. His reputation deserves more discretion."

"And Noah Brenner's reputation means nothing?"

"He's just a stupid farmer. He'll get some government bailout for this and be fine. Listen to me on this, Garit. I know best."

"You know best? How? How does it benefit your readers and this town to keep information from them, or worse, feed them lies?"

"You're too young to understand, boy. You're too idealistic and too young and too stupid. They all go hand in hand, you know. So just cool your jets a little and do your job or I'll find someone who will."

"Is that a threat?"

"If I wanted to threaten you I'd do it with this." He pulled a drawer open and drew out a small handgun. He held it up, vertical to the ground, near his ear.

"Now get out of my office and do your job."

Garit glared into Wally's eyes, determined to defy the threat and show no fear. He turned, then turned back. "Let me tell you something, Wally," he spat. "You think I won't just walk away from this job right now, in this instant?"

"No, I don't think you will. You have nowhere else to go. Your debts will follow you wherever you go."

Garit snarled, walked back to his desk, and punched the back of his chair.

"You know, Wally? You're right," he said, walking back into Wally's office and ignoring the pain running through his still-healing fingers. "I don't know how you know about my parent's debt, but it's true that I have nowhere else to go. But I sure hope, before I work up the guts to leave you high and dry, that you get taken down hard. I'd just love to see that!"

"Get out of my office and back to work," Wally snarled.

Garit stared at his computer and tried to write, but nothing sank in. Suddenly, his phone rang, blessedly tearing him from the rage that hung like fog over the bog of his soul.

Before he could say "Garit West" into the phone, he heard a vaguely familiar voice that he couldn't identify. It was breathing heavily. Loud popping and humans shouting and cattle bellowing cluttered the voice.

"Get over to Brenner's" the voice rasped. Bring a camera. Now!"

52

Garit drove to the top of Brenner's Hill.

The blacktop driveway was in better shape than the rutted, gravel road that led to it. The air hung thick as leaking insanity. It smelled like musky, freshly turned earth mixed with diesel fuel and heavy equipment fumes. Gunpowder lingered like cigarette smoke on a nonexistent breeze.

Garit slid the company Kia sloppily into a small opening amid five pickups, two with large trailers attached, parked just off the blacktop. Huge piles of dirt dwarfed earth-moving equipment alongside them. They were silent, but radiating heat from their engines in the mid-morning cool.

When he turned his car engine off, Garit heard pops, echoing against the farm buildings and bouncing back, only to be muffled by the piles of dirt. Then he heard cattle bellowing.

Garit rushed toward the sound, his brand new Canon camera batteries fresh and ready to go on a new 4G memory card.

Between the two large piles of dirt, deep in a pit that stretched in a narrow rectangle about fifty yards wide by forty yards long, stumbled a few remaining cows, panicked from the noise and the smells and the confusion of the killing floor.

At least ten cows lay in the cool earthy pit, some twitching muscles, reactions of a body turning into a carcass, wasted and senseless.

Ca-Wham! Sounded one of the rifles. Garit looked to see four or five men, each dressed in jeans and T-shirts covered with flannel against the cool morning air.

Garit laid on his stomach on the crest of one of the dirt piles and, nearly unconsciously, checked the camera's light meter and adjusted the camera, which was set on manual mode.

He pressed the rapid fire shutter as he saw one man fire his gun. Garit watched as the bullet tore through one of the last standing cows' heads, sending her nose into the ground as her flesh tore away from the crest between her ears. But she refused to die. She struggled back up, blood gushing from her head and pouring down her face. She bellowed and shook her head, but was not answered. A second shot rang out. Her face shattered when the bullet invaded her skull just below her eye. Finally she collapsed onto her side, and a third bullet went through her side, just above her front shoulder, ending her suffering.

Finally, all lay motionless. The sound of the silence laid heavy, as sickening as the scene in the pit, and Garit heard weeping behind him.

The men with the rifles held their ground atop the dirt mounds on the west end of the pit. One looked through binoculars.

"There," he shouted. "The one with the white leg!" More shots blasted the air. A weak moan lifted from the pit, followed by another shot, then silence. More moans, weaker this time, then more shots. Finally, like mercy itself, the spotter cried "That's it!"

Retching, Garit moved away from the pit. He held his camera high above his head as he slid down the dirt pile. He walked in the direction of the weeping. His legs were heavy and slow to respond, and he felt as if the blood in his heart was too thick to let his legs overcome the weight of the scene he'd witnessed.

On the other side of the driveway, under a grand, two-hundred-year-old Sugar Maple, was Noah. He squatted on the ground in the shade, his back against the tree and his arms around his knees, rocking back and forth. Swells of grief rose and receded like milk pumped and sucked from a milking claw into the dairy pipeline.

Garit snapped a few frames, hesitant to come too close. Finally, he crept closer, and as he approached, he heard Noah repeating the same word—the only one that had been in his mind. "Why?"

Garit kept moving, unnoticed by anyone, though he was in plain sight. The camera was like a part of his hands, and he squeezed the shutter release again and again and again.

He walked, dazed, fighting his urge to throw up, toward Noah, unsure of what to do when he got there. But then, from somewhere Garit could not tell, came Coney.

He boldly approached Noah, who stopped rocking and sobbing long enough to look up. Then he burst out in a fresh wave of grief and torment, sobbing inconsolably like typhoon waves, merciless against a weakening earthen wall hastily built.

Garit kept approaching, unseen or ignored by the two men. His camera shutter opened and shut, opened and shut, opened and shut, as Coney dropped to his knees at Noah's side.

A cloud crossed the sun, and Garit instinctively adjusted the camera's f-stops. Coney stretched his weathered arms around both sides of the weeping man, his work-toned muscles hard as sanded hickory in the filtered sunlight.

Noah reached his right arm up from the elbow and gripped Coney's wrist, and they both slumped under their heavy burdens, weeping loudly. The camera shutter opened and shut, catching tears falling to earth and crashing like fists into a soft, unprotected belly. The men rocked together, silent but for the anguish pouring from their noses and eyes and mouths.

Garit came closer, still shooting, his own eyes foggy from tears and sympathy and brutality.

Coney rose slowly, like a flame growing above a wick, and sat back down on the ground next to Noah, one arm across his shoulder.

"I had to do it, didn't I?" Noah blubbered, finally. "I couldn't live with myself if people were getting sick because of my cows, could I?" Coney remained silent. "I'm a farmer. I have responsibilities." Noah sobbed. "I couldn't take the chance. A cow's life or a human's? What have we been taught all our lives, Coney? Humans are more important, right? Made in God's own image? Isn't that the truth?"

Coney wiped his eyes.

"Everyone I know understands that a human life—no matter how miserable or how worthless we may think—is worth more than an animal's life," Coney said. "Anyone would have done the same as you did if they had to make the choice."

"I had to do it," Noah said, his back straightening slightly from his haunches. "I had no choice. Even if it means I'm out of business, it was the right thing to do." A new wave of grief overtook him.

"What were your choices, Noah?" asked Coney, when Noah became silent. "Why did you have to kill these cows?"

Noah spilled the whole story, intermittently breaking down with grief. Garit's shutter opened and shut, opened and shut. From the inspector's visit to the computer designation of adulterant to his decision to ask local hunters to perform the task he couldn't, Noah blubbered it all out. He ended with his call to his brother-in-law to scrape a giant grave behind the barns. Coney stood, looking as numb as Garit felt.

"Who was this inspector, Noah? What did he look like?" Coney asked.

As Noah described what he remembered, a chill rolled down Garit's spine like ice water dripping down his bones and legs, soaking his socks and making his feet too heavy to move.

"How could PBB get into your herd?" Coney asked. "Did you see any symptoms? Curved hooves, loss of appetite? Skin and bones?"

"It was too early to show. I had to put them out of their misery, didn't I? I had to show my animals mercy or I'm no better than a torturer, right?"

"You're a merciful man, Noah," Coney said. "You've always been."

They embraced again, and Garit kept the camera shutter moving. Open and shut. Open and shut. Open and shut. Again and again, again and again. Open and shut.

Garit kept his finger on the shutter as the hunters filed by Noah and Coney, each one squeezing Noah's shoulder silently as they passed by on their way back to their trucks.

Garit stepped up from his shooting angle on his belly as Coney and Noah rose.

"Excuse me, Noah." He approached softly and spoke in a voice he never thought he could produce. It was almost smooth, yet unnatural in his own head. But it was all he had.

"The way you described the inspector gave me chills," he said. "You described one of the jerks who beat me up a couple weeks ago. Clean cut? Perfect hair, close shave, wore a tie?"

Noah looked at him as if he were a misfitting piece of a puzzle that had been forced into place. Finally, he nodded.

"That's the guy. But why would a milk inspector want to beat you up?"

"Why would a guy who beats people up have a job inspecting milk?" Garit retorted dryly. "And didn't he seem a little young for a special investigator?"

Noah stared, confused.

"What if he wasn't really a milk inspector?" Garit asked at last.

"Wait a minute," interrupted Coney. "You said this guy was from what, special investigations? I've never heard of such a thing at the state."

"And how can a state that's short on financing fund a special unit?" Garit asked.

"He had a seal on his car that said MDA special investigations," argued Noah. But Coney was already on his phone.

"Sam? Coney. I'm OK. Say, Sam, any such thing as a special investigations wing in your shop? Didn't think so. I think we may have someone impersonating one of your boys up here. That's right. Told Noah Brenner that his herd had PBB. Right. Convinced him somehow. Maybe he hacked into his computer, I don't know. Well, check into it, will you? Noah's shot thirty head. Thanks, Sam."

Coney didn't have to say a word. When he punched off his phone's connection, Noah's jaw was open, and he twisted his head slowly as if trying to shake off the truth, grab it by the throat and make it confess to lies. His body followed in jerky motions as he got up and paced a circle. The bulldozers fired up loudly. Noah stopped, looked back at Coney. Their eyes met for a moment, and Noah dropped to his knees, gushing out rage and sodden anger and tears that could drown a muskrat. He pounded his fists into the ground, leaving impressions that Garit photographed, open and shut, open and shut.

"Why?" Noah looked up at Coney at last. "Why would someone do this, Coney? Why?" He fell on his face in the scant grass under the shade tree and wept long into his elbow. After what felt like a very long time, Garit's eyes met Coney's. He laid aside his camera in the grass and joined Coney.

They approached, and with one on each side of Noah, they touched him on the shoulders. They gently pulled him from the ground and braced themselves under him. He seemed too weak to stand on his own. He finally stood with unshaking knees with Noah and Coney, and they watched the dozers return the earth flat again. Noah's voice was raspy when he finally spoke.

"I think I'll just let it go to weeds for now," he told Coney. "Ugly for ugly." The two farmers wept again. Garit picked up his camera and slowly walked away.

53

Garit drove to Sventon, silent and alone
except for the camera and notebooks on the passenger seat.

He parked the Kia behind the offices that held the *Sventon Sasser*
and Botsdorf's law offices. He hung the camera around his neck and
walked into the newspaper office. It was nothing more than cubicles and
offices, and Garit walked down the hallway, looking for signs of life.
When he heard stirring from a corner office just off the main entryway,
Botsdorf emerged, dressed in a T-shirt that hung outside his suit pants.
It had a dark picture of Homer Simpson, praying, in fading colors.

"Well, Garit!" Botsdorf thrilled, moving briskly forward to shake
Garit's hand. Garit shook it, aware of making his own grip firm, and
was impressed by the firmness of Botsdorf's. "What did you decide?"

"Well sir, I'd like to sell you a photograph."

"Freelancing, are we? Can I assume that your action got you fired
from the *World*?"

"I'm still there, but I don't know how long."

"Oh, this sounds interesting," Botsdorf smiled. He stepped aside
and waved his hand invitingly toward a chair. "Sit down and tell me
the story."

"I'll probably talk your ear off. Do you mind if I vent a little? Get
a little advice?"

"Feel free. But let's look at that picture."

Garit popped open a side door on the camera and pressed a lever to push out the memory card. Botsdorf took it and sat behind his desk, slid the card into a slot on the laptop computer and motioned for Garit to come around and look over his shoulder.

"Holy Lord, save us," Botsdorf prayed gutterally when he saw the first few shots of blood spurting from a cow. "What is going on?"

"Noah was scammed like nothing I've ever seen before," Garit replied. "I don't have it all figured out, but someone's out to get him, that's for sure."

Botsdorf kept the photos rolling quickly across his computer screen. Finally, he reached the portion of the card that held the photos of Noah under the tree.

"These are really touching," Botsdorf choked. Tears were spilling.

"About here," Garit replied, pointing, "I've got an ethical problem. Maybe you can solve it for me. I've heard you're an old-school newspaper guy."

"The only thing that makes me old-school is that I'm old," Botsdorf said, still looking at photos, but at a slower pace now.

"I know a man's grief should be private," Garit said, "but what was my role when I saw this? What was my duty? As a reporter, I should get the story, try to talk to Noah, answer the questions everyone wants answered: 'Why?' Noah kept muttering it over and over in these shots. Was I then a reporter or a human being? Was my responsibility weighted more heavily to get the story or to console a human being, one who seemed as helpless as a turtle on its back?"

Botsdorf scrolled through the pictures of Noah and Coney.

"This nearly broke my heart in a thousand pieces, and that ain't easy to do these days," Garit said. "Look at these two farmers. They're just trying to make a living. They're both decent, trustworthy, good-hearted people who wouldn't harm a flea if it were their choice, but they're man enough to know—" he stopped and sobbed—" hard choices have to be made. These are real men. Not like the rest of the men I've met who's lives are all in a tizzy if they have to go to Florida on vacation because they can't afford Alaska. These guys have real problems on the farm, and then some inhumane terrorists decide they want to screw with them! And why? Is it just for entertainment? What's up with that? These farmers make choices no one else in society ever has to make, except maybe for the decision to put down the family dog a couple times in their miserable little lives." He paused.

"Most people just stop having pets after one or two of those decisions," Botsdorf said. "They prefer to live without love rather than endure the pain that comes with it. But farmers have to choose between life and death every day. They have to make choices that hurt today but have long-term benefits. Most people don't possess that kind of courage and mercy anymore. Like dehorning calves. Hurts the poor little things like crazy, but two, three days of hangover and headache is nothing compared to the damage of a horn in the rib cage as an adult."

"How can a person ever get used to things like that?" Garit asked. "What drives a man to care so much about humans—I mean, they're just numbers in the larger picture, represented by how many gallons of milk they buy. That's how most of American industry thinks of people. Just numbers. Statistics in board meetings. How can a man who's just been burned by some miserable hoax destroy his own business to protect those very people? He killed those animals even though it broke him, and I don't mean financially. And all for the sake of those despicable humans, consumers. It's incredible, Bots. No ordinary human being can do it. Only a farmer can do it. His own self-interests come second. How rare! How precious, rare and untaught! How unlike America. How angering. How maddening. How much wrong crying out in need of what's right!"

Botsdorf paused on one particular photo, where Noah was looking directly into the camera, his mouth wide in the middle of an anguished howl, and Coney's profile beside him, three distinct teardrops falling from his cheeks, one falling off his chin in mid-air.

"I learned a lot today, Bots," Garit said. "This is how farm men, real men, express their sympathy. It's heartfelt, plain and simple. No unnecessary words. It's what masculinity really is, which makes today's definition of it as false as a sock down your pants. I learned there is no shame in weeping or in what Noah thought was merciful killing. Love, even for an animal, sometimes means doing dastardly things. Real men do them, and they don't second-guess themselves, at least not for long.

They don't join cults or follow rock bands. They don't kill themselves and they don't get fooled by shallow, selfish women."

"Wow," said Botsdorf. "No bitterness in your past!"

"Why does everyone keep saying that?" Garit groaned.

Botsdorf's eyes leaked tears onto his desk when he scrolled to the last few photo frames, the ones of Noah pounding his fists into the ground.

"In the face of all I saw today, all that grief and helplessness, there's something missing, too," Garit said. "How could this simpleton Noah not be filled with rage? Anger here was so justified, so righteous, so natural, that it's just wrong not to show anger. I mean extreme anger. Sure he pounded his fists a little, but I never got the feeling that he really was angry enough to be, like, vengeful. Those cattle don't mean anything to me, and I'm beyond anger! These things cry out for justice, but who will step up and perform it? Who's left in the world who will stand up?"

Botsdorf shrugged. "'Who knows but what you've come into the world for such a time as this?'" he quoted.

"I don't know what that means, but some son-of-a-bitch will have to pay for this," Garit snarled. "The world will be off-kilter until the bill is paid. Maybe that's my whole purpose for being here, if there is a purpose. I'll make sure the guilty people pay, no matter who they are. And pay big. Sick sons of bitches."

"These pictures are a good start," Botsdorf said. "These are gold, man. I'll buy them all. What about a story?"

"Well, I still work for Wally, so I should write it for him, unless you're offering me a job."

"I can't do that right now, but I will pay you for the photos. You write a story for Wally, and send me anything you want after that. When I get something from you, I'll assume that you're done with Wally. No guarantees, but if I run something, I'll pay you well."

"Alright. But I need to keep one shot for the *World*. Let's dicker over price later, OK? I'm about as drained as I've ever been right now."

"That's because you're not just a good reporter for your age anymore, Garit. You're a good reporter of any age. I read your Deadfrick story. I couldn't have done it any better. You have a nice style. And in this case, sure, you have a great story to tell, but you're part of something bigger than a story now. You're in deep humanity now, Garit, and you have to write it from inside, not outside."

He thumped his chest. "It's no longer about a reporter being an objective observer. You're waist-deep in vengeance. You're in the middle of community, love and hate, envy and violence. All the human emotions known to man are there inside you, raw and eloquent, and you need to write them, and now. You owe it to your readers and yourself and to God to write it with all the emotion you have. You have an obligation to use all the bitterness events like this bring out in you, because they are common to man, and every reader out there will empathize. On top of that, you have a mystery to solve. You have responsibility to sort out what appears to be haphazard and find the order in it. You will find it, whether you believe it or not at this moment. You're in life now, son. Kick its butt!"

54

Garit took his memory card and drove back to Jovial and his apartment. He plugged the card into his computer's card reader. He allowed the pictures to run continuously on a slide show program as he began to work the story. Through anguish and recurring gut-wrenching weeping, he did several phone interviews, and worked well into the night.

He put the finished story on a flash drive, rubbed his eyes and yawned. He'd never known such exhaustion, even after he knew his parents had yielded to the evil they had embraced. Absentmindedly, he opened a new message box and attached the story to an email for Wally. But in his weariness, he didn't notice his mistake. He put Botsdorf's email on the top line. For the message line, he wrote: "For the next edition."

This is the story that appeared the next morning, along with photos, on the *Sventon Sasser* website:

The Killing Pit
By Garit West

The bullet lands a little higher than intended, pushed in air heated by diesel exhaust fumes and warm blood. It collides with Cow Number 1046's skull, and the top inch of her head flies up and away, gushes of crimson following like wolves fighting over an aging, slow creature's guts.

She staggers, and her knees buckle, sending her nose into the soft subsoil. She shakes her head, terrified. Confused, with blood flowing over her eyes, she stands back up, bellowing. A shout from a man with binoculars rings over the pit, and another man aims his rifle from atop a massive dirt pile. One clean shot lands behind her shoulder, and she drops. Another shot rings out, thumping her like a muffled grunt, and she lies still.

Behind the scene sits Noah Brenner, his arms wrapped around his knees in a fetal position. He's widely known for producing the highest-quality milk in all of northern Michigan. He thought he was showing mercy, he said, but the cruelest trick of all is that destroying 30 cows to prevent their suffering was likely unnecessary.

Brenner, between waves of heart-rending anguish, tells of an alleged state milk inspector who showed him papers the day before.

"The inspector said the papers proved that the cows had been poisoned," Brenner said. "I confirmed that with my own computer system, but it may have been rigged to show false positives. I wish I had known that before I had my cows killed." He breaks down in anguish again. "But I couldn't prolong their suffering. That's not humane. That's torture" he sobs.

Officials with the Michigan Department of Agriculture said they could not identify the alleged inspector based on descriptions provided by Brenner. They also said there is no "special investigations" unit in the department, but Brenner said the inspector had official-looking identification.

"I didn't question his credentials," Brenner said. "With all the confusion going on with the health department lately, I figured there probably would be an investigation at some point. And it all looked authentic."

Brenner was allegedly involved with a recent illness that ran quickly through 10 Jovial residents. The Jovial County Health Department traced the illness to a contamination allegedly from Brenner's milk, sold in the Farmers' Own Store. Tests on the milk to determine what caused the illness will get underway when the Health Department finds milk that matches the proper lot numbers of the batch that allegedly made people ill.

"Unfortunately, most of the milk from that lot was destroyed when it was learned it might contain contaminants," said Health Department spokesperson Fran MacInerney.

"We're actively tracking some down, though, and the public should be assured that no more of the contaminated milk is in the food chain. There is no health risk anymore, and the people who were affected are all recovering nicely."

Sam Sperrson, Michigan's deputy milk quality division supervisor, said anyone impersonating a milk inspector and falsifying records will be prosecuted "with vigor" for their actions, which may also have involved computer tampering.

"It's not out of the question for someone who's good with computers to be able to hack into a system like Brenner's," said Dr. Carol Flaskean, a computer science professor at Northern Michigan University who also designs feed delivery and diagnostic systems for farm businesses.

"The type of system typically used by farmers to test feed for contaminants can easily be manipulated to show that a trace mineral such as manganese, for example, is a contaminant," she said. "Without a lot more information in the system, it won't say what the contaminant might be. It would just show as an unknown contaminant.

That's standard computer language for something it's not sure about."

Brenner said all the cows he had killed to ease their pain had been shown by the computer to have eaten PBB, the same fire retardant that swept through Michigan's food chain in the 1970s. At least, that's what the alleged inspector told him.

"He couldn't explain how it could have gotten in my feed, and I didn't think it was possible," Noah said. "But his test results showed it, and when my computer said these 30 cows had eaten an unknown contaminant, I couldn't just let them suffer. The inspector told me PBB wasn't being tested for anymore in these systems. He said his tests at the state labs were more sensitive than mine, and he had the results in his hand. In black-and-white. I had no choice when I saw that. I wouldn't sell them into the food chain, even though I probably could have gotten away with it."

Coney Dogues, president of the Jovial Area Farmer's Association, speculated that the contaminated milk in the Farmers Own Store and the false inspector may be connected.

"These two tragic incidents are too close to be disconnected," Dogues said. "And I'm still not convinced that the illness wasn't a case of sabotage. There's been a lot of animal rights activity around here, and tampering with milk is well within their means and their methods. But to falsify evidence and basically coerce a man into doing something so loathsome, something that will scar him forever, is way beyond activism. It's criminal activity, and it has to be dealt with by law enforcement," he said.

Jovial Police Chief James Dulogski refused to comment, saying the incident is under investigation.

As for Brenner, he said he hopes the incident ends when health department tests come back and clear his farm of any wrongdoing.

"I know that there was nothing in my milk that could have made anyone sick unless it had been tampered with," he said. Dogues agreed.

"Noah Brenner is as conscientious a man as I've ever know in my life when it comes to his cattle and his milk," he said. "Everyone in the Jovial Area Farmers' Association is anxious to clear his name so he can once again supply the best, highest-quality milk in this state to the customers of the Farmers' Own Store."

Neither Dogues, Brenner, or officials with the Health Department would speculate on who might be behind the alleged crimes, but said investigations would continue.

Expect follow-ups to this story in future editions.

By mid-morning, the *Sventon Sasser's* website carried a home-page photograph of Noah and Coney, the one with Noah bellowing out his agony and Coney's tears in mid-air. Forty-eight-point text said very simply: "Who's responsible?"

Dozens of photos of the brutal scene were available for viewing, and they were setting records for opens and time spent on the site. Comments on the *Sasser's* website were overwhelming. They called for arrests of people who could contrive such an evil plan against a farmer, although one anonymously called for an end to factory farming.

Dan Pinckney and Jim Deadfrick read the story, then the comments in Deadfrick's basement.

"It's four-to-one in support of the farmer!" Pinckney cried. "Why isn't he in jail? If he'd done this to people, he'd be in jail! He has no respect for life!"

Deadfrick was silent. He clicked through the photos section, smiling.

"Stop it, you sadistic bastard!" Pinckney shouted, and grabbed the laptop. "What did you do? I was with you on the formaldehyde in the milk, but this is not what I signed on for, you son-of-a-bitch! Making a few people sick is one thing, but killing innocent animals is another. Who's going to pay for this?"

"Who *is* going to pay?" Deadfrick repeated, calmly. "Noah? He's just a pawn. Sure, he's evil if for no other reason than he's a factory farmer, but he's no mastermind. No, the person who has to pay is the kingpin, the purveyor of the attitudes that made people shoot cows for fun. Cut the head off, and the body dies. That's in the Bible," he lied.

Pinckney clicked back on the front page photo, stared at it. Then he read the story again.

"We've got to figure this out," he said, pacing. "Let's be logical, Jim. What do people know?"

Pinckney paused, and raised his hand as if to put papers in a mail slot.

"Fact," he said, jabbing his hand in the air. "People got sick from drinking milk, Noah's milk. Fact: Test results aren't back yet. Fact: test results will probably never come because the farmers' store manager destroyed the evidence. That's all pretty clear. Now. Fact: Noah shot cows, thinking he had PBB, but accused some nebulous inspector. Conclusion: Noah is hiding something. He's trying to get himself off the hook. Fact: he's being supported by the factory farmer president."

He paused, tears in his eyes as if some relevant, cruel truth had just been revealed.

"Fact," he said. "You have a full-page ad coming out that points out that our organic store doesn't sell Brenner's milk."

"Fact!" Shouted Deadfrick, jumping from his seat on the couch. "Conspiracy! There's no other answer, Danny! These guys probably had something to hide and wanted to kill these cows and destroy the evidence anyway. Our boys putting formaldehyde in the milk just scared them, sent them running. We did a public service! We've exposed their true colors. You've finally done something more substantial than some stupid sit-in or picket line. Congratulations, man!" He patted him on the back.

"But why did the cows have to die?"

"Do you want people to drink contaminated milk?"

"But it wasn't contaminated! You contaminated it. The cows had nothing to do with it!"

"How do you know that? If they were clean, why did Brenner and Coney Dogues kill them all?"

Pinckney shook his head. "Stop it!" he shouted. "You're confusing me!"

"Look at this, if you want clarity," snarled Deadfrick, grabbing the laptop away from Pinckney's grip. "You want to know why you have to get to the source of this and fix it? Look!" He opened the laptop and pulled up the pictures again. He scrolled down to the comments. "Look at these stupid sheep!" he said. "They're swallowing this West boy's propaganda hook line and sinker. And how do we know these are real photos? Could be just a bunch of Photo Shopped images meant to divert people from the real issue—contaminated milk—and gain sympathy for the slavers. Look at it, Danny! Look what they're doing!"

He pointed to a new graph on the site, one that had been posted only seconds before.

"Look at this new graph," Deadfrick said, and pointed the computer at Pinckney. "Public opinion is overwhelmingly in sympathy with Noah, the guy who just murdered thirty cows in cold blood. Look! Ninety-one percent say they would buy milk from the store again when Noah gets back on his feet. They're all fools, little Danny. They'll drink poison if it salves their own consciences! They'll believe anything if it makes them feel better, and they won't feel better because they still kill animals and butcher them, and eat them. They're a bunch of cannibals, and they have blood on their hands. But they aren't the real problem either, are they? Are you listening to me, Danny? It's the pushers—the sellers of contaminated milk—that have to be chopped out by the roots, just like drug pushers in your school, indoctrinating the youth, the future of America. Sons of bitches! What kind of game are they playing, anyway?"

"That's right," Pinckney exclaimed. "How could PBB get into cows, especially that herd? Who could treat animals so cruelly as to poison them and shoot them?" His eyes widened, his pupils dilated. He was standing at the edge that Aspen/Cindy had not been able to push him toward.

"Then they get some pliable young reporter to use for their own purposes, and dupe him into a story that brings sympathy! What a great plot!" He giggled madly, and Deadfrick smiled.

"Now you're getting it!" he said. "Are you going to let them get away with it?"

"No, dammit, they will not get away with it," Pinckney snarled. "This is all so wrong! It can't continue. They'll pay alright. Justice demands it. Brenner will pay, even if he *is* just a pawn. He's still a factory farmer. I'm sure he's committed all kinds of crimes against non-human animals. All those cow shooters will pay. All the voters who voted against Proposition One will pay. And all the farmers. Especially the cruel, heartless slavers. Especially Coney Dogues. He's the pusher man!"

Deadfrick smiled.

55

Coney soaked his upper body with the house water hose and changed his shirt. He grabbed a cold Indian Head beer from the refrigerator in the garage and let himself fall into the cushion on the porch swing. Before he'd taken his second sip, Jenn came out and sat beside him.

"Rough day, huh?"

"You got that right. Where's Fulton been all day?"

"Carlos is taking his daughter off to college, so Fulton's packing celery with the migrants. He said he wanted to be sure it was ready to go by morning. Not to mention watching out for these terrorists. Everybody's a little spooked now since the stuff with Noah. How 'bout you, babe? Doing alright?" She massaged his neck with her left hand.

"Well, I couldn't cut all the hay I wanted because of all this nonsense with Noah." He sighed. "Might be tough to get the corn silage up in time."

"Well, you didn't have to be at his side, you know," Jenn answered. "Most people would have just let him deal with it himself. But that's not you. That's not what a disciple is called to do."

"Do you ever wonder if it's all worth it?" Coney asked. "Will the rewards of heaven really make this all worthwhile?"

"You know it will."

"I do know that, deep inside. But sometimes it gets to you, you know? This is the kind of thing that makes you wonder if God really is in control. But then, I remember that I'm not in control, that's for sure. I'm sure glad I'm not. I can't understand my own mind most of the time, much less anyone else's. How do I forget that so fast?"

"Because you're human," Jenn said, stroking his arm. "Just because we can't see the plan behind it doesn't mean there isn't one."

Coney's cell phone rang. He looked at the screen and put the phone on the cushion beside him.

"Frank." Coney said to Jenn. "He's called every couple hours all day long. He's afraid to do his job since the milk disaster, and he's turned every little decision he should make on his own into an exercise in risk prevention. And that's not to mention the calls from Noah, and the health department, and a reporter or two. I can handle most of it from the phone while cutting hay, but it's hard to keep my mind on task. I had to shut it off just to get that field over by Woodmore's done. I got so distracted I hardly heard this new ping coming from the haybine. I ran over a big woodchuck mound, so the blades are dull now, and something's loose, for sure."

"Let me get you something to eat," Jenn said. She returned from the house with two cold chicken legs on a paper plate, a handful of carrots from her garden and another ice cold Indian Head.

Coney devoured the food and leaned back in the swing. The dogs lay contentedly on the grass just in front of the porch.

"Look at the sunset tonight," he said as he relaxed. "Look at the way it's such a vibrant orange. Look at that color spilling onto the rows of calf hutches. It's as if God invented new colors just so we'd notice." They sat in silence for a moment.

"God has a strange way of shoring me up," he said. "Not strange, I guess, just mysterious. Just when I need it, he gives me a dose of beauty in nature or moves my spirit with the turn of a phrase or a song. Just look at this sunset. He's an artist, not an accountant or a lawyer, and am I thankful for that!"

He smiled and picked up Jenn's hand. "The sky is God's canvas, and he's a fantastic painter."

"No doubt about it," Jenn said, and patted Coney's knee. "Just relax, babe. I have to take care of some paperwork before it gets too late."

She kissed Coney on the neck and went inside.

❦❦❦

No more than thirty seconds after he saw Mulder and Scully sit up straight, he heard the confusion, too. A distant roar of a souped-up engine, combined with thumping bass from some acid rock song. The dogs rushed toward the road, and their voices showed far more than mere annoyance. Coney's adrenaline began to pump with every menacing, agitated woof.

A loud pickup truck, jacked up on over sized tires and a rebel flag in the rear window, barreled down the driveway. Coney jumped up, but the truck didn't stop. It turned toward the west and headed for the calf hutches as the engine revved higher. Above the roar and the bass beat, Coney could hear "YEE–HAWs" coming from the cab. He couldn't see who was in it in the disappearing light, and that didn't really matter.

He ran toward the truck as he recognized the song. *It's All the Same*, by Acrid Reins.

The first row of hutches spun and lurched wildly as they were hit by truck tires. The truck spun hard to the right and ran over three more hutches. Two had calves in them. Homeless, frightened calves bawled and ran. Some ran straight toward the road, panicked, and in the fading light, Coney couldn't tell if they were injured or not. He ran in a beeline to try to head off the calves as he screamed a seldom-used profanity at the truck.

"Jenn! Get the gun!" he shouted. A car breezed past on the road, making the calves stop for a moment. Another car was not so lucky, and struck a calf, sending it into the ditch, but it drove on.

The dogs ran quickly past Coney, instinctively going to round up the calves. "Get 'em, kids!" he yelled.

Just as the dogs caught a few of the calves and turned them back toward the barns, the truck came around again and weaved between hutches, tipping them over as calves bellowed in pain and fright. Their water, bedding, and feed spilled across the ground like guts of a bean bag chair, flying and scattering.

Coney could smell the mayhem, mixed with newly churned earth and exhaust of a high-revving, eight-cylinder truck. It smelled like dark disinfectant used on young castrated pigs, mixed with blood and mingled with stale cheap cigar smoke.

Coney ran first west, then east, dodging the truck between the scattered hutches, gaining at least some protection.

"What are you idiots doing?" he yelled. The truck headed back to the road, spinning its huge tires, rutting the lawn as it hit the driveway.

Coney was already tending to injured calves when Jenn came on the porch, squinting in the dusky light.

"Jenn!" Coney shouted. "Get the shotgun! I think they're coming back! There's three calves down here. One's leg may be broken. Get the gun!" He pounded his fist into the soft ground and tried to count the damage. Four calves, as best as he could tell, were unaccounted for. Six might never recover from their injuries. But then he saw Number 4449. Coney could see, even in fading light, tire tracks on her neck. He rushed to her as she struggled for air. She tried to get up, but couldn't. Her back was mangled and pointing in three different directions. A lung probably punctured. Her breathing was heavy and labored. "The shotgun!" Coney screamed, and threw himself to the ground, breathing heavily as anger hammered his lungs.

He rose to his knees and screamed a guttural, instinctive howl. He heard a whimper behind him.

Mulder was lying on the ground, struggling but unable to rise. Dirty tire tracks ran across his entire length, nose to tail, and his head was flattened.

Coney ran to him, hugged his neck close to his, but couldn't weep. The dog's breathing was shallow and gaspy.

He hugged the dog tightly when he heard Scully, barking menacingly, running toward him. She leaped over his crouched frame as he spun to see three men behind him. In the silhouette of the barn's flickering mercury light, he saw a man step to the side, and with a baseball bat, smashed the dog in the side. Coney heard her yelp. An aluminum bat he didn't see struck him in the back, between the shoulder blades. He bent backward in pain as another blow hit him in the face. His knees bent backward with the force, and boots began kicking his ribs over and over like a pitching machine firing rhythmically.

"An eye for an eye, you stinkin' farmers. You're ruining the planet!" Someone growled from behind him. He heard another voice as the kicking subsided. "Set them all free," the nearer voice yelled. "Freedom or death! We are the avengers! We are the merciful! Better to die now than endure years of suffering!"

Two of the men ran off, and the kicking resumed. Coney curled into a fetal position and faded in and out of consciousness, waking with the pain of each new kick to his spine, head, butt, legs, and crotch.

Dan Pinckney hadn't experienced anything this surreal since he was in college and ate blotter acid at a party. His rhythmic kicking wasn't tiring at all, and it didn't hurt his feet a bit. He was outside his body, but it would not relent from its evolved anger.

He was a ten-year-old, standing at a small farm on which the barn had been turned into a medical clinic. He was watching a veterinarian do something to pigs. He watched while the farmer sorted them from a pickup truck, caught them and held them by their back legs over the side for the procedure. Little Danny was with his dad.

"Why do we have to buy flea powder, daddy?" he'd asked on the drive. "We don't have any pets."

"There are more ways to get fleas than from pets, boy," his father replied, and went back to scratching between his legs.

The first pig's scream bit through little Danny's eardrums like a drill at high speed, and he clapped his hands to his ears as he watched some legs that felt foreign and removed from him, kicking the man lying on the ground in front of him.

A slit was made in the piglet, and when the vet squeezed, out popped a small, barely formed testicle. A few swipes of the knife, ear-piercing squeals, and some dark liquid disinfectant was splashed on the little cuts. The pig was tossed back into the truck, where it looked none the worse for wear and scampered to the farthest corner. Little Danny looked at his father, who was laughing. He looked down at Danny, then nudged him.

"Watch this, boy."

The vet tossed the testicles off into the yard, where three dogs rushed to them, one unsuccessfully. There would be more.

After two more pigs, Danny screamed too, and began to cry.

"Daddy," he screeched between squeals. "Why are they hurting those pigs? What are they doing?"

"Castration," grunted his dad. "Cuttin' their little nuts out." He reached spryly between Danny's legs and harshly squeezed, smiling. "You ain't there yet, eh?" He laughed loudly, like he did when he came home late with a toxic smell in his mouth, which was frequent. Even his laugh couldn't cover the piercing pig squeals.

The next pig was wiggling and squealing, and Danny began sobbing and crying. "Daddy, why can't the little pigs keep their nuts?" It took him some time to get it all out between sobs, but his father continued to laugh.

"Their nuts make their meat too tough," he said. "You wouldn't want old stringy boar meat on Easter Sunday, now, would you boy?"

As he began to realize again that it was his adult legs kicking someone, Pinckney screeched like an angry raccoon.

"I don't want ham this Easter, daddy! I never want ham again!" He kicked his father in the shins. His father backhanded him across the mouth, drawing blood.

He stopped kicking. He looked around him, dazed, and saw the truck, screeching its tires on the driveway. He looked down at Coney, shook his head.

"Serves you right, slaver. You're all high and mighty, aren't you? Where's your god now? He's supposed to be vengeful? Then why do I have to do his work for him? Why's he treating you like you're an animal?" He laughed demoniacally, snorted back phlegm from his sinuses and spat on Coney, then jumped into the truck. It roared down the driveway, away from the bleating of dying, suffering calves and a confused, whimpering, paralyzed dog.

Garit's phone rang at 11:31 p.m., just as he was falling asleep. Fulton mumbled something about Coney. His voice sounded hollow, drained of the life it normally exuded, though somehow it was calm and peaceful.

When Garit got to the hospital, he hugged Fulton and Jenn just as Coney was being rolled past on a gurney. It stopped for a moment when Coney held up his hand.

"Is that my family?" he asked the orderly, and began to cough. They all ran toward Coney. Fulton spoke first.

"Who did this to you, Coney?" he choked. "I'll pay them back double."

"No you won't," wheezed Coney. "You'll forgive 'em. How are the dogs?" Fulton would not answer.

"Tell me!" Coney demanded.

"Mulder was already gone, but Scully I had to put down," he said, his voice cracking.

"Thank you," Coney wheezed, turned and rolled his head jerkily, and his eyes squinted, squeezing back the deepest pain Garit had ever seen in another human. It seemed to flow directly from Garit's own broken and bleeding heart.

Jenn wiggled between them and squeezed Coney's hand, smiling at him crookedly. Coney smiled at her and called Garit's name.

He rushed toward Coney as if he were his long-lost father and touched his arm.

"I'll get the sons of bitches for this," he spat, his head swelling with ache.

"Forget it. The milk is in our fridge in the milk house." Coney coughed again.

"What are you —"

"Test it. It's Brenner's," Coney interrupted. "Ask Fulton."

"I will," Garit said as a doctor came through.

"Keep him moving," he ordered. Coney suddenly lurched, arched his back and cried, with a broken, choking voice: "Why? Lord? Why did they have to kill my animals. Why my dogs?" Tears bounced from his eyes and he began to cough again, and the sound gurgled like a rock plopping through thick seaweed.

The doctor looked at Jenn as Coney disappeared behind self-closing doors.

"I'm going to sew up what I can, get him stabilized," the doctor said. "Then we'll set the leg in the morning. Right now I want to get that punctured lung back working and put him out so he can rest and heal those ribs. He's going to be sore for a long time. If we have to, we may put him in a controlled coma until the swelling inside his skull can be brought down."

"Get to it, Doc, and give him your best work," she said, her easy smile suddenly drowning and falling down into her quaking chin.

The three sat in the waiting room, silent for at least an hour.

"Fulton, what's this Coney said about the milk?" Garit finally broke the numbness. Fulton shook his head as if coming out of a stupor.

"Oh. The day of the press conference, Coney told me to grab several gallons of milk from the store and put it in our fridge at the farm."

"So there is milk to test."

"Already been sent to the lab. We opened one gallon and sent samples to the state police, the health department and the FBI. One we kept sealed, so we have proof of the lot number. All of them have little tiny puncture holes filled with wax! Almost impossible to see."

"How long before the samples come back?"

"Don't know. These things take time."

56

Coney was still in surgery when Garit jerked awake from his slump in a waiting room chair. It was 8:50 a.m.

"Why don't you go home, Garit?" Jenn said, squeezing his arm. "I know Coney appreciates your concern, but there's nothing you can do here." Garit nodded. "Where's Fulton?"

"He left about 4:30 to do the milking." Garit nodded again, and dragged himself into the Jeep. He was late for work.

Wally heard Garit's heavy footsteps coming toward the stairs to his apartment, and rushed from his office into the hallway, blocking Garit's path. He was holding a laptop computer.

"Clean out your desk and get out!" Wally shouted, after a suitably angry glare.

"What for?" Garit argued wearily.

"What for? What for! How about selling stories to the competition!" He held up the laptop, running through photos of the cow killing.

"I sold photographs that I took with my own camera, not stories."

"Then why is your byline on top of the story that goes with these photos?"

Garit looked at his story.

"Botsdorf must have stolen my story, Wally," Garit growled through clenched teeth. I sent this story to you last night."

"How nice of you to send me a story that's already been done by my competition!"

"Shoot, Wally, you probably wouldn't have printed it anyway. You wouldn't print the Deadfrick story."

"I'm the owner of the *Jovial World*. I risked my own money to be the owner, and I've brought it where it is today all by myself. It's my right to print what I want."

"No, it's not! This is not your personal little world like some highschooler's diary. You have a public trust as a publisher to print all of the truth, not just what suits your own interests."

"Don't give me that college classroom theory crap," Wally spat. His breath smelled of weak coffee and something alcoholic. "The name of the game in the real world is survival, and if I have to kiss the rear of a jackass like Deadfrick now and again, I'll do it and never look back."

"You're suppressing the truth! Deadfrick is a criminal! So is Pinckney. And so are you if you hold back information that the public needs to know!"

"Enough with this noble ethics crap. It doesn't jibe with the real world, boy. Think what you want. Just think it someplace else. I'm not going to talk about it anymore. You're fired. Pack up your desk, then pack up my apartment and get out. You have until tonight."

"And how are you going to put a paper together all by yourself?"

"I guess that's not your concern anymore, is it?"

Garit collected a Styrofoam cup of pens, the only thing of his own on his desk, and went upstairs and called Jenn's cell phone.

"I'd like to take you up on your offer," he said when she answered.

"What offer is that?"

"To stay with you guys awhile. I was just fired."

Jenn gasped. "You just feel free to stay as long as you need," she said.

"I'll help with the chores to help pay my way."

"Thanks, Garit. That would be helpful. Just use the guest bedroom off the kitchen. I don't know when I'll be home. Coney's finally out of surgery, but I want to stay until he wakes up."

"Thanks, Jenn. This means a lot to me."

"You mean a lot to us, Garit."

That evening, Garit parked his Jeep in front of the farthest garage door on the Dogues farm. To the west, under a sinking sun, were dented and battered calf hutches strewn around like tinker toys. The silence and absence on the farm reminded Garit of his moments viewing his parents' bodies at the funeral home.

Their coffins were positioned side by side, and Garit wanted to scream, but he knew it would be absorbed by the thick morbid silence that pulled at his feet as if he were in a whirlpool of draining quicksand.

He didn't say goodbye, and he didn't cry in those few moments. But as he walked out, he knew he'd never forget the feeling of that moment. It came back strongly now.

He went into the garage fridge and grabbed an Indian Head beer. He wrote the item on a list he pulled from his pocket. He would pay back the Dogues's for every penny of their hospitality. Somehow. Then he slumped down in the porch swing, but it felt wrong because it had always been the place for Coney and Jenn.

As the mercury light was turning itself on, Fulton came out of the milk house. He nodded at Garit, then went into the garage. He came back with a beer and sat on a chair next to Garit. He popped the beer open and took a long drink.

"So how'd you sleep in the hospital chair, man?" he asked, grinning. "Didn't look too comfy to me."

"Well," I'm sleeping here tonight."

"Jenn told me. Coney's awake, but in pretty bad pain, she said. Punctured lung, right leg broken in two places, broken left arm, three broken ribs, fractured jaw and just general soreness. But they got the internal bleeding stopped."

"I can't even imagine," Garit replied, stoically. "Who could have done this, Fulton? Why?"

"We both know who did it. Why is another question."

"I don't know who did it!"

"Can't you guess? Who did all the crap to Noah? Who injected the milk with something? Who's behind my whole court case?"

"Deadfrick? I thought he'd be too smart to commit assault!"

"Oh, he wouldn't do it himself. He hired his goons, and this time, Pinckney was right with them all the way. In fact, he's the one who did most of the damage to Coney!"

"That little weenie could beat up Coney?"

"When you have baseball bats, you have quite an advantage, don't you think?"

Garit sighed and slooped his shoulders. "Do the cops know all this?"

"The cops haven't even been to see Coney yet, as far as I know. Insurance agent was out today, though. And Botsdorf."

"That bastard!"

"What do you mean?"

"He stole my story. That's why I got fired. I sold him photos from Noah's, but told him I still worked for Wally and he'd have to get the story first. Then I see it on the *Sasser* website the next morning."

"Could have been just a misunderstanding. Bots isn't the type of person to steal a story. How did he even get the story if you didn't send it to him?"

"I don't know, man. All I know is that I haven't met a single person in Jovial yet that has any integrity." He sipped his beer and looked at Fulton.

"Except for Coney," he said as his chin began to quiver. "And you." Fulton jumped out of his chair and gave Garit a brief leaned-over hug. Garit cleared his throat. "And Jenn. What do you guys have that nobody else seems to have?"

"Do you want an answer, or was it a hypothetical question?"

"You have an answer?"

"Are you ready to hear it?"

"I'm ready for anything except a bunch of bull, man. Whatever you do, don't lie to me to make me feel better."

"Some people can't take what I'm going to tell you. It seems a little too far-fetched."

"If I could take the cops telling me my parents gave all their stuff to some idiot cult leader, moved to a commune and drank poison so they could go off to Nirvana wacky land, I can take anything."

"We have Jesus." Fulton got up to get two more beers.

"What does that mean?" Garit asked when they'd both popped their cans. "I mean, neither one of you seems all that religious."

"We're not religious. We're Christians. Deadfrick is religious."

"I was going to ask what the difference was, but that answers that, in an obtuse sort of way."

"You want it sharper? The difference is just about a relationship with God," Fulton said. "Coney is God's friend. Deadfrick just pretends."

"How can anybody be friends with God, if there is such a thing?"

"Not a thing. A person. Not a human person like us, but I guess the word person is about as close as I can come to describing him."

"If that's true, how do you know all this? How did you figure it out?"

"It's not something you can figure out on your own intellectually, man, although it makes sense to me that the world isn't just random. There is a designer. Look around here at the sunset. That's evidence to me. No one can figure out God. If we could, he wouldn't be God, above time and space and humanity. But anyone can be in a relationship with him. There's a song that says 'it's more like falling in love than something to believe in, more like losing your heart than giving your allegiance.'"

"And just how do you fall in love with something—sorry—someone you've never seen?"

"Just start by surrendering to him, man. What do you have to lose?"

"I'll think about it." They finished their beers in silence.

"So what can I help you with on the farm tomorrow?" Garit said as he got out of the porch swing. "I need to try to pay my way as much as I can."

"Well," said Fulton, holding back his suddenly quivering lip, "we have graves to dig."

The next morning, with the sun just beginning to warm the late-summer day, Fulton dug a deep trench beyond the dry cow pasture with the Bobcat while Garit started hand-digging a smaller grave inside a small fenced plot. It was overgrown, but sticking out here and there were crude markers from other long-dead pets. Garit stuck to his digging task, unwilling to look at the reminders of death surrounding him.

He and Fulton loaded dead calves into the Bobcat's bucket, and buried them with no words.

When the trench was covered, the two hand-dug until the smaller grave was deep enough. They went back to the house, where Jenn was waiting. Fulton and Jenn carefully placed the two dog carcasses, wrapped in old blankets stained with their blood, into the Bobcat bucket. Fulton drove the Bobcat, and Jenn led Garit on foot to the pet cemetery.

There, amid the other makeshift markers, they tenderly placed Mulder and Scully in the bottom of the hole, noses facing each other. They looked into the holes, sobbing for what Garit thought was hours, and finally, Jenn spoke.

"Father, we are crushed deep inside for these wonderful dogs you let us take care of for you for a little while," she sobbed. "Thank you for their lives and their time with us. They were good dogs, just like my own kids, and I loved them like they were real children. I don't know why all this happened, Father, but I know we are like gold to you, and whatever this is all about will refine us, even though we are so crushed and broken because our dogs are gone, taken from us brutally and without sense. 'The Lord gives, and the Lord takes away. Blessed be the name of the Lord.'"

They wept bitterly and leaned on each other, then waited for their tears, lingering as if they would never go away. Finally, Jenn broke the embrace and threw the first shovel full of dirt into the middle between the two dogs. Fulton was next, and then Garit, and soon the hole was filled, with a slight mound on top. Jenn pounded a single stake into the ground, on which was written the dogs' names, and they walked back to the house, saying nothing.

Two days later, Garit went to the hospital.

"Hey, Garit! Glad to see you." Coney smiled when he saw him, although it was only half a smile. The other half of his face was too swollen to respond.

Garit smiled back, but he wasn't prepared for what he saw. Coney looked tired and drained and white. Every movement, every breath was obviously painful. His right leg was set and elevated, and there was a single tube coming from his right nostril.

"Wow, that's some shiner you got," Garit overcompensated. Coney's face was black and blue, with one eye completely shut and the other swelled with various diverse colors, yellow, purple and deep dismal brown.

"Thanks for helping with the chores," Coney said. "Jenn and Fulton say you've been a big help."

"I don't know about that." The two sat in silence for a moment.

"I know who did this to you, Coney," Garit finally blurted. "I've been thinking about nothing else for two days, and I intend to nail them to the wall. Sons of bitches. They need to take as well as they gave you!"

"And what good will that do?"

"Somebody's got to pay for all this, Coney. Who's fighting to stop this from happening again? Have the cops talked to you yet? Have they even launched an investigation? Do they even know about it? First they get away with beating me and now you? How can they get away with killing dogs and calves and ruining property and tricking Noah into killing his cows? Where's the first shred of justice?"

"Just relax," rasped Coney, who paused and worked hard to get some air. "You're not going to do anything. You're going to forgive them and stop being so angry. Look deeper into your own soul. This isn't even why you're angry, man."

"I have every right to be angry—for you! I don't get you, Coney. Wouldn't a friend be happy that another friend was willing to defend him? Doesn't everyone need someone to watch his back? Isn't that what friends do?"

"How does your anger watch my back?" Coney asked. "Do you think Pinckney and Deadfrick care that you're angry? Do you think they even know? If they did, it wouldn't bother them in the least. Does anger bring justice, or does it just bring rash, poor judgment?"

"I don't care. They can't get away with this, and I intend to make sure they don't."

"You have to do one thing for yourself instead," Coney said. "You need to forgive the people who did this, and then work your way backward."

"No. I won't forgive them. I'd rather bash their heads in."

"I think your time would be better spent getting the story out."

"That won't happen. I've been fired."

"Go to Botsdorf. I know he'll buy it."

"He's a scum-bag man, He stole my story about Noah."

"I doubt that. You should talk to him, straighten it all out. If you don't write this story, what are you going to do?"

"I thought I could work on the farm. It's about time I got my hands dirty, and you need the help right now. Nothing more honest than that, right?"

"Only if you're honest with yourself. God has a strong mission for you, and it isn't driving a feeder wagon or milking cows or cutting vegetables. No. You have to write the story, but not because of me. You have to write the story because it's important for people to know what kind of violence can be accomplished in the name of a cause, especially when it's as totally misguided as Pinckney's. But you have to forgive, or it will eat you up inside. Then they win. Not you or me."

"If I write a story that could put people away for years, like you want me to do, how is that forgiveness?"

"I didn't say that you just walk away like some kind of wimp. Actions still have consequences. Forgiveness is not about giving up. It's about keeping bitterness from taking hold. If you let it fester, you'll end up as bitter an old man as Pinckney and Deadfrick. You're too valuable for that."

"Retribution would be so much more satisfying. That's what I want! I want revenge, but it doesn't matter anymore. I'm done writing. It just doesn't matter, Coney." Garit's voice cracked, and he gasped back tears.

"Nothing I write will make a difference," he said, recovering. "A ball bat to the head? That will make a difference. That's justice. That's proper payback. That's all anybody around here seems to understand anyway. On top of that, I will not work with any of the scum that are involved with news anymore. I can't be in such a corrupt society."

"What, you're all full of righteous indignation now? Get over yourself, Garit. I don't mean that harshly, believe me. But you will not stop writing if I have anything to say about it." Coney paused and winced as he adjusted himself to sit more upright.

"It's not your call, Coney. It's my life, and it's my call."

"Bull!" Coney shouted, then wheezed as he inhaled deeply, as if there was too little air in the room. "You are not in control of things, Garit, and it's time you realized that."

"I have enough control to bring two lunatics to justice."

"You're confusing justice with revenge. It's only by the power of a just God that I've chosen to forgive the people who've done this to me. When I actually will have forgiven them, I don't know. I still intend to testify against them, if that's what it takes. They have to be stopped. But forgiveness means that I carry no grudge against them. I don't want more violence. A grudge is not justice. Every action has a consequence. That's God's law just as sure as the Ten Commandments."

"So you think it's alright for you to pay the price for Pinckney's violence?"

"That's not my call," Coney said. He tried to take a deep breath, but the pain stopped it short.

"I may not understand why it had to be me, but I do know that I don't see the big picture. Only God sees that."

"Why should I trust a God who lets someone like you suffer so much? What's that all about?"

"I don't know why this is happening, but one thing seems pretty obvious to me, man. You're here to write. Writing about me and my dogs and cattle and the animal rights agenda is just the start. Don't pigeon-hole yourself. There's a lot more for you that God has planned, and there's more for me and Jenn and Fulton too. We just can't see it all right now. We're stuck in this moment of time. I have a new mission just like you do. Mine is to stop people like Pinckney and Deadfrick. I ignored that mission before, and maybe it took a beating for God to show me what I've been neglecting all this time. I knew they were evil people, but I didn't do anything to stop them. That's my greatest regret, and I will pray to be forgiven for that. Now, besides loving my wife and family, I have another, more immediate purpose. It's not revenge, it's just making myself an instrument for God's use. Forgiveness has to come first, or my mind will be clouded with revenge and anger, and it will blind me to the right way to go."

"I'll never understand this God stuff," Garit replied. "Fulton said maybe I never will."

"You have to forgive first too, Garit, or your stories will be slanted and petty. You're better than that. Step back, get the lab results from the milk and blow this thing wide open."

"But I can't, Coney. I can't write it for the *World*, and I refuse to write it for Botsdorf because he has absolutely no integrity. I will not work for people who betray public trust and personal trust. I can't forgive that!"

"Well, you have to do something to let off all this steam. Maybe just write it, as therapy. Get it off your chest. Who cares if it's published right now?"

Fulton and Jenn were on the porch as the sun was setting two days later, when Garit finished the story.

"That was exhausting," he sighed as he popped open a beer and sat with them.

"So why write it if it won't get published?" Fulton asked.

"I don't know. But after I talked with Coney, I saw my role in a different light, even though I still don't understand much. I'm not just a regurgitator of facts, I'm a tool in the hands of a God—Coney's God—who wants me to do something with the talent he's given me. And I guess it's alright to be used."

"Coney's said it a thousand times," Fulton said. "We're just tools in God's tool chest, and it's not up to us to figure out when He needs a hammer and when He needs a screwdriver."

"I can't pretend to know about that, and I don't understand why I can't figure it out rather than have it be an emotion, like you said. But this cosmic dude must be real, because Coney is no idiot. Something about the way he handled all this stuff rings true, somehow. And even if it isn't all true, the peace and ease Coney showed me is by far the best false religion I've ever seen. Not like the peace of suicide. That's the coward's way out. That was Joan and Harold's way out."

"It takes courage to forgive them too, you know," said Jenn, softly. "I never took you for a coward. But you'll never find the kind of peace Coney has until you forgive them."

They were all silent for a moment, and Jenn yawned and excused herself to go to bed.

"So the story's done, huh?" Fulton asked. "Bet it's pretty long."

"Yep. Because It's about everything. I wrote about the beating, even wept when I wrote about Mulder and Scully. I wrote with brutal detail about calf cadavers bloating on the side of the road. I wrote about the bravery of the dogs, barely dodging cars themselves to round up the calves, only to be brutalized moments later. I wrote about inhumane suffering of a broken spine on an animal and a punctured lung on a human. I wrote about cover ups, pollution, deception and hypocrisy. It's the best thing I've ever written. It's passionate and factual, dramatic but not reaching for effect. It's angry and righteous. It's inspired." Garit paused a long time.

"There's something else?" Fulton asked.

"Just one thing. God, for the first time in my life, seems real. At least I think he's real. Maybe. I can't say why, but I think there really is a God after all. Maybe he's cruel and unfeeling to make this stuff happen. Maybe he's really not in control at all. But maybe he is. I don't know what it all means for me, but there has to be a plan, right? This world just can't be all haphazard. That's what my parents believed, but they didn't have a clue."

"Believing is a start, man. A good start. So where will your story be published?"

"It won't. I'm done writing. If God had a purpose for me as a writer, it's done. My new purpose is to become a farmer." Fulton chuckled.

"What's so funny?"

"Never mind. But I would like to tell you something. You've really worked hard on this story, right? It's almost like you gave birth to it?"

"I suppose."

"Then why are you willing to let it be stillborn?"

"Because there's no one worthy in this town to let it live. Wally's a moron and Botsdorf's a crook."

Fulton pondered a long moment.

"Did you ever wonder why Jenn and Coney got Mulder and Scully?"

"Never even thought about it."

"They were a present to Jenn from Coney after they had a stillborn child." Garit stared at Fulton.

"It was their one and only chance to have kids, as it turned out. A nearly full-term baby died before he even had a chance. Can you imagine what they went through? Maybe you can, because your parents died."

Garit wiped away a tear. "So what's your point?"

"You figure it out. I'm going home. Congrats on knowing God is real. Keep going down that path."

57

Botsdorf left Garit six messages—both voice and text—on his cell phone during the next week. Garit listened to or read each one and deleted them. He was weary at the end of every day from the farm labor he'd never experienced before. Soreness lingered from his injuries. Carlos, the most trusted of all the Dogues Farms seasonal workers, labored circles around him, and Fulton was away most of the time managing his own tasks. But neither one criticized or put pressure on Garit to perform better or faster, so he settled in to do simple, physical tasks they told him to do.

It was the peak of vegetable season, and there were no lack of menial duties that demanded attention. Manure still had to be pitched by hand from group box stalls and paddock pasture fences still had to be moved. Coney could do it in half the time, Garit assumed, but as he'd experienced in the days following his parents' deaths, time seemed to have little relevance. Most of the labor did little to tax his mind, so he became focused and preoccupied with purpose. His, Fulton's, Jenn's, and Coney's and, for the first time in his life, God's purposes, if he were real. Doubt clouded his mind equally with belief.

One morning, Garit caught up with Fulton as he was hurrying to his truck.

"I think there's something wrong with those surviving calves," he said. "They don't seem to feel all that good."

They went to the up-righted hutches. Only five of them held calves, and twelve were still strewn about the area in front of the barns, askew, upside down or tipped sideways like vandalized grave markers, reminders of the fallen victims of perverted, misguided passion. Fulton called Carlos and they both examined the calves.

"Good catch, Garit," said Fulton. "They're all in the early stages of pneumonia. I'll call the vet on my way to the packing shed. You probably saved their lives."

"See there?" Garit grinned. "I've saved lives. Proof that I'm supposed to be here on the farm, helping you."

"What, you think your life purpose is to save a few calves? I think you're underestimating your role in this world."

"The animal rights people say there is no higher calling than having compassion for animals."

"Seriously?" Fulton jabbed. "After what you've seen, you'd even consider anything those wackos say? You think they know the first thing about compassion? They have zero regard for people, even though they say humans and animals are equal. Instead of raising the bar for animals, they've lowered the bar for people. You've seen how they are. Even their compassion is cruel. It's all described in Proverbs."

"That's their problem, not mine."

"Exposing hypocrisy is not a writer's problem?"

"I'm not a writer."

"Well, you're no farmer, either, man. Look, I know you mean well, and you have filled in here pretty good. But let's face facts. You're not a farmer. Never were, never will be. You're not some kind of savant with a mysterious skill that allows you to identify respiratory distress in calves. Carlos or Jenn or I would have seen it if we'd been feeding calves. But you were, and you saw it. That's it. It may be divine grace that you knew something was wrong, but it's not evidence of purpose. Evidence, to me, are the calls I've gotten from Botsdorf wondering why you won't return his calls. Calves will always get sick. A publisher will not always want your work. What more proof do you want?"

"Some kind of sign from God would be nice, if he's really there."

"What more do you want? You have a prominent publisher who

wants you to call him. Seem like a sign to me. Don't expect to hear God's voice in your ear, man. It doesn't happen." Garit shook his head.

"I'm new to this God business. I have way too much to learn, I guess. I've seen way too many people who say God is love, but act out of hate or greed. Like Deadfrick. Like Botsdorf! It's all a giant fraud!"

"But what about Coney and Jenn and Noah?"

"What about them?"

"Don't you think it's evident that God makes a difference in their lives? Do you think they would throw away an entire philosophy because a couple people misuse and misinterpret it?"

"I don't know if it's God or just that they're good people."

"Nobody's good," Fulton said. "What standard of good gets you into God's good graces? Only God is good, and he doesn't grade on a curve. If he did, that would prove he's a liar. Unconditional love means there are no grudges for what people have done."

"A good God allows people to be beaten half to death and lets animals be killed for no reason?"

"You can't know there is no reason. Human perspective is limited to our own minds and experiences. Look Garit, do you think it's God's mission to make people's lives all unicorns and ice cream? You think a good father just gives his children everything they want whenever they want it?"

"If he doesn't make your life better, what good is he?"

"Oh, but life *is* better with him. It's better because we can cope with the crap that goes on in the world. It doesn't take the crap away. Let me ask you this, Garit. What drew you to Coney and me? What made you want to be friends with us and not with Pinckney or Deadfrick?

"I don't know. You weren't ass holes?"

"No. Sometimes I can still be an ass hole. I'm completely flawed. I've been known to smoke weed and drink and deface public property. I use Melissa and then ignore her. But in the long run those things are superficial, flesh trying to drown the Spirit. This life, and the reason you were connected with us, is not about behavior. It's about getting rid of that human nature—the anger and bitterness and revenge—and replacing it with God's nature, which is always love, even when it doesn't seem that way to us, blind as we are. You were attracted to us because there's love inside us. That's God. He's irresistible. Even if you don't believe in him, he gives you the ability to love. And he allows you to reject him, because he loves you too much to force you to love him. Love by its very definition can't be forced. You never even considered him before now, but you still loved your parents, right?"

"No. I hated them for what they did!"

"Somehow I doubt that. If it's true, does it make you feel better? Did you ever lose sleep because you were thinking about how much you love them? No. It was hate that made you lose sleep. Believe me, Garit. I wasted a lot of time hating the person who killed my parents. But my hate couldn't change anything. My hate didn't impact his life at all. Forgiving him did change things. The man who drove drunk that night might not have changed at all, but I have. Forgiveness is tremendously freeing, Garit. I don't have to walk around angry all the time. That just robs you of life. I don't want bitterness to infect me. I want love to infect me. That's a lot more peaceful. And that's what trust in God does."

That evening, when the hospital elevator doors opened onto Coney's floor, Garit saw Noah Brenner waiting, wiping tears from his eyes.

"Hi, Garit," Noah said enthusiastically, his demeanor recovering quickly. "Hey, are you working for the *World* or not? Haven't seen your name in there for quite awhile."

"No, I got fired. I'm just helping out Jenn and Fulton for now. Until Coney gets back on his feet."

"Well, I got a story for you that should be front page," Noah said, his voice cracking slightly. "Do you know what Coney did for me? Do you have any idea?"

"No, I don't, Noah. What did he do?"

"Tell you what. Come on out to my place first thing tomorrow and see. And bring a camera. They're going to deliver thirty cows to my place! Coney—and he did this from his hospital bed—knew insurance wouldn't cover me, so he ignored his doctor's orders and spent his days on the phone, calling all kinds of farmers. Twenty-three farmers, thirty cows. All top-quality. He even donated two himself." Noah shook his head to shake away tears.

"Also, I'll be shipping milk again to the Farmer's Store within a day or two."

"So the milk's been cleared?"

"You haven't heard? It was formaldehyde. Injected into the plastic milk bottles. They even found the injection holes."

"Congratulations," Garit said, reaching out his hand for Noah to shake. "We knew it couldn't have been your fault."

"Well, thanks for your support, too. Your story really shifted public opinion my way. I appreciate it."

"I'm just sorry about it all," Garit said. "Sorry your personal business and grief was out there for the whole world to see."

"It all happened for a reason," Noah said.

Garit walked into Coney's room and sat down in the chair beside his bed to wait for him to detach from his cell phone. He hung up, looked at Garit and smiled stiffly.

"What's the matter?" Garit asked. "Still hurt to smile?"

"It's getting better," Coney replied. "But you look like you swallowed a spoonful of jitters. What's going on?"

"I just found out what you did for Noah," Garit said, holding his own voice strong against it's attempt to crack. "I don't know what to say, but I tell you what. It frustrates me that I can't tell your story."

"Ain't much to tell. Anybody would have done the same."

"But it wasn't anybody. It was you. The one guy people would have said deserves to just lay in his hospital bed and feel sorry for himself. What made you even think of organizing a donation of cows? Most people would have just been thinking of themselves after being beaten half to death, and rightly so."

"Oh, it's not as dramatic as all that. Hey, I needed something to do, man. I can't just lay here. I'm bored out of my mind when they aren't trying to get me to take pain killers. I hate those things. They make me feel dopey all the time. They're either arguing with me over that or sticking me with needles. Don't they understand that there are worse things in life than a little pain?"

"Don't change the subject."

"The subject is you writing a story, isn't it? Noah's story? Mine? I happen to know that Bots would publish them both and then some."

"I told you before I can't deal with liars."

"What makes you think Botsdorf is a liar?"

"He printed my story without my permission."

"Are you sure?"

"Positive."

"Well, he has a different story, Garit. He told me you sent him the story and said it was for his next edition. Why would he think that?"

"Because he's a liar?"

"I suggest you be careful before you make that accusation."

"It doesn't matter anymore anyway. No one's been arrested for beating you up. No one's paid for the violence done to you. Someone has to pay, Coney! That's the real story."

"You're still stuck on someone paying? It's not even your debt, man. Maybe you need to figure that out for yourself before you get back to writing."

"I told you I'm done with that. At least in this town. Maybe I should just pack up and leave. Go back home."

"What, you're a quitter all of a sudden? Why don't you write my story first? Get you back in the groove."

"It's all written. Except for this happy ending with Noah. But nobody in this town is worthy of it."

"Wow. I didn't know you were so arrogant."

"I'm not arrogant. It's a fact. Yours is a great story, but if it won't make people change, then it's just stillborn." He instantly regretted the reference. Coney did not react.

"Look Coney, I think I understand a few things now, and not just about Jovial, but about life, thanks to you and Fulton and Jenn, but it's tough to find a purpose in all this violence. Isn't discovery of purpose supposed to bring peace? And then I get a story right in front of me that's full of redemption and the good that can come from the soul of man—one single man—and I can't do anything about it! God, apparently, won't do anything about it! That, to me, shows that even if he *is* real, he just doesn't care."

"Just because you can't see what He's doing doesn't mean he's not doing anything," Coney said. "You couldn't see any of the work your lawyer was doing either, and then, bang, just at the right time, you get a camera."

"Just dumb luck," Garit said. "Coincidence."

"Seems to me it takes a lot more faith to believe that than to believe there's a plan."

"I'm not outright rejecting the idea of a higher power," Garit said. "I just don't understand how it can change anything."

"It's like science," Coney said. "We agree on the facts. But how you interpret them makes all the difference. Deadfrick believes in God, but what good does it do him? Does it guide his actions?"

"Who knows?"

"God will let you ignore him if that's what you want. But for me, it's personal," Coney said. "I discovered some time ago that the world's way of doing things is nothing but a vapor. I need Jesus in my life, not just a vague recognition of a higher power. It's easy to ignore such vagueness. Not so easy to ignore the God-man, standing right in front of you."

"I really don't understand that right now," Garit said, wishing to avoid a subject he might never be able to understand. "But I know one thing, and I can't shake it. These people have to pay for what they've done! Aren't you even mad about Pinckney? I mean, how can you be so calm about this? You were assaulted, and the person you know did it is still running around a free man! Where's the justice? Where's your God of justice now? Why won't he do something? Anything!"

"What do you want, Garit? A lightning bolt? Fire from heaven?"

"Might be a nice touch."

Coney rasped out a laugh. "That would be a nice touch. Maybe a little over-dramatic, but effective, right? God has more class than that." He paused, breathing laboriously. "I want to be angry, Garit. Believe me. It still creeps in, but not for long anymore. Not that long ago, I would have been laying here stewing, plotting revenge. But what good did anger ever do me? All it ever did was make me wallow in all that toxicity. I don't want to live like that, always stirred up and pissed off.

Anger and revenge makes me think only about myself and the pity party I want to sink into. My anger doesn't serve God's purposes, and they're a lot higher than mine. We can choose to refuse anger. All it does is raise my blood pressure and make my mind rage and focus on all the wrongs that have been done to me, and then I want someone to pay. It's all focused on self, and that's what leads to all this anger and bitterness. It's not my place to make anyone pay or to insist on staying in this vicious circle. That's God's job, and I ain't him!"

Garit smirked.

"My parents thought they were going to become gods when they drank the poison they thought would take them to the planet wacky." He paused, then looked up at Coney. He smiled. Coney was listening.

"They traveled all over the world following some asinine pursuit of God or Nirvana or a higher form of consciousness, and never found it. And yet you never left this community, and found God in a way that's more real than anything—anybody—I've ever met. You're probably the only real Christian I know, Coney. And you're way different from the people I've known who told me they're Christians. You didn't have to say it. I just knew. And so will anyone who knows what you did for Noah."

"I told you it's not that big a deal. We farmers take care of each other. And remember that no one suspected that Jesus was God. He didn't behave the way the religious folks thought he should. Do you think they killed him because he was preaching love and tolerance? They killed him because he challenged them and their selfish interests. He didn't hate people or carry grudges. That's human nature. God's nature is a much better way to live. Easy to follow, but yet extremely hard to follow. Just love other people. Pretty hard sometimes, isn't it? But it's deeper than the deepest hole in the ocean."

The nurse came in to tell Garit visiting hours were over.

"They tell me I might finally be out of here by Friday," Coney said as the nurse helped him sit up so she could straighten the bed and check the tubes going into his arm, which made him wince in pain.

"Just in time for Founder's Day!" the nurse said, cheerfully.

Garit reached out to shake Coney's hand.

"Maybe you're right about the camera," Garit said. "Maybe the whole reason is so I can know that my dad wasn't a total jackass. He did one or two things right."

"Are you getting the idea that he loved you?"

"I guess maybe he did, in his own weird way."

"Remember God loves you lots more than that."

Jenn and Fulton were on the porch sipping lemonade when Garit arrived back on the farm. Garit sat next to them, silent and brooding.

"What's on your mind, Garit?" Jenn asked finally. "You've been awfully quiet."

"It's about Coney," Garit said. "Not what he said. What he is. I've never met anyone like him, and Fulton said it's because he has God living inside him. That seems wildly strange to me, but it doesn't matter, I guess. I just want to be like Coney. I don't want to live in turmoil and anger and bitterness all the time. I want to be the guy who arranges to restore a friend's cattle just because it's the right thing to do. I want to have that same kind of peace and forgiveness inside that Coney has. That you and Fulton have. How do I do that?"

"Will you let us pray for you, Garit? Will you pray?"

"Maybe some other time," Garit said as a wave of warmth traveled from his head down his back. It made him hesitant, as if his true feelings—if he knew them himself—would be exposed. "All this God stuff is too new, and it doesn't really make a whole lot of sense. I've been taught my whole life that it's just a myth."

Jenn leaned nearer, grasped Garit's hand with hers, and Fulton's with the other. "Do you trust me?" she asked. Garit started to pull his hand away, but something inside him kept it there.

"Father," she began, "we're here as humble as children, begging you to work in your child Garit's heart to change him into what you want him to be. Bring him your peace, and when he asks, forgive the things he may have thought unforgivable. Give him the strength to forgive just as you forgive all of us every day of our lives. Bring him to know without doubt his need for you, and let him grow in you until he bears a big, bumper crop of fruit every day of his life!"

Garit felt a warmer wave of heat flow from his head down his back. It wasn't embarrassment, but comfort. At least he thought that's what it was. He couldn't be sure. He released Jenn's and Fulton's hands and looked into the sky, filled with stars and a crescent moon.

"OK, God," he said into the sky. "I'll try it your way!"

"Good!" exclaimed Jenn. "Welcome to the family." She sighed charmingly. "So, are you going with us to pick up Coney tomorrow?"

"No," Garit said. "I think I have some pictures to take."

58

The unusual heat of early summer had
given way to a cool breeze off the Big Lake, and Founder's Day dawned
with Garit at Noah Brenner's farm, shooting photos of happy faces
greeting cows calmly walking off livestock trailers.

Garit pulled off his sweatshirt as the sun warmed him, and the
breeze refreshed him. *Thank God for all this nice weather*, he thought, even
though he couldn't understand where that foreign thought came from.

When Garit got back to the farm late that morning, Coney was in
a wheelchair in sweat pants and T-shirt, sitting on the deck, sipping a
steaming cup of coffee.

Garit smiled broadly as he sat on the deck chair next to Coney.

"Ain't you a sight for sore eyes? How you feeling, man? When did
you get out?"

"About an hour ago. I feel a lot better home than in that hospital,
that's for sure," Coney replied, smiling, but it disappeared quickly. He
looked around the farm as if expecting happy, white and bubbly animals
to bounce his way any minute now.

"The place isn't the same. Kind of empty." He shed a few tears, and
Garit joined him with a gentle hand on his shoulder.

Jenn came out from the house.

"Garit, you better get cleaned up for Founder's day. Fulton will be
by soon. We're all taking the day off."

"You going, Coney?"
"Just as I am."

With considerable pain and a pace that frustrated him, Coney slowly and methodically pried himself out of the truck in front of the Farmers' Own Store, two blocks from the Jovial City Park and the kickoff celebration for Founder's Day. Band music played from an innovated stage built out of plywood and two-by-fours by the city's public works boys. Some John Phillip Sousa march, Garit surmised.

The stage backdrop had been put just in front of the tennis courts and behind the skate board area, and faced west, hiding Alan Jovial's effigy from the crowd.

As they walked from the east ahead of the slower Jenn, pushing Coney's wheel chair, Garit nudged Fulton and pointed. The statue of Alan Jovial had brand new bright red underwear painted on it.

Fulton roared and looked back. He shouted at Coney and Jenn: "Look!" and pointed. They guffawed.

The Founders Day crowd slowly milled toward the stage to witness the annual official announcement of the start of Founders Day—now called Jovial Day—with a shotgun blast into the air from the Mayor.

Suddenly, the growing crowd's direction shifted like corn falling out of a bin, and glommed onto Coney when Jenn, beaming and beautiful, wheeled him around the stage limits and onto the park grounds. First one person shouted "Hey, it's Coney!" then another, and before Garit knew it, the couple was surrounded by people who wanted to see him, or speak with him or simply pat Coney on the back and wish him well.

Oblivious to the crowd's action, Mayor Benz walked on stage, cradling a shotgun in his left arm as if it were a baby.

The high school pep band stopped when he stepped to the open standing microphone. He tapped it, sending a screech through the park that made dogs bark a half-mile away.

Soon the crowd hushed itself and the Mayor spoke, the mic screaming slightly again as he stepped toward it, then back.

"Good people of Jovial," he shouted into the mic, "Let the Jovial

Day celebration begin!" He fired the shotgun into the air, and the crowd cheered.

The band began playing again, and a man in a suit walked on stage and whispered into Mayor Benz's ear. They walked off the stage together.

Garit was watching the crowd around Coney and Jenn when he heard a commotion to the left of the stage and turned around. Six Michigan State Police uniformed officers had lined up several people at the side of the stage, and were applying handcuffs. The mayor stood quietly, already cuffed, and Dan Pinckney was chanting "meat is murder" as the police pulled his hands behind his back. Observing from the crowd, Garit noticed, was a solid detective with a white beard and cowboy hat. He touched his finger to his brim and nodded at Garit. Garit saluted him.

Another, bigger commotion was out of his sight, so Garit ran toward the scene at the other side of the stage. He outraced the rest of the crowd and saw a police officer holding someone on the ground with his knee as he forced the handcuffs on him.

"Don't you know who I am?" Shouted Deadfrick from under the officer. "I'm an elder in the church! I've brought this town into the twenty-first century! You have no right to treat me like this! You have no proof!"

"Oh, but we *do* have proof!" said a voice behind Garit. He spun to see Betty, and she hugged him as the police began hauling their cuffed men away toward police cars.

"See," Betty said, "Deadfrick had gone through all the city's computer files and deleted his dirty deals over the years, but he made a mistake. He didn't think about those carbon copies until it was too late. You, my friend, had hauled them all away to the library by the time he went into the basement. He figured if they weren't there, they must not exist. Good work Garit!"

"Good work, Betty," Garit beamed.

They turned as Botsdorf opened the microphone on stage and asked for everyone's attention.

"Folks," he said, "for you who don't know me, I'm Botsdorf, owner of the *Sventon Sasser* and other assorted publications. I want to tell you a little bit about all this commotion going on up here. First of all, I'm going to give a shameless plug, and let you know that you can read all about it, in great detail, in the new, special edition of the *Jovial World*, which I now own."

"Woo hoo!" Garit heard Aspen's voice, followed by similar refrains from other female voices. He couldn't tell where they came from.

"Now, to the business at hand. I'll be brief," Botsdorf said. "The mayor, superintendent of schools, owner of the organic store, former owner of the *Jovial World*, the police chief and several more people have all been indicted by a grand jury, and so were arrested under order of that grand jury. They're being charged with crimes including conspiracy to defraud the federal government, embezzlement, assault and anything else related to years of corruption. Don't worry, you'll understand it fully when you read the *World*!"

Suddenly, from the crowd's perimeter, appeared dozens of pretty girls, high schoolers, Garit guessed, dressed in tight shorts and tighter white tank tops, all bearing arms full of *Jovial World, Special Edition* newspapers.

Garit took a paper from a very cute blonde, who smiled at him and looked back over her shoulder as she continued her job. Then he looked to see the headline.

"Jovial Officials Indicted," it read, and above it, a picture he had taken of Noah Brenner during the cow killing. Garit looked right below the headline for a byline. Aspen Kemp, Botsdorf and Garit West. He looked up to see Fulton, who held up his own copy and pointed to the byline.

"How did that happen?" Fulton asked. "I thought you didn't trust him?"

"I should have trusted him, and not myself," Garit said. "I decided that you were right. I wasn't doing Coney any good letting my story be stillborn. So I sold them to Botsdorf. While I was in his office, he showed me the story I sent to him about Noah. I had just made a mistake and emailed it to him instead of Wally. I asked him for forgiveness, which he did, without hesitation."

Botsdorf resumed his speech as pretty young girls continued to distribute papers.

"This is a despicable tale of dirty deals, collusion and deceit," he said, his voice growing nearly as dramatic as it had been in court. "Jim Deadfrick was indicted for defrauding the U.S. government on multiple counts for his years of dubious grant proposals. The paper you now have in your hands references websites where complete lists of his grants, with the deceptions highlighted, were kept. And the Mayor, along with present and past members of the city council, are under investigation for colluding with Deadfrick to defraud the government. The entire city council is under suspicion of abusing its power by making laws under false pretenses, designed to get grants.

"The sheriff is under investigation for writing false reports about gang activity. And Wally East is being investigated for promoting fraud through his editorials, along with some questionable financial dealings. Seems that Deadfrick had cut Wally East in on the whole deal to get grants for Jovial through a federally-administered private foundation program that sent law enforcement money to cities for fighting gangs," Botsdorf said.

"And Superintendent Pinckney? He's been arrested for his alleged assault on Coney Dogues, who I see has attracted quite a crowd over there." He pointed. "State police are looking for two young men who helped him with the assault along with computer fraud in the cow-killing case of a couple weeks ago. That's about it. Read about it in the *World*, folks! And enjoy Founder's Day!"

The band started up again.

Garit felt a tap on his shoulder. He turned to see Aspen behind him. She reached out her gorgeous arms and pulled Garit toward her strongly, and put her mouth by his ear.

"We nailed the bastards, Garit!" she whispered. He stepped back, held her at arm's length, his hands squeezing her gorgeous bare arms. "I guess we did."

Botsdorf walked up through the crowd, a huge grin on his face. "So what do you think, Garit? Did we treat you fairly in the paper?"

"I haven't had time to even look through it all."

"It's all there, son. Even your Deadfrick story. A few updates since you wrote it, but it's all there, including what you didn't know. Deadfrick also is being charged with environmental crimes. Seems that when he bought the abandoned part of the Jovial Woollies and Undies factory, he made a deal to store formaldehyde illegally. It's how the JAAR goons got it. It's a story that will have to be fleshed out in the next few months. But it's your baby, Garit. Not a bad topic for my new staff writer's first story!"

"What are you talking about?" Garit said with anticipation.

"A job, son. I want you to work at the *World*, under my ownership. I acquired the place from Wally just last night. You'll be the reporter, Aspen will be the editor. I don't know what to do about that sports guy." Garit looked at Aspen and grinned.

"That OK with you, boss?" Aspen hugged him again. "We'll make a great team," she said.

59

Two weeks later, on the Friday evening
that kicked off the Labor Day weekend, a jovial crowd milled on the
lawn and the large porch on the Dogues farm. Several copies of the first
regular edition of the combined *Jovial County World and Sasser* were on
the picnic table, a decidedly smaller pile than just a few hours ago.

Coney sat in a wheelchair on the deck with a walking cast on his
leg and a soft cast on his arm. One eye still drooped, but otherwise his
face was nearly back to normal.

Jenn cooked steaks on the grill, and Botsdorf, Fulton, Garit, Aspen,
Noah Brenner and his wife, Detective Sheridan and his wife, and
Betty were sated and sipping Indian Head beer, ice cold from a large
galvanized pail filled to heaping with ice.

At the center of the crowd, Garit had news, and the guests were
eager to hear more about it.

"We just broke the news on our new website a few hours ago," Garit
said. "Dan Pinckney's body was found last night. Police found him
bloated and hanging in his basement, his neck bound with a leather
belt. It was an old belt, one he'd had since he first came to teach at Jovial
High, and it still bore the stamp that read 'genuine leather from Jovial's
finest cowhides.' A note was pinned to his shirt."

"What did it say?" Someone asked. Garit looked to the detective,
who nodded his OK.

"It said: 'I didn't know. I would never cause such suffering to animals. They deserve forgiveness. I have found none and deserve none.'"

"What about Deadfrick?" Someone else asked.

"He disappeared after his arraignment, but police found him four days ago in the back room of a casino in Illinois—sorry. Ohio." Aspen was the only one who laughed.

"He was drunk and hovering over a mirror with lines of cocaine on it when the door was kicked in. He's fighting extradition to the Jovial County Jail, and his ex-wife refused to bail him out or even visit him."

"And Wally," interrupted Aspen, "is out on bail, but living in the Sventon Motel/ Hotel and unemployed."

"One more thing," Garit said. "Those two thugs Deadfrick hired are in jail, hopefully with no one to bail them out. Cops said they caught them at an animal rights rally in Chicago. Their truck still had white fur wedged into the front bumper."

The crowed thinned out after awhile, and the remaining inner core of friends lingered. The talk turned sober as sunset neared.

"Did you ever fear for your life when Pinckney was kicking the stuffing out of you?" Garit asked Coney.

"You know, I never feared anything," he said after a moment of thought. "There really wasn't any time to do anything. But there is one thing about that night that I never told anyone. Not even you, Jenn." He paused again, took a long slug of beer.

"I died that night," he said. "Not for long. I got just close enough to see the pearly gates. How I knew they were made of pearl, I don't know, but they were fantastic, and more real than anything here. I saw animals, one little child, and my parents, though I'm not really sure about that. They were far away, holding the child. I wanted to keep going, to run or fly or whatever I was doing, toward those gates, but I got jerked back. It was real, folks. More real, in fact, than us sitting right here, right now. No walking on clouds, no hazy dreamlike state. Real. Solid earth. Fertile land. Well-constructed gates."

The crowd was silent for a moment. Aspen broke the silence: "Well,

Heaven's loss is our gain, Coney. I'm very happy you're here and kicking up your heels, so to speak." She hugged him as tightly as she dared. The crowd chuckled, and each person raised a beer can to toast Coney.

It was almost dusk when a white truck pulled into the driveway, and it startled everyone on the porch. The truck bed was divided into caged compartments.

A small, wiry woman with leathery skin got out of the truck and walked toward the porch gathering.

"Is this the home of Coney and Jennifer Dogues?" she asked.

"Yes, Ma'am," replied Coney, standing unevenly.

"I got something for ya," said the woman. She walked to the back of her truck and opened a cage. She reached in and when she turned, she had two Great Pyrenees pups, one in each arm. They looked a little bewildered and sleepy in her arms, and she brought them onto the grass between the driveway and the porch and put them down.

The female immediately squatted to pee, and the male yawned and shook his head playfully.

"What's this?" Coney asked. Jenn said nothing, but leaped from the porch, cooing as she lifted the little boy in her arms, and then laid down on the grass to let the female climb on her.

"They are so precious!" beamed Aspen, and Garit couldn't disagree.

"Noah, what's going on?" Coney asked. Noah was grinning from ear to ear.

"It's a gift from your fellow farmers," said Noah. "You didn't hesitate to help me, or anybody else over the years, for that matter. This was the least we could do."

"But these are fine purebreds, Noah. Must have cost a fortune."

"Worth every penny to see that look on your face, Coney. And look at Jenn! That's priceless."

Jenn hugged the two pups, tears streaming down her face, her sobs turning the hearts of everyone on the porch to supple, fertile mud.

They watched the delightful show as the woman pulled some papers

372 | Paul W. Jackson

from her truck cab, along with a small bag of puppy chow, and handed them to Coney.

"These two are brother and sister, from the best stock you'll find in the Midwest," she said. She turned, said "Bye, babies" to the pups, who by now were all over Jenn. Then they bounced around to meet the other people, Fulton first, then the rest.

She backed out of the driveway as Coney reached to embrace Noah, crying himself.

"I don't know what to say, Noah. This is the best gift any man has ever given me."

"Don't mention it, Coney," Noah replied, straightening himself. "Hey!" he cried finally. "What are you gonna name them?"

Several suggestions started coming out, among them Sony and Cher, Wally and Beaver, Bonnie and Clyde, Bill and Hillary. Coney listened to them all as he settled back with great effort onto the porch swing.

By the time the pups were pooped out and Jenn had laid them gently on the porch swing cushions between her and Coney, talk was getting lower. Longer periods of silence became more common, but it wasn't uncomfortable. It was peace.

"I know exactly what to name them," Coney finally said softly to Jenn, but everyone could hear.

"Their names are Pearly and Gates."

And so they are.

THE END